Glint & Shade:

THE SCARECROW HUNTERS

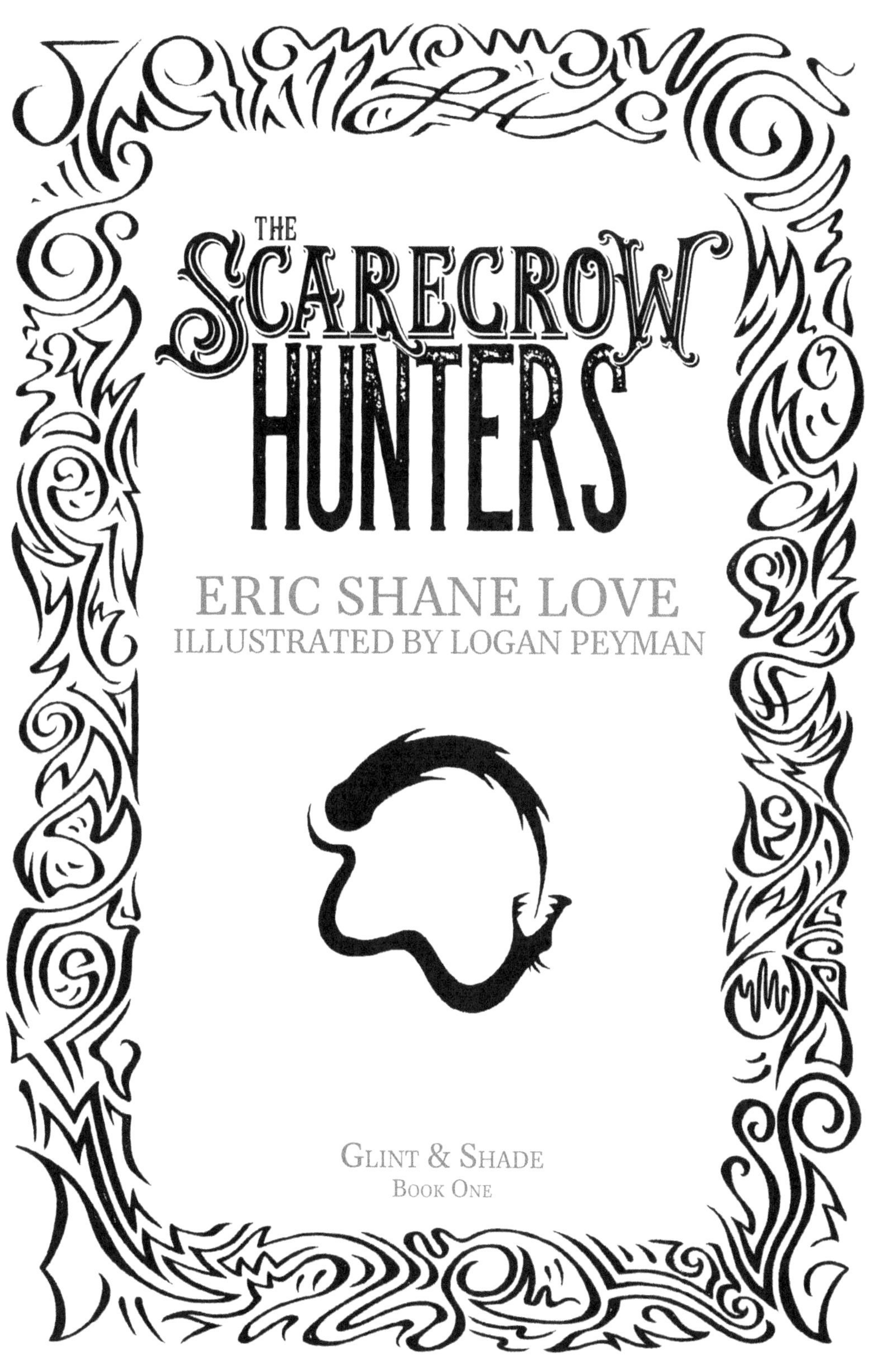

THE SCARECROW HUNTERS

ERIC SHANE LOVE
ILLUSTRATED BY LOGAN PEYMAN

GLINT & SHADE
BOOK ONE

First paperback edition January 2022

Book design by Anja Scholte
Maps and illustrations by Logan Peyman

Trade Paperback	979-8-9853173-0-5
Ebook	979-8-9853173-2-9
Audiobook	979-8-9853173-1-2
Also available for Kindle	

www.ericshanelove.com

BACK AND BACK FOLLOWING THE EXILE OF THE GREAT WITCH, THE DUMAS CAME FROM SHADOW INTO SHADOW, A STUPEFIED BOY SHUFFLING BEHIND THEM. THE FOREST WAS A LOW PLACE, FILLED WITH A BROODING, SHAPELESS RAGE AND DRIPPING WITH MALICE. BUT THE MEN WOULD MAKE IT LOWER STILL, THE BOY'S BLOOD SEALING THE PACT. THUS BEGAN THE KOHLAS . . . AND BY THIS, THE DUMAS FED THE *SLEEPING DRAGON.*

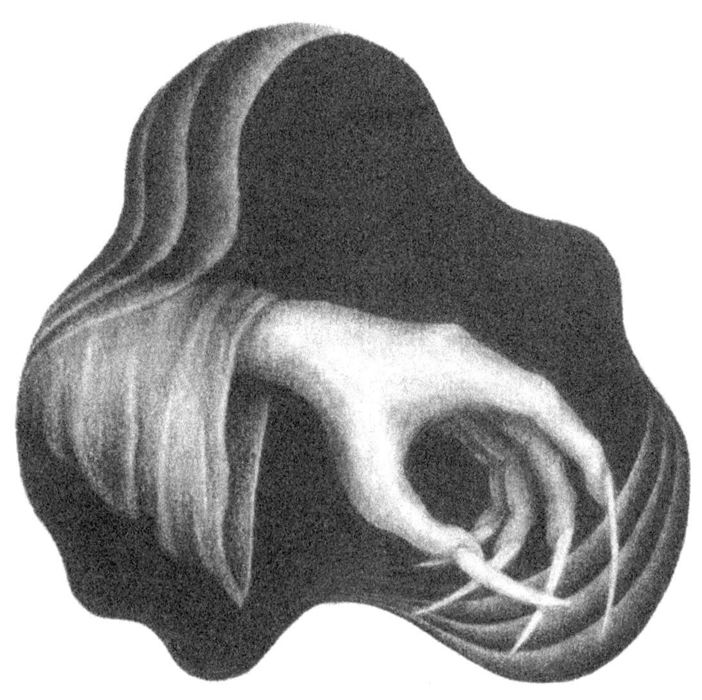

THE WINDOW THAT WASN'T THERE

Eliot was mad. His splintered mind was at odds with the stifling heat of the room. The heat on his skin. It skittered up the flesh of his arms and torso, across his frantic heart, and down into his belly. It was eating him from the inside out.

A blast of hot breath tore at his thoughts, bringing him upright with a gasp. He put his hand to his chest. He had felt the tip of a blade slice into his flesh just beside his nipple. He had felt wet blood pour from the wound, felt a wet tongue lapping at it. He had felt repugnance. When had that been? Now his chest was only slicked with oily sweat. It was bones and skin, but otherwise unmarked. What had cut him? And when? Though he seemed unhurt, his head ached. A wedge drove down between his eyes and out the base of his skull, his mind torn on either side.

He heard shuffling nearby as through a wall. Not in the room with him, then. But what room was this? And how had he come into it? Eliot stood, his body rippling with fatigue and, what else, atrophy? He had no memory of this place. It was dark save for one small slit of light coming from the far wall. In the darkness, he sensed no furnishings. Only a cold open room made of petrified wood and stone.

Again, he felt his chest. It remained whole, though his heart thrashed like a cat caught in a sack. He felt his stomach and arms. His face and neck. Down each leg. He was whole. Then why did he feel so broken?

With unsteady legs, he shuffled toward the scant light. It came through what appeared to be a small vertical window. Misshapen and ugly. As he reached it, a thing occurred to him that caused his pickled skin to shiver: the window was alive.

It was not a window, and it was not real, but Eliot thought of it as both. It was rough and narrow and sliced like a scythe straight through him. The window acted as a tether somehow between his two halves, but he had lost his connection to one of those halves. Eliot shook his head to dislodge the madness caught in it. He felt claustrophobic. He took a deep breath and again shook his head. The madness held firm.

"What am I?" he asked. He'd meant to say, Where am I? But that wasn't what came out. He looked down at his naked torso and saw, by the greasy light sliding through the slit in the wall, he was shiny with sweat. Head to toe. His dark skin was luminescent from its sheen. And yet he was cold. His skin was all gooseflesh, his nipples hard. Where were his clothes? His hands trembled. He tried to steady them against the wall, but that made them worse. The wall was at once hard as stone, yet soft as yielding flesh.

From beyond the wall he heard a crack like a bullwhip. Pain seared his head, hot and angry. Nausea swept through him, and he bent double but could not vomit. He heard a voice—his voice—mumbling. Vertigo pulled at him, and he tumbled to his side. Again, he heard himself cry out. He'd heard of such transcendent moments for those departing. Tales of men or women meeting themselves as they passed out of life and into what came after. Passing themselves on the path as they entered the pasture next: one moving on, the other lingering for answers.

But Eliot was not dead. Not yet. Death was there, however, and it had a face. He felt it.

Eliot stood. It was a slow act, but with deliberation he pulled himself upright to see through the opening. The light bleeding through it was dull; still, it burned his eyes. He could just make out a man sprawled on the dirty floor of the adjacent room. Eliot squeezed his fists and willed himself to stay upright as he watched the man writhe in agony. Man? No, this was a boy. Maybe fifteen years. Eliot grew nauseous with realization: the boy was no stranger.

It had been years since Eliot'd had a good look in a mirror, but he knew his own face—pulled in anguish. He knew his frame, drawn taught through trunk and limbs, shuddering with pain and effort. He knew the bleeding chest, tree bark thin.

The boy writhing in agony was Eliot.

Eliot heard a small shrill voice laughing from somewhere a little farther away in the dark. How far, he could not say. It was not part of Eliot, and its coldness mocked him. It pressed its way into his thoughts like a dart, but he cast it off. He focused instead on his tortured body.

His doppelgänger was twisting beneath an unseen torment. But Eliot understood that whatever force was working on the body, its target was the ruin of his mind. He perceived his division: his mind caught, trapped on this side of a black, sweating wall with his body—his actual body, not the dim, naked reflection he'd examined on this side—exposed to ruin on the other. This realization racked Eliot. He trembled and felt a bit of his mind get sucked into blackness.

Wait, he thought. *If I can think, I must be in control.* But just the idea of control made his head hurt to burst. He tried to focus but couldn't. Again, he felt revulsion stir in his belly. He felt the need to throw up and the inability to do so.

His body's eyes were open but showed only white flecked with red. The lips drew into thin lines, teeth grinding like mill stones beneath them. His heart beat so hard it was visible in his chest. His body's tightened fists pounded the rickety floor.

He heard the laughter again, freezing and hateful. It had grown in its malevolence, now a snare of poisoned fangs constricting his ability to think. Eliot beat his fists against this side of the seething wall. He had to act, but how? He could not get to the body on the other side of the wall. His body. He looked closer. He was bones and skin, little more.

Eliot scanned the wall in front of him. Could there be a door? The so-called window he looked through was tall and thin. It pulsated, growing smaller or larger as he breathed. There was no knob. Nothing to grasp hold of. No, there was no door. Just this little slit chipped out of an otherwise solid wall, like an accident. Or a wound.

Eliot saw the boy gasp and felt it burn down his throat into his chest. Just now, Eliot could not hear the cold laughter, but he felt it. A rabid dog chewing on his bones. Darkness surrounded him, pulling him, tugging on his thoughts. It would be a reprieve to give in. He might find rest in this darkness. Even if it came robed in death, he longed for rest. The pull whispered sweet things into Eliot's ear: darkness is your salvation. Death is rest and peace. But Eliot feared the darkness as well.

There was a gust of wind, but it did not touch him nor his body on the other side. It was not in either room. It blew deeper . . . inside his mind. Its edge was cold and fierce. And strong. It was so strong. This wind was desolation, and it was hungry for him. Eliot heard the laughter rise again with the fury. It was louder. It was closer. The wind and the darkness sucked at him with nausea.

On the other side, his body convulsed. The force of this crossed over. It ripped at Eliot's mind and burned away at the seal that held his reason intact. He was faltering. The ragged straps that remained of his sanity flew in tangles, clouding his inner vision. Reality, like a pylon within his head, shook with violence. He placed his palms flat against the wall. It breathed, swelling with the inhale. Shuttering with the exhale.

His body went still. As Eliot watched, it became an empty sleeve. The deepest load-bearing part of Eliot's mind was faltering. In his delirium, he bit down. Blood welled from his lip.

Eliot watched blood drip from his body's mouth. He saw a lifeless hand move to wipe it away, then felt a hand against his lips. A realization came to him. His body was not separate from him, or not so separate as he'd believed. Eliot was watching himself, not a replica. Not a mirror image. He looked down again at his chest, lit by the pale light coming through the slit. This chest, here on this side, had been whole before. Blood had not been here before, but it was here now. He heard laughter—cold, dead laughter—coming from somewhere in the shadows of his mind, shrieking in his darkness. But not just in his mind. The laughter was physically there, on the other side. The one laughing was not inside Eliot's head, but he was coming.

Eliot stood on the edge of madness, one step away from tumbling over it. He had little control over his body. He would watch his body die and his mind would break. It would break, he knew. That hateful wind tore at his mind in a furious howl, and his body seized. More of his mind dropped like broken stones into a deep well, and its falling tore open a fresh gash in his madness. Like a rip at the seam of his consciousness, he opened: a bleeding wound.

A vacuum expanded inside him, only this went against the pull of the darkness. He felt himself falling into it. Hurtling toward an unknown. The slit in the wall was there. His body was on the other side. But in his mind, he fell into something new and unexpected.

He divided yet again. In his periphery, warm light blossomed from the chaos. This was strange, and it did not fit here. It was light . . . literal light that came from within somehow, blinding and brilliant, surrounding him from behind. Bending to encircle him. He fell into it until he could no longer see his other self through the festering little hole, until nothing but dazzling yellow filled his vision. It was not hot. It was warm and comforting, though so brilliant it hurt his eyes. He snapped them shut just as his thoughts abruptly snapped open. The light came from a deep place inside him, deeper than the destruction and the wind. The light was good even as it pained him.

And with it came yet another voice: a third voice in the mad chorus. This, too, was familiar . . . . A voice he'd driven from his thoughts years before. This voice had represented betrayal. Abandonment. Now, it called to him from a place of hope.

"I am the adeglåst," it said. "And this is my oath . . ."

Eliot landed hard against those words, no longer falling. No longer reeling. They were sturdy beneath him, holding him up. "I am the adeglåst," she said again. "And this is my oath." Eliot sucked in a breath, hot, acrid, and sour. Those words, what had they meant? They burned a truth beyond his understanding. He felt them singe their way through the layers of his paralysis. They cut deeper and bore their way along the outlines of his consciousness, a hot alloy to bind together his severed parts.

His vision returned as the light receded. He saw his own body jerk on that floor. He saw his agony. He saw his eyes drawn tight. He saw his thin bloody chest, his heart beating its mad cadence beneath tight ashy skin.

Then a fierce gust of that evil wind ripped away a linchpin in his mind. He felt a chunk of his sanity collapse. There now was blackness in its place. He reeled. His stomach clenched into a tight knot. But those words remained, those mysterious words. They continued their work of binding him together.

Eliot did not understand what was happening. He knew his mind had splintered from his body. But had this been his doing? Was the division a product of light or darkness? Life or death? Even now he could feel his mind giving way, like the deep root of a rotten tooth. Beyond that, however, he felt something deeper, something out of his reach. The voice and its magic trussing up his brokenness. Obligating his pieces to mend. Pulling them together. Binding them.

From without, he felt something else clawing its way to get in. Death was not its goal. The owner of that hideous laugh meant for Eliot to suffer, meant for Eliot to go insane. But it did not want Eliot to die, not yet. He could not say how he knew this, but it was true.

The light and the oath distracted Eliot, stalling his mental collapse. His thoughts diffused and re-centered, grounded to the voice and her words. Eliot focused on her words: adeglåst. Oath. The conflict between mending and rending tired his mind. He was failing, but he pushed himself. He had no choice. He was drunk with fear. Then the voice was in his head again. He recognized it—yes, he did. It was his mother's voice. It was how he remembered her voice. Or was it imagination? His head hurt so. This oath, was it a memory or a fiction? A memory. Yes, he believed it was a memory. It was powerful, real or otherwise. It held a compulsion potent enough to pull him from his madness, if only for a moment. But no. Not just a moment. He was still here. Still here, in the memory.

Movement called his attention back to the other side. His body writhed now as if a snake were coiling up it, but beneath his skin. It started at his feet and crept its way up his legs, the sensation both hot and cold at once. Wherever it touched, it burned. It burned hot. It burned cold. Eliot felt it. This was new. He felt the touch on his clammy skin even here on this side. He shook his head. He was not separated. The separation had been in his mind, but now his halves, body and mind, were coming back together.

Eliot registered a smell. This scent was from the memory, long ago. In it, he had been young. A child, no more than six. The scent connected to that sweet, steady voice. A voice made of love, strength, and fanatical resolve. He knew his mother's voice, and he knew this smell. It was the scent of his childhood. He smelled his childhood. Rain in springtime. The mud from the creek near his cottage home. Like his mother's voice, it was the smell of juniper blossoms, honeysuckle, and jasmine. The smoke from the hearth fire and burning leaves in autumn. The smell was all those things and more. It was a warm smell. A safe smell.

Misery tortured his body. He felt the anguish to his bones on both sides. Then he saw in the darkened room something he hadn't seen before. Something hidden from his view. As his parts fused together once again, his eyes saw through the glamour. He saw spindly fingers creeping up his bare legs. They belonged to hands that appeared too old to be useful, gnarled and meatless. Yet they were strong and tracing the length of his body. The nails like blades were clawing as the fingers crawled, trailing ghastly arms behind them in the darkness, disembodied and hungry. They were poisonous.

Eliot breathed deep that warm, safe scent and heard again those words and believed in their magic. This memory, fighting to get out, loosed by the breakdown of his sanity, had long been buried. If the owner of a memory is its father or mother, this one had been an orphan. But no longer. At once, this memory filled him, and he reclaimed it. His memory reclaimed *him.* Not just a single image or a scent, but everything. He chose to accept this memory's truth. He chose to believe in it. With blazing ferocity, he felt the warmth of sun and heard bird song. He tasted the air, and he saw his mother's eyes.

He remembered. He remembered everything. Where he was. How he came here. Who was laughing. Why he must survive. A fury awoke in him, born from new freedom and driven with outrage. It was a fury to match that of a thousand wild devils. He became one again. As one, he was on the floor clinging to his sanity for his very life, his chest burning with poison inside and out.

Eliot opened his eyes and began to fight.

CHAPTER ONE: WIZARD IN A BIRCH WOOD

The rise was not steep, but it was broad. Eliot scaled the slope, dodging trees. Early dawn invaded the forest. Bare trees reached with grizzled knuckles to clasp the low gray sky and yank it down on top of them. The sky grew lighter, but he could not see the sun. It was coming, he knew. His chest burned from the frosty air; plumes of vapor escaped his jagged mouth. He stopped to look at the woodsman beside him. Talker, he called this one. They had never proffered their names, so Eliot had given them names when he was seven years. Talker nodded. Go on, he was saying. Words would give them away here, and they were unnecessary besides. Eliot was not new to the hunt. He understood this game, both its vague satisfaction and its manic peril.

Up the rise he flew, hovering low to the ground. His body knew this stance well. His legs were strong and thick, unlike the rest of him. He reached inside his cloak and removed a small knife. Just in case.

Atop the rise, the land flattened in a field and leaned into a birch wood on the far side. Something had disturbed the grass: a clear path cut through it. *This must be the way,* Eliot thought. He made for the tree line, but Talker grabbed his collar and yanked him off his feet. He looked up to see the woodsman's expression. Was that fear?

"What?" Eliot mouthed.

The woodsman did not reply. A clap sounded from the end of the field, toward the sunrise. There was the sun, as Eliot expected. Hunched in its growing amber waited Stalker, the woodsman who did not speak. His silhouette poised, ready to strike, Stalker had gone ahead of Eliot and Talker, as he often did during the chase. Stalker would stir their prey to instigate the hunt, returning only after the hunt was over, never while it happened. But here was something new. Here was Stalker, mid chase. Further, he had clapped. The hunt was silent, always. Eliot and Talker were hushed wraiths in pursuit, yet Stalker had risked giving them away with his clap. More curious, Talker made no objection. Eliot could not make out Stalker's features, but something in his stance betrayed emotion. He, too, was afraid.

Eliot stood. "What?" he asked, an edge to his voice. And if he were honest, a bit of fear.

Talker looked at Eliot. "Shhh," he said. "This way."

He pulled Eliot's collar toward Stalker.

"But the scarecrow?" Eliot protested in a whisper. They'd tracked the creature up the rise to the field and across it. Eliot's eyes drifted to the trees lining the perimeter. The birch wood. That is where the thing hid.

"No," Talker replied. "The scarecrow is not here."

Eliot wanted to protest. He trusted the woodsmen. They knew their work well, and he was just an apprentice. That's the way he saw himself, at least. But he had learned much over the six years of his quest, and this felt wrong. He knew better than to protest, though. They knew more than he about the creature they sought. The scarecrow was . . .

Light filled Eliot's peripheral, burning his eyes. Talker released Eliot's collar and shielded his own face. Eliot saw Stalker had pulled his scarf around his face as protection. Eliot turned to the birch wood. It was aflame with white light. The brilliance came not from within the forest . . . it *was* the forest. The trees were glowing. No, not glowing. Emanating. They were pulsating with light. His eyes hurt to look at it, but he could not look away.

That's when he saw it.

"Scarecrow!" he cried. He felt immediate shame. He had never laid eyes on their prize before, and when first he did, he cried out like a child. In that moment, he had forgotten his training. His body was alive with energy. A frantic dread commingled with raw excitement, and Eliot trembled from the current.

"No!" Talker shouted behind him, all pretense of silence gone. "That is not the scarecrow."

But it was. It had to be. The creature stood at the forest's edge. He was tall and lean. His arms and legs went on forever, it seemed. His eyes glowed yellow. Yes, they glowed. In his hand he held a pipe. The bowl burned yellow as well.

Wait, in his hand? Did the scarecrow have hands? Eliot wasn't sure. Talker had never described the creature. Rather, Eliot had used his own imagination to craft the being in his mind: he saw the scarecrows in countless farms, spindly things with branches for arms, a burning gourd for a head and straw for guts . . . . Only in this iteration, Eliot saw those parts animated by an ugly evil that preyed on innocence and fidelity. Hands had never featured in the image Eliot conjured, but this was the scarecrow: it had to be. On its head it wore a wide-brimmed hat. It lifted its free hand toward Eliot, and he felt the skin on his back tighten.

"Eliot," Talker said. "Come." He spoke the words with an even calm, but fear crippled their effect and rendered the words impotent. Eliot couldn't obey. He could not run from or to this creature. He could not move. The creature could, however. It stepped from the tree line into the field. Just one step closer, then two. The light behind it dimmed, as if to allow Eliot a better look. In the same instant, the rest of the birch wood burned brighter as white crystals jostled among the radiant branches. It was a cool light. It attracted Eliot, drawing him closer like a moth to flame. It did not have the same effect on his woodsman companions.

Stalker ran into the field toward where Eliot crouched with Talker. Eliot had a realization. The creature from the birch wood repelled the woodsmen in a way he was not affected. This meant he must act. Perhaps he must do what the woodsmen could not. Still, he could not move, and he was now uncertain this was the scarecrow. This was a man. But his friends, the woodsmen—this thing was hurting them. Even so, his legs would not obey when he told them to move. He shut his eyes and breathed deep. Then again. Before he could talk himself out of it, he found his legs and sprang toward the man. Things happened quickly then.

Behind him, he heard Talker cry out. Beside him, he saw Stalker running. In front, he saw the wizard in the wide-brimmed hat with the smoldering pipe reach toward him—and all went twisted in his head. He felt a corkscrew of pain pierce the back of his skull and rip behind his eyeballs. It was a pain so intense, his skin broke out in sweat and he vomited as he fell. His head was breaking open. In his mind he heard a voice speaking riddles. Eliot screamed. It was a child's scream. He remained a child. The years of his kohlas had not yet made him a man. He was a thirteen-year-old boy who had just pissed his pants and was screaming like a newborn.

He lay on his side, his eyes bleeding tears. He watched whiteness ripple through the field, flattening the grass and vaulting his woodsman friends into the air. He heard brittle cracking as they landed in knotted heaps, still.

Then there was mercy: Eliot passed out.

His eyes opened, breaking the crusted tears that bound them shut. Eliot sat up. Talker was waiting before him, watchful. Stalker paced at a distance, his eyes crooked in Eliot's direction.

"Where are we?" Eliot asked.

"The Dark Wood," Talker said. "But don't speak. Eat."

Of course, the Dark Wood. Even after so long, it still caused a creepy tingle to climb across Eliot's skin. The wood always seemed on the verge of pouncing, like a black cat poised to strike a tiny bird. Talker passed Eliot a bowl of stew, though he kept his distance. There was trepidation in his movement. There was concern on his face; Talker looked as though he expected Eliot to spring on him. This was new for Eliot. Was the woodsman so worried about him? Or afraid of him? Eliot took the bowl. As he did, he saw Talker's fingers remained clear of his own.

"Were I in danger?" Eliot asked.

Talker only motioned with his finger: don't talk. Eat.

Eliot did as he was told, but his mind raced. His head still ached, and his body trembled. He felt tightness in his joints and muscles, and there was a cut on his leg. It must have happened as he fell.

He didn't taste the stew as he ate, but his body knew to do the deed with or without his help. Eliot was in his head.

He had seen the scarecrow, or some other fiend besides. That alone was a startling development. For more than six years, he'd pursued the scarecrow. Often they found the trail fresh. Never had he seen the thing, however. Now, Eliot rethought what he believed about his kohlas.

The first doubt regarded the creature he sought. It was possible the scarecrow was less a creature than a flesh-and-bone man. This did not square with his instruction from Talker. Even for the woodsman who spoke, words were sparse. Still, Talker had made clear the object of their quest: the scarecrow was a mythical being, a creature whose lust for flesh and bone was itself magic enough to imbue it with dark life.

The scarecrow was not a man . . .

But if that were the case, who had they encountered on the fringe of the birch wood? That brought up another troubling detail Eliot could not square: this man, a wizard Eliot liked to think, had frightened the woodsmen. But the woodsmen could not be frightened. Or was that the imagination of a child? He had not imagined their fear. Eliot had seen it as clear as the birch light illuminating it. Worse, he thought he'd seen the wizard's power issue forth and topple the woodsmen. Had he imagined that?

Eliot considered all this. Could it be the scarecrow was a wizard? Or at least, a man possessed by the same dirty magic that might fill with ugly life an inanimate object like a scarecrow?

"Eliot."

Eliot looked up. The woodsmen squatted a short distance from him, both watching him. Eliot realized he'd finished his stew, was in fact trying to eat the wooden spoon. Embarrassed, he handed the spoon and bowl back to Talker. The woodsman wouldn't accept it. He nodded toward the ground, and Eliot placed them in the grass near the fire. Curious, he scooted forward. Both woodsmen flinched. It was slight but obvious. They were afraid of him, afraid of becoming infected by him, Eliot thought.

"Were I in danger?" he asked again.

Talker shook his head, but there was little truth in the gesture.

"Were you?" Eliot asked.

Stalker stood and bounded away. Talker remained, softening his stance.

"Danger is not the right word," he said.

"I don't understand," Eliot said. "That man . . . who was he?"

Talker shook his head.

Eliot waited, but Talker offered nothing more. So Eliot went on. "The light were blindin', aye? It were magic light, then . . ."

"Hush, boy. Evil doesn't reckon well with talking. Your words give it power."

Eliot sighed. "I felt somethin'," he began. He did not want his words to empower the creature, but he believed if he did not get the words out of his chest, they would burn their way out. "I felt somethin' in my mind." Eliot stirred the fire with a twig. It caught alight and burned as he dug in the ash and embers.

"I . . ." Eliot faltered. Did he want to say this out loud? Would it betray just how much a child he remained? Could he keep it inside himself? Should he? He shook his head and tried to speak again. He couldn't.

Talker came then and knelt by his side, extending his hand toward Eliot. The woodsman then stopped, hovering his hand near Eliot for a long moment. Then he rested it, squeezing Eliot's bony shoulder. Talker's hand filled Eliot with warmth, the reassurance of it making Eliot want to cry. But he could not cry. He could not act like a child. The point, the entire purpose, of this quest was to become a man. The woodsman's hesitation to touch Eliot, to even approach him, had once again made him aware of his otherness from the woodsmen. This difference always made him feel insecure. Now, Talker's touch was life.

"It was not the scarecrow," Talker explained, "but neither was it a kind thing. It is not our quarry, and so we must leave it be."

Eliot looked at Talker. The woodsman's face expressed kindness. And something else: pity. The woodsmen were a mystery to Eliot, but a comforting mystery. He knew they were magic beings. They were still men, however. He smelled them, and that was proof enough. It was not a pleasant odor, but he didn't mind it. Like so much about the woodsmen, this peculiarity was a comfort to Eliot. Not at first, perhaps. But he recalled little from the very beginning. The woodsmen were his teachers, his bards. They were his personal khamun. They fed him, instructed him, protected him. He had never felt like one of them, but he always felt at home with them . . . until now.

He could not help but wonder over the differences between them. He had accepted his kohlas. It was the way things were, the way things always had been, the way things would always remain. The kohlas was, like any other cumatu, a rite of passage. The kohlas was his journey into manhood, and for that he guessed they could have been hunting a badger or an auroch. They could hunt anything. What, then, should he learn from hunting the scarecrow? It was a genuine threat, but one never seen. A monster, but doubtless one strategic in his tutelage. The woodsmen had taught him the quarry was not so important as the journey, but was that true?

Strange, but Eliot felt like he should have protected the woodsmen against the wizard of the birch wood. That made him want to laugh. It was a caustic, humiliating thought: what arrogance to assume he could protect the woodsmen when he could not protect himself. Was it possible he might fail his kohlas? Tears came then. He tried to stop them, but he couldn't. Talker squeezed harder his shoulder, a father's gesture.

But Eliot had no father. Once he had. Once he'd had a mother, too, but she'd abandoned him. She had left him and his father without a word, and he could not forgive her that injustice. His father had done his best with Eliot for the brief time remaining before his kohlas began, but Eliot had seen the man's pain. He had known his father bled inside over his wife's betrayal.

Eliot had grown up in the valley of Gal-Braith: he knew his father would be dead long before Eliot returned home from his quest. Though it was the way of every kohlas, it made Eliot sad. But the way was the way: it was, always had been, always would remain. Sadness was part of life, but betrayal? It was unnecessary.

And of all things, his mother's abandonment so many years before made Eliot weep now. Not that it hurt that she left. He'd healed from that long ago. He understood he would never see his father again, and even that he could accept. He could even receive the thin affection from his woodsman companions. On every other day, he had resigned himself to this, allowing them to care for him in their own detached way. He saw it for what it was: charity. They did not love him, not really. They had a job to do. He was their ward. But he knew they cared for him. The nuances sometimes troubled him, but not like this.

Eliot's grief had nothing to do with the woodsmen, nor with the birch wood wizard. It had little to do with his father or even his mother's betrayal. Rather, it had to do with the voice he'd heard under the spell of the wizard's magic. The words were fuzzy, but the voice was not. Eliot did not cry for what he'd lost. He cried because his mother's voice had filled his head.

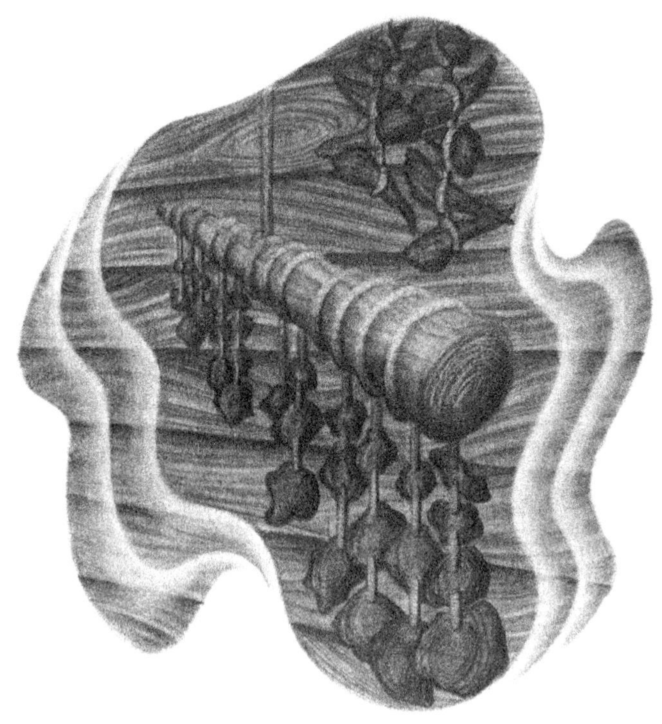

CHAPTER TWO: ITCHY SUSPICION

Little happened in the weeks following the incident at the birch wood. Mornings became boring with routine. Eliot rose each day to find his breakfast prepared, the woodsmen already awake. This was their way. He'd never witnessed them sleeping, but he knew they must. They allowed him to break his fast at his own pace. The change was in how they looked at him. Or at least he thought there was a change; he was uncertain. Eliot knew his cowardice had shown in the field. He had hesitated to go after the strange man, if it was a man, in the birch wood. Talker had called Eliot away, but Eliot couldn't believe he'd wanted him to run from the wizard. It was a test, whether or not the woodsmen meant for it. A test Eliot failed. Worse, he could not get out of his head his mother's voice.

It was possible Eliot imagined the difference in how the woodsmen saw him, but there was no question about the pivot in the hunt. The woodsmen were more earnest, and their urgency had shifted. They no longer employed their usual slow steady method. Instead, they began a frantic race, winding in and out of the Dark Wood, the woodsmen always pressing to keep moving. This differed from what Eliot had experienced over the years that had passed since he began his quest. Often they'd traveled in loops. They'd followed the scarecrow's path, and doubling back was common. Now, the path was more or less straight, but always threading in and through the Dark Wood. This made sense to Eliot: the scarecrow's behavior hadn't changed, only its reaction to their pursuit. Eliot followed the signs left behind by the creature. Its path was clear. The change came not so much in where they went but how. They moved with more haste, as if to tire the creature out. To break down its defenses. Or was the scarecrow the object of this new fervor?

"Have I done somethin' wrong?" he asked over his breakfast one morning. Mist hung low in the trees. That could be a signal spring was close. Or it could be nothing more than heavy clouds dragging along the uneven earth.

Talker tsk'd. Eliot hated the dismissal.

"Answer me," he said. There was anger in his voice, but he meant it to disguise his shame. He was angry only with himself.

"You've done nothing wrong," Talker replied.

"Then why do yeh treat me more like a child than ever? I'm no babbie . . ." But he was. He'd acted like a baby, that was certain.

Talker came closer. "You are no child, but you are not yet a man. This is as it should be."

His certainty would have been comforting had Eliot believed him. He did not believe. Eliot shook his head. "I couldn't go after him . . ." Tears burned his lids and threatened to appear yet again. Eliot brandished his anger and drove the tears back into his baby chest where they belonged. "I could not protect yeh."

Talker chuckled. "You've never been able to protect. We've needed no protection."

Eliot looked at the woodsman, remembering what he saw in that field. "Then how did the wizard—"

"That fiend is no wizard," Talker interrupted.

"Ahh," Eliot exclaimed. "Yeh say it, but I saw him. He were a wizard."

Talker grabbed Eliot by the arm. "Wizards don't hide in forests."

Eliot shook his head. It hurt from trying to sort it all. "Aye," he conceded. "It weren't no wizard, then what was it? Who was he?"

"No one."

"Then why'd he scare yeh—"

Again, Talker took Eliot by the arm. This time, his grip was tight. "We were not afraid for ourselves, young one."

"Aye, it were me. The babbie, like I said."

Talker shook his head. His dark eyes rolled in his pale face. Releasing Eliot's arm, the woodsman stood and walked away.

Eliot stirred the fire, a squat dull thing in the morning gloom. "It were powerful magic," he said. Talker began packing camp. Eliot went on. "I never knew magic like that existed." Talker did not respond. Eliot shook his head. It was too much. He was desperate to tell Talker what he'd experienced in the field, but did he dare? The voice of his mother haunted him. It managed to double his shame. He hated her. She had been nothing but a painful memory, a distant one rarely conjured. Now she was a menace. She had left him as a child, but now she refused to leave. The bitch.

Eliot looked up. He realized he'd been stabbing the fire with his stick. Talker had stopped packing to stare at him. The woodsman's eyes were wide.

"What?" Eliot asked.

Talker dropped the pack he was stuffing. He did not speak. He did not look away from Eliot.

"What?" Eliot asked again; this time his anger was real. Talker's silence annoyed him.

"What did you see?" Talker asked.

"Nothin'. What do yeh mean?" Eliot fidgeted with his cloak, a loose thread distracting his fingers. Talker came to kneel before Eliot.

"Boy, what did you see in the field?"

"The forest glowed, like. And the man in the wide-brimmed hat, he were—"

"No," Talker interrupted. "Not what you saw of the field. What did you see in here?" He tapped Eliot's forehead. His finger left a greasy stain. Eliot's fear vanished. Could Talker somehow see inside his head? Did he know of Eliot's shame? He had not wanted his mother's coddling, but what else could explain her sudden presence in his head?

"Nothin'," Eliot replied too quickly.

Talker's voice grew softer. "It's all right, boy. Tell me."

"Nothin'! I saw nothin'." And this was true. He hadn't seen his mother. He'd heard her. Had he felt her as well?

Talker watched Eliot's face. Eliot screwed his emotion down flat. He could not betray himself. After a few moments, Talker relented. He returned to packing up camp.

Eliot was a strong young man now, even at such a young age. Even skinny to the point of being skeletal, he'd lost the clumsy gait of childhood. Cords of flesh rippled his lean body with tiny plates of muscle and coiled around his emaciated frame. The dark skin he'd gotten from his father was ashy, almost gray from the toil and filth of his quest. His face now bore tufted patches of hair. His wit and judgment were those of a young man, yet his heart was thin and frail. He did not feel disappointment, but it had taken root inside him. Disappointment in himself. The fervor of the hunt remained, but often only as a perfunctory instinct. A reflex. Most days, he felt competent. But some days, he doubted his ability to finish his kohlas. But the woodsmen's faith in him appeared to remain intact, and his in them. He hoped they were right about him. He had no reason to doubt them.

The moon waxed and waned. Weeks passed into months, and months into seasons. As always during the day, a scrim of leaden clouds diffused the sun's light. Only the moon was free to light the boy's progress with any clarity. This was worse in the wood, but the sun had abandoned Eliot even in the fields and heathland. With each step he took, Eliot moved further into melancholy. For days at a time he might forget to eat. Often he slept only when his legs collapsed beneath him. Never showing need for rest nor food themselves, the woodsmen gave less attention now to Eliot's need of such things than they had before the birch wood. They still made him eat and sleep, but with less regularity. All three seemed possessed by lethargy in all things save the hunt. The woodsmen showed modest approval at his industry, seeming satisfied with his focus and content once he was again immersed in the hunt rather than the birch wood. They still threaded in and out of the Dark Wood, but Eliot no longer wondered over their pace. He trusted the woodsmen. They knew more about the hunt than he did. But the hunt retained an intensity that exhausted Eliot. Their frenzied pace worked: twice Eliot believed he was near upon the scarecrow. And many times he read signs in the hunt that told of the creature's waning strength. But each time, the scarecrow outmaneuvered them or otherwise vanished into the near perpetual shadow. The woodsmen refused to relent. As a result, Eliot grew anemic: a rawboned haunt chasing a phantom through darkness.

Their speed did not mean they were always on the verge of wresting the scarecrow. For every day it seemed Eliot was near to grabbing it by its dirty coattail, there were countless days the scarecrow seemed little more than a fiction. Most times the scarecrow's trail was almost impossible to discern. Stalker still ran ahead often to flush out their game. Talker and Eliot came behind. And always, Eliot only ever saw what the fiend left behind, not the thing itself.

Eliot's mind drifted. He was always fatigued and often distracted. His mother's voice plagued him. His insecurity ate at him. His fear he'd disappointed the woodsmen shamed him. He might lose entire days in this way, pulled inside his thoughts. On one such day the trail was not so distinct, so tracking was perfunctory. The distraction in his head was so effective, it took Eliot a while to recognize the two unknown companions trailing beside him. The mongrels, two hounds maybe a year old, were flea-bitten and almost as gaunt as he was. They kept a safe distance, wary eyes keen on his movement. He slowed his pace. They slowed. Crouching before them, he reached out a friendly hand. One hound huffed; the other wagged its tail, hopeful yet cautious. Perhaps they were waiting for Eliot to keel over. They looked starved.

He called to them, but they were too hesitant to accept his invitation outright. He watched as the one nearest crouched low and scuttled closer. It leapt away just before Eliot could stroke its muzzle. The two hounds spun round each other in a playful dance before turning again to study him. A sound in the distance, one Eliot could not hear, caused both hounds to turn and run toward it. Eliot followed.

They were running through an open moor peppered with saplings and heavy brush. The heathland was hilly. The hounds ran down into a gully, and Eliot followed. The hounds made a sudden sharp turn up and over a hill. As Eliot reached the top of the hill, he stood on a brief flatland cleared of heather and grasses. In the center stood a tiny cottage. A bonfire was burning in the yard.

Two small children and an older boy were standing beside the fire. They had been tossing apples wrapped in dyed corn husks onto the flames. Now they were looking at Eliot, the two children squatting to pet the hounds. The older boy, who stood facing Eliot, was no more than thirteen, Eliot figured. Near his own age, perhaps a bit younger. Around the house were tween lights filled with burning tallow. Along the eaves of the small cottage hung bright, painted shards of glass and wagon wheel parts fastened by leather straps. Eliot recognized them as fricks, though they were not the same as those he knew from home. The family was poor and had used what they had on hand, just as his family had. Fricks often adorn homes during Sauingrey, the Hidain signifying the end of harvest and beginning of winter. They were chimes designed to mimic the zyphlen bells of the faye and intended to confuse the more mischievous pixies into passing by while doing no harm.

Eliot had interrupted the family's celebration. It was a meager celebration. But everyone celebrates the Hidain in some fashion. Where had summer gone, Eliot wondered.

"Heigh, kin," the boy said. It was a greeting used to welcome family and close friends on special occasions, but on the boy's lips it sounded more like a request: "Be kind," it seemed to say. "Be friend, not foe."

"Heigh, kin, and may yer hearts be sunny," Eliot responded in typical fashion.

The boy seemed to ease at this. From inside the doorway of the little cottage, a woman appeared. She was speaking as she did so but stopped when she saw Eliot. She looked past Eliot, over his shoulder toward the heath. Alarm and recognition crossed her features.

"Royo," she called. "Gainé . . . Trillé . . . inside. Now."

The boy turned to look at her and then back toward what she'd seen. His face grew pale and his eyes widened. The other children had already made their way inside the cottage, the hounds at their heels.

Eliot turned to see what had frightened them. Across the heath on the facing rise were the woodsmen. They were walking toward Eliot and the cottage beyond him. Eliot turned back as he heard the door of the cottage slam. He took a step closer, wanting more than anything to offer the family inside comfort. To tell them they were safe. Why would they fear the woodsmen?

Soon, the woodsmen topped the hill behind Eliot and passed him without a word. As they approached the cottage, the bonfire and tallow flames dimmed as the wind picked up and flustered the fricks. Stalker went to the door and knocked as the other turned to speak to Eliot.

"We will catch up," Talker said. His meaning was clear: Go. This is not your concern. But Eliot couldn't move. By now, the tween lights had each fluttered still and dark. The fricks were a dissonant jangle of haunting noise. The bonfire, a basket of colorfully wrapped apples beside it, sputtered lower and darker. The woodsman at the door took hold of its handle and opened it. Both woodsmen stepped inside and shut the door behind them.

Eliot waited. He listened, but no sound came from within. He wanted to approach, to open the door and step inside and see what his companions were up to. He did not. He could not. He was afraid of what he might find. There was no explanation for this. The woodsmen had ever been kind if distant to him. Still, he felt dread. He knew nothing about this family. The mother seemed to know the woodsmen, but what of that? Instead of going to the door, Eliot drew closer to the bonfire. It recovered as the wind died down. The fricks were quiet. Too quiet, perhaps.

Eliot dozed, the smell of burning apples in his nostrils, but he did not sleep. There was no moon. The Sleeping Moon, they called it. Or the Dead Moon. It foretold of magic when it fell on a Hidain, but Eliot could not recall what it might mean or if he trusted such superstitions. All moons foretold magic in his experience.

The door to the cottage opened, and the woodsmen reemerged. Their appearance gave no sign of their business inside. Eliot stood. Inside the doorway of the cottage he saw Royo, the boy who had greeted him as a friend. Filthy tears streaked the boy's face, and Eliot felt a grave sadness, though he could not say why. Otherwise, the boy seemed unharmed. Over Royo's shoulder, his mother took hold of the door and shut it against the night and all its terrors.

The hunt continued. The three still moved at a brisk pace, though not so intense as before. Stalker left the chase for longer periods of time and with greater frequency, returning in a week or two at most rather than a matter of days. Talker gave no explanation for these longer partings, and Eliot spared little thought for them. He had a scarecrow to find. In the time since the birch wood, an event that came to define a shift in the kohlas for him, Eliot had discovered a renewed vigor in his quest. The scarecrow was all that mattered.

Why it mattered was a question Eliot could not answer. He did not trust himself to answer. He trusted the woodsmen, but he could not trust their confidence in him. A growing suspicion in his gut suggested it may be far worse than misplaced confidence. This suspicion itched inside him, too deep to scratch. The woodsmen seemed less interested in finding the scarecrow than before, only in chasing it. Eliot could not define what had changed. Perhaps Eliot was to blame. They'd seen him for what he was, and their hesitation was valid. Eliot's doubt only urged him forward, though. He must find the scarecrow no matter what the cost. He must prove himself once again to the woodsmen. He must prove himself to himself. This rabid ambition once again drove Eliot as it had in the beginning. What he should do with the scarecrow once he found it was a matter for which he had no strategy.

Such a thing would be evil. It must be. Crafty, too. The scarecrow now left little if any trail. Often, the trail would be lost for days, even weeks, before Eliot would pick it up again. The signs were not obvious, and they were becoming more rare. They had never been what one might expect: strange scratchings or footprints in the earth, a thread of cloth left snagged by a branch, or a wasted campsite of cold ash. Most often he found the mutilated body of some small animal as a sign of the scarecrow's passing. Why the creature killed these animals was not clear since they were never eaten. Perhaps it was sacrificial. Eliot thought it must be. Always, he pursued. He tracked. He'd grown efficient at seeing what little there was to see. Talker did not often interfere with Eliot's task.

His quest had been his entire world for almost seven blurred years, most of that time in solitude. Eliot thought back on how his quest began. Boys from his home, a valley known as Gal-Braith, began their kohlas on their seventh birthday. All boys. Once he'd joined the woodsmen, Eliot had succumbed to its madness just as every boy before him. It was a thrilling hunt in the beginning, one marked by possibility. From birth, all boys were educated about "the way." Few people called it their kohlas, not until the boys were older. "The way is the way," his father said to him countless times. "It is, always has been, always will remain."

This maxim was sacred to Eliot, and in the earliest days on his kohlas, he'd felt divine. Like a stiff burlap sack pulled over his reality and drawn tight enough to drive out everything but the quest, Eliot saw only his kohlas. It was all that mattered. He missed that simplicity now. For in time, that sack of truth had stretched, loosening. He no longer saw his quest with wide-eyed expectation. Now, he felt more absurd than divine. Thinking the kohlas silly made his face burn red with shame, but didn't he find it odd after all? Reality made little sense anymore. The stretching allowed in just enough light to reveal inconsistencies in the logic of his quest. These gaps were enough to make him distrust his ability to finish the quest. He knew the truth of it remained: the way was the way. The question was, was he up for it? Eliot relied on the woodsmen to instruct him. They had always done so even as they allowed him to grow, to carry his own weight. Never had they treated him like a child even when he was. Could he justify his growing self-doubt? He could not. He should not question his teachers' wisdom. But neither could he shake the disquiet that had rooted in his heart. It tasted of despair and flared with disappointment and grief. In response, he did the one thing he could: take hold of the sack and pull it tight again.

He was not a child, or at least, he could not remain one. Thirteen years was regarded as the time a child becomes an adult, and he had turned fourteen in spring. But in Gal-Braith, age was only part of his growth. The kohlas was a ladder. It would last beyond a boy's thirteenth year. It was the process by which he grew out of childishness and into manhood over time. Perhaps that was the origin of his current struggle: letting go of his old self was a hard matter. Perhaps this was a critical part of the work of the kohlas in him. Perhaps this was part of the way.

But for Eliot, this no longer felt a quest to become a man. It was an empty challenge. He was empty. He feared he would remain a child for all his days. Still, he kept going. He had to. He could not allow his fear becoming known to Talker or Stalker. When doubt scurried past his burlap defenses, he brushed it away as he might a spider on his skin. If the itch of its furry legs did not go away, Eliot did not linger on his doubts. He could not allow the growing sense of pointlessness to divert his attention. He had a task. He would accomplish his task or die in the effort. He could not waste time trying to answer questions that likely had no answers.

And he knew how he must finish this quest: the solution was to do the work. To put his mind to it even when his treasonous heart clung to infancy. To wrest his emotions and bridle them with purpose. With that vigor and determination, Eliot could complete his quest. He must.

CHAPTER THREE: HAUNTED DREAM

Autumn had fallen hard, yet a rogue summer storm pressed itself in among the cooler days and falling leaves. Eliot was picking his way along a rough patch of stony ground when a gale, a lingering fragment of the former season, bullied its way in from the coastal region far to the east. For hours, Eliot pressed on, the woodsmen following his lead. Toward late evening, however, storm clouds pleated the sky and the wind, already malignant, bore the painful darts of hot rain. Eliot pushed on until he lost his footing on slick stone and fell. As he righted himself, he saw Talker point with his chin. Eliot turned to look. Up the rise was a cave opening. Stalker stood just outside it with a torch in hand. Eliot agreed: there was no use fighting the storm.

Inside the cave was cool, but not so cold as Eliot would have imagined. The scarecrow had never ventured into the tight spaces beneath the earth, and for that Eliot was grateful. Hunting the scarecrow in these hollow hills would have been nearly impossible.

Eliot ate roasted roots and allowed himself the pleasure of their campfire's heat, thankful for the cave's presence amidst the raging storm. The steady thrash of wind and rain against stone outside lulled him, and the heat of the fire and a full belly pulled him toward sleep. His weariness flared in his joints and limbs. His back ached. His head throbbed dully. There was nowhere to go, no hunt to be made on this angry night, so Eliot stretched out on the cave floor and slept.

The storm's wind blew in circles the fabric of Eliot's sleeping thoughts, and he dreamed a strange dream. He was sitting at the base of a large shade tree in his father's yard—a tree blown down two seasons before Eliot's kohlas by another dreadful storm. Eliot's back was against the massive tree's trunk, its bark digging into his young skin. The breeze whispered, a gentle murmur. On it danced the red, gold, and yellow leaves of autumn as they fell in their lazy descent. He heard his father off to his left chopping wood, anticipating winter. Before him, coming from inside the warm little cottage, was his mother.

She was tall and elegant. Her long hair wreathed her head, a deep golden shawl. Her brown eyes were just a deeper shade of gold. Her mouth was set in a permanent smile: not a full smile but just enough.

She walked a few steps into the yard and placed a hot pie, fresh from her oven, on an old stump. "To air," she would say. To let it cool. Eliot believed it was to torment him and his father with its spicy-sweet fragrance. They weren't allowed even a bite until Mother said it was time.

She looked over at Eliot and smiled. Dusting her apron with her slender fingers, she walked the short distance between them, crouching before him and taking his face in both her hands.

"My sweet boy," she said, and she bent to kiss his cheeks. She always smelled like a hearth fire or summer twilight. It was a clean, honest smell. "Yeh know I am," she said.

"You are what?" Eliot asked, but rather than answering, she leaned away from him to look into his eyes. She sighed, contented. Her hands slid from his face to take hold of his.

"My sweet, sweet boy," she said again. "I've made yeh a pie." She laughed when she said this. The smell alone tortured him. Seeing the pie just over there, cooling in the quiet afternoon, its scent filling the yard with invitation, filled Eliot's belly with agitated grumbles. He knew the smell would draw his father from his work. He knew his mother knew these things, and it gave her pleasure.

Eliot laughed. He loved his mother. He loved her gentle way of calming his father when he became irritated, loved her charming way of convincing Eliot that even his least favorite tasks were not so bad if he did them with a smile. He loved her pies.

But his mother wasn't here. This was a dream, and Eliot didn't know her pies or the way she calmed his father, or her musical laugh. Not anymore. His mother had abandoned them, and his father rarely spoke of her afterward, not to Eliot. This wasn't surprising. His father spoke little by any standard.

As Eliot woke, the gauze of his dream superimposed over the reality of the cave for a lingering moment, imagined happiness evolved into disappointment before festering into ripe anger. He sat up, propping his back against the cave wall. Across the fire, Talker sat mending their packs while Stalker stood at the cave's mouth, his back to the others.

Eliot's anger manifested as tension in his body. He wanted to pound something. Instead, he sat quietly, waiting for the storms to pass, the one outside the cave and the one inside his chest. He took deep breaths, an effort to steady himself.

His mother. He'd given little thought to her since he began his quest. Why had she returned after all these years? Since she left, sometime after Eliot's sixth birthday, Eliot felt little love for her. Over time, what began as confusion became anger. Eventually, that anger grew into hatred. She abandoned him. With time, he'd trained himself to forget her. This dismissal had worked for Eliot for a very long time; now, his equilibrium was being challenged.

The dream was strange, but not for any amount of novelty. It was strange because of its tardiness. He'd dreamt it before. In it, he'd always felt love for his mother. He knew he must have felt love for her in real life—otherwise, her leaving would have meant little—but he did not remember it. What he felt in his dream was real. At least, it seemed real to Eliot.

What did he remember of her? His mother was an outlander: she was not from the valley. Her skin was lighter, though not pale like most in Gal-Galleen, but its olive shade stood in stark contrast to his father's complexion. Like most in Gal-Braith, Eliot's father was black as night. She had not wanted Eliot to begin his kohlas, he remembered that. She wanted him to remain a boy on the farm. She meant to coddle him. She would have held him back. Eliot's father would not allow this. His mother had lived much of her life as a vaga on the sea with her father. She did not understand the ways of the valley or the importance of every boy's quest because she was not raised there. That explained her irreverence for the kohlas. Beyond that, he remembered little save her desertion. Her betrayal . . .

But why should she matter at all? Dreaming of her infuriated Eliot. Worse, in his dream, he'd loved her. His hands began to shake, and to distract himself, he studied Talker as the woodsman busied himself with the matter of mending packs.

In the cave's tightness, the woodsmen's odor was more pronounced. Eliot had to admit: they stank. He must stink, too. He knew this. On the hotter days of summer, he smelled his own armpits: it was a savory, oniony smell. Worse, he sometimes smelled a sweet, tangy odor from between his legs. He did not bathe often, had not bathed in months, but when he did, it was because of this: his own body disgusted him. But like sleeping and eating, the woodsmen never appeared to bother with bathing.

He watched Talker, and the woodsman's focus over his work allowed Eliot to see the man. The woodsmen were queer, but their eccentricities were endearing to him. For the first time in as long as he could remember, Eliot looked hard at Talker. It was not just their odd behavior or dress that made them peculiar, though that would be enough. They wore an archaic vesture fitting of woodsmen: furs, leather straps, and heavy boots. They wore these year round, despite the weather. Around their necks they wore thick woolen scarves. On their hands, heavy leather gloves. Only their faces shone beneath their oversized woodsmen wraps. Their garb had once been colorful. The ghosts of that color shone through in places, faded and gray. Color was common with most khamunic orders, another reason Eliot assumed the woodsmen had magic. Their ragged clothes were unlike any dress he'd ever known.

Even in the orange light of the fire, Talker's skin was pale. Eliot didn't think the woodsmen had hair. He didn't remember seeing either remove their wrap, but he had seen their wraps get pushed askew from time to time during the hunt. Beneath was shiny scalp. Their skin appeared oily yet dreadfully dry—their scarves and shoulders were often adorned with flakes of their skin. Even now, Eliot saw little drifts of transparent flakes collecting in the folds of Talker's scarf. They were fish scales dried by sunlight. His pupils accounted for most of his eyes, dark saucers of black oil in a bloody soup. The woodsmen's ear canals were red and inflamed. The condition formed a husk in and around the ear. These things taken as a whole gave the woodsmen an uncanny appearance. No wonder the family on the heath were afraid of them. They looked infected.

Again, Eliot wondered over their magic. They'd never performed spells in his presence, but he did not doubt they had magic. Eliot believed they were fayelee: imbued with the power of Lynthian mystics. They were holy men; this he knew. And as khamun, he knew they must have been trained in sorcery. Granted, Eliot would never ask them about it, but he knew enough to suppose. Perhaps their magic had kept them alive for a very long time, their corrupted bodies betraying that fact. Or perhaps the power took as much as it gave. What did their magic cost them, he wondered.

Regardless, Talker and Stalker were faithful to Eliot. He thought again of his mother's betrayal. He thought of his father, how he would never see the man again. Emotion welled in Eliot's chest. He became overwhelmed with gratitude for these two strange men. As if sensing it, Talker stopped his work and looked up. Eliot averted his eyes. Did they hold tears? Would Talker see them? The woodsman did not speak. When Eliot looked again, the man had returned to his work.

Closing his eyes, Eliot rested his head on the stone. What about his dream? Whatever bewitchery the wizard had used against him at the birch wood, it had put his mother in Eliot's head. Or rather, perhaps it had stirred memories of his mother from the filthy floor of Eliot's mind. Yes, that was it. The way silt clouds a mountain stream when the water is disturbed, his focus was now polluted.

What troubled him most about the dream was not his mother or how he felt toward her in it. It was how real it felt. Could the dream be a memory?

Early in his kohlas, he'd had the dream regularly, but as his kohlas continued, the dream became less frequent. Sometimes it varied. Sometimes she came out with a fresh baked loaf of bread. Sometimes she brought hot tea flavored with cocoa and sweetened with honey. Sometimes she sat beside him in the grass. Sometimes they napped in each other's arms.

But always at the end, his father came in from his labor. His father was young in the dream. Handsome and dark, his shirt open against the heat of his work. His sleeves rolled up to reveal thick, strong arms. In the dream, Eliot's mother always ran to him and they embraced. She became the moon cradled by his night. He kissed her the way a young man kisses his beautiful young wife. Eliot would think his mother so beautiful and his father so strong. When had Eliot stopped having the dream? When had he forgotten it?

It was a good dream, he must admit. Eliot remembered always waking with the belief the dream was reality. It would take several moments before he'd come to his senses and realize he'd been dreaming. That his mother was gone and his father was not young, handsome, or strong. His father was gone, too. Then, looking back on the dream, Eliot saw how silly it was. He knew actual people wouldn't act that way. His father, returning from work, would be sweaty and smelly, more likely as not half covered in dung or mud. His mother would not have been so thrilled to embrace him in that condition.

And she wouldn't have looked as though she'd just walked fresh from a warm bath. Her face would be oily with sweat from the heat of the stove, from baking whatever she'd just removed from the oven. Baking like that in the middle of the day was an awful idea, except in winter when the heat was welcome.

And he himself wouldn't have been lounging in the yard. There were too many chores to get done. He would have had too much work to do for napping. No pageant so perfect and endearing could ever happen, not in real life.

Why, then, did the dream seem real? He'd always loved it. It may be silly, but still he'd loved it. And here he was, years since the poison of that recurring dream last came to him: Eliot was once again forced to revisit his father's farm. The wind and rain battered the world outside the cave, but inside Eliot retreated into his mind to escape his own thoughts. But his weary body betrayed him. He drifted into sleep again. With sleep, his dream returned. Except something was different this time. Something was off.

"My sweet, sweet boy," she had said. And she leaned in to kiss him one more time on his forehead, a shower of autumnal leaves drifting about them. When she leaned out, her golden eyes were gone. In their place were two leaking black holes. They looked seared into her skull with a burning stick.

Eliot drew away from her as far as the tree would allow. She was still too close. He could smell her now, but it wasn't a pleasant smell. This was the smell of body odor and soured milk. Of turning meat. His mother smiled at him, sweet and benevolent. A kind, honest smile. And it was incongruous. The juxtaposition turned her smile evil.

Her eyes were dead, and in their shadows Eliot saw movement.

He heard his father coming up from behind her. Knew he would look like the hero from some children's tale. But then, not this time. Eliot's mother turned to look over her shoulder, and Eliot got a good look himself at the man. His father was a corpse. He was naked and his ashen skin hung from his body like melting wax. His large frame was reduced to a thin wraith. There were large rotting sores covering him. His penis was gone, a ragged, fleshy wound in its place. Fluid seeped from fissures in his torso. The wind picked up, but instead of smelling his father's rotting flesh, Eliot smelled the fresh baked pie, sweet and enticing.

Eliot's rotting father was smiling, though a third of his mouth was gone. It looked as though rats had eaten it away. His gray tongue lolled out through the remaining gap. Eliot's eyeless mother stood and went to the man. They stood in profile to Eliot. They embraced, rusty moon against stormy night. She kissed him. A chunk of meat fell from his father's face, revealing gray bone beneath and something wriggling just beyond the ruptured spot, trying to avoid sunlight. His father's naked emaciated body quivered when his wife wrapped her arms around him.

Their kiss was the same as it ever had been, one of a young man kissing his beautiful wife. Only he was not young, and she was not beautiful. He was a corpse, and she was a monster. Warm light from the low-slung sun filled the yard. It was the golden hour. Aphids danced in the amber. It was a wonderland, and at its heart stood the grotesque. Then his mother ate his father. She gobbled bones and flesh and wriggling things, the gore slopping onto her face, hands, and chest.

Eliot screamed. No sound came, yet he screamed anyway. He heard the sounds she made, his mother. He heard his father's body being chewed in her mouth. The crunch of bone. The rip of torn meat. The slurping of vulgar fluids. Impossible except in nightmare, Eliot's mother ate his father until there was nothing left. She looked at Eliot with her eyeless face, smiled at him, and waved. Her mouth and hands were filthy from her revolting work.

Then she turned and walked back toward the cottage. As she passed the pie, she looked back at Eliot and said, "Pie's cool, my sweet boy. Yeh can eat it now."

Eliot woke with that scream trapped in his throat. His chest burned. Stalker was beside him, Talker a few steps further. Eliot looked from one to the other, trying to make sense of where he was. The cave. The storm outside. Yes, he'd been dreaming. He'd had a nightmare.

The woodsmen studied him, concern on their features. Eliot scratched his chest. It burned, but also it itched. Disoriented still, Eliot closed his eyes to push the memory of his dream—and his mother—out of his head. He felt a pressure on his hand, stopping his scratching, and opened his eyes to see Stalker above him, his hand on Eliot's. The woodsman pulled Eliot's hand away, and, by the firelight, Eliot saw his fingertips were bloody. Had he scratched himself to bleeding? He felt heat in his eyes and a hitch in his lungs. He was going to cry. He could not cry.

"Eliot, get up," Talker said.

Eliot realized the concern in Talker's expression was replaced with purpose. Eliot stood.

"Storm's almost passed," Talker said. "Help with the packs."

Good enough, Eliot thought. Any distraction was welcome. Talker had removed the contents of their packs before mending the torn places and lay everything against the far wall, drying them by the heat of the fire. Eliot beat the articles of clothing against the cave walls to clean them and loosen their stiffness, then he rolled them in tight bundles and returned them to the packs. They had canvas, twine, and stakes for pitching tents. He had his coat for when the weather turned cold and his cloak was not sufficient protection against it. There were other items, supplies useful on a journey. Many they used daily, others they used little at all. But when they needed them, they were there. All were essential.

Eliot considered all this. What he did not do was think about his dream. He did not think about his mother. But like any faithful spirit, the specter of his dream haunted the corridors of his mind. Like a devout ghost, it consecrated Eliot's thoughts: an altar for burning.

CHAPTER FOUR: NAMELESS DANGERS

Eliot pressed himself into the hunt. This had the benefit of distraction, but also it was effective in stirring their prey. Eliot ran, with Talker behind him, through a thick young forest. The limbs of the trees were low, so Eliot was mindful of his eyes as he ran. Autumn had swept the leaves clean from the trees, which made seeing through the diffused light of the early morning easier. They had been running since the middle of the night.

The scarecrow's path was plain. There had been a trail of blood left from a kill. Eliot guessed it was a pug rabbit from the look: it was too much blood for a tiny creature and not enough for a dog or badger. They must have interrupted the scarecrow sacrificing the animal. The scarecrow had fled, bleeding carcass in its grasp. Eliot could follow that bloody trail even by the thin moonlight until it ran out an hour before. Ever since, he'd been running on instinct.

His lungs were heavy with damp air. His throat was dry and scratched. He needed to rest, but wouldn't. The scarecrow was close, and it'd been a long time since he'd felt it so near. This could be the day he caught the fiend. It must happen someday. Why not this one?

Eliot did not have the luxury of hope. He had to channel the fullness of his energy into the chase. He had to focus on the challenge in front of him. So he ran, pushing thoughts of capture from his head. The land dipped. The two hunters ran down into the trough and up the other side, never slowing their pace. Eliot's breathing was quiet but labored. He heard nothing from Talker. That was typical. A limb slapped against Eliot's temple, bringing tears into his eyes. He swept them away and kept running. He tried to breathe deeper, to slow his need for air and regulate the noise as much as his breathing itself.

There was another dip, another rise. Eliot stopped for a quick breath, holding on to a tree for support and scanning the forest floor for signs. He looked at Talker. The woodsman nodded toward sunrise. Eliot shook his head, but the woodsman insisted. Eliot ran west. For a moment, he heard nothing behind him. Then Talker was beside him, grabbing his arm and pulling him in the other direction. Eliot yanked his arm free. He was the tracker. Yes, the woodsmen were shrewd hunters. Yes, they knew far more of the scarecrow than Eliot. But Eliot had always been the tracker, even from the first days of his hunt, and he felt how close he was to the scarecrow. Why would Talker question him now?

"Eliot."

The sound shocked Eliot. The woodsman had spoken aloud. Why? Eliot slowed, looking over his shoulder. Talker had stopped, his hand extended east.

"Eliot, please."

The words formed a request, but they didn't sound like one.

Eliot shook his head. "This way," he heaved, swallowing bile.

"No, Eliot."

Eliot had stopped and was leaning against a tree. He could not run much farther. With a look to Talker, he lifted his shoulders in a shrug. A question: why? But not just why east, why speak during the hunt? Why not trust Eliot to do his job? Why was Talker so earnest? All of this confused him, but more, it frustrated him.

Pointing in the direction he'd been running, Eliot said, "The way is here."

"No. It is not."

Eliot bent, propping on his knees. He had to think. He had to push past his irritation and find reason. Talker had never questioned his lead so directly, but he'd often made suggestions. The woodsman had never been proven wrong, but Eliot knew what he was doing in this case. Could this be a test? If so, to what end? Should he trust the woodsman, or his own ability? What would Talker want from him? He looked again at the man. Talker's expression was flat. Again, he didn't understand why Talker had risked giving away their position by speaking aloud. It was unusual. And if their quarry was as close as Eliot suspected, it was more than risky. Eliot huffed. He looked east. He did not want to go that way. It felt wrong. It felt insulting. He looked west.

Something occurred to Eliot. He recognized this place. He looked at the forest surrounding them. Yes, this was familiar. Nervous buzzing filled his belly. He stood to get a better look. Talker took a step toward him, his face now animated with worry. Eliot ignored it. He felt anchored by his recognition. More solid.

"This place," he said. This was the place, he knew it. Energy pulsated down his arms into his fingers. His feet itched to run, to push. To seek. To find.

"Eliot!" Talker came for him, but Eliot was running.

Through the knuckled trees he ran, up the broad slope to the crest of the rise. Excitement and fear built in his chest. There it was: the field almost exactly as the last time he'd been here. On the far side waited the birch wood. Talker was almost to him. Eliot sprinted across the field.

"No!" Talker shouted. The force of his emotion stopped Eliot in his tracks. He turned to face his companion.

"What?" All attempts at quiet were gone. Stealth made impractical by Eliot's annoyance.

Talker shook his head, panic in his eyes.

"What are yeh afraid of? He's not here," Eliot reasoned. Again, Talker shook his head. "Tell me who he is! I know yeh know."

Talker took a step into the field, his eyes scanning the tree line. *He is afraid,* Eliot thought. And at the thought, his own fear reached down his spine. Still, he knew the birch wood hid secrets . . . Secrets that may be vital in finding the scarecrow. Or vital in silencing his mother. Secrets he had to uncover. Fear did not release him from this obligation: he had to go. He took a step back toward the birch wood. Talker froze.

"Eliot, listen to me," Talker began. "We have worried about you since last you were here. The man put something in your head, aye?"

Eliot swallowed. How much did the woodsmen know? "What makes yeh say so, aye?"

Eliot took another step toward the birch wood, almost beneath its canopy now. Talker scanned the tree line again. The forest wasn't glowing. The only light was coming from the sunrise. Eliot looked across the field toward the dawn, expecting Stalker to be there as last time. He was not. Eliot was mildly disappointed at this, but not surprised.

"Eliot, you must come from this place. You must come with me."

"Why?" Eliot asked. He took several steps toward Talker, but not to obey his wishes. "This is the way, aye? The way is the way . . ."

"No, Eliot. This is not the way. This is . . ." Talker faltered, again searching in the forest's shadows for something. "This is something else."

Eliot saw Talker's hesitation and fear, and he pitied the man. Seeing the woodsman vulnerable stripped Talker of something vital. Eliot could not bear the intimacy. The disgrace of it. His teacher was the personification of surety and instruction. Yet here was his insecurity, exposed. Eliot felt sorry for him, but Eliot also felt disrespected.

"Then what is it? Tell me. Or don't yeh trust me?"

"It's not a matter of trust, boy."

Eliot shook his head. Again, tears were there. Damn them. He had to choose. Should he respect his teacher's wishes, or should he trust his own instinct? He felt himself poised on the blade of a knife. If he listened to Talker, he may never learn the secrets in the birch wood. But if he ignored Talker, he would cross a line he could not come back from. "I go where the trail leads," he said, his back straightening. "The trail leads here." Eliot turned and started for the forest.

Behind him, Talker bellowed, "You go where we allow you to go, and nowhere else."

Face scalding, Eliot stopped. His heart was a sudden stampede in his chest. By now, he'd reached the birch wood. He turned to face the woodsman.

"Allow?" he asked, his voice low.

Talker's face softened, but just. "Eliot, listen to what I say. Listen, I beg."

"Which is it, yeh beggin' or allowin'?" Eliot felt his hands shaking. Felt his knees quake. Felt his heart barrel ahead at breakneck speed, beating so hard it thundered in his ears.

Talker took several steps toward Eliot, his posture rigid and his face tight. His hands reached out in supplication. Again, Eliot felt shame on behalf of his teacher. And again, Eliot suppressed it.

"Boy, there are many things you do not know."

"Aye, then why don't yeh teach me? Why do yeh bark yer orders at me instead?" Again, hot tears burned his eyes. Hot shame burned his face. He'd never spoken this way to Talker.

"There is a time for teaching. And there is a time for trusting. Now is the latter."

"Based on what? Aye? I'm no child, yeh know this." *Oh, for that to be true,* Eliot thought. He stuffed the thought into a crack and went on. "I'm no boy. I'm close to bein' a man. I'm fourteen years, or did yeh not notice?" His voice broke, though he could not say if from anger or disgrace.

But what he said was true. Eliot was fourteen. And for the first time, it occurred to him he had lived as long on the hunt as he had before it. He felt a sudden gripping sadness at the realization. The sadness fought against anger and shame for purchase within him. In answer to this conflict, Eliot turned to the birch wood.

"Eliot," Talker called, but this time it sounded less like he was speaking to Eliot as he was speaking an oath. "Come back to me."

Eliot stopped moving. He brushed his hand along the rough trunk of a birch tree, the white bark thin and peeling. The tree thrummed beneath his palm. There was power here. Magic, as he'd suspected.

"Eliot, come back to me," Talker said again, his voice a flat cadence.

Shame won against Eliot's sadness and anger. He claimed to be almost a man, yet he'd acted like a child. He had been petulant. He heard his own words repeated in his thoughts: "I'm no boy," he'd said. "I'm close to bein' a man." The words whined in his head. He turned back and walked toward Talker. The woodsman's stance softened. Eliot wanted to go back in time and remove the last several minutes from their shared history. Why had he spoken that way to Talker? He'd felt insulted and disrespected, and he had repaid Talker in kind. But Talker was the teacher. Talker had ever been faithful. Eliot had revealed his own immaturity here. It was raw and hideous, and it made him want to hide. As he reached Talker, the woodsman cupped Eliot's chin, forcing him to look into the woodsman's eyes.

"You are not a child," he said. "You are strong and wise, but you do not yet understand all there is of the world. There are unnamed dangers. Many unnamed dangers."

Eliot nodded. Talker motioned with his chin toward the dawn, now blazing on the horizon. Again, Eliot nodded. And again, they were running.

They did not catch the scarecrow that day. Eliot tracked the creature for several more hours, their pace slower than before the field. Before the birch wood. Talker was right: the rising sun revealed the scarecrow's tracks were plain. It had not gone into the birch wood. Had not even come close to the field.

Midday, they broke off the hunt. Stalker returned shortly thereafter. Eliot sat cross-legged, staring at a small tumbling brook. He broke fast with strips of jerky and a handful of autumn berries. He had little appetite.

Why had he argued? What good did he believe would come from it? He remembered arguing with his father once, weeks before his kohlas began. He couldn't remember what they argued about, only his terrible guilt after. He felt the same guilt now.

He was stubborn, always had been. "Just like yer mother," his father had often said. Maybe he was just like her. Maybe he couldn't finish what he started, either. Eliot held his breath to break his emotion. He shut his eyes and thought of nothing.

"It's my fault," a voice said beside him. Startled, he looked. Talker was sitting next to him, staring at the brook. Then the woodsman turned to look at Eliot. "I push you, and you always do your best. But I do not stop to tell you I am proud. And I am."

Eliot's tears came unbidden. His breath caught, and his chest hitched with each inhalation.

Placing a hand on Eliot's knee, Talker said, "Eliot, you are a good boy. And you are right, you are no longer a child. You have many questions. I cannot answer all of them. You need to trust me when I have no answer. Can you do that?"

Eliot thought about the question. Snot was making it hard to breathe. Yes, he realized, he could trust Talker. He gave a vigorous nod, throwing tears from his eyes and mucus from his nose. He snorted, rubbing his face with his sleeve.

"You are a good boy," Talker said again.

Eliot knew his emotions should embarrass him, but he was too proud for that. Too grateful. Talker removed his hand from Eliot's knee, stood, and walked away. Stalker approached and dropped Eliot's camp pack next to him. They were finished for the day, then.

Eliot watched Stalker walk away and join his comrade. Then he blew snot from his nose into the brook, wiped his nose again on his sleeve, and began unpacking. He should sharpen his blade and check his coat for wear. Every day seemed cooler than those preceding it. It would be wise to ensure his coat was winter ready before winter arrived in full.

"I will prepare your meal tonight," Talker said from across the camp. This was a simple kindness, and not uncommon. But Eliot sensed Talker meant to extend the connection they'd shared earlier for just a bit longer. Gratitude threatened fresh tears.

"Rest now," Talker continued. "There will be time after you sup for tending your pack."

True, it had been a long day. He hadn't slept the night before and had run most of the day. It was still afternoon. It made sense he could rest for a bit and still have time after dinner to do what needed doing. This was a nice bit of forest, besides. They weren't in the Dark Wood. He hated that place. It was lighter here. In fact, a band of warm sunlight cut through the trees, a rare and golden jewel. He stretched out in the light and cradled his head on his arm. He was asleep in moments.

He had no dreams of mothers or monsters. He had no dreams at all. And in what felt like a single moment, he was awake again. But by the look of the forest, hours had passed. Strange how sleep could swallow hours and compress them into seconds. He noticed the fire first and Stalker second. The woodsman crouched over him, a small red jar in his hand. He patted Eliot's chest and tucked the jar away in a fold of his coat.

Eliot reached for his chest to scratch it, realizing it was itchy again. Stalker grabbed his wrist and shook his head. No, he was saying. Don't scratch it.

"Why?" Eliot asked.

"Because it is infected," Talker said, walking up with a steaming bowl: soup. Stalker left them to continue his silence alone. Talker handed Eliot the soup. His stomach complained, so he fed it.

"What happened?" Eliot asked between sips; the soup was hot. He had to go slow. "What is infected?"

Pulling Eliot's shirt by the neck, Talker revealed the dirty ash-dark skin beneath. Eliot was shocked at how thin his chest was. He saw muscle, yes. But he also saw bone. Besides that, he saw angry festering welts. They crisscrossed what of his chest he could see. He touched one of them, grazing it with his fingertip. It was hot and furious, and even the slight touch was enough to send searing pain into his chest. Eliot cried out.

"Leave it," Talker said. "It will heal in time."

"But how did it happen?"

"Poison vines," Talker said. "They fill the forests."

Eliot knew most things that could be found in the forest, or the field. He did not recall any poisonous vines, not since summer. One more reason he should pay better attention. His mind wandered, following that thread. Talker, still beside him, was fussing over his own pack. Eliot pulled his knife from its sheath and a whetstone from his pack, then spilled water from his waterskin onto the stone. As he set to his task, he heard Talker mumbling beside him. Talker did not, in fact, talk that much. He never mumbled. Curious, Eliot shifted his weight so he was closer and could better hear.

Over and over, the woodsman repeated a single phrase. It was a slow chant, almost inaudible. The rhythm was soothing. Eliot tried to make out the words, but they were not in any language he recognized. Perhaps they were Lynthian. Perhaps after all this time, Eliot had caught his teacher in a spell. He stilled his sharpening to hear better. Yes, he thought he understood.

Turning to Talker, he asked, "What does that mean?"

"What, boy?"

Eliot concentrated, then repeated the words as he'd heard them: "Gho gret kee," he said and tumbled to his side, vertigo spinning him. His head went empty. His chest flared hot. Talker cradled his head and sat him upright again.

"No," Talker said. "Do not speak those words."

"But you . . ." Eliot began, stopping himself when he became light-headed again. His chest was burning and itching. He may not be a child, but he was no magician. "Aye," he said. He set again to sharpening his blade. The world was full of mysteries, and most seemed best left alone.

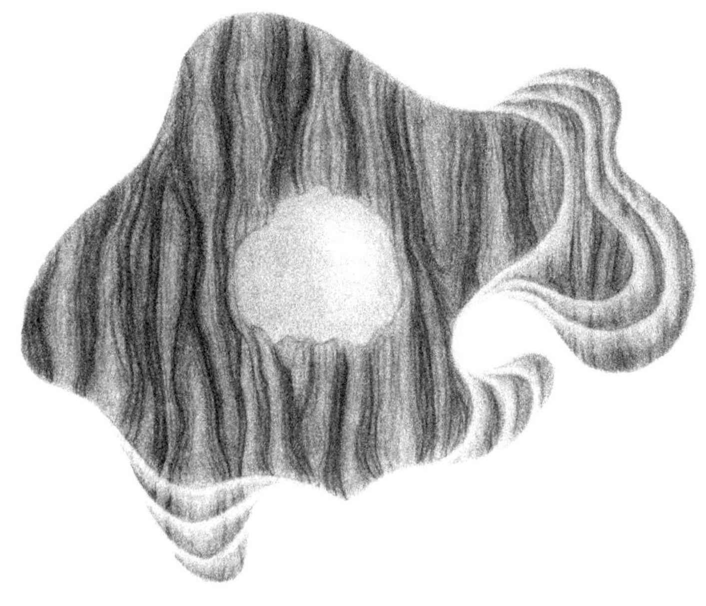

CHAPTER FIVE: LAUGHING FOREST

Eliot slept little that night. Even exhausted as he was, his nap ruined sleep. The moon was not full, but it was bright enough to see the open forest. The fire had burned out long before. He guessed it must be early morning, a few more hours before he would get up. Falling back to sleep was not an option. Instead, he thought back on the dreams of his mother.

The first dream had awakened something in him, something that brought him incredible shame. The second dream had frightened him. But of the two, only the first felt genuine. Perhaps they were part of the wizard's magic. The wizard . . . Talker insisted the man in the wide-brimmed hat was no wizard. Then what was he? And who? If his magic induced the nightmare, how had he done it? Was he in Eliot's head?

A thought came to him, turning his feet to ice: What if the stranger in the birch wood knew Eliot? What if he was no stranger at all?

Nonsense. Eliot had never seen the man. And there must be magic that uses what is already in a man's head to torment him. That was more likely, Eliot thought, but he was uncertain if this was a product of logic or hope. He thought again of his mother.

He missed her, he realized. That shamed him. Why would he miss someone who gave so little regard for him and his father? Even after so many years, her betrayal still hurt. His dream was sweet . . . not the nightmare retelling, but the original.

The wind rustled the leaves on the forest floor as Eliot settled deeper into his thoughts. One thing was becoming obvious to him: the dream was born out of memory. It was not an invention of his mind. And the pie had been . . . what kind? He could almost taste it, but he'd had no pie in seven years and couldn't be sure he remembered the taste. It had not been his favorite pie; he remembered that much. But any pie would do. His mother baked the pie and brought it out of the cottage, placing it on the stump to cool.

But Eliot was not seated with his back against the old tree. No, that tree was gone. The stump where the pie cooled was all that remained of it. How had the tree fallen, he wondered. It was a storm. And he remembered it had been earlier. He was young then, too young to remember much, perhaps. But the morning his mother brought out the pie was clearer. Or becoming so.

She'd placed the pie on the stump and walked over to him. Eliot had just collected the eggs from the coup, and his mother came to him. She took the basket from him and laced her fingers through his. "My sweet boy," she'd said. In the present, tears burned Eliot's eyes.

How had he forgotten this? Now it seemed so plain. Bleary-eyed and heavy with torpor, he stared into the trees overhead. Eliot watched the campfire light dance among the tree limbs, faint and yellow, and he remembered more: she'd made him a pie. It was not his birthday or a special occasion, yet she'd made him a pie. And she came to him, took his egg basket, and led him by the hand to sit in the shade of the trees. "My sweet, sweet boy," she said again.

And then she'd warned him. But of what? He could not remember, but he did remember how it made him feel. At first, he was afraid, but she kept talking, and his fear became comfort. She comforted him. She'd made assurances, but of what? Why could he not remember?

And that made him curious further. If he could not remember this, what other memories had he lost? And not just from before his kohlas began, but after? He heard shuffling from the far side of camp. The woodsmen were stirring, but he was not ready yet to engage them. He closed his eyes against the dancing light of the campfire on the branches overhead.

Eliot knew most things that had happened to him before his quest would matter little after he finished it, but he also knew he wanted to hold on to as much of them as he could. They were all he might keep of his father. And his mother. Ashamed or not, he realized he wanted to keep hold of her, too. The yellow light from the campfire sneaked its way through his closed lids, so he rolled to his side, away from it. Listless, he needed more time alone in his thoughts.

He had loved his mother. He'd always known that, even if he'd been unwilling to admit it. But the pain he felt now over her loss revealed just how much he'd loved her. She was the bright, shining center of his life before she left him. Not his father: he had been a surly, silent man. His mother had been radiant. But why did she leave him? Her betrayal was unforgivable.

There was more movement behind him. He did not want to, but he opened his eyes. The forest stretched out into darkness before him, but up close the light from the campfire burned the trees gold. Something about this troubled him. It occurred to him then the campfire had burned out long before now. This uncanny yellow light was something else.

Icy fear licked up Eliot's spine as he turned. The woodsmen were not in the camp. Rather, here was the wizard. The man in the wide-brimmed hat with golden glowing eyes and pipe in hand stood, facing Eliot. The campfire was dead. But the flames inside the man's skull were not. His eyes filled the forest with a radiant warmth.

Eliot scuttled away from the man on hands and knees. Before he made it far, he was lifted onto his feet, and his feet were running. The darkness before him was split in half by a golden ray emanating from behind him. His chest battering and his eyes watering, he ran for his life. The forest flew past him. He didn't think he'd ever run so fast, but even still he doubted he could outrun or outlast the man.

Then the light was ahead of him. Eliot was in pursuit. He was chasing the strange man through the forest. He was gaining on him. They ran to set the night on fire, Eliot closing the gap between them. Compelled. The man's eyes burned in the darkness, his pipe more so. Eliot could smell that burning pipe, and he ran harder.

Through the forest they flew and into a field . . . the field. Across the field they ran, and into the birch wood. Into the glowing audience of birch trees they fled, Eliot so close to the man with the pipe he could almost grab his cloak. He could feel the man's warmth. And then the smoking man turned and Eliot was on him. Face to face. Chest to chest. Light came from the smoking man's mouth, and Eliot saw black.

A shaft of white light. Glowing trees. Snow petals. Soft earth. Enormous trunk.

Eliot pulled himself along the ground. He could not feel his legs. He could not open his eyes except in thin slits. Shafts of light came in at these: white light, not yellow. He tried to focus, to will his eyes open, but they were dead. Like his legs. He pulled, slogging his way along the forest floor. The forest was alive around him. He heard it thrumming. The white light came from the trees. He saw that much. They glowed, pulsating. The birch wood vibrated with magical energy.

Eliot could not keep going. He had to keep going. He tried to open his eyes again. This time, they opened more. Not much, but it was enough for him to see the snowflakes—snowflakes!—filling the lambent wood. But he did not feel cold. He took a moment, breathing deeply. The ground beneath him was so soft, so warm, so inviting. He could sleep here. He could sleep here forever. His sore bones begged for it. Perhaps he would sleep. Perhaps forever.

No, he had to return to camp. He had to escape this bewitched forest. He opened his eyes again, this time almost to half. Was it snow he saw? Or was it soft petals? Birch trees do not have soft white petals. Then what? The forest was alive with them, whatever they were. He risked a cautious look around. He was in a glen, and at its center was a gigantic tree. The largest elderbirch he'd ever seen, its trunk broad. At the tree's heart was a glowing stone. At the sight, Eliot's head went fishy.

Eliot rolled onto his back. The glen tilted around him. The leaves around his head fell down to his shoulders, then to his elbows. The ground tilted further, and he was on his feet. He was walking. Eliot was walking through the luminous birch wood, marveling at the laughter of the trees. Yes, they laughed. Song came from the crystal petals dancing among their branches. Eliot was smiling. His heart hummed.

Then Eliot saw black.

Click, click, click. Eliot knew that sound from somewhere. His head was so heavy, but with sleep, not pain. He gave in and slipped back into darkness.

The tree was huge. It stretched into the sky, to the sky and perhaps beyond. The stone in its heart glowed, a radiant jewel. But no, it was not a stone. Not exactly. The wind blew a fiery white dance through the birch wood. The forest was in full bloom. Green and white and magical. Eliot wondered.

Click, click. Eliot stirred, soporific. Rolling onto his side, he propped on an elbow. The woodsmen were near, watching him with cautious eyes. Weary. Wary. He looked beyond them, into the trees. There were the skulls. Yes, he knew he recognized that sound. He tried to sit up, but the ground spun beneath him and he was on his back again. And then he was in darkness again.

The smoke was sweet and savory. It was heady. The song was funny. The dance was funnier. Eliot laughed.

Click. Eliot sat up. He was in the Place of Skulls. He did not see the woodsmen at first. Then he felt a hand on his shoulder.

"Rest," Talker said from behind him. "Your fever still burns."

Then there was a cup to his lips. He sipped. His chest burned a furious, mad itch. He wanted to scratch it. That was when he realized they'd bound his hands. The tonic in the cup was bitter and warm. It turned his stomach, and Eliot fell to his back again. The skulls rattled in the trees, their familiar *click, click, click* almost a comfort. But not quite. He remembered this place now. How long ago had they come here? More important, he remembered other things. He remembered the glen. He remembered the smoking man. They had met before.

Sleep regained its hold on Eliot, but it did not banish that memory. Rather, it released it.

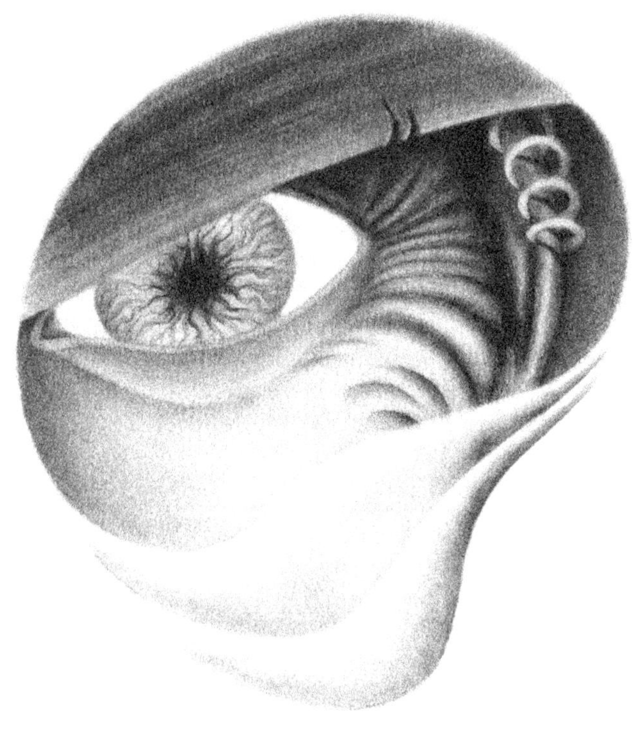

CHAPTER SIX: THE SMOKING MAN

Eliot paused at the forest's edge. Something tight gripped his shoulder, pinching it to the point of pain. He turned and saw it was the hand of Stalker. But he did not yet think of him as Stalker, did he? No, this memory was from before that.

"We do not go this way," Talker said with a sneer.

"Why?" Eliot asked.

"Because it is not our way."

"But why?" Eliot asked again. "If the scarecrow . . ."

"Our scarecrow did not enter this forest. Of that I am certain," Talker said, his voice heavy with condescension.

"How can yeh be sure?" Eliot, only a few months into his kohlas by now, thought it curious the woodsman referred to the scarecrow in the possessive. It wasn't *the* scarecrow, it was *our* scarecrow.

"Trust me on this, boy. This is not our way." The other woodsman's grip on Eliot's shoulder tightened. Eliot pulled away.

Eliot would never challenge the woodsmen. The newness of the woodsmen and their peculiarities remained a source of fear and anxiety for Eliot. In time, he would grow to trust them. He would grow fond of them, Talker at least. But at just seven years and fresh on his quest, he remembered trepidation. Besides, he had no cause to challenge them. They allowed Eliot to lead the charge, and he was young. On rare occasions they changed his course, but he was learning. And each time they course corrected, it was sensible. But this time, something was off. He took another step into the edge of the birch wood, but the woodsmen did not follow. Eliot did not think they would follow him inside the trees. He wondered if they could not. But he was certain this was the way the scarecrow had come. Eliot took another step.

"But why?" he asked. It was a simple question, but it had always annoyed his father. He could see the same annoyance in the woodsmen now.

"That is a hollow question." Talker's disdain was clear.

"Why do yeh not answer it?" A simple question demanded a simple answer. Nothing more.

"Don't be insolent, milly." The woodsmen turned in unison and walked along the forest's edge, leading east away from the birch wood and back toward where they'd come.

Eliot had to choose. He deliberated for a moment and turned to follow. He had no reason to ignore or disobey them. He had no desire to raise their anger. Perhaps they knew something of the place he did not. But as he turned to follow after them, he saw in his periphery a flash of shining yellow just inside the tree line. In his gut, Eliot felt anticipation leap.

"Wait," he called out to the woodsmen, but neither turned. He looked back into the dim forest but could make out nothing but the shape of ancient trunks, thick and white. Out of the corner of his eye, he saw movement. A tall man with long legs and long arms who wore a wide-brimmed hat cantered among the trees: not a man . . . the scarecrow.

Like a hound sighting a rabbit, Eliot tore into the forest in pursuit. His breath sounded in his ears like storm winds. He'd found the scarecrow, and so soon into his quest. The creature seemed to amble along, ducking in behind trees and out from behind others farther ahead. For all of Eliot's effort, he could not catch up. He could not account for this. Was the scarecrow magic? It had to be. If it walked like a man, magic must enliven it. How had he not considered this before now? He felt icicles stab into his seven-year-old belly. He gave no thought to the woodsmen and knew not whether they followed. Anticipation had erased the woodsmen from his thoughts. Again and again Eliot saw that lanky shape moving amongst the trees. It remained far enough ahead to prevent Eliot from seeing much. Each time he caught a glimpse, he pushed harder. He ran faster.

After several long minutes in a full sprint, Eliot came into a glade. The space was dim but not dark even though it was late. A gentle snow fell even though it was too early for snow. The air in the clearing was comfortable, not cold. Eliot felt something queer—something he had no catalogue for. A tingling on his skin. What was this place?

In the center of the glade stood a towering birch tree. The base of its trunk was as large as a small house and just above head height was a grave cavity filled with shadow. It had not always been in shadow. A glowing orb had been set in it. But how did he know that? The bark down low on the tree was a rich chestnut brown. However, by the height of two grown men it faded to a brilliant white so the tree itself looked a specter. Its white bark glowed like the other trees in the strange forest, only more so. Wait, the trees were glowing? Eliot realized the glade was hazy with unnatural light, a stark contrast against the darkness of night. The light did not originate in the sky but rather came from the forest itself. Witchlight, only Eliot did not feel it foreshadowed death. Quite the opposite, Eliot felt life. This was no ordinary birch wood. And the enormous tree was no ordinary tree. It was talismanic.

The tree's branches reached in every direction, and Eliot heard soft humming as their fingers rubbed together in the slight wind. The snow falling among those branches danced like floating crystals or wayward stars. There was magic in this place. Deep magic. High magic. At once, Eliot felt thrill and dread. Was this a vaultine? A low place? Good or bad?

At the base of the tree, sitting on a large upturned root, was a man. Not the scarecrow, as he'd hoped. He remembered his initial disappointment at this, and how his disappointment faded into wonder. And how he understood at once he had never met a man like this. The man's face was downcast so his large-brimmed hat covered his features. When he turned to look at Eliot, Eliot felt exhilaration course through him. *Friend,* Eliot thought, though he took a step backward. Wariness made him alert to potential danger. Wouldn't an enemy, and especially a fayelee enemy, disguise himself as being a friend? An asp coiled within the fluff of a puppy . . . waiting for a curious boy to come close enough to strike.

The man's face was white, but his eyes were glowing yellow. This made Eliot uneasy, but there was a kindness in his smiling, fiery eyes. A cloud of mystery shrouded him, but Eliot felt he saw the man with more clarity than made sense. Was this a glamour? The man had a thin, wide smile that stretched the width of his face. To his lips he held a long fine smoking pipe the bowl of which glowed yellow, the same yellow as the man's eyes. A soft tendril of smoke rose from the pipe in a wispy grin. The smile on the man's face was one of utter delight.

"Looky-look," the smoking man said in a congenial, playful tone. "What seek you, boy?"

"I seek an enemy," replied Eliot. He stood aslant from the man. His feet apart, his knees loose, and his hands soft fists at his sides. He was ready to run or fight.

"Mayhap you found one," smirked the smoking man. "Mayhap you have. Tell me, why think you to find an enemy here in this magical place?" The man lifted his hands in a grand gesture, taking in the surrounding wood. At the move, the glittering crystals chimed and the trees themselves sang.

"I do not know," stammered Eliot. "I don't know what this place is." *I don't know what you are, either,* Eliot thought. He swallowed. He felt happiness swirl within him. It must be a trick. A devil's trick. He moved another step back. The man in the wide-brimmed hat smiled, and the brilliance of it almost drew Elliot back in.

"Then truly I say to you, boy, wisest thing may be for you to find your way out, and that quick." At this, the smoking man stood. He was tall, taller than either of the woodsmen, and seemed to unfold endlessly. Towering above Eliot, he moved close. Eliot wanted to flee for his life and hide, but he could not move his legs. Eliot smelled the man's burning tobacco, but it smelled unlike anything he had ever known. It was intoxicating, a scent that left him unsteady. He shook his head to clear it, but he chuckled instead. He slapped a hand over his mouth. He knew he must be a comical site: his eyes wide and his hand hiding his rebellious smile. Eliot's vision softened as the man leaned closer. "Wisdom may yet keep you here, hmm?"

The smoking man laughed a gentle laugh.

The smoke from his pipe rose from the bowl and reached out to Eliot with purpose. Eliot wheezed and made to run away. Instead, he fell into the man's arms. The moment they touched, Eliot felt peace encircling him. He wanted to give in to it. To live within it. This alarmed him. He understood then he was no match for magic. He understood this stranger could do with him as he willed. Eliot could not stop him. The man lifted Eliot and held him close, kneeling with the boy and placing him among the roots of the enchanted tree.

Moving in close, so their faces were only a breath apart, the smoking man sniffed. “You are a ripe one, are you not?” After a chuckle, he went on, “But no one can blame a wild thing for being wild, aye?” In a whisper, as though they were fellow conspirators, the man added, “but I still smell her on you . . . and aye, that’s good.”

Her? Who did he smell? For a moment, Eliot knew. For a moment, Eliot smelled her too: juniper blossoms, sunshine, and hearth fire. But in a moment, her smell was gone and his head was fuzzy again.

Then, changing the subject, the smoking man said, “You really oughtn’t be making your way through a vaultine by yourself. Even good magic may be testy.”

Eliot realized the man was right, not about good magic—Eliot knew nothing of magic—but about the other thing he’d said: Eliot was alone. The woodsmen had not followed him into the forest, just as he first suspected. Perhaps the magic of the forest would not allow them in. Fear choked him then. What if the woodsmen couldn’t get to him? What if his disobedience had led him into a trap? What if the woodsmen, his only allies, had abandoned him for being insolent? Eliot froze with panic. His knees trembled, knocking together like walnuts. He was stretched out on the forest floor, vulnerable and exposed. The smoking man loomed over him, his glowing eyes boring into him. Their gaze pressed him into the soil. His arms were so heavy that he couldn’t lift them to cover himself, much less fend off an attack. He’d never enjoyed the company of the woodsmen, but he wished they were here now.

The smoking man continued, “It isn’t right for a boy like you to be running through a magic wood with no thought to consequence. What think you now, Eliot?”

Eliot? Had he called him by name or was the smoke working deeper into Eliot’s brain? Eliot stammered, but the smoking man cut him off. “Shh, now. Be quiet. Lucky for you, says I, that I was here to intercept you.” Once again he laughed. It was kind laughter but unnerving. Eliot’s head was both light and heavy. He wriggled in the leafy bed of the forest floor to push himself away, but as he did, vertigo whipped him back against the ground.

“Do not fear me,” the smoking man said. “Fear only what chases you.”

“But nothin’ chases me,” Eliot made to say but his lips didn’t move. The smoking man answered as if they had.

“Oh come now, my boy. You are clever. Surely you know that you are being chased. Don’t you? Or do you believe still that it is you who are the hunter?” He tsk’d twice with his tongue. “Oh no, child.”

Eliot felt the smoking man’s grip tighten, and his eyes stung as the smoke from the pipe filled them. “I am not a child,” he said. He was seven, but where he came from, that was the age he began growing into manhood. But even as he made this statement, he felt its foolishness. He felt foolish for believing it. For ever having believed it.

“You are not a man. Not yet, and far from it.” The man squatted on his heels, all knees and elbows. “Eliot, do not race to become a man. Instead, you should remain a boy for as long as it pleases you. But alas, that choice was not given to you, aye? And that makes my heart weepy.

“And that thing which you pursue is not your mark. It is folly to believe it. Folly and death. You are the mark and know it not. It is not my duty to save you, I’m afraid. I do not intend to give you aid. I have, however, a tiny thing which may bring you hope in some dark moment. Of this matter I will speak little. You are young even if you are not a child. I am old. And old men say no more than they choose.”

Who was this stranger? Eliot wondered. And why did he want to sit at this man’s feet for a lifetime just to bask in the radiance of his smile? The smoking man spoke in riddles. Eliot was not fond of riddles. The man was not from Gal-Braith, that was certain. Had he been from the valley, he would understand the value of the kohlas. The importance of every boy’s cumatu—every boy’s coming-of-age rite. The reverence it deserved. The respect that bordered on worship. Wasn’t it a sacred thing? And weren’t sacred things meant to be revered? Eliot did not trust the smoking man. Or rather, he did not want to, but trust came unbidden. It came like sunrise.

The man’s voice was high and light, his dialect foreign. The man was celestial. He moved Eliot into a more comfortable bed of leaves and twigs nestled among the roots. The roots pinned Eliot in, but they comforted him like a swaddled baby. He now looked straight up into the white branches of the giant tree, crystalline flakes exulting among the luminescent arms. The smoking man danced out of Eliot’s range of vision, singing as he went. A flutter of sparkling diamonds rushed in the man’s wake as his lilting voice mesmerized Eliot further into reverie. Eliot’s vision shimmered around the edges as the smoking man sang of a magic glass and a sacred tree and the birth of light.

A tale of tales
I have to tell
A merry tale it be
A story of old
And one so bold
As ever a tale they'll be

The fire kindles
In a pot
A pot of glass and tree
It burns to light
The world alight
It shines on me and thee

That magic glass
That sacred bough
It sets our marrow free
And showers down
In endless round
All good and lovely things

A tree sprung forth
From river mouth
And stretched, towering
The sandy bed
A cryst'line bed
Gave us gifts like these:

Up from the glass
That formed the bowl
A light was loosed and see!
The world became
Awash, ablaze
Bounded by the three

It showers down
In endless round
A pitch to make us free
As ever a song
Could carry along
The hearts of those who sing

Eliot smiled. He could not see him, but he heard the smoking man's dancing feet shuffle amid the crunchy leaves on the forest floor. Then the silhouette of that enormous hat came to hover above Eliot's face. The man was so close Eliot could smell him. He smelled of a riverbed. His yellow eyes twinkled, fireflies in his head, and he laughed.

As the smoking man drew away, he held aloft a small pouch pulled tight by a string. "And what do I offer the young lad, hmm?" he asked in a sing-song voice. He unfastened the pouch and removed a small brownish-purple object from inside. Held between the smoking man's thumb and forefinger, Eliot saw a large bean. His wonder increased.

"Hidey-ho," cried the smoking man as he did a quick pirouette. "My little master mayhap recognizes the prize?"

It was a juniper-bean. They grew on his father's farm. He'd loved them as part of their husking celebration to bring in each new year, their colorfully dyed husks covering their yard in rainbow. He'd eaten them roasted on frigid winter days, raw by the handful in the summer heat. But there was another way to eat them, wasn't there? Eliot could not say why, but the bean moved him. It transfixed him, connecting him somehow with a memory that lay just outside his reach. And even though Eliot could not say why, seeing the juniper-bean filled him with warmth. The warmth was life and hope, like warm pie fresh from the oven.

"Yes, yes, my little one," cried the smoking man. Then he put the bean in Eliot's mouth, who chewed and swallowed it. "Now," the man continued, "Breathe deep and sleep." He blew on his pipe, creating a cloud of fragrant smoke that filled Eliot's vision. The smoking man sang again, this time a lullaby.

Fireflies
Swimming in moonlight
Teasing twilight's dusty shades
Night songs
Tickle time since gone
To the smile of Edön Grey

The willow weeps
The melody
Of sweet mem'ry's lovely strain
The humming brook goes
And the thistle knows
The secret of Edön Grey

Though he tried to stay alert, Eliot's eyelids grew heavy. There were things here he needed to see, but his eyes were so very tired. Perhaps he could see them in dreams instead. He felt himself being heaved from the ground and smelled the riverbed and the char from the pipe. He felt strong arms holding him tight, and he saw one last glimmer of the ghostly tree, a spirit in this magical place. A beacon. The sensation of the man's arms cradling him infused Eliot with contentment. He realized he could stay in this place. He could be happy here, being held by a stranger with actual fire in his eyes. The thought made Eliot jolt, and he tried to shake himself from the euphoria threatening to take hold. His mind spun, and he felt nauseous. His unease was palpable and stood in stark contrast to the contentment threatening to fill him. But oh, he wanted to be filled. He needed it. Yes, caution be damned. Eliot wanted this. He would suffer the sickness to prolong the pleasure. He was no longer apprehensive. Perhaps he should be, but he settled instead into a cozy bliss. This man could do with him what he pleased. Eliot dipped deeper into his stupor, the remaining fragments of his worry flying away like dandelion spores on a wind. He could not resist. He no longer wanted to. Eliot felt safe. Why should he fight that? He heard the smoking man's chuckles, and they pulled Eliot feet first into a heavy sleep. As he drifted down, song followed him. The smoking man sang: the song remained the same, but the cadence altered.

Fayelee tales wish for the magic
And make-believe wants to dream such dreams
As the creatures of the forest linger
Linger while Edön sings

Enchanted, the little ones they slumber
As the weaver spins softly night's seams
And fire leans gently from star field to kiss
To kiss little Edön sweet

Who was Edön Grey? Eliot wondered, but he knew she must be beautiful. Eliot was sifting into a deeper sleep than he had ever experienced. The sway of the smoking man's gait lolled him further, until he slept the contented sleep of a cradled infant. The man's song burrowed into his marrow.

Dandeli'ns
Drink in the milky night
As the moon shines down his violet haze
Laced with stardust
The singing breeze must
Go the way of Edön Grey

Very soon
The sleepy moon
Follows the stars' parade
As the golden glow
Warms both lilies and thorns
To delight of Edön Grey

As peaceful reverie shone on the boy's face, the smoking man's voice faded into the air, and his hand pressed hard against the boy's chest. Searing warmth transferred from him to the boy as the smoking man spoke a secret incantation. The boy did not stir, but the oath did.

"Late," the man said, "but not too late. May it yet bring you good in the years ahead, Eliot. And just on time."

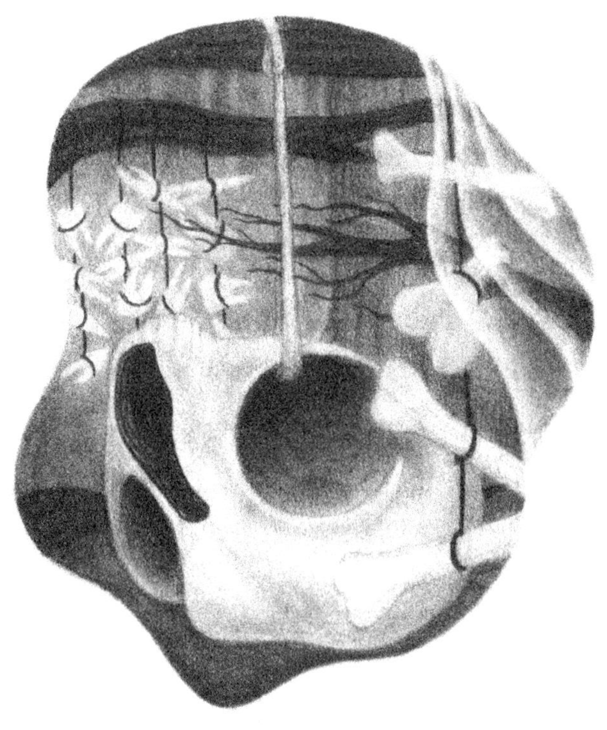

CHAPTER SEVEN: INFECTED

Eliot woke with a start. He was in the Place of Skulls, but he hadn't been moments before. He'd been in the glen with the smoking man. That's what Eliot had called him the first time they met. Even though it was just a memory, Eliot's body thrummed with the raw energy of the hypnotic birch wood and the enchanted tree at its heart.

As his mind sharpened, he felt the skin on his chest and stomach. It was alive and crawling with a fierce itch. He wanted to scratch it. To scrape his very skin away, but he could not. His hands would not obey. He went back to his memory of the smoking man.

How long ago had that been? Less than a year into his quest, so six years at least since. It was a strange experience, one not easily forgotten. But he had forgotten it. Utterly. Even seeing the smoking man again in the field did nothing to dislodge the memory. Then again, perhaps it did. That night he'd dreamt of his mother. Perhaps the man's magic had uncoiled something in Eliot's mind that allowed the memories to surface once again. And if these, then what others?

The woodsmen appeared with fresh game. They saw him awake, and Stalker cut his hands free. He had bound them with strong leather.

"You were hurting yourself," Talker explained.

"How long did I sleep?" Eliot asked. His body ached and his chest and stomach itched, but there was a fresh burning sensation on the skin of his lower abdomen. He pulled up the tail of his shirt to see. An angry rash started beneath his naval and ran down below his waistband. It speckled his dark skin with red dots, but there was a pattern. He scratched it as he pushed his breeches lower to see. The rash continued to his inner thigh, in the cleft of which he found a small open wound seeping blood and puss. The rash could have been drawn on, he thought. A coiling, curling band of wrathful flesh.

He looked around. Talker offered a waterskin, which Eliot used to wash the spot and then drink. Such skin irritants were common. Whether from poor hygiene, the exertion of the hunt, exposure to poisonous vines and biting insects, or a combination of all, burns, bites, and rashes were an accepted reality of his quest. Though he was not a healer, Eliot had gleaned insight on how to treat them. He stood. His legs were wobbly, but they worked.

"Mayhap you should not move just yet," Talker said.

"How long?" Eliot asked again.

"Your fever lasted many days."

"Days?" Eliot asked, startled. "I slept for days?"

Talker nodded.

"Mayhap that's why I'm starvin'," Eliot replied. He thought again of the smoking man, wondering if he should say something to Talker. Not yet, he reasoned. Perhaps after he cleared his head of sleep.

He found a tuft of gilly weed growing near the creek bed and gathered a bunch for his wound. There was a stone altar in the center of the creek, and the bones of animals cluttered the open area of the camp. Bones, their majority skulls, hung from the trees and clicked with maddening regularity. Eliot hoped they were animal bones. He remembered the woodsman had called this the Place of Skulls, and the first time they'd come, he'd given little thought to it other than it scared him senseless. He was young then. Now, he understood this was a sacred place. A Dun-twille, most likely. It appeared ancient, but he could not say if this was true. Even at fourteen, he knew little about such things. He studied the flat surface of the stone altar. It was a cyth, he knew that much: a surface meant for divining. On it were carved ancient Lynthian runes. He shuddered to think what acts may have been performed here.

As Talker prepared Eliot's dinner, Eliot chewed the bitter grass and formed the gilly weed pulp into a pasty ball before applying it to his wound and rash. It might slow the spread and even draw out the offending poison, whatever it was.

Eliot turned to Stalker, who had kept to himself since Eliot woke. "Do yeh have any of yer ointment? In the red jar?" he asked, but Stalker did not show any sign he'd heard.

"We cannot give you more ointment," Talker said, "not now, anyway."

"Why? Won't it help?" Eliot asked. If it would help heal his burning itch, he wanted it.

"Not now," Talker said, handing him his dinner instead.

Eliot finished his meal. The skin between his legs now itched with a madness, though it burned less. That was a good sign the gilly weed was working. He hefted himself from the ground and moved around the camp, his legs and back stiff from disuse. He needed to work them. Besides, moving distracted him from the discomfort of his inner thigh.

"You should sleep," Talker said. It was close to dark.

Eliot did not answer. He'd slept for days. He did not need more sleep. The bones in the trees went *click, click, click.* The creek gurgled. Otherwise, the forest was silent. After a moment, he sat hard on the ground and took in the horizon. He scratched at his chest. It was not so painful as his thigh, but it was not much better. Perhaps he should scrub himself in the creek before the weather turned colder. But not now. His belly full, sleep called to him once again like an estranged bedfellow. He felt weak, knew the fever may yet be wearing off. Next day he would eat and hunt. But now, he would allow his body a little longer to heal.

He slept, but his dreams were not merciful.

"Yeh did not think the story would have a happy endin', did yeh?"

Eliot was dreaming about a strange old woman. She was stuffing a sack with turnips and looking at him with keen milky eyes. Her skin was dark, like his. She was Braithian, perhaps.

"Well," she said. "Did yeh?"

Eliot did not know how to answer. He scratched the skin beneath a bristly scrap of hair on his cheek. He scratched an itch between his legs. The old woman's questioning bored him. She, however, was not finished.

"Answer, boy. Yeh didn't think the story would have a happy endin'. Not even one so young as you would expect that. No one makes it out of such a sorry tale. Not alive and whole, leastways."

Eliot thought for a moment. "Any story can have a happy endin', and I am not so young."

"No," she said, venom in her voice. "Put that from yer filthy head. Not all stories are built for happy endins, and this is no babbie's tale. Yeh know that."

She shoved the sack of turnips into his hands, but it was no longer a sack of turnips. It was a basket of rotting gourds, the kind with faces carved into them at high festival time. The tween lights' visages, fitful and spurting with the flames burning inside, jeered at him. Their flesh melted with heat and decay.

He looked back at the old woman. She was young and healthy. Beautiful, but her skin was not so dark as before. It was his golden-haired, olive-skinned mother. She smiled at Eliot, reaching a hand to caress the now smooth skin of his cheek. He was a young child again, no longer fourteen.

"Ah," she said, her voice a sweet melody, "my sweet boy is a dreamer."

She stood, walked to the window, and looked out. In the distance, Eliot saw bright orange light burning the horizon. His mother turned.

"Yeh cannot spare to hope, my boy." She looked again out the window, a tear washing her cheek. "And yeh cannot spare not to."

Her meaning was lost on him. He shook his head in confusion and found it hurt. From the basket in his lap, the gourds were singing:

When the moon turns to blood
The boys all eat the wormy meat
When the moon turns to blood
The boys all eat the wormy meat

The woman at the window turned again to Eliot and rushed forward, her hands reaching out to him. "Boy," she said, "yeh don't have to run. There are other ways . . ." But as she spoke, her voice, which had been sweet like her face, changed back into the gravelly voice of an old woman.

Then her jaw came unhinged and her mouth fell open like a trunk. From inside, a flurry of blackness threatened to escape, and Eliot heard the basket in his lap fill with laughter. He looked at it in horror: the gourds were eating one another. Something sharp struck him on the nose, and he looked up in time to see a murder of crows issue from the woman's throat, cawing to turn the night red. Their bright red talons clawed at his chest as they flew.

Eliot jerked awake, the nightmare still trundling through his heavy head. The crows were still at his chest, ripping at his flesh. He scurried backward, only then realizing he was awake, and it had not been the crows scratching his chest.

Stalker's hand remained extended from the place where Eliot's chest had been, the tips of his leather gloves red. But this was not blood red. In his other hand he held his jar of ointment.

"Calm down, boy," Talker said, sitting across from him by the fire. "It's for your healing."

"What?" Eliot asked, the depth of his slumber a stubborn burden and reluctant to leave. He shook his head. "My healin'?"

"Aye," Talker replied, his voice calm. "Your chest. You asked for ointment."

"And yeh said I couldn't have it."

Stalker capped the ointment and left Eliot's side.

"Wait," Eliot called after him.

"Do you want it or not?" Talker asked.

"Will it hurt me?"

"It will cause pain, but that is the price of getting well."

Eliot had madness on his skin and madness in his head. He should have healing for one, at least, he figured. He nodded. Stalker returned, opening the jar as he did. The smell was caustic and heavy. It burned Eliot's nose. No wonder it also burned his skin. Stalker dipped a finger into the jar and then lifted Eliot's shirt to apply it.

"Should I take it off?" Eliot asked.

Stalker shook his head. Eliot couldn't see how bad the rash on his chest and stomach was, not in the dim light. And Stalker helped little, lifting his shirt only enough to apply the ointment. The pain was intense. Eliot squirmed at the abrasive cruelty of the job. *It better heal me,* he thought. Pain flared, and he had to fight the urge to run. As a distraction, he talked.

"The man in the field," he said, wincing and squeezing his eyes shut against the pain. "I met him before." He hadn't meant to bring up the smoking man, not yet. But perhaps better the smoking man than his mother.

Stalker's hand stilled. The camp was quiet. Eliot opened his eyes. The woodsmen stared at him.

"Did yeh hear me?" Eliot asked. Talker nodded. Stalker recapped his jar and walked away. "What?" Eliot asked, regretting he'd said anything.

Talker did not offer an answer, so Eliot went on. The woodsmen's reaction puzzled him. He may as well search out more of this mystery.

"It were early, less than a year after I left my da's farm. Do yeh remember? I'd forgotten it," Eliot said. "Strange, aye? To forget and all. He were a—"

"He's a villain," Talker said.

"Why say yeh that?" Movement in Eliot's periphery drew his attention. It was dark here, but as he scanned the tree line, he swore he saw coiling gloom among the bones. As if a large snake, one as big as his leg, was coming for him. His heart skipped, but it was a trick of the firelight. What he'd seen was a tree root, nothing more. Talker's voice called him back.

"There are many unnamed—"

"Aye, I know. Many unnamed dangers, and I'm just a child and can't understand 'em. But why say yeh that? What makes him a villain, aye?"

Talker shook his head, his face sad. "You must trust us, boy."

"But that don't go both ways, yeh reckon? When will yeh trust me back?" Eliot kept his voice level and light as he spoke, careful to keep any hint of emotion out of it. He did not mean offense, nor to press this issue. He'd found himself firmly put back in his place the last time he had. But like the itch on his skin, this resilient agitation itched in his brain.

As Talker turned to him, Eliot thought the woodsman's face seemed more gaunt than usual. The skin around his eyes and ears was inflamed, or so the trick of firelight made them appear. Infected, Eliot had thought about the woodsmen. They looked infected. This seemed truer now more than ever. What about the smoking man could instigate such unease in them? Stalker had left the camp by now, no doubt sulking in the shadows.

"He wants you," Talker said. "For himself."

Eliot said nothing to this for several moments, the weight of the words cumbersome in his belly. He swallowed and forced himself to ask, "Who is he?"

"He is an enemy, has been a long time. He has no love for you."

"Who is he?"

"A villain."

"Aye, but who is he? A villain in one tale is the hero of another, so who is he? How do yeh know him? Where did he come from? And how does he know my name?"

"He knows your . . ." Talker began, but stopped himself. He looked panicked, and Eliot could not help but catch some of that panic himself. It spun out with the anger rising in him, making his thoughts oily.

Then he heard something. A distant rattling in the trees. He looked around them. Again, he saw movement in the gloom. He saw darkness writhing, shadow twisting in a black helix. But no, there was nothing there. Just trees and bones.

"What are yeh not tellin' me?" Eliot asked, as much to distract from the discomfort of their surroundings as to get an answer. The rattling continued, and it seemed closer. He stole a glance into the forest, but there was nothing. *Dry branches in a furtive wind,* Eliot thought. Eliot hoped. Why he should be paranoid now, he could not explain. He'd spent countless nights in this dreadful place. Why should the Dark Wood seem fit to come alive just now? Perhaps it was the bones. They'd camped in the Place of Skulls before, but not for so long.

Talker stood and walked over to Eliot, kneeling before him. He put his hand on Eliot's chest.

"I cannot name him," the woodsman said. "To do so would give him power. If you see him, run from him."

Talker's gravity struck Eliot. He didn't know what to say, and before he could say anything, Talker was speaking again, and Eliot's chest was blazing. The rattling in the trees was lightning strikes in his head. The darkness among the bones a hungry serpent.

"Gho gret kee . . . Gho gret kee . . . Gho gret kee, ehl koh let kee." Talker repeated the words until they swam through Eliot's head. The clattering wood trilled a dirge of nervous chatter and knocking. His skin agonized, a burning tunic of flesh. The forest bent toward them. Limbs like jagged teeth came for him. Eliot started to scream but rather fell through a black tunnel into a dreamless sleep.

CHAPTER EIGHT:

THE WAY IS THE WAY IS THE WAY

In the following days, Eliot did the one thing he knew how to do: hunt. He set about his task with renewed vigor, and each day he felt weighed down by a shift in the woodsmen's attitude toward him. They wanted to move slower, often suggesting a different route from the one he chose. They had doubted him before, but this felt different. He feared they'd lost all confidence in him. Rather than broach the subject with Talker, he pressed forward in the quest, determined to prove their doubts unfounded.

They left the Place of Skulls but remained in the Dark Wood. Eliot hated the place. He believed every dry and fretful twig was an affront to him, to his childhood, and to his quest to find the scarecrow. And since that night after his fever broke, and the forest seemed to come alive, Eliot could not escape a blanket of fear for the place. But that had been his raving imagination. The product of the bones and a days-long fever. Still, the Dark Wood was the perfect terrain for a creature like the scarecrow. Nowhere did the scarecrow's tracks seem more difficult to decipher than here. Tracks were everywhere, as though the forest itself were the scarecrow. To further complicate things, his dreams echoed over and over in his head, a torrent of emotion ripping through him each time. But he could not allow that to hold him back.

So he tracked. His eyes were keen to find signs of his quarry, and so they did. Everywhere. Discerning which signs were legitimate was the challenge. Not waiting for their guidance, he pressed ahead of the woodsmen. He did not need their approval, not yet. That would come later, he hoped. His outward focus was singular, but his thoughts were frenetic. His mind's eye grew fractured. Everywhere he saw his mother's face. In the undulating shadows beneath the canopy of limbs. In the dark shapes coiling near the forest floor. The scarecrow was there, too. Spindly arms and burning eyes darting in among the trees, and not just the scarecrow. The smoking man led the charge. Eliot seemed always in the man's shadow, just beyond his magic. And on his heels, Eliot felt the woodsmen's disappointment. With each step, he saw all over again Talker's dismay when Eliot had mentioned the smoking man.

But Eliot could not abide such distractions, so he tracked, pushing his body into service. But always he saw golden hair. Always he felt burning eyes. Always he sensed crouching darkness, hungry to taste him. Always he was lost, craven, obsessed. Even in the cool air, sweat made his hair heavy, sticking to his face in clots. He chewed his lower lip to bleeding. His eyes darted back and forth, roving the landscape for signs of his prize. Finding the scarecrow was his sanity, so he must find it at all costs.

"What are you doing, Eliot?"

Talker's voice broke the spell of Eliot's chase. He crouched amid thistles, studying a thatch of hair caught in the tangle. He turned his wild eyes on the woodsman and found empathy there. Scolded by the man's concern, Eliot looked back at the fur, most likely deer, and blinked his eyes dry.

"Huntin'," he said, but he understood this was not the answer Talker sought.

The woodsman crouched beside him. "You are pushing yourself too hard."

Turning on him, Eliot asked, "Am I?" He spit the words. "Is that why yeh can barely look at me?"

Eliot yanked the fur free of the brambles and stalked away, but the woodsman wasn't finished.

"What has soured in you?" he asked.

"Me?" Eliot asked, turning to face his teacher. "Nothin'. It's not me who's changed."

He watched for emotion to alter Talker's countenance, but none came. The man was stoic as ever. Eliot remembered how unsettling the woodsmen had been at the beginning. How he had feared them and longed for their approval, two opposing forces pulling within him. Pressing him forward. Now, he did not fear them. He respected them, but he had no reason to be afraid. He wished he could say he no longer required their approval.

"You have changed, boy," Talker said. His words were soft, but they offended anyway. Eliot stomped up the rise away from Talker. "Do not walk away," the man said. His words were no longer soft.

In Eliot's head, he knew Talker was being reasonable. The truth of it shamed him. Even so, his body had spun as if by its own volition, and Eliot was before Talker, his finger thrust up into the woodsman's face.

"You have changed!" Eliot shouted, his voice raw and shaky with emotion. His eyes wild and wet. "You do not trust me! You try to slow me down, to tell me where to go. I am the hunter! This is my kohlas!" His body trembled, his face hot and swollen. Anger and remorse constricted his throat. All he wanted was Talker's approval. That he would shout at him was illogical. He felt compelled by another Eliot, one unwilling to see reason. But he was in it now. Might as well press on.

"Ever since that damned man showed up in the birch wood, yeh've treated me like a child. Like I were too stupid to see for myself. You question everythin' I do. You told me to sleep when all I'd done was sleep for days. It's like yeh want me to fail. Like yer makin' me fail!"

"When have I made you do anything, milly?"

"When you used yer magic to shut me up!"

Eliot had no idea how furious this had made him until he'd spoken the offense aloud. He'd had no idea it had been gnawing at him for days. A torment just around the corner, where he could not quite see it.

Talker had used magic to put Eliot to sleep.

With both hands, he pressed hard against the woodsman's chest, but the man didn't budge. Rather, he took Eliot by the arm and flung him to the ground. From the forest floor Eliot saw Stalker, skulking in the shadows as if waiting to lunge. Eliot looked up at Talker, his fury blurring his vision. His chest was a wreck of pain now, the itch a firestorm all the way to his crotch.

Talker stood erect, looking down at Eliot. "Come to me when you are reasonable," he said and walked away. Eliot watched him go, anger and shame burning his face in equal measure. He looked to Stalker. The woodsman sheathed the knife in his hand and turned to follow his companion. Emotion boiled within Eliot, but that emotion had taken possession of him moments before. Had driven him to put hands against his teacher.

What was he doing? Eliot wondered. What madness had taken hold of him? He had a right to be angry, but to disrespect his teacher? No. He squeezed his fists into his eyes and shook out a silent scream. It turned to sobbing. In the distance, he heard that sound. That rattling, unsettling sound. He ignored it. He wanted to erase the entire day. To make it as though it had never happened. He must face the woodsmen. He must show them his shame and accept their reproach. They had reason to doubt him. He'd proven it just now.

The wood chattered around him, click-clacking as if vested with haunted Hidain fricks. Eliot sat on the ground, his knees pulled into his chest and his face buried between them. He remained this way for a long time, unwilling to move until his emotions were flat. He took long controlled breaths and practiced his apology in his head.

"You are my sweet, sweet boy," he heard his mother say. He clenched his fists. "You don't have to run," she said in his thoughts. Eliot bit his lower lip. He took another long steady breath. *The way is the way,* he repeated in his head: a chant to center himself. *The way is the way is the way . . .*

"But there are other ways," his mother said.

"No, there isn't," Eliot replied.

Eliot realized the forest surrounding him had grown silent. The Dark Wood did not entertain unnecessary noise. This was a primary reason the place felt so eery. But what of the rattling? And how had Eliot not considered this before: sound of any kind was out of place here. Outside the noise made by him and the woodsmen, the Dark Wood was silent. It was always silent except in the Place of Skulls. So how had he heard rattling here? Eliot wiped his tears on the knees of his breeches, scratched the irritated skin of his inner thigh, and stood to look around.

The darkness came alive with noise and movement. The rattling before was only the first drop of rain compared to this cyclone. Sharp cracks of wood and stone clamored around him, burrowing into his skull. But worse than the sound were the fingers. Grizzled claws the size of boulders reached for him from the forest. The trees. It was the trees. They came for him. They bent together into a wreath of teeth and claws and razor-bone talons, encircling him. The ground beneath his feet erupted. Bands of coiling tree roots caught his legs. And in the roots he saw eyes staring at him. In those eyes, he saw his ruin.

He screamed, but something long and hard and rough gagged him as it forced its way into his throat. His eyes went wide as, above him, the sky coalesced into a frenzy of glossy, diseased skin. It quivered with lustful energy as a fissure opened within it. Pulsating lips surrounded a concave tunnel of blurred blacks and dirty blood-reds. It was a gaping, festering thing sweating yellow-tinged fluid. The labial horror dripped its viscous discharge onto his face. Into his eyes. The root shoved deeper into his throat. Talons wrapped round his stomach, squeezing the life from his body. And the mouth above him lowered. Closer and closer it came, a hot, stinking breath burning his face. The smell briny and old. Bitter and spoiled . . .

"Vai stech theo lok!" A voice boomed in the chaos. "Ack! Vai stech the-andy tay! Hold fast!"

The wood retreated. The hold on Eliot's legs pulled back into the earth. The root in his throat left with vicious speed. It left him choking, swaying on dumbstruck legs. But the mouth did not move. It pulsated, salivating above him. Eliot fell. He scuttled backward, but where could he go? The voice. Who had spoken? Who had commanded the Dark Wood?

"Hold fast! Do not break covenant!" Eliot knew this voice, but he'd never heard it with such volume. With such power.

Eliot followed the sound. Talker stood, his short sword drawn. Stalker beside him, sword in hand. Both looked to the mouth. Both appeared ready to die if necessary. Eliot ran to them.

"Vai stoche therry lok! Nay, the-andy tay . . . Hold fast, I say. Do not break covenant. Hold fast or be driven back." Talker's face was homicidal with fury, his voice formidable. Stalker's body trembled, but Eliot did not think from fear. The mouth receded into the darkness. The trees fell into place. The death-rattle ceased, and again the Dark Wood slid into a black, fitful peace.

Talker turned to Eliot. "We leave now. We leave the Dark Wood."

"What—" Eliot began, but Talker interrupted.

"Now!" he shouted. Without another word, they left.

“I’m sorry,” Eliot said. They hadn’t spoken since it happened, whatever it was. They’d left the wood as quickly as possible, Eliot positive he’d called certain doom down upon them. Had the woodsmen not known what to do, Eliot would not have survived.

Talker was building the fire, and Stalker was skinning a goat. Neither looked up as Eliot spoke. So he went on.

“I shouldn’t have . . .” *Damn it all,* he thought. Did he even know what he’d done wrong? One thing he knew for certain: “I shouldn’t have shoved yeh,” he said. Of all the things that had happened, this was the ugliest to Eliot. For this darkness had been his alone.

Talker paused his work to look at Eliot. He did not speak.

“I made that happen,” he said, trying to make sense of it. “The Dark Wood, I did that somehow.”

“Leave it,” Talker said.

“I can’t,” Eliot said. “We could have died.”

Talker shook his head. “No. We would not have died. It was a test; one you failed.” He went back to his work. Eliot felt his heart drop.

“A test?” But of course. Forests don’t eat boys. That was ridiculous. Then why did Eliot’s throat feel as though something had skinned it? Why were his legs bruised? Then again, it made sense. This was his punishment. He had been insolent. He’d acted against his teachers. He’d defied his kohlas. He’d brought shame on himself, and with it, physical pain.

“I . . .” Eliot shook his head. What he’d said in the Dark Wood was true: the woodsmen had lost faith in him. He could not take that back. The test proved as much. That he’d failed proved their lost faith grounded. “I should be more reasonable,” he tried, hoping it was the right thing to say. If he meant it to make Talker talk, it didn’t. He tried again, sitting down across from Talker.

“I’m afraid,” he said. He felt his chest tighten at the admission and the truth of it. “I’m afraid I’ll fail. I’m afraid I can’t do it, and I gotta.” He shook his head again, pleading with his tears to go away. They fled, but straight down his face. “I am just a child, I know it. And I hate myself for it!” Again, he pulled his knees tight into his chest and hid his face in the crook of his elbow, biting down on his emotion. He pounded the earth with his fist, hating his childish tears. His itchy skin mocked him, adding to his humiliation the indignity of an insatiable craving to scratch his crotch. If the earth opened at just that moment and swallowed him whole, or perhaps a giant mouth in the sky, he would have been grateful. Still, the thought of that mouth made him shiver.

"Eliot," Talker said. Eliot did not look up, could not face the man. "Eliot, look at me."

Eliot took a moment but did as he was told. He looked into Talker's weary face. The man looked aged, more withered and gray than normal. More than even a few hours before. Had he been crying? The skin around his eyes looked raw. Fresh shame flooded Eliot, but Talker did not wait.

"Every boy feels as you do. Every boy believes he is not enough. Every boy is tested. Every boy fails the test." Talker leaned forward, pronouncing his next words with care. "You are exactly what is needed."

Eliot felt the risk of believing this. He wanted to, but he shook his head.

"How? How can I be?"

"The way is the way," Talker said.

Eliot laughed as fresh tears blotted his filthy cheeks. He hated his kohlas. With everything in him, he hated the whole damn bit.

"Eliot, do you remember when first you began this quest?"

Uncertain where this was going, Eliot looked at Talker. He nodded, though he had remembered little of those first years until the last few months. Then he shook his head. "Not really," he said. "Only bits and pieces."

"I remember," Talker said. "You were a scared little boy, but you didn't want us to see that. Instead, you gave yourself to your kohlas. You grew. You learned. This is the same."

"How is it the same?" Eliot asked. He could not hide the incredulity in his voice. He tried to press it between respect for Talker and a forced reverence for the kohlas. "I've gotten us nowhere. We've been huntin' this bloody scarecrow for seven years, and I have nothin' to show for it." He heard his tears in his voice. They mocked his sincerity.

Talker did not respond right away. He just looked at Eliot. Finally, he said again, "The way is the way."

Eliot scoffed and buried his face. His body shook with anger, shame, and confusion. He was disappointed. His chest and stomach were a maze of poisoned trails leading down his body. The rash quickened even as he thought of it, the need to scratch unbridled. He threw back his head and wailed, using both hands to claw at his chest, stomach, and crotch.

"No, Eliot," Talker said, but it was Stalker who grabbed his wrists. Eliot had forgotten Stalker. This was common when he and Talker spoke. But he was here now, and his features betrayed his emotion. Stalker was livid.

Eliot tried to pull his wrists free, but Stalker would not let go. No matter what Eliot did, the woodsman's strength overpowered him. For the first time in almost as long as he could remember, Eliot felt fear of the woodsman.

"Eliot," Talker said, "it will not do for you to scratch. That will not heal it. Trust us."

Talker seemed sensible enough. His pragmatic way only intensified Eliot's humiliation. Stalker released him, and Eliot rubbed his wrists.

"Can I have more of the ointment? It's like near unbearable."

"Later," Talker said. "For now, I will prepare a poultice of weed and mud. It will still the itch."

Stalker brought Talker a bunch of gilly weed and a jar filled with wet black soil. Swamp mud. It was easy to find in the lower areas of the foothills, but not so here.

"We were preparing for this," Talker explained. "My companion found these on his last errand."

The woodsman set about administering the poultice, crushing the herbs between two stones, mixing it with the mud. Then he placed the mixture in a bowl and set it on the fire's edge to warm. He called Eliot over to him.

Talker sat on the ground as Eliot stood before him. Slow and methodical, Talker dipped strips of torn cloth into the bowl, squeezing out the excess fluid. He nodded, and Eliot pulled up his shirt. The heat from the fire felt good on his back, but it could not compare to the relief of the warm concoction on his chest. The forest was bathed in night shadow as Talker wrapped Eliot's torso in the medicinal cloth. He pulled down Eliot's breeches and wrapped his offending leg and thigh down to his knee. Eliot tried to see how bad the rash was, but in the poor light he could make out little. The relief from the poultice was undiluted bliss.

After Talker finished, Eliot pulled up his breeches and sat again by the fire. Most of his body was warm now from the wrap. For the first time in weeks, he did not feel like peeling himself to the bone.

"It is time we change strategy with our scarecrow," Talker said.

Eliot's face wrinkled. "How do yeh mean?"

"We have played at its game long enough. Tomorrow, we head west."

"West? But how can yeh know that's where it'll be headin'?"

Talker looked at Eliot, his face placid but set. Eliot did not think his teacher would suffer debate. The woodsman looked poised to say, "There are many things you do not understand, boy . . ." Eliot did not think he could handle such a derisive statement. Not now. He remembered his former shame, that which only now had burned down to ash in his stomach. He used it to fortify himself against bringing on further rebuke.

"The scarecrow has a pattern," Talker said. "It will lead us in circles unless we force its hand."

"What?" Eliot asked, unable to hold it back. He shook his head and started again. "How do we force its hand?"

"We head west."

"And that'll do what?"

After a moment of excruciating silence, Talker said, "There are things you do not understand."

"Oh, damn it all!" Eliot cried. "I know I don't understand plenty, but that don't make no sense. Head west? And the damn thing'll, what, follow us?" He took a long breath, his eyes apologizing for his mouth.

"There is a pattern, Eliot. A pattern we know that you do not."

Eliot bit down on his tongue to silence it. He huffed, trying to use the breath to quell his returning rage. *You were sorry only moments ago,* he thought to himself. *Don't make yourself sorry again.* He took a slower breath and steadied himself.

"Alright, I can understand that. Will yeh leastways explain the pattern to me?" He tried to fill his voice with the tone of sensibility. Instead, it sounded petulant in his ears.

"It is easier if you trust instead."

Eliot took another, slower steadying breath. "It's easier, I think, if we all understand the strategy, aye?"

Talker looked at Stalker, who threw a stick onto the fire and strode out into darkness. Talker turned again to Eliot.

"The scarecrow is unnatural, aye?"

Eliot nodded. This was obvious. And he could guess where Talker was going with this.

"His ways, too, are unnatural. Not like ours."

"How do yeh know?" Eliot asked, doubt rounding his words into ovals. "I see no signs that—"

"There are other signs. Signs you don't see in the earth."

Eliot had nothing to say to this. Talker continued.

"The stars, the moon, the water, the earth . . . all have voices if you know how to listen."

"Yeh've been readin' the moon then?" Eliot asked, looking up into the darkness above them. The sky was scraped in black with coal ash. There was no moon or stars. For a moment, he saw in his memory the mouth bearing down to eat him and shuddered. When he looked again at Talker, the woodsman's attitude had soured. Eliot put up his hands.

"Aye," he said. "I'll not press it. We'll do as yeh say, but . . ." He put his hand flat on his chest, adding weight to his words. "I do not think that is the way. I'll trust yeh, but I need to say it. Here and now. Tomorrow, I'll not say a word. Promise. But now I gotta say it: I do not think this is the way."

Talker did not respond right away, but after a moment he nodded. "The way is the way," he said.

Was he joking? Eliot wondered. Had the woodsman made a joke? Talker did not smile, but Eliot did despite his reservations.

"Aye," he said, "the way is the way." If it wasn't a joke, it should be.

"Now," Talker said as he stood and walked to where Eliot sat, "we will apply the red ointment to your rash. But first, I'll make you sleep to ease your pain."

Talker moved his hand toward Eliot's chest, but Eliot flinched away.

"You do not like me to use my magic?" Talker asked. Eliot shook his head. "There are other ways to help you sleep, but they will not feel so good in the morning."

"Can I just wear the poultice? Yeh only now put it on me."

"No, boy. The poultice hides the pain. It does not heal it. And it wears off quickly."

Eliot wasn't convinced that was true, but he knew one thing: he had to trust Talker. He had to learn to accept his wisdom and not fuss over every thing he did not understand. Just then, Stalker wandered back into camp. Eliot did not feel the same need to trust Stalker. Something about the woodsman made Eliot leery, and it was more than his prickly personality. If he were honest, Eliot had to admit he did not like Stalker. The woodsman always had the look of a hungry beast, and Eliot felt like little more than a chipmunk next to that. But Talker was a good man. And he meant only to instruct and aid Eliot in his quest. If by association alone, Stalker was the same.

Finally, Eliot nodded acquiescence. Talker placed a hand on Eliot's chest and spoke the words that drove him into a deep, dreamless sleep. But in a far corner of the curtain covering Eliot's awareness, in a place where the fabric grew thin, a voice whispered to him in his darkness. "You don't have to run," she said. "There are other ways . . ."

CHAPTER NINE: INTO THE DARK WOOD

True to his word, Eliot made no complaint the next day when they packed up camp and headed west, not bothering to look for signs of the scarecrow. He did not understand this new tack, but neither did he begrudge it further. Perhaps it would give him a chance to sort things in his head. Their pace was not lazy, but it was much slower. Both woodsmen seemed preoccupied with something. Perhaps there was more to see than what Eliot had the skill for.

As they trekked, Eliot thought. The encounter in the Dark Wood dropped a shadow long and wide across his mind, but despite that, his conversation with Talker muscled its way to the fore of his thoughts. His outburst with Talker the day before still glared white hot in his memory. Something in the woodsman's tone had opened new vaults of remembering for Eliot. That word he'd used, milly, was a disrespectful term. Talker did not call him milly, not anymore. But there was a time when the woodsman did not treat Eliot with any measure of respect. He thought back on his earliest days of the hunt, how he'd existed under a blanket of fear of the woodsmen. They were strange creatures to him, every bit as wicked and vile as any animated scarecrow. That was before he grew to understand them. Before he stopped judging them based on their manners and appearance and more so on the way they pushed him. Taught him. Protected him. Still, that word had resurfaced, and it bothered Eliot.

Worse, the exchange made Eliot remember other things. Talker asked him what he remembered of the early days. He had remembered little, but the longer they marched, the more memories returned. Lost in his head, Eliot recalled the moments just before he left his father to join the woodsmen on their quest. He hadn't thought of it as his quest, not in those moments. He could not recollect many details from the morning of his kohlas except for the ominous clouds clustered over his father's farm and the Dark Wood. They'd felt crushing, that he remembered. And he remembered the thrill mixed with terror as his feet brought him—against his will, he thought—into that low place. Had he seen anything in those early days like what he'd experienced the day before, he would have died of fright. The truth that such hungry darkness had dogged his every step through the low place in the many years since his seventh birthday turned Eliot's stomach sour, filling him with a new terror. For even as horrified as he was at the beginning, Eliot was blissfully ignorant of the danger the woodsmen had led him into. The danger of the Dark Wood.

The Dark Wood gathered around the three, swallowing the light and past from behind them. Even the shadows in his father's yard seemed like noonday brightness to the darkness here. The wood's greedy attention pressed at their backs as the woodsman put Eliot on his own two feet. There was no need to compel him now that he was here. Eliot commanded himself, compelled by an inner, insatiable lust. Terror dogged him, but that was secondary to his mad need for this, his kohlas.

Eliot relived the shock he'd felt entering the wood for the first time: it had been madness motivating his compulsion, he realized. All his life he'd been warned against the Dark Wood's terrors, and now it engulfed him. It overwhelmed his senses. He remembered little of what he saw in those first moments; his mind had spasmed into blankness from fear.

But he remembered his first impressions after the paralysis had lifted. A dense, dry moss carpeted the forest floor littered with gnarly roots. They reached out from the ground like mossy bones from an ancient battlefield where giants and trolls may have warred. The trunks of the trees were several times as thick as a man. They were pockmarked with knothole eyes that did not see and crusty mouths filled with teeth that did not bite. Or at least Eliot had believed they did not see or bite at the time. But there were other eyes watching. From above and beside and below, and these had both teeth and hunger.

The sky was blotted out. This was a forest of night. Eliot felt its pull, its ravenous thirst to taste him. To push inside him and pull him apart. It was a hateful thing Eliot traversed. The woodsmen had assured him of his safety in those early days. Yes, the Dark Wood wanted the boy for itself, but an ancient pact prevented it. He'd been taught this truth since he was born. The woodsmen reminded him of the pact. But this did little to calm Eliot's nerve.

With no other choice, Eliot pushed forward, the dry floor mantle crackling like flames beneath his feet. He knew little of hunting, but the woodsmen seemed content to allow him the lead. He'd never tracked, but his focus was uncanny. He no longer controlled his thoughts nor the impulses by which they drove him. He was breathing the hunt. It consumed him. Willful and cooperative, Eliot gave in to its conspiracy.

And as he gave in, something took possession of him. He was unaware at seven, but looking back, it was impossible not to see it. Hunger had filled him from thought to foot—an ache for the hunt. This desire surpassed his fear, though that resilient force remained for quite some time. In Eliot's feverish state, he felt eyes on him. He felt desired, coveted. The forest lusted for him, his flesh and blood, but that did not matter. The woodsmen were with him. He was their ward. They must protect him. He weaved in and through the dense forest. Its smell of rotting leaves and moldy earth was the odor of old death. But Eliot's fervor insisted his focus concentrate on one thing and one alone: finding the scarecrow.

He'd found his footing as a tracker by instinct. His eyes zeroed in on a broken twig, then a crushed bush, then a scratch in a tree. And like that, Eliot was on the trail. Thinking back on it, he wondered if he'd found any actual sign of the scarecrow in those early days. The creature's wit was fierce. He could now go weeks or longer finding no sign of the beast, and yet the markings he'd found at seven were so obvious. Could the thing have played him? Or had the woodsmen placated a child playing at being a scarecrow hunter? Either way, the child had found his purpose.

Eliot had moved at a gallop through the Dark Wood. He remembered the deafening silence as the wood swallowed all sound. He'd used it. He could hear himself, and he could hear the woodsmen. Sometimes in the near silence he heard what he knew must be the scarecrow, scratching its way ahead of them just out of sight. Any sound was a beacon in the wood. He knew his sport was just ahead. Always just ahead.

Remembering this, Eliot smiled without humor. That nearness to catching his prize always there, even at the very beginning. For over seven years he'd lived with the disappointment of always just missing the thing he sought. A cavity of nothingness grew inside him because of that gnawing inefficacy, and he'd tried to fill it with the hunt. It was like trying to stave off starvation by sipping water.

As he ran on that first day, Eliot's eyes adjusted to his new dark surroundings. In time he could spy crawly things and climby things and slithery things, most small and hidden, both like and unlike the rabbits and squirrels he'd known from home. There were crouching shadows like that of dogs, but otherwise unlike dogs altogether. There were things that flew and hissed and dripped venom from angled teeth. Things that curled themselves around knuckled branches and drooped below to perchance grab a running boy. He did not see but felt the craven hunger of the place. In other circumstances, he would have stalled in his resolve. His legs would have rebelled. His heart would have failed. He had feared both the malevolent forest, and his new comrades. But even so, Eliot did not falter. The Dark Wood was the landscape of his pursuit, the woodsmen its facilitators, and his pursuit was everything.

Only a sick frenzy could explain this paradox, his madness. That, or witchcraft. The Dark Wood is a low place, he'd had no doubt of that even then. But how low? And why? His people in the valley of Gal-Braith spoke only in guarded whispers about the pact set in place here, back and back, and that rarely. But if there was darkness here and he its pawn, the kohlas was his salvation. It was a share of every boy's sacred supplication. The object of his nightly prayers. His baptism into manhood. And so Eliot had embraced the fever of the hunt even as his own fear and disappointment hollowed his core. But now Eliot wondered what else may have driven him then.

For beneath that fervor, Eliot was still a little boy. And he was terrified. He remembered this, too. He did not understand this new thing that had taken possession of his heart. He tried to ignore his fear. The way was the way. A boy could not wrestle fate and win. And no matter how terrified he felt, he wanted more than anything to become a man. To make his father proud. The quest had ripped a boy out of one world and thrust a zealot into another. He embraced the new and turned from the old. He was running deeper into the Dark Wood, but he was also running from who he had been. For his shame, he'd wanted to cry. He'd wanted his father. Worse, he'd wanted his mother, long gone by then. But he knew what he had to do, so he pressed forward.

Deep inside the seven-year-old Eliot, the glue of fear had held him together even as it chilled him, bone and nerve. It clawed at him like a frightened cat stuffed inside a gunny sack. And yet, his fervor drove him onward despite his fear. Looking back on those days, Eliot realized he'd hidden behind the force that had taken hold of him on the outside and allowed it full reign of his body so that he would not feel the fear and despair that otherwise surely would have ended him. It had been his only recourse. His only means for survival. Fear itself was enough to still his heart. If he had been left to what was inside, Eliot would have fallen to the forest floor and never again risen.

Remembering that fear paralyzed him in the present. It came back to him as real and fresh as those first days. Where had that fear gone? Had it gone? He thought maybe not. Rather, perhaps it had taken new shape inside him. He was older, yes. But most days he felt like little more than that seven-year-old boy who had walked into the Dark Wood with two gray strangers. Now, he trusted the woodsmen to protect him. He trusted them to teach him, but he hadn't believed that on his first day.

He'd had to master his weakness. Control his fear. It had to be made into something new. In the process, Eliot had let go of the fragments of the boy of spring—that's what his mother had called him, the boy of spring—cocooned the pieces in the most secret places of his core, and gave himself over to the hunt. His fear became a madness, a furious and volatile preoccupation. Onward he went, always ahead.

Looking back, he saw now what he could not see then: his choices were not entirely his own. There had been an outside force working on him. Yes, it began at his birth. It was the faith of his people in the kohlas, and that became his own faith in time. He had a curious thought: if he had been born in some other place and brought to Gal-Braith now, would he have believed in the kohlas? Or would he, like his mother, have thought it wrong? He had not wanted to leave his father's farm on his seventh birthday, but not doing so was never an option. It was his duty to the valley. To himself. So he would have done what was needed, no matter. The way was the way. But in those first moments, mad fervor had gripped him which, remembering now, was altogether unnatural. It was the obsession for a hunt that made little sense. Moreover, terror had been his constant companion: terror of the woodsmen.

"I've been thinkin' about what yeh asked me, about what I remember," Eliot said. They'd been traveling close to a week, on a straight course heading west. They were not speeding in that direction, but they were not meandering either. It felt to Eliot like the woodsmen had a destination in mind. Winter had settled in among the scrubby countryside, wet and miserable, and Eliot wrapped his cloak round his shoulders against the night as he ate dinner.

"What do you mean, boy?"

"Before, back in the Dark Wood. Yeh asked me what I remember about the beginnin'." Eliot took a bite of rabbit. It was undercooked and tough as leather, but it was warm and delicious in his mouth.

Talker stopped his work to look at Eliot. "And?"

"I remember, I were scared slap to death of both of yeh."

Stalker, off by himself in the firelight's edge, stabbed a stake into the ground. He picked up another stick and began carving. Talker nodded.

"Aye, you were."

"But why?"

"Look at us, boy. You were right to be afraid."

"I know yeh look—" What could he say? That they looked like corpses? No, he couldn't say that. But come to think of it, they did. "I know I were jest a boy, and yeh were frightful to look at, but it were more than that, aye."

"Speak plain. You must sleep soon."

Ah, sleep. More of the woodsman's magic. More black sleep with silent echoes. And his itch was no better. Maybe it was worse.

"I don't think it were yer look is what I'm sayin'."

Talker waited.

Eliot looked away, out into the forest. "I got the feelin' yeh didn't like me. Like yeh wanted to . . ." This was so foolish.

"Say it."

Eliot looked at Talker. "Like yeh wanted to eat me."

Stalker stabbed another stake into the ground, picked up another stick, and began whittling. Talker looked over at his companion, then back to Eliot.

"Have we ever hurt you?"

No, they hadn't. Other than the murky red piss they smeared on his chest and thigh each night, they'd never hurt him. They'd done nothing in the years he'd been with them to cause him any actual fear. To make him doubt them. And it could have been the simple childish fear of a seven-year-old boy in the beginning, but that did not account for the strange madness. He could not think of any other word for his unaccountable fervor in those early days.

"It weren't just that. The fear, I mean. I felt . . . somethin' came inside me. Like somethin' moved in, aye."

Stalker stopped his work. Now both hunters were looking at Eliot with an intensity that made his itch worse.

"Go on," Talker said.

"Well, that's it, is'n it. It were like someone else were movin' my body. And I was just stuck inside it, like, screamin' to get out."

The woodsmen shared a look, then both returned to their chores.

"It's nothing but the pale memories of a scared little boy," Talker said, explaining it away. He looked again at Eliot. "Does any being other than yourself command you now?" Without waiting for an answer, he returned his attention to the work at hand.

The woodsman's words didn't convince Eliot in the slightest. If anything, he had more doubt now. Something in the way the woodsman wouldn't address his fear, or his—what was it, possession?—filled him with apprehension. They were keeping something from him, but what? And to Talker's last question, hadn't he himself suggested the woodsmen determined where Eliot was or was not allowed to go?

It was true: they'd never hurt him or given him reason to distrust them. Yes, Stalker was angry, moody, and intolerant, but he'd never put a hand against Eliot. Only Talker had done that, and that only days before when Eliot pushed him to it. That was self-defense. No, they meant him well and Eliot knew this. Whatever inconsistencies he may find in his memory and his reality, it was his responsibility to sort them. To do his part of the hunt, to succeed.

West is where they were heading. Toward the Dead Plain and the Western Mountains beyond it. Where they would end up, he did not know. But he knew this: he would play his role well. He would do right by the woodsmen, by his father, by his kohlas. He would find the scarecrow. He would finish his course. He would not lose faith. His kohlas was all he had, after all. That, and the woodsmen.

CHAPTER TEN: AN ABHORRENT FANTASY

Pre-dawn quiet sheathed the land when Eliot woke. The sky was cloudless, and the moon was bright. It was low strung, hidden behind the distant ridge, but it provided enough light to ward off darkness. Most of it, anyway. A heavy blue mantle saturated the world, slumbrous and ample.

Eliot waited for his eyes to adjust. He had grown accustomed to Talker's spell wearing off at dawn each morning. This was earlier than usual, but his stomach grumbled at him to break his fast, so he sat up . . . and froze. A large dark shape crouched near the remnants of last night's fire. The woodsmen were not in the camp, not that Eliot could see. They never were first thing.

In the low light, Eliot did his best to make out what he was looking at. It had the shape of a man, if the man was squatting. He saw shoulders, knees, elbows, and a head. A big round head. Was it the smoking man in his wide-brimmed hat? The shape shifted its weight, and Eliot saw it was digging through Talker's pack. Its fingers moved with quiet dexterity. Eliot prayed for a similar skill as he braced himself to stand. *Quiet*, he thought.

He made it to one knee before the shape turned. Eliot again froze in place, hoping the smoking man hadn't heard. For a moment that stretched the length of the horizon, neither moved. Both waited for the other. Was this real? Eliot wondered. Or was he imagining this?

The shape stood, and it was not the smoking man. What Eliot had mistaken for hands were rust-colored talons, crusted with sulfuric resin. The cloak it wore billowed as though from an inner wind. As it stirred, Eliot smelled it: a rancid, vile thing that caused his eyes to run water. He batted them to better see.

The creature rose to its full height. It was enormous, larger than any man Eliot had ever seen. Bigger than a bear, only this creature was thin as a sapling. It turned its wicked head to face Eliot, an abhorrent fantasy come to life. A dull orange emanated from within its eyes and mouth, carved from an oversized gourd. It snarled at Eliot but made no sound.

The scarecrow.

Eliot sprang from the ground, his knife in hand. He stabbed at the creature's throat, but it parried with ease. With one nimble arm, it tossed Eliot across the camp and into a tree. The breath left his body almost fast enough to pull his spirit with it. He tumbled to the ground, wheezing. The creature was on him, lifting him by the neck until they were eye to eye. He stabbed with the knife, but the scarecrow blocked it. Eliot expected this. With his other hand, he punched into the creature's head just beside its eye. The gourd cracked, hissing foul steam up the length of Eliot's arm. He screamed as his skin boiled, and the creature dropped him.

Eliot slashed at the monster's legs, once. Twice. On the third try, his blade found purchase. The scarecrow brought down its other leg on Eliot's head. It split his skull, Eliot knew it. Sparks of flame circled his head, and darkness blotted his vision. He swung and swung with his knife, desperately. Then he calmed himself. He stilled to listen. He heard nothing but his own breath. He held his breath to better hear. Still, his heartbeat pounded in his head.

His vision returned. Blood trickled down his forehead. The brawl summoned his mad itch back to clamorous life. Still, he waited, his breath tight in his chest. The move came from his left. He saw it in his peripheral just as he heard it. He twisted, exhaling and driving his knife upward. The scarecrow came down on his blade. A screech split the silent dawn, and in a moment it was gone.

Had he wounded it? Eliot couldn't say. He'd stabbed it. He felt his blade enter it. But enter what? It seemed made of wood and stone. Would a blade even harm such a creature? But it had fled, and he'd struck its face: that seemed to hurt it. It must have vulnerabilities. But to what extent he'd wounded it, Eliot did not know.

He stumbled to his feet but fell right back to one knee. The skin of his right arm was blistered. His head was pounding. And his body from neck to knee was a ripe anguish. Two figures came for him, but he could not react. Already, he was fading to black.

THE VALIANT, FIRST STAVE

The hungry are known by way they eat
The thirsty by way they take a drink
The cruel by way they take

The lonely by way they lay in wait
The lusty by way they taste the sweet
The sweet by way they taste

The dark is known by way it hides
The söklyn by way they shine at night
The light by way it shines
The strong by way they love
The weak by way they hate
The living by way they live
The horde by way they die

The faye, the brute, the dahnee
known by way they shine
The babe, the sick, the dumas
known by way they cry

So it is, so it will be
So it was, back and back
and on and on

And the Dragon's fire shone bright
as it chased across the night sky
the Comet's tail . . .
And all the world trembled in their wake.

CHAPTER ELEVEN: THE BOY OF SPRING

"Tell me again," she said.

"I've told yeh woman all there is—"

Laila was baking, her arms white with flour to the elbow. She looked out the window to spy her boy. My little boy of spring, she called him. But Eliot must have run round back. She turned again to her husband.

"Tell me again, then."

"As you say," Asha replied. "I were a boy of seven on the day of my kohlas. It always begins on a boy's seventh birthday. As I told yeh, I remember little. One thing that remains clear in my mind is how hot it was that day, and how cold my blood ran when first I saw them."

"The woodsmen?"

"Aye, the woodsmen."

"Tell me more."

"Love," Asha said. "There is no more to tell. I left. I came home. My father was dead. That was my kohlas."

"From the sound, that is every kohlas," Laila said. Her bitter words were not aimed at Asha. She hoped he understood this. More important, however, was that he understood how earnest she was. "You have no memory of what happened to you all those years in between?"

"No, lady. I do not."

Laila considered this. Asha was, she believed, a good man. He was honest. Still, his inability to remember ate at her. He should remember something. He had lost so much of his life. Strange, he didn't seem to feel that loss himself. At least, if he did, he did not show it to his wife.

"But why?" she asked again.

"Laila." She knew Asha was trying to be patient with her. She was not from the valley. She could not understand this strange and vulgar religion. "It is the way of things, and the way is the way. There is no escaping it," he said. Bitterness framed his words, but his voice was steady. He did not make eye contact with her as he spoke. Escape was an impossible option for which he did not believe they could afford to hope. On that, they disagreed.

"But why, Asha? Don't just quote scrip from a religion that makes no sense, give me a reason. Why should we send our boy on a foolish quest? Just to satisfy the superstitions surrounding silly old myths about a Dark Wood? That's not enough . . ."

"Shh," Asha replied sharply. He reached out and took her hand in his, his eyes shifting to look out the window into the growing twilight. He looked toward the wood itself as if the forest might march its way up the hill and gobble them down.

"Are yeh that fearful, love?" Laila looked at her husband with both pity and frustration. "It is a dark place, I'll grant yeh that. But I've seen many'a dark places. Many low places as it were. I was born on the water, and aye, I lived there, too. But these feet o' mine have walked the streets of many ports. I've heard the tales of many cultures. I've visited the island folken in the Glass. And the weirder ones, as far north as the ShooShoos. I lived more'n two years in the Screw and counted pirates among my friends. Aye, and ever'where I've ever' been, and in ever' culture I've ever known, boys grow to become men all on their own without need for such a wicked and senseless thing as this kohlas."

Asha squeezed his wife's hand as though it might trigger her mouth shut. His head bowed as if in prayer, and his broad shoulders shrunk before her. She understood his superstition: to speak such things aloud was to invite grave mischief. But she was not afraid, and she needed to help him see.

"And what o'the girls, then?" Laila asked. "Am I to believe the valley's daughters are of such little consequence as to not warrant such a grave errand themselves? Lucky they are, says I, to be so overlooked. But why the sons?"

"He will come back to us, love. That I promise."

"But how can yeh? How can yeh make any promise when yeh don' know what happens to him once he leaves? I've seen when your eyes go blank, Asha, like there's nothin' there behind 'em. That's what your kohlas left yeh with. Yeh think that's normal?"

Asha did not answer. She realized he did not think it was good. He did not want it for his boy. But in Gal-Braith? Yes. It was normal.

"I'll not have my boy raised by woodsmen we do not know," Laila continued. "Woodsmen who do not love him. I'll not risk 'im goin' off only to come back years later to find you cold in a grave and with no memory of where's he been. And me, who knows where I'll be? The mothers don' factor into these stories, do they? No, but the fathers . . . Aye. They're always dead time their sons come home. Yeh told me yourself. So it was with your father, and his father . . . and fathers and fathers so far back and back as anyone can see. Aye?"

Asha squeezed her hand again, pleading as if he could feel the darkness outside pressing itself against the window. Night had fallen. The wind picked up and the skeletal fingers of the sturdy oak outside the kitchen clicked and clacked against the pane as if wanting to come in. The pie, half assembled, lay forgotten on the table.

"It's senseless," Laila continued. "Asha, hear me. It makes no sense, none at all, to send off our boy like that, with the dark like who come from that place. It's unnatural, and it's senseless."

Asha shook his head as if to loosen her reasoning from it. She saw how her words landed in the soil of his heart and threatened to take root. She understood there existed a tricky balance in the valley, one she could not comprehend. Perhaps her words felt good in her husband's heart, warming him like a good song. She could hope as much. Hope, once caught, becomes a dangerous thing.

"Let's leave, love." She implored him. Laila looked at Asha, holding his eyes to hold him within herself. Laila saw he felt the sting of hope in his chest. She saw, too, it was not enough.

"Yeh know we can't," he said at last.

"And why can't we? Tell me that. Yeh make enough coin in Galleen. We can save up, start fresh anywhere. Jump a ship. Take our chances."

Asha shook his heavy head, sadness furrowing his brow.

"Why?" she pleaded. "Love, why? Will that Dark Wood come chasin' after us? Will it track us down and take our son away? Is that yer fear?"

Yes. It was that simple. Asha believed it would. He looked away from his wife.

"I will not give up my boy for some mad chase," she said after a time. "I'll not stand by while yeh let it happen. I'll play no part in it."

And she meant it.

Spring was a riot of color. Eliot had once been the boy of spring, but that was long ago. Now he felt out of place in the season's festival. His arm was healing. His head, too. There was no lasting damage from his encounter with the scarecrow. Not this time. And in the weeks since, his wounds had retracted to again allow the fury of his itching chest and stomach to take prominence in his thoughts . . . Just behind the scarecrow.

Eliot felt foolish. He had doubted Talker's wisdom to head west. He'd made such a fuss about it. And will the scarecrow follow us, he'd asked. The question had been an accusation. The groundwork to later make his point: heading west was the wrong thing to do. He'd said as much. But the scarecrow had not only followed them. It had attacked Eliot. It had taken a while for Eliot to agree to Talker's sleep magic after that, only once the woodsman agreed to enchant their camp against interlopers. But Eliot had put his hands on the scarecrow. He could have died as a result, but he hadn't. The woodsmen had come, but only after Eliot had made the scarecrow flee. At least that was a source of pride. He'd stood his ground and driven the fiend away. Next time, he would not let the scarecrow escape.

It was hard to believe. After seven years, he'd finally encountered the object of his quest. Almost eight years, Eliot realized. His birthday was soon. Sometime in spring. He had forgotten exactly when. For that matter, it could be now. Eliot thought again of the scarecrow. It didn't sit well with Eliot. Why now? Why had the scarecrow shown up after eight years of hiding? He absently scratched at his chest.

A sweet aroma filled Eliot's world. Immediately his thoughts of the scarecrow were replaced by another. Smell must harbor its own magic, Eliot thought, for this one conjured a memory in his mind he could not look away from. Eliot was following at a distance behind the woodsmen through a shallow ravine, a gentle brook his constant companion. Its mesmerizing song a lullaby to his senses . . . until he smelled it. Along the water's edge grew brambles of interwoven briers and creepers, among them a congregation of juniper-bean vines bursting with fragrant blossoms. Like honeysuckle or jasmine, juniper blossoms were the sigil of spring for Eliot. And therein lie the magic: their balmy essence had carried him back to his childhood. To his mother. The memory of her desaturated his thoughts, leaving him with a swamp of emotion.

He saw it all. The argument. The bundle of flowers clutched against his chest. The falling darkness outside the window. I'll play no part in it, she'd said . . . but how could she abandon her child?

Many memories had been bricked up in a dark forgotten recess of Eliot's mind. But like tugging a loose thread on the bottom of a rice sack, grains of memories kept falling out one by one into the bright light of day. And here, once again, Eliot found himself confronted with one so beautiful yet heartbreaking, it was painful to look at.

He had been outside. It was early spring. The trees were still mostly bare, but the juniper-beans were redolent with blooms. He'd picked a bunch for his mother and sneaked in the back door to surprise her, but he'd been the one surprised. He'd stumbled upon an argument between his parents, an argument about him. They were talking about his seventh birthday, which was almost a full year away.

He'd folded himself in the nook between the door and the potato bin, the juniper blossoms clutched against his chest, and listened. He could not see his father from his vantage, but he could see his mother. She was tall and regal. Even sitting in a chair and wearing a flour dusted apron, she looked highborn. He'd often thought she must be the most enchanting and beautiful creature to live. This filled him with pride. She sat upright. There was no slouch to her posture, as though she, too, understood she was queenly. Her cheeks were always ruddy, flushed the deep rusty colors of sunset. But her eyes were pools of honey.

His mother had warned his father she would not abide it, Eliot's kohlas. Eliot could not believe what he had heard. It should have been no surprise when she left. But it had been a devastating surprise.

"I will not give up my boy for some mad chase," she had said. "I'll not stand by while yeh let it happen. I'll play no part in it."

His father had gone to her then, knelt before her. Eliot knew they would find him out, but they were too caught up in their own worry to notice him. "Love," he'd said. "Don't be like that."

"Like what?" she'd asked. Eliot saw she was angry. Her hands were trembling. His were, too, but for a different reason.

"Laila, the way is the way."

"I'll play no part of it. I'll leave you . . ."

Cold emotion filled Eliot's chest. *I'll leave you . . .* How could she say that? He shook his head, emotion like round pebbles rattling his brain. She had left him, that was without question. And she had told his father she'd leave them, but was that all? Something felt unfinished. Eliot revisited the memory, removing himself from the emotional reaction it caused in him. Separating the memory from the way things would turn out.

"Laila, the way is the way."

"I'll play no part in it. I'll leave yeh," she'd said. "We both will."

Eliot stopped walking. Is that what she'd said?

"I'll take our boy and go. Asha, hear me. I don't want to do that, not without you. But I will. Come . . . Come with us, love."

Eliot's knees went soft for a moment as his stomach filled with fluttering phantoms. In his head, a switch clicked and there was an avalanche of sensation. It fell down his center in a rush, pulling into his core a violent truth: his memory had lied to him before.

"We can't leave," his father replied.

"I can," she said. "And I'll see to it my boy never takes a step on that damned quest."

The rice sack ripped open in Eliot's heart, spilling its truths onto the floor of his soul. His mother never promised to abandon him. She'd promised to keep him from this, his kohlas. She'd vowed to take him and run.

But she hadn't. She left without him. Why?

The woodsmen turned, no doubt to question Eliot. Why had he stopped walking? Something in what they saw prevented them from interfering, and Eliot did not care. He dropped his pack to the ground. His vision had gone glassy and distant.

As though by its own momentum, the scene in Eliot's mind continued to play out. He remembered later that evening, he'd brought his mother the juniper blossoms. His spirit was flat by then, but she'd mustered her own when she accepted them. Her smile was pure light. She pulled him into her lap; he would have hated this on any other day—only babies sat on their mother's lap—but that day it was a gift. She pressed her lips hard against his forehead.

"Let this be a seed planted in my boy of spring," she said after her kiss was done. She'd said this so many times in his life. It was a custom among the seafaring people, she'd explained. They called it adeglåsia, a Lynthian word that meant oath speak. Adeglåsia was the practice of imbuing a promise into another. True, it was little more than superstition and similar to some found in the valley, but Eliot liked it. It was a thing he and she shared.

"It's like this, love," she'd explained to him. "I speak my intent into you, and it's held there by the salt of the furies." Or the faye of the forests and mountains. Or khamunic incantations, or the song of the Edön, or the whispers of the Eri. The source of power changed depending on where the belief was practiced, and she'd heard tale of it all her life among the many folken of the seas and lands she'd traveled with her father. The important thing, she believed, was not the specifics of the culture but the faith of the speaker, the adeglåst. And of all the things of which she was certain, her own faith in the power of love was strongest. At six years, Eliot could not have claimed to understand any of it, but he'd liked it. At almost fifteen, he understood more, but not near enough. It was just enough to raise more questions.

He lingered with his mother in memory. "See, love," she'd said, "I've seen goodness and beauty all around us, and I've collected them. Aye, like you and your flowers. Now, I push them out from myself and into you." She'd smiled at him, her radiant face warming him. Her eyes pools of liquid love. "It's hope, my boy of spring. Hope of kindness, love, and quality. That's what I push into you, deep in here." She put her hand on his chest. And could he feel it kindle there? Yes, he thought he had felt it.

She then described the sponge of him soaking up the oath, her promise. How she believed the stain of her hope permeated her boy. She had breathed deep his scent. Eliot remembered and felt his body tingle as it had then.

"Aye," she said, her voice a prayer. "That is the smell of hope." Then she had looked across the table at her husband, whom she loved. Eliot saw the hope in her eyes then.

Looking back, Eliot wondered if the seed of hope had been working in his father. He believed it may have been. His mother had believed it. He saw that much in her eyes, also. Hope was nearly kindled in his father, but it did not burn. Hope is yet a stubborn thing, however, and once kindled, very difficult to kill.

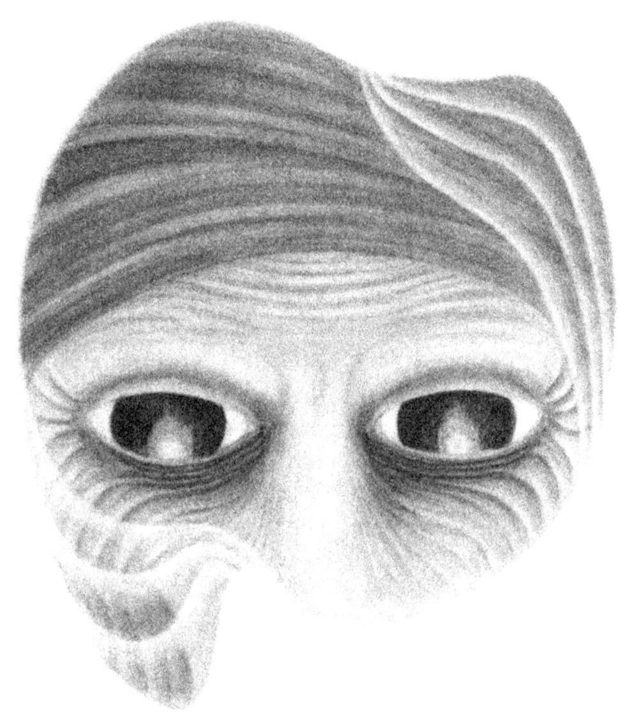

CHAPTER TWELVE: WHEN MEMORIES LIE

"My mother . . ."

The woodsmen shared a look. Stalker turned and left the ravine.

Approaching Eliot, Talker asked, "What of your mother?"

Eliot gave way to the weight of his revelation, falling to sit in the grass. Tears streaked his face already, and more threatened to come. He felt as though a hook had reached inside him and was pulling out his guts in one long train. Words and ideas clouded his mind, too fat to make their way out of his mouth just yet. He was top heavy, his shoulders and neck strained beneath the weight of his head. He fell on his back, the sky turning above him.

"My mother . . ." he said again.

"Eliot," Talker said, his voice gentle and threaded with alarm. "What of your mother?"

Eliot rolled to his side, pulling his knees into his chest. He could not bear the pain of this invasive new truth. Her betrayal was much easier to manage; his hatred for it, and her, easier to feel. What must he do with this revelation? Worse, what should he do with its implications?

"No, no, no," he said, his voice small. His thoughts swelled, pressing out against his skull. His heart, however, was clenching in a fist, growing smaller and tighter. His lungs, too. Breathing was labor.

He tried to think: what would have caused his mother to abandon him if she'd loved him? He could find no logical answer. The big ugly shadow of truth kept looming in front of him, but he wouldn't look at it. He couldn't. He was afraid of it. If she would not abandon him, then where had she gone?

"My mother," he began again, but Talker had taken him by the arm and pulled him to his feet. It was not a violent act, but neither was it kind. Eliot tried to open his eyes, but they squinted against the memory. Talker slapped him across the cheek, and Eliot's eyes flew open. Even so, it took several moments for his vision to clear. His eyes were sticky with tears, and his mouth was salty with snot.

He looked at Talker. "My mother," he began, his voice thin as grass blades.

"Your mother is not here," Talker replied.

"No, she—" Eliot began.

"She is not here, but you are. Or you need to be."

Eliot had a moment of clarity. Talker's words affected him more than his slap. Eliot's brow twisted as he planted his feet and pulled his arm away from the woodsman's grip. The two stared at each other, Eliot's anger blistering his palms.

"What do you know of my mother?" he asked.

"I know nothing of your family, boy."

"My mother!" Eliot cried. "What do you know of her?"

Talker's head tilted. He studied his pupil. "What do you know?" he asked after a moment.

Eliot shook his head. "I don't . . ." He couldn't answer. He did not know what he knew. A cyclone of emotions braided themselves with his bowels, threatening to rip him open. "She didn't . . ."

Talker grabbed Eliot's tunic and pulled him closer. "What have you seen?"

Again, Eliot felt hot anger rise at Talker's insensitivity. He slapped the woodsman's hand away, stepping back as he did. He looked at Talker, questions and accusations on his face.

"Eliot," Talker said, his voice mollifying. "Tell me what troubles you. Mayhap I can help you."

Ignoring the woodsman, Eliot asked, "Is my father dead yet?" The question appeared to take Talker by surprise.

"I know not your father's condition," he said, his voice even. "I do not know your family."

"But yeh took him on his kohlas, aye? So yeh do know him . . ."

Again, Eliot felt as though Talker was studying him. Like he was trying to identify a strange bug.

"Your kohlas is yours alone, and it is all I see."

"Answer the question," Eliot said, unable to keep the anger from his voice now.

Talker's eyes narrowed, the corners of his mouth lifted. "And do you think to command me, milly? You are not in charge."

"Aye, that I know well enough. Now, leastways. But yeh knew my father, and his father, aye?"

Talker's face lost most of its arrogance. "We will talk about this, but not now. Later. We should keep moving."

"No," Eliot said.

"Eliot, now is not the time."

"No."

Stalker appeared once again over the rise, storming down toward them. Before Eliot could register what was happening, Stalker had grabbed him by the back of his neck and pushed him forward, forcing his feet to walk.

"Kinsman," Talker said, but not to Eliot. Stalker ignored him. "Aht dech toosht," Talker said. Stalker stopped, his hand gripping Eliot's neck so hard it added to the pressure in his head. The woodsmen looked at each other, something inaudible passing between them. After a moment, Stalker released Eliot's neck. Talker nodded at his companion. Then to Eliot, he said, "Eliot, this is a difficult thing to discuss. But we will discuss it, just not now."

"When?" Elliot asked. He could feel anger radiating from Stalker like heat from a stove. And like a match to tinder, fear lit up in Eliot's belly. Still, he would not leave this. Not yet. "When?"

Talker looked at Stalker. Again, Eliot felt something pass between them. When Talker looked again to Eliot, he saw kindness in the woodsman's features for the first time. Walking to Eliot, Talker placed a hand against his cheek. The rare expression of tenderness did nothing to ease Eliot's inner turmoil. If anything, it fanned it further. But he held his tongue. He allowed his teacher to speak.

"Tonight, we will talk. We will not take a single step again until you are satisfied we have answered your questions." He removed his hand but held Eliot's gaze. "Are we agreed? Does this satisfy you for now?"

Eliot wanted to kick him. To rip his scarf from his neck, or choke him with it. But he saw the strain in the woodsman's face. He seemed to grow sicker by the day. His eyes were set in bowls of inflamed red skin. His ears were worse: they glistened with viscous pink fluid. In his mouth, his gums were retracting, revealing elongated teeth tarnished with rusts and yellows. Nausea joined the other forces vying for attention in Eliot's stomach, a cacophony of emotion and bile. He had to look away from the woodsman's face. Despite his anger, he felt pity for the man.

Words wouldn't come. He nodded.

Talker turned and began walking without another word. Stalker did not move at once. He was staring at Eliot. He looked equally unwell, but unlike Talker, his mouth was a thin coil of malice. Eliot felt the woodsman's anger, and what else? Did he hate Eliot? Stalker broke their gaze and walked away. Eliot picked up his pack and followed, allowing the space between him and the woodsmen to breathe.

"The kohlas is a sacred agreement, aye," Talker said. The fire was warm, a little too warm for Eliot, but he ignored it. The night would grow colder. In time he may welcome the warmth. Besides, he was more concerned with Talker's explanation. "The covenant has existed between our peoples for an age. You should not assume we know your father. We are not the only broi-dain who guard the covenant, though once there were more of us."

Eliot couldn't reply to this. Everything the woodsman said raised questions. Sacred. Covenant. Broi-dain. Once there were more . . . Where did he even begin?

"I cannot tell you all you want to know," Talker said. "The pact is sealed in secrecy. But this I will explain: the kohlas is long honored by your people and ours alike. It binds us to each other. We do not wish you or your family harm, for that would not serve our mutual purposes."

Talker had never used so many words. And still, the more he explained, the less Eliot understood. For the moment, it seemed, Talker was finished.

"And my mother?"

"We do not know your mother."

Talker did not often use the words I or me. He referred to himself and Stalker together: we. Eliot wondered if this was a simple act of inclusion, since only one of the two spoke, or if it had broader meaning.

"Aye, but do you know somethin' about her? Somethin' that might explain why she . . ." Eliot shook his head, forcing his emotion deeper.

"Why she did what?" Talker asked.

Eliot looked at the woodsman. "She left us, my da' and me."

"No, boy. I cannot tell you why she left."

"Can yeh tell me about the Dark Wood?"

"The Dark Wood?"

"Aye, was it always a low place?"

Talker did not answer right away. He glanced toward Stalker, but Stalker did not look up from his task of mending an old waterskin. Like as not, they would need fresh supplies soon. Stalker continued his task, but something in the way he held his head suggested he, too, was invested in their conversation. As though proving as much, Talker turned back to Eliot, satisfied, it seemed, in what he found when he looked to Stalker.

"What you call low may not be low to others," Talker explained. *One tale's hero is another tale's villain,* Eliot thought. Talker continued. "It is a vaultine, but I cannot say it is low."

"Vaultine?"

"It is a place of power."

Eliot considered this. "But it is hungry. It nearly ate me. That doesn't make it low?" His question settled in the night air, and he couldn't swear by it, but he believed the night grew colder.

"Why ask such questions?" Talker asked. "Is a wolf low just because it eats the shrew? Is a bear low simply because it might eat you? It is a wild thing, not a low thing. Before that day when you grew agitated, had you ever felt threatened while in the wood's shade?"

Yes, Eliot thought. *Every second.* He did not answer the question, however. That answer belonged to him alone. Talker was crafty to shift the blame of the Dark Wood's violence onto Eliot, but did he believe it was truly Eliot's fault? Eliot did not know. His mind was raw and bleeding. Though it surprised him, he realized he could not handle more conversation on the subject of his kohlas or his mother. He needed rest.

"Thank you," he said. "For talkin'." The ghost of a smile appeared in Talker's eyes, and the woodsman nodded. Though he feared sleep may not find him for some time without Talker's magic, Eliot unrolled his pack and prepared to rest. As he lay back, his skin pricked with awareness. He glanced at Stalker. The woodsman was watching him. Eliot closed his eyes, a new sensation tightening in his stomach. For the first time since his earliest days of his kohlas, he'd felt genuine fear for Stalker. It was a solid, coherent fear. Eliot believed Stalker would harm him if pushed to it. He was uncertain how strong the push would need to be.

He felt a hand on his chest then, and his eyes snapped open. He grabbed Talker by the wrist, but not in anger.

"Mayhap no magic tonight?" he asked. Talker did not remove his hand, but neither did he speak his incantation. The two waited as though someone else would answer the question. Eliot felt his heart beating hard in his chest and wondered if the woodsman felt it in his palm. The more seconds passed, the more aware Eliot became of the beating. His heart was racing.

Finally, Talker nodded and removed his hand. Relief flooded Eliot. So much so, he may have shed tears if he hadn't squeezed shut his eyes. He knew his mother would come to him in his dreams. He hoped for it. He had questions for her.

CHAPTER THIRTEEN: NIGHTFALLING

It was not his mother who came to him that night. It was another lady, one withered and seasoned by long life.

"Yeh look a wee bit like yer mother," the old woman said to Eliot while she packed potatoes in a sack.

Eliot paused in surprise. "My mother?"

Eliot often accompanied his father to neighboring farms for trade. His father was outside with the old woman's husband, bartering over the value of a bushel of greens and casks of malt honey-cider.

"Oh, don't mishear," the old woman said, "it's just a wee bit'o her I see in yeh. Mostly, it's yer father in yer face. No, t'aint but a trace, mind yeh. Mayhap a squirrel more."

"Aye? How?" Eliot stammered. The wound his mother left behind when she disappeared six months earlier still seeped raw emotion, fibrous and knotted. He didn't like to think about her usually, but this simple comment began an itch just out of reach in Eliot's head. He needed the old woman to scratch it.

She must have seen the desperate look on his face, and after a brief glance out the window where the men negotiated their trade, she turned to look Eliot full in the face. She sat down in a chair next to where Eliot stood.

"I see her in yer eyes, lad. She's there, clear as summer sunshine." She giggled as if this was the happiest thought she'd had in months. Eliot stared, transfixed. The woman continued as much to herself as to Eliot. "Oh, the men round these here parts, they think they run it. Aye. So they do. Us women are scarce. Don't know how I made it this long." She said this matter-of-factly, but Eliot sensed the woman did know—and only dared not admit it out loud. Her eyes wandered about the room before snapping back to Eliot. "They'll not be runnin' me out soon. I'm just a wee bit stronger'n all that, and I've staked my own claim here. No, I'll be stayin'."

Eliot sat, again taking in the room. He knew he was dreaming. He also knew this was not a dream. The quality was too clear. Dreams run like a river, the surface diffused and uncertain. This was not like that. This was more like still, deep water, and as clear as crystal moonlight. He returned his gaze to the old woman. The potato sack was half full. He'd seen this tableau before, only then it was a dream. And then it had been a turnip sack.

How do you relive a memory you don't remember? he wondered. And just as he thought this, he heard himself ask, "Why did she leave me?"

The old farmer's wife looked at Eliot, her eyes shining, and took his small hand in hers. Her wrinkled, calloused fingers were a warming comfort. Still, comfort was not what he needed.

"Why'd she leave?"

"Yer mother didn't leave yeh, love." She paused, mustering the strength to continue. Eliot felt emotion building in his chest, and he knew this was not the fruit of the memory. This was from an awareness of the coming revelation, something his six-year-old self could not have discerned. "Yer mother died, son. I'm sorry to say it."

Eliot's reality cantered, both in his present and his past. The dreamscape sloped toward eventuality, and Eliot knew dread for what was coming. He dreaded it but leapt headlong into it.

"But she—" he heard himself begin, but confusion and pain clamped his throat shut. He swallowed. "She said she'd leave us," he heard himself say. But his older self knew this was not true. That had been a false memory.

"No, love. She would not have ever left yeh, not with breath in her body." The woman's eyes were wet diamonds in her dark leather face. Eliot, the child, felt the weight of her words crushing his chest. Eliot, the dreamer, felt the words pull his chest open.

"How did she die?" both Eliots said in unison.

The farmer's wife released Eliot's hand to strike the tears from her eyes. "She came to me one day. She'd had a mind to leave this place, to take yeh with her. She said she were afraid."

"Afraid of what? My father?"

"No, no, boy. Yer da' was good to her, as best as he was able leastways. No, she were afraid . . . . She didn't think he'd go with yehs. She were skeert of the way things be."

Young Eliot's brow furrowed in the memory. "I don't understand," he said. But Eliot the dreamer saw with intense clarity the meaning of her words. He needed the truth, even if it filleted his flesh from bone.

In a whisper, she explained, "The way our boys are took from us. The way they come home empty. The way a mother can't quite stay. The way a father is never really there, yeh know, in the heart. The way things be."

The way is the way, Eliot said in his head as liquid fire gathered in the hem of his dream. He wrestled for control of the moment, to see if he could bend it. He only felt the strain of his effort pull him up, as if to draw him out of the deep well of the memory. That he did not want. So he let go instead. He let go and felt himself settle fully into that six-year-old boy he once was, that boy of spring.

Eliot looked at the sturdy old woman who sat before him. Her face was weathered to a dark brown suede. Her wrinkles folded around her face rather than sagged away from it. There was a fire in her eyes. He could see why she had endured so long in a land unsuitable for most women. He could also see weariness.

"Why're things that way?" Eliot asked.

"Don't know, boy. Never made no sense to me. But then nobody asks me what I think." She took in a deep breath and held it for a moment. She exhaled and continued. "This thing, I know yeh heard of it, this kohlas. This is how the boys leave us, go off on some adventure, and return to us as men. Only I say, those boys don't return. The men who come back to us are missing somethin'. I say it's needless."

"Then how would we become men? It is the way . . ."

"Bah! Same way a calf becomes a cow. Or a puppy grows to a mutt. Same way anyone becomes anythin'. Yeh grow into it. Simple as that."

"But, the kohlas—" Eliot stopped. Of course he had heard of this thing. For weeks he'd thought of little else. It was the eve of his seventh birthday, and the thought of what would happen next day petrified him.

"Ah, forget that for now," the farmer's wife said. "Yer mother. That's what yeh want to know. What happened to yer mother."

"Will yeh tell me?"

Again, the woman looked out the window at the men in the yard. She nodded at Eliot and began again, but he stopped her.

"Yer afraid they'll hear yeh, aren't yeh?"

"Afraid? Not me, boy. I don't have the energy for fear. I'm an old woman. Yeh see that. No, I am not afraid." She had that defiant spark in her eyes as she said this, but her brow softened. "But there are different kinds of fear, I s'pose. Anywhat, the men won't care for what I have to say. But I give no credit to that. It's not the men I want to keep my words from."

Eliot did not like the sound of that. His feet went cold in his boots. He wasn't about to ask what she meant, and she didn't seem inclined to explain. Instead, she continued her story. The blaze was back.

"Yer mother wasn't like the weaker ones that sometimes come along. She was a fiery one, that." Eliot knew she referred to the girls who wed the men after they quit their quest. "She had feelins and ideas. She were strong. And she loved you and yer father, but she hated this valley with its secrets and its darkness. She hated it, I tell yeh. 'Gal-Braith is poisoned,' she'd say. She wanted to leave. She wanted to take you with her. And yer father.

"She'd come sometimes, tellin' me 'bout her plan. She was workin' on yer da', tryin' to win him over to her way of seein' it. And it seemed like she were mostly there. They could talk about it without fussin'. That were progress. And it were certainly more than most would have gotten from their men. He was almost to see it her way, she thought, but this place takes a'holt of a man. And it don't like lettin' go.

"Last time I saw her, she thought the three of yehs were close to runnin' off. To leavin' the valley for good. She told me he'd agreed to leastways travel a piece, to see what they could see. And so the three of yehs were leavin' next day. Mayhap you'd come back after a few days, mayhap not. She thought not.

"She'd brought me a pie. We'd often trade pies, yeh know, but the girl could bake in ways I never could. I sliced it up, and we had us each a piece. I had fresh milk, and I put a dab of honey in it. We had us a little supper with that pie, just the two of us. It were a good thing to go out on, a good memory to keep of her. I were very fond of yer mother. I saw myself in her. What I might've been, leastways." Eliot saw emotion rise in the woman's cheeks and flush tears into her eyes, but she swallowed them and pressed on. "I couldn't have no babbies. We tried and couldn't. My husband just accepted it as fact, and I was relieved. I hate to say it, but I was. I didn't want to risk losin' a child to some horse-shit kohlas." She spat and then steadied herself with a deep breath.

"But then again, ever' woman longs to be a mother. And I couldn't be. So I saw myself in yer mother. She had a fierceness about her. That I recognized right enough. But also her unwillin'ness to leave things be. No, she fought hard for you and yer da'."

Eliot listened, watching the woman cycle through emotions, springing up into defiance and sagging back into grief. He could see that cycle had worn its way into her features over her many years. Eliot liked the old wife, he realized.

"When she left me that evenin', she were so excited. She had found a way out for you three. She had won." The woman patted Eliot's hand, a nervous gesture, he thought, and then she scratched against the grain of the table.

"What happened?" asked Eliot. "Is that when she—?"

"Aye, boy. Yer mother never made it home." Her hand fretted about her lips, her stumpy fingers trembling. "I said she died. Before, I said that. There's more to it than that."

Eliot blinked. He held his breath.

"She left here, and it was just late afternoon. She had plenty of time to get back home before full dark. T'weren't more than an hour at most. And that if she walked real slow. And that girl weren't walkin' slow. She were too excited."

"Did she take the road? Did anyone see what happened to her?"

The woman's hand covered her mouth, emotion making her aged face quiver. Then she shook her head, her hands moving to ferret with her apron in her lap. "No. She didn't take the road. Leastways, I don' see how she mighta. There's a path that used to lead straight from here to the back side of yer daddy's farm. But it cut awful close to that wicked place—"

"The Dark Wood?"

"Aye, that's what they call it. But the darkness there has little to do with that forest, I s'pect. That darkness is ever'where in this valley.

Gal-Braith seems to be a sluice for it. It just concentrates there, like water pools in the lower places. Aye, and that's it. It's a low place." Her voice was a rusty whisper now.

"Why is it low?"

"'Cause all the people believe it's low. Somehow, long before anyone who remembers came along, somethin' happened there. Somethin' woke up."

"Woke up?"

"Best way I can s'plain it. Mind yeh, this's just what I think. No one knows. Not really. But I say somethin' that shoulda been left alone was roused. Something bad happened, and it happened there, where the Dark Wood is now. So the people here 'bouts steered clear of it. Old superstition is a powerful thing, boy. Time passed. The forest grew. It became a low place filled with darkness." She leaned close, her hot breath the smell of burnt cabbage. "The darkness what takes our boys from us. Our boys who come back with dead eyes, if they come back at all."

Eliot shuddered. He could see the Dark Wood from the window of his cottage. His world was separated from it by a rickety wooden fence.

Fingers snapped in front of his face, and he blinked to find the old woman looking at him. "You see that place in yer mind, don't yeh?"

Eliot nodded.

"Don't even look at it that way. And never, ever go into that place." Her hand whipped out and gripped his tightly. "Eliot, listen to me." She had spoken his name. He couldn't remember her doing that before. Eliot looked into her eyes and saw a gravity there that made him uneasy. He swallowed his nerves.

Eyes wide, he said, "Aye, lady?"

"The day will come soon when yer own father, who I know loves yeh in the only way he can, yer own da' will tell yeh it is yer time to make yer way into that place, that ever' boy does it. When that day comes, yeh run, boy. Eliot, hear me. Run th'other way. It's a lie. That place will do nothing for yeh but steal the life in yeh. Aye, and replace it with somethin' black."

Eliot's guts cranked inside him. The day would soon come? He hadn't the heart to tell her it was next day. Her hand, which had been gripping his with an uncanny strength, came to rest on Eliot's chest. It trembled as she lay it flat over his heart.

"Yeh have yer mother's eyes, but she's in here, too. I can feel her there. She was a strong'ne. So're you. She's in yeh, boy. That place took yer mamma. It took her, boy, sure as I draw breath. The low place stole yer mamma away 'cause it knew she could break its spell. It knew she understood it for what it is. What it really is." Her solemnity shrunk her voice to little more than air. Eliot strained to hear.

"So when yer day comes to pass through it, you run th'other way. You remember: it's all a lie. Yer father—"

The door to the cottage opened, breaking the spell of the moment. Eliot's head snapped toward it as the old woman stopped talking. Her husband stood in the doorway. Behind him, in the yard, was Eliot's father. When he turned back to the woman, he realized that her eyes, now full of tears, had never left him. Those tears seemed almost to put out the fire in her eyes, but not quite. There was still a hot blaze there. In fact, she looked crazy.

Her husband called her name. She held the boy's gaze for another moment, then looked at her husband. The severe, frantic look of remembering fled her face like a wisp of smoke in a strong breeze.

"Yeh done all yer yammerin' out there?" she asked. "The two of yehs gotcher trade all worked out then?" The strong old woman was back, ornery and beautiful.

"Yar," her husband responded, his voice a gravel pit. "Yeh done bewitching the boy? He looks pert near scared nuff to hightail it straight out the back wall!" And he laughed an old man's burlap laugh.

"I'm done," she said. Eliot went to move away from her, but she grabbed his wrist hard and pulled him back to face her. That fire was there in earnest now. "Don't forget yer tater sack, boy."

Then she pulled him even closer. Her breath was tinged sour with tobacco. In a whisper so the men couldn't hear, she said, "And don't forget this." She patted his chest again. "She's there. Do not doubt it."

He swallowed as the old woman sat back. "Yeh have the look of yer mother," she whispered. "When the time comes, you remember her. You answer her. And yeh run th'other way. Don't let it take yeh like it took yer mother, boy. The way it took yer da'. Don't let it steal yeh." She spoke so softly by the end, her words were almost lost to him. She seemed lost in them.

The old wife's eyes let him go then. Eliot dragged the sack of potatoes off the table and hefted it over his shoulder, bending under its weight. Just before he went out the door, the woman called out again, near enough to a shout to count as one. "Don't you forget it, boy!" Surprised that she would betray their conspiracy in front of the men, he froze, his gaze frantic as he looked back at her. It felt like he'd been caught doing something dirty. He didn't know why he felt this way. He hadn't been the one telling a little boy scary stories. He hadn't been sharing secrets he wasn't allowed to tell.

But he realized he didn't want his father to know what he and the old wife had been talking about. And now, she had broken their unspoken truce to keep their conversation a secret between them. She ignored the panic in his eyes and instead raised her hand and pointed at the window.

"Don't forget it, boy," she said again, pointing at a pie cooling in the open window sill. "Take the pie with yeh when yeh go. And when yeh eat it, remember the crazy old woman who made it for yeh." Eliot saw her trembling finger, but more than all that he saw mad clarity in her eyes. He nodded understanding.

Eliot's father stepped inside and protested. "We didn't come to steal yer pie, good lady."

"Good lady," the old woman spat, getting up now from her chair and busying herself with housework. "Don't think to tell an old woman no when she's made up'er mind 'bout somethin'. Take it and go. We got work to do here, and I s'pect you do as well. Go on!" She made a shooing motion at them, like they were both little boys come in from the creek, dripping and covered in mud.

Chastened, Eliot's father took the sack of potatoes so Eliot could grab the pie from the sill. As he did, Eliot looked at the old woman one last time. Tears were streaming down her weary face as she looked at him. Her bottom lip trembled. Emotion filled a deep well within her. She gave a resolute and final nod, spilling giant tears over her wrinkled lids.

Eliot again nodded. There was understanding, gratitude, and quiescence in the gesture. He took up the pie, its warmth spreading in his palms. And the smell . . . it seized his attention. He had not asked what was in the pie, but now he knew. It wasn't his favorite, but it would do fine. He turned to thank her, but a searing heat stabbed his chest, and he was hurtled out of the dream and into a flurry of light and darkness, starscape reflected on turbulent, inky waters. Just as his consciousness blinked out, he heard the phrase "gho gret kee" and smelled the fragrant headiness of juniper-bean pie.

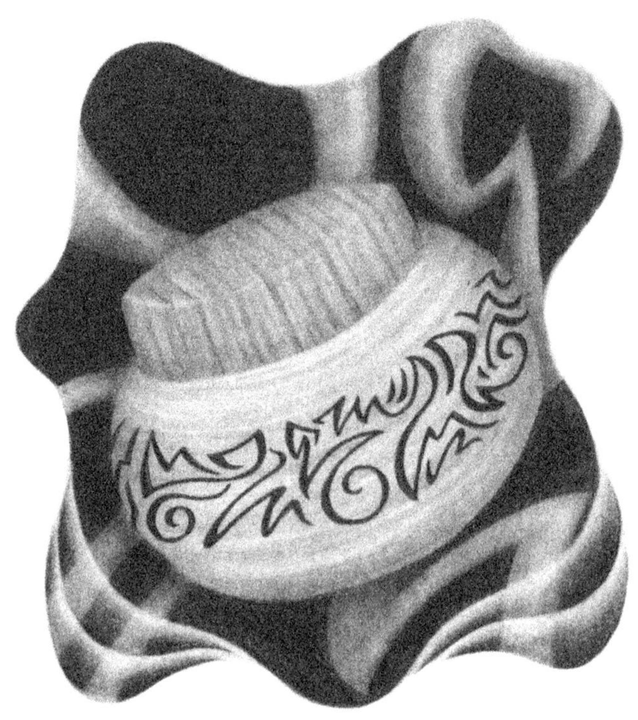

CHAPTER FOURTEEN: A GLEAMING FURY

Soft light filtered through the gray canvas of morning. Eliot sat up, wiping sleep from his eyes. The camp was empty. Good. He rolled and hefted his pack and set off at a trot in a nearby copse of trees. He needed time to think. He needed time alone.

He pushed his way through the tight brush. It was as crowded as his thoughts. He was quick but also quiet. He knew the woodsmen would find him. They were hunters, after all. And they would soon need to begin their trek for the day. But before all that, Eliot needed some time to sort the clutter in his head.

There existed duplicates of his mother: one an old image, a faithful if painful image he'd grown used to. In that iteration, his mother had left him. She'd betrayed him and his father, abandoning them. But he now saw that was not a true image. That revelation evoked the second version: his mother had never abandoned him. Rather, she'd meant to protect him.

To take him from the valley before his kohlas began. What prevented her? Had the Dark Wood taken her? Had it killed her the way it had tried to kill him? The idea made him dizzy.

And there was also the matter of the old wife's pie. He'd smelled it still: it had been juniper-bean. He knew. His mouth watered. He tasted the tangy beans. In the glen, he'd eaten a juniper-bean. His head swirled around that truth. That tangy morsel of truth . . . Did that make the smoking man an ally or a tormentor? If an ally, as Eliot suspected, why all the mystery? And why did the woodsmen see the smoking man as a danger?

And here was yet another matter needing address: the woodsmen. He'd asked Talker to let him sleep with no magic. He'd asked, and Talker had agreed. He'd agreed; what then explained the sudden silence of his memory? What clamped those images shut, his memory in a dream . . . and who else could have spoken that Lynthian phrase echoing in his head? Turning his thoughts white with frenzy.

There was no one else.

Eliot felt heat in his face. He felt pressure in his chest and neck. His hands clenched and unclenched, clenched and unclenched. His jaw tightened. He had always trusted the woodsmen. Hadn't he? Not at the very beginning, perhaps. But he was a frightened child then. He had learned to trust them. They had proven themselves trustworthy. Right? Yes, yes, and yes. Over and over and over. But when had they proven themselves? And how?

Betrayal stirred Eliot's guts. His own betrayal. The woodsmen had been faithful in their tutelage. They'd kept harm from him. The Dark Wood would have swallowed him had they not intervened, but were there other moments they'd protected him with such obvious intention? No. His kohlas would be impossible without them; that was true. But that was another problem: his kohlas would be impossible without them. That thought was heavy with implication. It was infected with meaning.

He stumbled through the bramble, steam billowing in his chest and head. Who was the damned smoking man? What was he playing at? Did the woodsmen know something about his mother? Where had she gone? Why didn't the woodsmen trust him? What were they keeping from him? What was he not seeing? Why did he feel so broken? Why was Talker's magic such an affront? Didn't it prove the woodsman still thought Eliot too much a child to handle . . . to handle what? The kohlas?

No. Eliot feared it was more than that. Worse than that. They did not believe he could handle the truth. Could that be it? Talker's magic helped him sleep, yes. But his sleep was dreamless. Void. A new thing occurred to Eliot. After Talker's incantation in his dream, after he'd felt pulled again into that void, something remained: he'd smelled pie. A small thing, yet it held meaning. Why did that matter?

Eliot thrashed his way out of the tangle of small scrub oaks and goat bushes, the tangle in his head tightening in a chaotic helix, and ran, reckless, into a solid object: Stalker. The woodsmen watched him search for his bearings to account for their sudden appearance.

"You struck camp?" Talker asked. Eliot didn't answer. "Good."

The woodsman turned and walked away, but Stalker stayed. He glared at Eliot, and that now familiar feeling of fear began to claw its way into Eliot's soul. After a few moments, the woodsman pointed with his chin for Eliot to follow Talker. Eliot stared at Stalker, anger replacing his fear and filling his vision with dancing particles of light. The woodsman would not intimidate him. He could not allow it.

It felt like a long moment before Eliot turned and followed Talker. He would have more time to think, more time to calm himself. They had a full day's journey ahead. He needed to speak with Talker, but later. And he needed to do so without losing his temper.

"But why?" Eliot was exasperated. And so very angry. He had not yet raised his voice to shouting, but it was coming. He felt it like the rising tide of a volcanic lake. It was evening, and they had chosen camp, but they had built no fire. No dinner was prepared. No packs unrolled. Rather, Eliot broached the subject with Talker the second Stalker left to fetch water. "I asked yeh not to."

"Boy, please . . ." Talker tried to calm Eliot, his tone soft and placating.

"Just tell me! Why'd yeh do it?"

Talker looked at Eliot. Did Eliot see curiosity in the woodsman's expression? Wonder? Confusion? Talker was so difficult to read. "What makes you think I spoke an incantation over you while you slept?"

"Because I heard yeh. After, like. While I was sleepin'. I were dreamin', and . . . and then I heard yeh." Eliot looked hard into Talker's eyes. "I heard yer incantation."

Talker made a dismissive movement with his hand. "You dreamt it, boy."

"No." Eliot still held the woodsman's gaze. If there was something to see in the man's eyes, Eliot would see it.

"Eliot, come. Calm yourself. We have work to do."

"The day is done," Eliot countered. "Our work now is this: why?"

Eliot studied the woodsman's dark eyes. Talker did not try to hide them. Like he had nothing to hide. But Eliot didn't believe that. Perhaps another tack would work better. He took a calming breath and settled his voice before speaking again.

"Aye, I know yeh look after me. I know this is our work. Our hunt." Eliot continued holding the woodsman's gaze. "That's why I need to know. I don't want yer magic to help me sleep. I need to . . ." To what? He needed to dream, is what he wanted to say. To remember. But he was certain he shouldn't say that to Talker.

As though hearing Eliot's thoughts, or divining them, Talker asked, "What do you see when you sleep?"

"What do *you* see when you sleep?" Eliot said, feeling childish the moment the words left his tongue. Then again, it was a valid question.

Talker's eyes narrowed. Finally, there was emotion there. "Eliot, we are weary of your distrust."

Eliot marveled over how Talker had turned this on him, had made Eliot the distrustful one. "What do yeh mean?" Eliot asked, his voice defensive. "I do trust yeh. You don't trust me. That's what we're talkin' about. I trusted yeh, and yet—"

"You trust us? Yet you call our actions into question. You question what we do. Why we do it. What we know. What we don't know. That is not trust."

Eliot's body rippled with tension. His breathing was a storm. "Aye, so askin' questions means I don't trust yeh? Wantin' to understand is, what, disrespectful to yeh? Don't twist this on me. I'll not play into that."

Talker shook his head. Eliot felt the condescension in the gesture. "Play is all you do of late," Talker said. His voice was thin.

"Why?" Eliot shouted. "Just answer the damn question! Why do yeh bury me in sleep each night with yer magic? Why do yeh want so bad to silence my head?" Was that it? Eliot wondered. Did Talker mean to shut out his dreams? To shut up his memories and their truths?

"Silence what, Eliot?" Talker moved closer, and the action made him uneasy. He bent toward Eliot. It was slight, but aggressive. "What are you keeping from us, boy?"

What are you not trusting us with, Eliot thought. That's what the woodsman was saying. Eliot stepped back.

"What are you keeping from me?" Venom made Eliot's heart itch as bad as the rash on his chest and abdomen. But he could only scratch this itch with words. "Yeh know 'bout my mother, aye. Don't yeh?"

At this, the woodsman stood straight again. His eyes reflected understanding.

"Ah," Talker said. "So we come to it at last. Your night terrors tell you lies about your mother, and you believe them. You believe it is we who lie to you, aye?"

The woodsman's words rolled over him, and Eliot felt how ridiculous it all sounded. His instinct told him Talker was right. How could he believe nonsense he heard in his dreams? But something deeper—or something closer to his core—told Eliot things were not that simple. His discoveries hadn't only been in his dreams. He'd also remembered things, wide awake in the full light of day. He stepped closer to Talker, bolstered by the truth at his core, no matter how reasonable Talker's argument seemed.

A venomous calm came over Eliot then, and he said, "Yeh say they are lies, but yeh offer no truth to counter them." Eliot paused, watching Talker's face. Willing some tangible authenticity to show itself in the man's features. "Yeh keep things from me. Yeh say yeh trust me, but yeh put me to bed each night like I were a babbie. And yeh can't even admit that much."

His anger curled up inside him, a snake waiting to strike. He felt the tension in his face, the drawing in his cheeks. His lips twitching. His hands shaking. His being shaking.

"Will yeh do that for me, at least that? Admit yeh used yer magic on me last night."

"And if we did, we did so to protect you."

"Do yeh admit it, then?"

Talker gave up the argument. Eliot saw it in the way his shoulders fell.

"No," Eliot said, his voice rising. "I am not satisfied!" The skin on his chest and stomach was inflamed. More than before. But not so much as his rage.

Now, at a crisp gait, the other woodsman returned. In one fist he gripped his red jar. In the other, his gleaming short sword. It caught the burning light of sunset and flicked it into Eliot's eyes. Eliot could not react. He had no time. Stalker lifted the blade and brought the butt down on Eliot's skull.

A vicious split rendered Eliot's head in pieces. Parts lay splintered in oblivion, the darkness of dreamless sleep. Not yet touched by Talker's magic, his thoughts were knocked out of his head by a solid blow. On the other hand, Eliot could still hear the woodsmen, Talker's voice and Stalker's movement. And in hearing, he visualized them.

"That was unnecessary."

Eliot's shirt was yanked up. The jar was uncapped. A hand set to apply the red ointment to Eliot's furious skin. Eliot wriggled against this, and he felt the woodsman's knee press into his hip.

"He is our ward. Not our pet."

Stalker pressed the biting red salve into Eliot's skin. His skin tightened and pulled against the abrasive liniment. Stalker seemed bent on skinning him. His knee ground into Eliot's hip. Eliot tried to cry out, but the split in his head lost him the words.

"Kinsman. Use just enough to keep the boy's mind clear. No more. We can not make more."

Stalker, finished it seemed with Eliot's chest and stomach, jerked down the boy's breeches. He began his ministrations all over, this time on Eliot's inner thigh and hip. Eliot's head hurt. His skin burned. And inside he was hot magma. He was gleaming fury. He was incandescent mania. Yet he could not move his body beneath Stalker's work.

"Gho gret kee, gret et ghosh."

Talker's incantation, altered. Talker's incantation, but closer.

"Enough, kinsman," Talker said.

Closer: "Gho gret kee, gret et ghosh."

"Kinsman!"

"Gret et ghosh."

The words were not closer. They were inside Eliot's head. And they were not Talker's words. A sphere of ice-cold blackness blossomed in Eliot's mind. It grew to encompass all he thought. It tried. It meant to, but it could not. Something held it back. A strange awareness held it back. And Eliot did not slip into the void. Rather, he stepped into a dream.

Eliot faced off against a dark man. They were clamped together in a death struggle. Every move by Eliot was met with its mirror. Every action expected and negated. Hand against hand. Strength against strength. But the man's identity was obscured. His dress was familiar, however. The weathered breeches. The stained tunic, a rip at the collar. The once thick coat, near threadbare in places. The cloak, chalky from years of wandering.

Eliot reached inside his own sooty cloak and retrieved his blade. His dark companion did the same. When Eliot thrust, he glimpsed the figure's face. It was his own. The blade dug in, and Eliot looked down in horror, seeing it caught between his own ribs. But rather than blood spilling forth, smoke hissed out. Fragrant and familiar, the smoke smelled yellow.

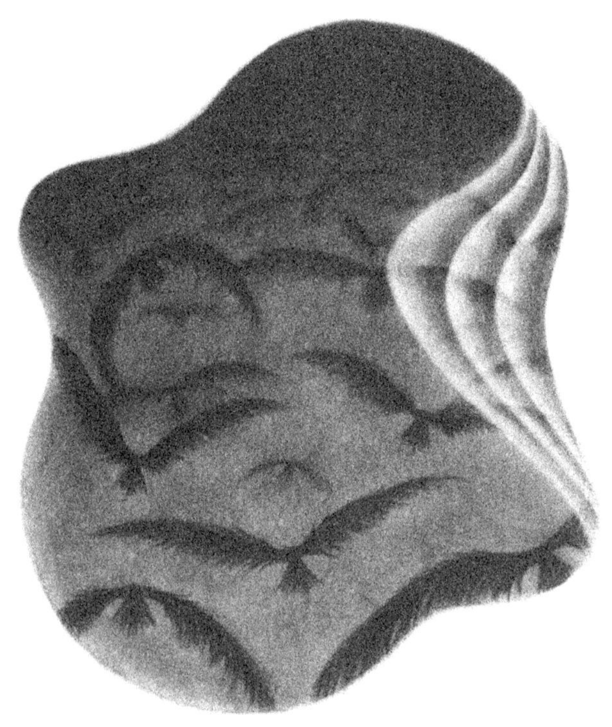

CHAPTER FIFTEEN: MURDER OF CROWS

Eliot walked through a mental haze. He spoke little in the days following Stalker's assault. His mind, however, was a hive of conversation. A cord had been broken. He felt it.

The skin of his chest and stomach burned. His anger burned hotter, as did his confusion. His feet moved by muscle memory as he followed the woodsmen. They had spent the last several days traversing a wide expanse of plain. They walked along its edge, hugging the tree line that marked the beginning of the Snake River basin. Still moving west.

Since Eliot did not begin a conversation, there was none. Sounds of shuffling feet and tinkling tack served as an arhythmic euphony to their travel, joining the chorus of wind and cicadas. Eliot could not help but glare at the short sword on Stalker's hip, the scabbard a dull mud brown. The knot on his head would not let him forget that sword.

Talker had not used his magic on Eliot since the night of Stalker's assault, not so far as Eliot knew. And Eliot slept little. He could not quiet the voices in his head, day or night. Things which once seemed so logical now failed to make sense. His mother was an open wound, one he could not look at just now. He would give that issue his full attention soon enough, but there was a more pressing matter.

The woodsmen made less sense to him than ever before. There was a reason he'd trusted them all these years. He knew this. He had been a boy, but he hadn't been a stupid boy. Considering that, Eliot grew suspicious of his attitude toward the woodsmen, now and at the beginning. He had remembered the first day of his kohlas, the fear he'd known, but he remembered little of the woodsmen themselves, only how they made him feel. And that did not sit well now.

His memory had been molested somehow, by some magic. He might concede it was his own doing, a repression of difficult truths, but that did not satisfy. Had the woodsmen done it? He began recalling things after meeting the smoking man in the birch wood. His magic, it seemed, jarred loose the door hiding his memories. But what began his memory loss? The woodsmen? The Dark Wood? The scarecrow? The kohlas itself? The woodsmen felt underhanded, but malicious? Had their ointment and incantations aided the release of his mental captives, or were they meant to suppress them further? If the latter, could their magic fail with such efficiency? Eliot feared the truth he may find. Perhaps this fear had prevented him from finding it, one way or another. Eight years. That was too much time to concede to lies. And long enough to make certain such deception never happened again.

The woodsmen confused him. They shared the same goal—to catch the scarecrow—but what motivated the woodsmen? Something Talker said lingered in Eliot's head: "We do not wish you or your family harm," he'd said, "for that would not serve our mutual purposes." What then was their purpose? What did the woodsmen gain from all this?

They hunted a scarecrow, but why? Eliot had never asked that question before the enchanted birch wood. Why would he? The chase was a necessity, one from which Eliot could not see a way out or a reason to find one. His people worshipped the damned kohlas, or close enough. They revered it as sacred. It had always been as much a part of his identity as the color of his eyes or skin, or his name. The hunt had always been a thing he must complete. It had always defined the shape of his future—if he had one. It was more than an obligation. It had been a part of him since birth. Was that why he hadn't sought an answer to the question? Hadn't thought to ask it? Had he always been willfully blind?

Why was a foolish thought. He wanted the truth, but why was a dangerous word. If he asked the question, he must decipher an answer. He must discern its truth. He must reckon with that truth, no matter what damage it caused. And his reason failed him. Why a scarecrow? Why alone with two men who remained strangers to him even after eight years together? Why the woodsmen? And why was this the way to become a man? That had made sense to him at six years. It no longer made sense at fifteen years. The logic of it seemed flimsy when examined in the light of day. And to admit as much was to admit a crisis of faith, a loss of something essential to his identity. And if so, who was he?

Around and around, Eliot cycled in and out of these corridors in his thoughts, as though his mind were a labyrinth without exits. Without beginnings. Weaving in and through logic and illogic alike as though they were twins, not opposites. It made sense in view of this vast canvas that he may have preferred hiding himself away in a tiny closet of his mind to avoid getting lost for good. Perhaps that explained his willful blindness, if he had it. Either way, he was good and lost now. His brain felt thin and raw as the structure of his understanding collapsed under the strain of reason.

The waterskin fell from Talker's grasp. Surprised, Eliot stopped. Talker had offered him the skin, and Eliot had walked right into it. He was seeing little in the world around him compared with what he saw in his head. He was not surprised, however, by the woodsman's offer of water. Talker had been more helpful than usual the last couple days. More conciliatory, his behavior bordered on kindness. Eliot looked at the woodsman for a moment before picking up the skin and drinking from it. He was parched and had not noticed. Having drunk his fill, he handed the skin to the woodsman.

"We will journey a little further, but not so much today." Talker waited for Eliot to respond, but Eliot only nodded. "How is your head?" he asked. He reached his hand to feel for the knot on Eliot's head, but Eliot pulled back.

Neither spoke for several moments. Talker pulled the waterskin's strap over his shoulder and scanned the slight slope of land rising to their right. The plain ended there and the river land began. He turned back to Eliot.

"Are you good to keep going? We can break here."

Eliot shook his head and started walking. Talker followed. Soon, the woodsman caught up with his companion—his kinsman, as he would say—and Eliot was left to himself. He scratched at the burning itch in his thigh.

After several more hours, the woodsmen broke to make camp. Eliot, however, kept moving. Though the horizon was bleeding with sunset, there were still a few hours left before full dark. The last thing he wanted was to spend another long evening sitting in silence while the woodsmen studied him. He heard them follow behind, making no protest.

It occurred to Eliot this was the first time he'd taken the lead since heading west. He led the way for some time, long enough to grow distracted again by his thoughts. He did not bother conferring with the woodsmen, and they made no effort either. That was well enough for Eliot. The sky and wind warned a storm was in their future, the clouds low and growing dark. Perhaps they should get to higher ground. The plain was flat, but along the edge of the river basin, the rise would offer a bit of elevation and some tree cover should the storm come in force. Eliot followed a deer path formed among the scrub and dense bramble. It was tight, but he could see it thinned ahead on a flat hilltop. That would make a good place to camp. But something caught his eye. So caught up he was in his reverie, he'd almost missed it. But instinct is strong, and here at least it served him well. Among the dog roses was a strip of cloth. Eliot stopped to study it. He pulled it from the thorn, which snagged it, and held it between his fingers. He smelled it: it was damp from blood. In the growing twilight he could tell little else about the cloth, but he knew what had left it.

The storm cloud, now dark as night, was moving fast and filled the sky overhead. Using the failing light, Eliot surveyed the thicket before him. It would not be possible to travel through the brush, not without leaving a clear sign of passage. There was no sign in the brush. That meant the deer path was the way forward. Sound came from the cloud above, but not thunder. Curious, Eliot looked and saw what he'd mistaken for a cloud was not just a cloud. Rather, a great horde of black birds swarmed. A murder of crows. Their great wings murmured as they filled the small barren trees surrounding him. They did not caw. They lit and turned their baleful eyes on Eliot, a million black feathers becoming a million black leaves with hooked beaks and vindictive stares. His skin crawled and rippled with gooseflesh. The crows stared like old acquaintances.

Eliot had seen crows before, but not so close. These were huge, bigger than any normal crow of which he knew. Their large luminous eyes stared into him to see his secrets. Their silence was disheartening. It was unnatural. It had to be magic as black as the birds themselves. What did the murder of crows mean? Surely crows would not collude with a scarecrow. The two were, at least in concept, enemies. Could the birds mean to aid Eliot in his pursuit? He doubted that, even if these were magic crows. And he doubted he would welcome their help in any case. Eliot looked closer at the crow nearest him. On its leg was bound a coil of dark red thread. The crow's head bent toward Eliot, as if taking his stock.

A racket ahead on the trail broke the uneasy calm. In an instant, the air around Eliot turned jet black as the crows took to flight, each one crying out. Their clatter made Eliot's head spin. He put his hands to his ears and squatted on the ground, shutting his eyes against the tumult, if only to buy himself a moment to think. The black birds flew round him, slamming into his head and shoulders. Each time he felt Stalker's strike all over. He covered his face as much as possible. Still, he felt cuts seeping blood. His arms were worse than his face. The crows ascended, and the sky became a black blur again, as if covered by a giant cloak. Then nothing.

Perplexed, Eliot stood. He looked around; the crows were gone. A black smudge smearing the horizon. In the vacuum of silence left behind, Eliot saw Talker for the first time since taking the lead. He approached, Stalker several paces farther back down the deer path. The woodsmen studied Eliot. Talker's expression showed as much confusion as Eliot felt. The crows seemed to unnerve the woodsmen, too, he saw. Then a howl broke the spell of the moment, and Eliot was off. He ran after it, headlong into the gloom. What pale light filtered through the building clouds was slight against the growing dark. His throat burned from heavy breathing and thirst, and the skin on his body was fitful. Propelled forward by an intense need to finish this quest, Eliot topped the rise and kept running down the other side. Fever filled his head and heart. The wet scrap of cloth was sticky in his hand, binding his fingers to palm. This would be it. He would be quit of this madness; he would find the scarecrow or die by the effort.

In blind hysteria, Eliot tore free from the tangled path and nearly plunged headfirst into a deep gorge. Having stopped only at the last step, he found himself pelted with stones. He found cover in the thicket and looked across the open distance. There once was a bridge here. Perhaps its ruin accounted for the racket, and if so it was not an accident. He strained to see in the dim light, but he saw no sign of his assailant. Another stone hit him. It struck against the knot on his head and sent pain lightning through his body. Tears flooded his eyes, and he rubbed them away as he turned in the direction of the stone's throw, squatting for cover. By the light of the rising moon, he discerned the shape of a crouching figure.

It stood. It was very tall and very thin. Its long arms hung loose at its sides and one spindle-barbed hand rolled two small stones together. It turned its head, but it wasn't a head. Atop its shoulders sat a huge gourd with malignant holes for eyes, a mouth, and a nose. A fire blazed inside the gourd, and Eliot could just make out a silhouette of thin sharp teeth ringing its monstrous mouth. The face twisted in a combination of hatred and infectious fear.

Eliot remembered his fear the first time he fought the scarecrow. He felt little fear now. Only resolve. Only anger over eight years of meaningless pursuit. And what had he to fear from this creature after having stared down the maw of the Dark Wood? No. Eliot was not afraid. He was livid.

The clouds parted. Eliot looked at the bloody cloth in his hand and thought, for the first time, the blood on the cloth could be the scarecrow's. The moon, now brighter and clearer, made possible a better look at the cloth. It glistened blood red. He looked across the ravine at the scarecrow.

The creature was hideous. The eyes in its grotesque, diseased head blinked and flame licked out from its mouth like a lapping tongue. Even confronted by such a mad image, Eliot felt matched to his prey. As he looked upon it, his resolve, however, began to waver. He was annoyed to find misplaced, tardy fear turning his stomach into a pool of ice water. His forehead was wet, sweat beading down his face. He looked again at the cloth, and his hand was shaking. He pulled out his blade. This was the way, and the way is the way. His lungs were heavy as if he were breathing syrup. Here was the culmination of eight years of his life. Here was the fruition of his quest. Why, then, was he filled with unaccountable dread? He was terrified, not by the horror with the burning gaze, but for something besides. If the scarecrow ended him, then that was the way his kohlas would always have ended. His fear was not that the scarecrow might win or that he might die. Something felt wrong here. Unaccountable. He could taste it like iron on his tongue. A spider of doubt had crawled into his head and was spinning an enormous web, but he could not see its design.

Eliot shook his head to clear it. This was the scarecrow. But now, seeing it from this distance, he failed to understand why, after all this time, it engaged Eliot twice in such a short span after years of concealment. Eliot stood. He left the protective cover of the bramble to face the grotesque creature.

"What do yeh want?" he shouted. There was no reply. Eliot searched the creature's head for signs of their last struggle. He saw none.

The scarecrow lifted its hand and pointed at Eliot. Eliot felt anger and dread jostle inside him, vinegar and oil. A trail led along the ravine's edge. Was there another way to cross? He looked back at the scarecrow. It waited here for Eliot to see him, but to what end? Could it be a trap? Eliot made no sense of this. A hunted thing does not taunt the hunter. "Do you believe still that it is you who are the hunter?" Eliot heard the smoking man's words in his head. Was this what the man meant? Was Eliot the scarecrow's prey? Surprised, Eliot found his anger boil to the surface again at this possibility.

"Do yeh want me? Why not come get me?"

Once again, there was no reply. Heat chafed Eliot's cheeks. He looked around, grabbed a handful of stones, and stood once again.

"Answer me!" Eliot threw a stone at the creature, but it flew wide. The scarecrow did not react. "Answer me, damn yeh! What are yeh?" Eliot threw another stone, and another. Both struck the scarecrow. One hit its left shoulder. The second hit the center of the creature's giant ugly head. The scarecrow did not move to stop the stones, but the dark expression on its face, silhouetted by the fire inside, changed. It grew more malevolent.

"What do yeh want from me?" Eliot cried, now close to angry tears. Feeling the desperation of his situation, the utter futility of the hunt, he threw his remaining stones. Here he stood, a literal stone's throw from the scarecrow, and yet an ocean might as well separate the two. Having spent his stones, he cried once more: "Answer me!" Tears streaked his face.

The scarecrow dropped the stones it held, and with three quick strides, it bounded into the darkness beyond and was gone.

Eliot could only stare after it. It could have set a trap and laid in wait by the gorge, thrusting Eliot over its edge. But it hadn't. It had destroyed the bridge. It had waited for Eliot to arrive, had alerted him of its presence. Had taunted Eliot with stones. What game was this? Eliot heard the woodsmen coming up the trail. None of this made sense, but he had just one option: he would follow the trail along the ravine. He traveled by the filtered light of the moon, following a precarious path. Following the scarecrow.

Talker came alongside Eliot. "We must stop, boy. It is too dark to see."

Eliot spun. "I'll not stop until I find the scarecrow. Until I finish this thing." Tears still wet his face, and he felt no shame. He realized he did not care if Talker saw his tears. He no longer cared what the woodsmen thought of him.

The woodsman was reasonable as ever. "Eliot, we are close. Now is the time for caution. For deliberation. Not rash action."

"Then be cautious. Deliberate, aye. I'm goin' to catch a scarecrow."

Eliot turned and stumbled up the path, the bloody cloth gluing his hand into a fist. Conflict raged a labyrinth in his head. What was he doing? Did he think he would find another bridge? How many could there be? Another crossing, then? A felled tree, or a rock ledge that narrowed the ravine enough for a jump? And was he so maddened by his frenzy he would risk his life in the dark?

He fell to his knees, sobbing. Talker was right. The damned woodsman was right. He had to be smart, to keep his head. Be smart . . . . The phrase percolated in his mind. Where had he heard it before? And why did it feel important now?

"Be smart," Eliot said, his voice little more than a whisper. Then he heard the words repeat in his thoughts, only this time it was not his voice speaking. His eyes caught moonlight and twinkled as he looked up at Talker. The woodsman, who should have been satisfied Eliot stopped, was pensive. Wary, even. Eliot perceived this subtle clue. Perhaps the woodsman was concerned over what he saw reflected in Eliot's eyes. And for once, Eliot believed he was close to understanding why.

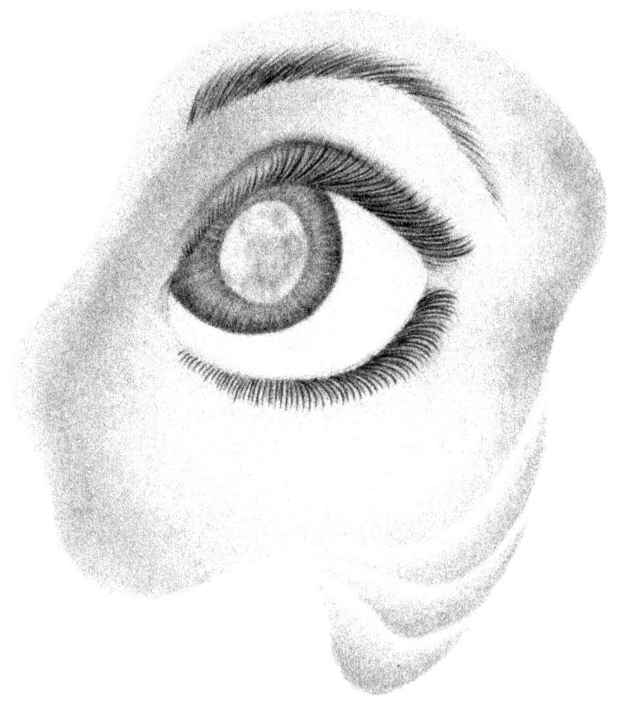

CHAPTER SIXTEEN: LURKING NEED

Eliot lay awake in the dark. The storm proved toothless. Deep in the gorge below, running water debated against rocks. The woodsmen kept busy with tasks. Eliot ignored them. They were always busy with mending packs or drying meats and vegetables or some other work, vital yet unimportant. They were not far from him, but neither were they close. Eliot did not think they ever slept. But his thoughts were not given to the woodsmen or their habits. He remembered his mother.

As a boy, Eliot loved to lie back in the field near his house once his chores were completed. He would wait for his mother to call him in for dinner and stare up into the clouds, willing them into shapes. He often drifted into a light sleep, the sun warming his face, as he imagined the butterflies fluttering around him speaking a faye language he alone understood.

Not long after he'd overheard his parents arguing, a strange compulsion took hold of him. He was napping in the field, enjoying a warm autumn sun. The earthy scent of honey carried on the mild breeze, all the way from memory to the present moment. Eliot could argue he was there again, six years old on the hill below his father's cottage. If he wasn't there, he watched with brand new clarity as if it happened all over again. And he felt it, too. But this time, what he saw and felt was new. Age and experience informed his understanding with new, uncomfortable truths.

His six-year-old self had slept awhile, his arm, now full of pestering needle pricks beneath his head, waking him. As he rolled onto his side, he spied a stir of shadows off toward the Dark Wood. He pushed himself onto his elbow to see above the field grass, moving like water in the breeze. The shadow was just a line of dark clouds coming in from the mountains. At its fore, the line was a civil gray, but farther at its heart it wore a deep black, the color and shape of pain. A storm was coming, an anthem for his childhood.

The breeze became a cold wind, and it silenced the dirge of the whip-poor-wills in the oaks. The butterflies were gone, swept away to wherever butterflies go when the winds blow cold and in earnest. Gone, too, was the sweet honey smell of early autumn. In its place was something darker, a scent that forebode the intentions of the storm.

Eliot felt the first splat of rain on his forehead. He remembered looking into the sky just overhead, quite blue and oblivious of the coming storm. He'd wondered about the improbable drop of rain, so ahead of its compatriots, then looked back toward the storm. It was moving fast. He understood the compulsion of the clouds. A similar force had built in him. He stood, looking down into the shadows of the forest and all its secrets on the other side of the old fence, his fingers scratching at his hip.

If he had meant to go to the Dark Wood, he did not remember now. But he found himself there regardless, standing next to the fence. It was old and derelict in most places and looked a miracle to remain standing. But his hands rested on fresh wood, proof of his father's recent repairs, the sap still seeping in places. He rubbed his thumb against a bead, its skin breaking, thick pine sap coming away. He licked it and then rubbed his thumb and forefinger, savoring the bitter sweetness. He tasted it on his tongue even now.

Then his foot was on the lower rail of the fence, and he flung his other leg over the top. Eliot, tasting the gummy residue of a dead tree on his tongue, was going into the wood. Without intention. Without thought. He just was. The place called to him. To his six-year-old curiosity, yes, but also to someplace deeper. To a need lurking in his inner shadows. To a lust there, gnawing at him to look and see. He would go into the Dark Wood. He would discover what the fuss was all about. In a matter of months, he would do this very thing, anyway. Why wait? Why wait.

Eliot, the young man, witnessed his younger self do the unthinkable: his smile was emotionless. His breathing flat. His mind clear. He felt drunk. Yes, even then, he'd known that feeling. He'd often feigned sickness during the winter just to have a few sips of his father's whiskey. It went down warm and made his thoughts go white. This was like that, but stronger, and Eliot liked it. But as he drew his leg up to cross over, hands yanked him back over the fence and into awareness.

Eliot remembered his confusion. What was he about to do? Sudden emotion saturated him. Where moments before he'd had no sensation, now his body buzzed with it. Fear. Confusion. Frustration. Weariness. A tide of unruly, gangly feelings surged in him. He looked away from the Dark Wood and into the eyes of his mother.

"Mah?" he asked, his voice thin and wet with fear.

"Boy, what devil's got into yeh? Yeh know never to go near that place, aye?" Eliot nodded, but it wasn't enough. His mother had him by the shoulders and shook him. Her violence hurt his neck and brought out his sobbing. "I told yeh, over and over, son. Do not go there. Do not ever go there. Alone or with others, aye? I told yeh that, aye!" She wasn't asking. She had been screaming. The fear in her eyes turned to panic in Eliot's gut.

"Mah," he said through tears, "I don't understand . . ." And he didn't. Eliot felt again the confusion clouding his thoughts: he would never go near that scary place. Never, never, never. But he had. Why? Now he knew.

"Eliot!" she sobbed. His mother pulled him hard against her chest, her breasts pressing into him. He felt her heart battering against his own. He felt her sobbing. "Eliot, my boy. Eliot." She held him tight. Breathing was difficult. But he needed it then. He needed it now. He needed to feel her that close. In the present, Eliot the young man began weeping. He was fifteen years, a grown man by any account in the region of Carde, yet he cried like that six-year-old boy of spring.

His mother released him, but she held him firm by the shoulders as she looked him in the eye.

"Son, promise me. Promise you will never go into that dreadful place. Promise me." Eliot didn't speak. She shook him again, shouting, "Promise!" Again, sobbing broke through her resolve. Seeing his mother weep was painful. Having caused it was worse.

“Aye, mamma,” he said. His own sobbing returned. “I promise. I promise.” His mother nodded, smiling through her pain. Through her fear and anguish. Her face contorted from conflicting emotions. It was red and slick with tears and snot. He would have promised her the sun to ease her suffering. Her pain was excruciating. “I promise, I promise, I promise,” he said, the words barreling out in a rush. He wanted the words to bear forth his promise and give it weight and power. To make it true. He grabbed hold of her, wrapping his arms around her. The boy of spring wept into his mother’s chest. The older boy of the kohlas wept into his sleeve. In the memory, he and his mother shook in each other’s arms, emotional debris cluttering their faces.

Then she pulled him back to look again in his eyes. She shook her head. Eliot, looking back on the memory, recognized that shake. She was trying to clear her head. To loosen and throw out all the dark things there. He knew that shake very well; he’d inherited it.

“Listen to me, love,” she said, her voice calmer. “Say it again. Say yeh promise.”

“I promise.”

She shook her head. “No, say it all.”

“I promise not to go into the Dark Wood.”

“And what else?”

He was confused. His face said as much. What else?

She said, “Yeh’ll not go into the Dark Wood, alone or with anyone besides.”

He nodded, fast and serious. “I promise not to go into the Dark Wood alone or with anyone else.” His tears were back in force.

“What if it’s yer da’ who brings yeh?”

He shook his head.

“Say it!” she shouted, but took a deep breath to steady herself. She began again, her voice measured. “Say it. Say it, love.” She smiled, nodding encouragement.

“Not even if da’ brings me.” Her brows lifted. She needed him to say it all. “I promise to not go into the Dark Wood even if da’ brings me.”

“Even if he says it’s all right?”

“Aye, mamma. I promise. But why would he? Why if it ain’t safe?”

“Shh, shh,” she said, wiping his face. Wiping away his tears. “Shh, my boy of spring. My sweet, strong boy. Don’t think of that. Just remember: always be smart. Yer my smart boy, aye? No matter what, yeh got to be smart.” Being smart made six-year-old Eliot feel grown in that moment.

Like a man, strong and capable. He could do this for her, he thought. That child's innocence was his ruin, fifteen-year-old Eliot thought. He had never been smart.

His mother shook her head. She saw something in her head that caused her pain. Eliot understood that as well. "No matter what, love, be smart. Always. Stay away from the Dark Wood. Stay far, far away." She was sobbing again.

How far away could he stay? he'd wondered. He'd grown up in the forest's shadow. He remembered being confused about that at six, but now he understood. They were leaving. She was taking him, and they were leaving to get far, far away. Fresh emotion swelled at the realization. There was a time he would have remembered this differently, had he remembered it at all. She would have tried keeping him from exploring his kohlas. She would have withheld from him that sacred rite. She would have prevented him from experiencing the glory of facing his fear. Of standing in the shadows of that ancient, hungry forest. Yes, it was hungry. He'd felt it then. It had wanted him, and he'd walked right up to it. But his mother had not prevented him from acting like a man as he might have imagined; she had saved him from becoming a meal. For a time, at least.

Back in the memory, she grew calm. "Now," she said. She pulled a cloth from her waistband and wiped his face. "Go home. Wash yer face. Don't let yer da' see yeh've been cryin', aye?"

Eliot nodded and stood to leave. Worry stopped him. "Aren't yeh comin'?"

"Aye, love. I'm right behind yeh." She nodded her assurance, and the six-year-old Eliot was satisfied.

He went home. But halfway up the hill, he turned. The sky was no longer blue, but the fence post was red. His mother's palm was red. She placed it against the wood, her back to Eliot. At the time, the boy thought she must have had an accident. Now Eliot understood: she was feeding the low place. She proffered an offering, something to slate its need. To make it forget her boy long enough for her to get him out. Eliot rolled to his side and curled into a ball on the edge of the ravine, the woodsmen near enough he could smell their stink. Fifteen-year-old Eliot understood his mother's offering would never have been enough. If anything, it had made the Dark Wood bloodthirsty for more.

In his memory, the storm hit in full just after they'd finished their supper. It rocked the small house, the wind moaning through the eaves like misplaced ghosts. The thunder was the sound of giants cracking their knuckles, expecting a feast. Just as six-year-old Eliot drifted into a fitful sleep, the anchor of autumn was broken and the storm blew it headlong into winter.

On the edge of the gorge, the storm of Eliot's childhood broke another restraint that had held his memories in darkness. His body thrummed with raw energy, the fruit of the violence in his mind. With each new layer of revelation, Eliot felt himself flayed deeper. His mind bleeding memories into his muscles and organs, churning them with fitful vigor. After an age of toil, Eliot fell into sleep the way he might fall into the gorge: straight down. He fell into a memory within a dream.

It was early dusk. Eliot had just finished washing up from his day's work. His mother was off to see the old wife on the neighboring farm. She had seemed earnest when she'd left earlier in the day. Perhaps it had something to do with Eliot's behavior the day before. He still did not understand why he'd gone to the fence.

His skin was polished from scrubbing as he pulled on a clean shirt. Well, a mostly clean shirt. He was hungry. His mother should be home soon, perhaps with a basket of still warm bread from the old wife. Or a pie. A thud, loud and heavy, shook the cottage. Eliot ducked and looked toward his bedroom door. His room was small, just a cot, a trunk, and a small window. There were few secrets in their tiny cottage: sound traveled through the cracks in the walls unimpeded. But this sound made Eliot's stomach somersault.

He walked to the door and took hold of the leather strap to open it, his other hand poised to turn the small block of wood holding the door shut. He hesitated. His heart was pounding. His father was home. His father was big and strong. Nothing could harm them so long as his father was home. Eliot believed this. Yet he could not account for his sudden and forceful fear.

He waited. After no further sound came from the other side, he turned the bolt and opened the door. No lanterns had been lit. Only the burning light of the setting sun filled the small living space. Eliot scanned the room for signs of . . . what? Whatever had made that sound. As if something heavy had been dropped. Heavy like a body. He scanned the room, but it was empty. There was the front door. The hall tree. The small square table. The door to his parents' bedroom. The kitchen. The cellar trap.

The potato bin and the trunk pantry. The back door. The room was lit with brilliant orange light except in the farthest corners where the failing sunlight could not reach.

Eliot studied these. In those shadows, secrets lurked. By the back door, there was nothing. There was no room in the shadows there. But the darkest shadow was beyond the door at the front of the cottage. He saw nothing there, either. But he had to know for certain. He walked into the room, skirting the center. He kept his back against the wall until he came to the pantry. He took an oil lamp and flint. He struck it alight. Yellow light brightened the room, but only the half closest to his bedroom. Small as it was, at least two lamps were needed to light the home at night.

Eliot swallowed. His breathing was quick and loud in his ears. He steeled himself. It's nothing, he reasoned. His father would have heard. His father would be here if something was wrong. He stepped forward one step, then another. With each tiny step he took, yellow light crept toward the far corner of the room. Yellow crawled along the floor, the ceiling, the walls, edging closer to any secrets hiding behind the front door.

Relief filled him as he reached the table. There was his father. His standing frame was huge in the small space of the corner.

"Da'?" Eliot asked. His relief flipped and slid like a razor through his understanding. Oily fear poured from the slit it left. It was his father, but his father was not right. His body was straight. Rigid, even. But his shoulders were slumped, his head bowed. The tufts of his hair hung greasy in his face, but they did not prevent Eliot from seeing his father's eyes. They were turned up. They were watching him.

Eliot stepped back, leaving the lamp on the table.

"Da'?" he said again, fear making his voice warble.

His father did not answer. Drool poured from his lips, slicking his chin and neck, soaking the collar of his shirt. "Da'," Eliot tried to repeat, but only air came. His back bumped against the doorframe of his bedroom. Should he go in and lock the door? What would a small wooden bolt do against his strong father? And why should he fear his father? He looked again at the man. Why shouldn't he fear him?

Neither moved. The sun continued its slant, the room's light tilting. The only movement was the orange sunlight, Eliot's frantic breathing and runaway heartbeat, and his father's drool. Time passed in a slow train until the orange light was little more than a band skirting the room. The yellow light from the oil lamp on the table was the only safe thing separating Eliot from his father. The one true thing that could keep the hulking man from crossing the room, from coming to get Eliot unseen. If he could see his father, his father could not get him. He could hope, at least.

The back door opened. Eliot cried out.

"Love?" his mother said, coming to her boy. "What's wrong? Yer face is slick with sweat . . ."

Eliot could not answer with his mouth, but his mother must have seen an answer in his eyes. She looked. Her gaze found her husband's form in the dim yellow light, and Eliot felt her body tense. She pulled him to herself. She was trembling.

"Come, love. We have to go."

She pulled Eliot toward the back door, still open. Eliot did not protest. He could not. He could not speak. Outside, she took his small hand in hers and ran.

"Mah?" he asked, his voice high and sharp. She did not answer. "Mah, I'm scared." He began crying. Outside the cottage and away from the fiendish image of his father, Eliot's tears came. As if they, too, had been too afraid to move inside the cottage. Eliot's arm was hurting. His mother was pulling it so hard, it felt almost as though it might come loose at the shoulder. "Mamma," he said again. "It hurts. Yer hurtin' me."

She stopped, but not at his words. They'd reached the road. She studied it, then stole a quick glance back at the cottage. Eliot looked. There was no sign of his father. Eliot edged closer to her, pressing his little body into her and wrapping his arm around her leg. He wanted to puke. His mother looked again at the road, and then at the small path that led away to the right. She looked back and forth between the two.

"This one's safer," she whispered.

"What, mamma?"

"But that one's closer . . ." She shook her head.

"What are yeh sayin', Mother? Yer scarin' me." His lip went fat and trembled.

She looked again at the cottage, then back to the road and the path. Eliot could not look at the cottage, not again. He could not risk seeing that image of his father.

"I don't know, I don't know, I don't know . . ." Her voice was quiet and earnest. Her leg was shaking.

She knelt, taking Eliot's wet face between her palms. She tried a smile, but it didn't fit. Eliot wanted it to fit, but it couldn't.

"Listen, love," she said, kissing his forehead. "We have to go, all right? We have to go now."

"But da'—" Eliot began.

"Yer da's fine, I swear it," she said, but she'd misunderstood. Eliot was not concerned with his father's well-being, only if he would follow them. Only if he could catch up to them. "Yer da's fine. We talked about it last night. After yeh—" She broke off. *After I tried to cross the fence,* Eliot thought. But she continued, "After yeh went to bed. Aye, yer da' and I discussed it. It's all right, but we have to go now."

She looked down the darkening path. The sun was behind the mountains. At least the moon was high and bright already. Eliot preferred the happy yellow light of the oil lamp over the cold light of the waxing moon, but it was something. He should have grabbed the lamp from the table. He should have grabbed a coat. It wasn't yet cold, but the air was chilled. He hoped his mother's coat was warm enough.

"Now listen," his mother said. "We have to take this path. It'll take us to my friend, Bickie. Yeh know her. The old farmer's wife, aye? Bickie'll help us." To herself she said, "She'll know what to do."

Eliot began crying again. He looked down the gloomy path. The wood line was tight on either side, and he knew, up ahead, it took a sharp right turn. It led down the far side of the hill and along the side of the valley wall. Close to the Dark Wood. Too close. He began sobbing.

"Shh," his mother soothed. "It's all right. I promise. It's all right. It's all right, love. But we gotta go now. And we gotta be quick and quiet, aye? Can yeh do that for me, love? Can yeh do that for yer mother?"

She was smiling again. He believed this smile more. He nodded. She took him by the hand and led him quickly onto the path. His arm ached from her pulling, but he did not want her to stop. He may never want her to stop. And he would not let her go, not for anything. The path turned downward, and she picked him up. Eliot wrapped his arms around her neck and buried his face into her shoulder. He felt the strain of the hill on her: the way her back muscles were tight and twitchy, the way her cadence beat their bodies against one another. He wanted to remain here forever, not on the path but in the crook of his mother's body. Her warmth and scent eased him, even if they did not calm his fear.

They reached the bottom of the hill, and his mother stopped. Eliot waited, but she did not move. He turned his head, peeking one eye to look. To see what his mother saw. There was nothing. It was all moon-blue darkness. He sat up in her arms. There was a cacophony of frogs and locusts to their left, the frogs who lived among the slick, mossy stones of the tumbling brook. He heard the brook, too, falling down the hillside on his left. He saw where its narrow, frothy white arm reached over the path at his mother's feet. And he realized the sound stopped there. To his right was silence . . . but not, it seemed, to his mother.

"Aye?" she said, her voice a whisper. She was looking into the darkness of the wood to the right of the path. "What is it yeh say?" she asked.

"Mamma?" Eliot said, his voice small and quiet. Sick threatened, a fat cat caught in the narrow pipe of his throat.

She stepped closer to the edge of the path. "What is it?" she asked.

"Mother. Mother, please." Eliot leaned back, away from the dark. He took his mother's face in his small hands and turned it toward his own, blistered with snot. "Mamma, yer scarin' me. I'm scared to death." Her face was toward him, but her eyes cut back to the wood.

She put the boy down, Eliot pulling his feet up to avoid touching the ground. But they did touch. She let him go, shaking her head, and stepped closer to the path's edge. Had he thought he would never let her go? He could not follow her toward that darkness. He reached for her but backed away.

"What is it yeh say? Speak plain. I don't understand."

She took another step. Eliot whined.

"Who is that?" she asked. "I don't know what yeh mean."

She was breathing heavily. Eliot watched her chest rise and fall in quick hitches. She talked as though someone were there, someone she knew well. His own breathing was irregular. His own fear ratcheted his heartbeat into a gallop.

Then the forest grew silent. All of it. On the left side and the right. Even the brook offered no further comment. Eliot lost feeling in his legs. Eliot's mother turned to look at him. In the soft moonlight, she was angelic. She smiled. Eliot did not smile back. Could not.

"I am the adeglåst," she said, "and my oath is unbreakable." Her smile widened. She looked at Eliot, the moon fat crescents in her eyes. Were tears there as well? She reached out her hand toward her boy of spring. "I am the adeglåst," she said, "and this is my—"

The darkness came from the forest and swallowed his mother whole.

Eliot screamed, panic thundering in his head. He screamed and screamed. And he ran. He beat a trail to home, to the warm comforting light of the oil lamp. Along the way, he threw up. It spoiled his mostly clean shirt. He ran inside and up to his father's slumping form, still mute and stiff in the corner. This was his father. Fathers had to help. Eliot slipped and fell, the wooden floor slick with something. It covered his palms, the seat of his breeches. His bare feet. The substance was cold and thick. Something dripped onto his forehead. He looked up. It had fallen from his father's chin.

Eliot trembled as he sat in a pool of his senseless father's drool. The room spun, and the air grew thin. As consciousness left him, before his head hit the hard floor, he whispered one word: "Mamma."

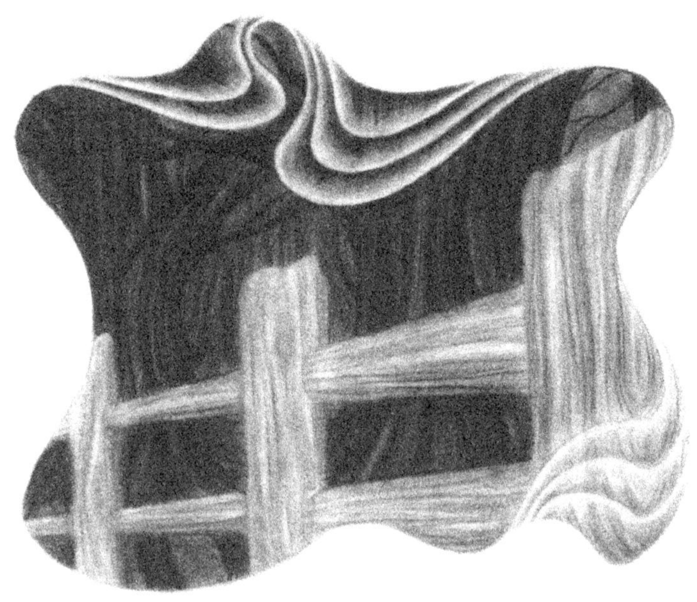

CHAPTER SEVENTEEN: THE WOODSMEN

Eliot's eyes snapped open. He had been there. He'd witnessed the Dark Wood take his mother. Anger wrestled his grief for prominence. He lay still, thinking. He wanted to weep, but he would not satisfy the dark magic that blinded his memory by feeding it tears. What black alchemy had robbed him of his mother and her true memory? What foul wizardry had saturated him with preoccupation over the past eight years? He would know. He would discover what cruel, vile fiend he owed retribution. But first, he would know what role his companions played in the sorry tale.

Eliot sat up. The woodsmen watched him from across the camp. It was morning, but early still. The soft light was ample. He could see enough.

"Is the Dark Wood the scarecrow's home?" Eliot asked. His jaw was tight and sore. His teeth screwed together.

Stalker turned to look at his kinsman, but Talker did not turn from Eliot. Neither did he answer.

"Tell true," Eliot said, the words slicing between his teeth. "The Dark Wood, is it the creature's home?"

"The scarecrow has no home, boy. To call it home would be misleading."

"Then lead me true, aye? What is the Dark Wood to the creature?"

"Eliot, what fever troubles you? Was your sleep haunted again?"

"Answer, woodsman!"

Talker looked at his kinsman. A kinetic vigor crackled between the men. Eliot studied them. Their deterioration was accelerating. Had he thought they'd looked infected before? They looked corrupted by rot now. Stalker wore hostility as clearly as he wore his glistening scarf. Eliot saw this in the morning light, clear as mountain water. Talker, he believed, held his virulence in check, tempering his angst with something milder. Something placating. It made Eliot want to spit.

"What is the Dark Wood to the creature," Eliot repeated, "and what is it to you?"

Talker looked back at Eliot. "Boy, we understand your curiosity. It is true, the mysteries of the scarecrow are vast. But I ask you—"

"Answer my damn question!" Eliot shouted, now on his feet. He clenched his teeth tight enough to shatter them. His hands were fists, his arms taught bowstrings. In a whisper, he repeated, "Answer me."

Stalker was on him before Eliot could react. The lanky corpse was fast, too fast and agile to seem natural. Eliot felt searing pain burn across his skin, neck to crotch, as Stalker's palm landed against his chest. Eliot heard the incantation rattling the rafters of his mind. He felt the heat of Stalker's magic bound into him through a circle on his chest, felt it wrap and coil and tighten in his gut, a funnel storm screwing its way into his belly. And he felt the surprising calm that came following a violent rip.

Eliot was standing in dark water to his waist. He had been torn in two. He could not account for this, but he felt it even now: he was not all here, wherever this was. All around was blackness. The water was warm. The air cool. This place was empty, but it was not emptiness. He wondered if the woodsmen's magic meant for him to come here. He did not think so. They preferred oblivion. And for all its emptiness and darkness, this was not quite oblivion. He turned. There was nothing here. Nothing except . . .

He walked toward a small rectangular light. Reaching it, he placed his palm against the glass. The window panes were warm, spring sunshine doing its work. He looked around. He was in his father's cottage. He saw the corner beyond the door, the one in which his father's insensate form had hulked. It was empty now save for happy spring sunlight. He looked again out the window. He saw his father take him by the hand and lead him down the hill.

Eliot knew this day. It was his seventh birthday.

Eliot stood with his father at the foot of the hill. Before them stretched the wooden fence and, beyond that, the Dark Wood. Eliot tightened his grip on his father's hand. Fear wrapped around his heart and threaded his mind like a spider's web, old and ugly. He'd thought himself ready. Excited, perhaps. But now that the moment was here, he felt only terror.

"Yeh know what today is?" his father asked. Eliot looked up. The man's face was greasy with sweat. His father did not look down.

"Yes, hommie," Eliot said. He used the respectful, less familiar term, hommie. It seemed appropriate. "It's the day of my kohlas."

His father eyed him. Eliot grew uncomfortable, but his father looked away again. "Do yeh know what that word means, son?"

"It is my life quest, hommie. My cumatu. It's the way I become a man."

"The way is the way," his father said. "Do yeh know where yer kohlas might take yeh?"

"Into the forest beyond the fence. Into the Dark Wood."

His father replied with a deep sigh. Eliot remembered the promise he'd made his mother months earlier, but she had left. She had abandoned him and his father. She had gone to see the old wife and never returned. Still, Eliot's promise spun out in his head like birthday ribbons, animating his disquiet.

"Hommie?" Eliot asked, daring to look again into the man's face. "I don't want to go." Silent moments slid past. His father made no reply except to sigh again. "Da'?" Eliot needed his father to look at him. Needed him to be with him, not a world away. "Mother said—"

"Yer mother left us," his father answered, his voice gruff with emotion.

"But she told me—"

"Eliot," his father said, turning at last to look at him. Eliot now wished he hadn't. "She left us. She left both of us. You know. You saw."

Eliot's face wrinkled, emotion spilling from his eyes. He saw what? He couldn't remember. He saw her getting ready to leave for her visit with the old farmer's wife. Saw her smile. But something was funny. He shook his head.

"Why did she leave?" Eliot asked.

His father turned away again. He did not answer.

"I'm scared, da'," Eliot said, a whine escaping his throat.

"Eliot," his father said at last, turning to face his son, "this is a difficult day, but it is the way things must be."

"Why?"

His father knelt before him. "Because." Eliot reached out for his father to hug him. To hold him. But his father placed his hands on his son's waist, holding him in front. Away from him.

"'Cause why?" Eliot's voice quivered, pathetic and weak. What bravery Eliot may have imagined he had melted like butter on a hot biscuit. In its place was a greasy smear of panic. He could not do this. The stench wafting from the forest had a taste as bitter as his own shame. His head spun, and he gripped tight his father's biceps.

His father looked into Eliot's eyes. Eliot looked for reassurance. For love. For a moment, hope caught in Eliot's throat: his father would relent. But the man turned his face away toward the dark forest as he stood. "Because it is. It is the way of things. The way things were, the way things always have been, the way things will always remain . . .

"The way is the way."

They waited. Hour-long minutes passed. The sun shone bright and warm on their shoulders. A gentle breeze blew through the field's high grass. Eliot heard it singing behind him. Birds argued in the trees up the hill. The spring day was unaware of Eliot's dreadful task.

The wind shifted. It blew out from the wood. The smell had been vague and unsettling. Now it grew hoarse and angry. Clouds moved across the sky, large ominous shadows crawling to cover Eliot and his father. They crept up the hill toward the cottage until the field and everything in it were cast in the whispers of winter shade. Eliot felt cold. Very cold. Dew still dampened the grass. The wind picked up the wetness and, in the shadow of the clouds, turned it to a chill on Eliot's skin. But the cold went far deeper than his skin and had little to do with the weather. He could not articulate this, but it was true. He took his father's hand. The wind stirred again the smell of the Dark Wood. It wasn't just the smell of decay, it was the smell of misery and fear. Eliot's stomach lurched. He tried fortifying himself, to swallow his terror. He didn't think it was working.

Eliot felt a tremor in his father's sweaty hand, still holding his. He looked up and saw the man's face convulsing. Sad tears stood out in his eyes, but anger showed at the corners of his mouth. His chest spasmed. Was his father afraid? He couldn't be. Eliot could not believe his father capable of fear.

"Da'?" he asked and heard his tiny child voice scatter on the wind. He asked again, "Da'?" He spoke louder this time and would have asked yet again, but something stopped him.

A sound. It stilled his father, too. Eliot watched as tension drained from his father. A new brand of fear lurched in Eliot's stomach. He would vomit, he was sure of it. His head was dizzy, and he fell against his father's side. Something was happening.

The sound came again, pulling Eliot to his senses. It was the sound of a breaking twig or branch. It came from within the Dark Wood. There was another snap, closer this time. It felt like the crack of a bone. Eliot knew his heart would break with fear, and he would soon die from it. Something was coming.

Thump, thump, thump, thump, thump. Eliot's beating heart trundled, heavy and clumsy, in his chest. It shook his frame. It whipped the walls inside his chest, bruising itself against his rib cage. His mouth constricted into a grimace. He heard a pitiful whine escaping his throat. He tasted salty mucus in his mouth.

He could not contain his fear any longer and gasped, "Father?"

His father did not answer. Eliot's heart beat *thump, thump, thump, thump, thump.* It would kill him. His own heart would rupture his chest. His fear would drive it like a mad horse. It would burst from his body like a rock from a slingshot, ending his life before a single step of his kohlas. He felt terror pulling him down, grounding him to the earth. He weighed as much as an ox.

He opened his mouth. Nothing came out. No air. No sound. Nothing to stop his snot and tears from coming in. His body was heavy, but his head was feather light. It bobbed side to side like laundry in the wind. Like dandelion spores. Without his neck tethering it to his shoulders, it would likely fly away. His vision clouded, his periphery little more than an oily stain of color. His tears were prisms in his lids, trapping light and hope and drowning them.

Then the woodsmen were there. The two men stood opposite Eliot and his father, the derelict fence between them. Eliot thought of them as men because there was no other word for what he saw. They stood like men. Had arms and legs like men. But they did not feel like men at all. Their faces were pale and grave, the skin ash gray except around the eyes. There it was inflamed, a blistered red. Their eyes were black disks. Their cheeks were sharp blades of bone above hollowed depressions filled with shadow. They had no lips, just a slit in the skin above their chins.

They wore hunting wraps on their heads and the strangest clothing besides. Their breeches were short and stained from countless journeys. They wore no cloak but had heavy coats that hung about their skeletal frames like rags hung on bare tree branches. The fabric was night dark. Their woolen stockings were the same ash gray as their faces. On their feet they wore heavy boots. Most peculiar of all, they wore gloves and scarves even though it was spring. The gloves were dingy gray, but the scarves were blood red and glistened as if wet.

They were wet, Eliot saw. He saw blood and puss draining from their festered ears, soaking into the folds of their heavy scarves. Eliot felt sick rise in his throat. He swallowed, feeling it burn as it carved its way back to his belly.

The woodsmen's appearance was not the foulest thing. Eliot smelled them. They were the source of the rotten stench he'd mistaken for the Dark Wood, what always had a dry and musty smell before. The woodsmen smelled wet with putrefaction. They smelled of decayed meat. It was oppressive, sweet and sickening. It burned his nose and made his eyes water. Eliot tried to step back, but his feet wouldn't move. He was paralyzed. His father's grip tightened. Whether to comfort Eliot or to hold him in place, Eliot wasn't sure.

The two men were hunters. Both wore short swords strapped to their belts. But they had no other weapons besides. No bow or string, no slingshot, no spear. No practical hunter's tool. As they stood with their comical wraps and scarves and strange outfits that hung loosely on their lanky forms, Eliot knew of what they reminded him. One woodsman spoke.

"Scarecrow." His voice was the sound of grating teeth.

Eliot thought the woodsman must have read his mind, for that was his exact thought: these woodsmen looked like scarecrows. Then he realized the woodsman had not spoken to him, was not, in fact, reading his mind. He was looking at Eliot's father.

"We are hunting a scarecrow. We've tracked it this way. Have you seen it?" His voice seemed little used, as though he was not well versed in spoken tongue. Even so, his words felt rehearsed.

Eliot's father shook his head. The woodsman turned to look at his comrade. When he did, Eliot saw clearer the steady flow of blood from the man's ear. Bile climbed again up Eliot's throat and into his mouth. The blood ran down into the hideous scarf. These two fiends were rotting from the inside out. Eliot knew it was so. The sight nearly stopped his heart cold. They were not alive. These were dead men. Long dead by the smell. The woodsman looked forward again, a razor-sharp and sinister smile on his face.

"We should like help in hunting this creature. Scarecrows are crafty and diabolical."

At this he turned for the first time and looked Eliot square in the eye. Cold so intense it hurt gripped Eliot's toes, squeezing them in a vice of agony. He stopped breathing. His fingers went numb.

The woodsman returned his gaze to Eliot's stoic father. "What say you to this?" he asked.

Eliot's father inhaled. Then, with equal deliberation, he spoke his lines in return. "I say this: take my son. He's a good lad. He will help with yer hunt."

Lead pummeled Eliot's spine. He squeezed his father's hand with both his own, pulling himself against the man's leg. He grew faint. That could not be his father's voice. It could not be his father's wish. This could not be happening. There was something wrong with these two dark woodsmen. This was not his kohlas. It could not be. This was violent folly, and unmistakable. If it was clear to a seven-year-old boy, it must be clearer still to that boy's father. The fiends stank of death. They bled from their ears. Was any other sign needed as proof these two were not safe? That they were not true men? These were devils. No, Eliot must have misheard his father. There was no way he would give over his son to these wretches.

Eliot looked at his father, pulling on his arm. His father's expression was blank. Placid, even. Eliot yanked his father's arm.

"Da'!" he screamed. He pulled and pulled till his father's arm must break. He pounded his leg with one fist, not daring to release both hands. "Father!" he wailed.

After an eternity, his father bent and gripped his son beneath the arms, lifting him from the ground. Gratitude overwhelmed Eliot. He reached his arms for his father's neck. He would kiss him. Yes, he would kiss his father's neck for saving him. His father might hate it, but Eliot would kiss him, anyway. He was crying again, loud and sloppy, but this was a cry of relief. How could he have believed his father would let the devils take him? His father loved him. It had always been so, Eliot believed it. How could he have doubted? He reached for his father. He closed his eyes against the nightmare of the woodsmen, reaching for the safety and sanity of his father's shoulders.

Then ice gripped Eliot's back. Ice grabbed him and held onto him. Eliot opened his eyes. His father's face was there, but not close. And his father was not looking at him. The man was studying the ground at his feet, his arms extended away from his body. Toward the fence. Toward the devils. Eliot felt the ice quicken its grip and realized the woodsmen had him.

Never had Eliot defied his father, but now he fought the man with all his strength. He fought to wiggle free from his father's iron grip. He now saw the stony gloves of the hunter reaching round his waist as his father walked him closer. As his father took him to them. Eliot screamed. He wailed. He shouted in his father's face, "Father! Da'! No, da'! Please!" But his father's eyes never looked up. All play at respect gone, Eliot reverted to the childish words. "No, pooey, no! Why? Why?" the boy screamed, his throat raw. His heart broken.

He was betrayed. First his mother, now his father. Eliot wailed, pleading with his father to see reason. To wake up from this insanity. He cried out to the goddess of spring itself for deliverance. For an answer to this cruelty. To this bitter betrayal. Eliot's argument and entreaty and accusation for his father all came in a single word, a single syllable, repeated over and over and over.

"Why?"

Eliot felt an arm wrap around his waist and pull him across the fence. He felt his father's hands pull free, cold emptiness left where before those hands had held him. He saw his father's arms fall limp to his sides, his shoulders droop, that slack-jawed drooling distance in his features.

Eliot thrashed, kicking against the fence as it passed beneath his feet. His skin stung with needle pricks from his scalp to his testicles, a crystalline pain knitting itself across his body in a wave. He felt angry frost in its wake. He cried out, his voice an arrow vaulted into the distant blue sky. The hateful sky that looked upon such treachery but did nothing. Already, like magic or tonic, the hunt was working on him. He felt it gnawing on him. Soon, cold wetness covered Eliot from head to foot, except in his breeches. They were warm with piss and shit. He would no longer be a boy of spring. That boy was dying.

Then a black curtain fell and his head filled with ink. It blacked over all things, save one. A furious hunger arose in him. The hunt was on.

Eliot was running. He did not remember waking, but already he was running. Then he wasn't. A tree, hard and unyielding, stopped his progress. He fell on his back, awareness coming back to him. He was next to the ravine. Lucky he hadn't run the other way as he woke. He would be in the gorge's belly then. His body was alive with pain, his skin a network of furious blades of heat. Where were the woodsmen? He spun on his knees, disoriented, and they were there. They looked surprised. They had not expected him to wake. Doubtless, they had expected their magic to hold him in darkness, not reveal their secrets.

Agony, excruciating and volatile, seared Eliot's flesh. Sudden recognition came to him. He stood, his gaze intent on the woodsmen. They did not come for him. Stalker held his sword. Talker held forth his hands, palms out. Placating. Eliot put his own hand against his chest. His stomach. It hurt so much just to touch it, even lightly.

"I know what you are," he said to the woodsmen. Then he pulled off his shirt. Shapes blistered his skin. He could not believe what he saw. Runes covered his body from neck to waistband. He'd seen runes like these before. Perhaps he'd seen these same runes. "The cyth," he said. "The altar in the creek bed." *Click, click, click* came back to him, the memory ugly. Hateful. He knew what he would find even before pulling down his breeches. He had to see.

The runes continued down into his inner thigh, but they were not all. He found a wound, infected, seeping, and hot to his fingers. It was in the fleshy part of his thigh. He looked at Stalker.

"Yeh were bleedin' me," he said. It wasn't a question. Not at all. "Like on the altar in the Place of Skulls. An offering to what?" He turned his eyes to Talker.

"Eliot, we can explain this. We have been trying to heal you against the dark man's magic."

"Shut up!" Eliot cried. "I know what you are!" But did he know? No. He was crying, and he did not care. "I trusted yeh. I believed yeh. And all this time, yeh were bleeding me. Yeh were markin' me. Yeh were—" Words failed. Eliot cried out.

"Eliot, be reasonable," Talker said. "It is not the way it appears. We have known his magic before. His ways are dark and ruthless. We wanted to tell you, to explain. But he uses our words against us. Think, Eliot. Think. Have we ever hurt you? Have we?"

"Yes!" Eliot screamed, his naked flesh the proof.

"What pain we've caused was meant to heal. We must first open the wound to treat it." Talker's voice was calm, soothing even. The woodsman's words seemed plausible. Reasonable. Eliot could believe him. Eliot could accept his explanation . . . had he not seen the truth.

"You lie!" he screamed. "Yeh've always lied. You have only lied. You were never my teacher. You were never my companions. I trusted yeh, and you lied! Yeh used me and my kohlas to fill yerselves. With what, exactly? My mind? My fear? My pain?"

"Eliot," Talker began, but something in his face suggested he knew he'd lost. That felt more true and more dangerous than the dead man's honeyed tongue. He stepped forward. Eliot stepped back.

"Yeh were rotten when yeh came out of that wood. Yeh smelled of death. Of decay." Eliot shook his head. How could he have not seen it? How could he ever have forgotten? Then he remembered the ink in his head, the black, oily madness that infected him when the woodsmen first took him. He wanted to laugh. All this time, he was the infected one. Not the woodsmen. They were just devils. "For a time, yeh were less so, aye? But then, somethin' changed. The birch wood. The stranger. Somethin' changed in me, and yeh started fallin' apart again. Rottin' again . . ."

Stalker moved. He would likely have taken Eliot, but Talker stopped his kinsman.

"No. That is not the way," he said to Stalker. The two stared at each other. They were communicating without words. Eliot felt it. He did not wait to think on it further.

He bolted, running up the path. He doubted he could outrun them, but he would try. If they took him again, they would have to kill him. He ran. He heard them following, closing the distance between them. But Eliot was running for his life.

The light was frail. It was dusk. He'd slumbered all day in his dark memory. Clouds gathered overhead. Clouds had dogged his steps for eight years, it seemed. And Eliot ran to outrun the storm, to outrun his past. To outrun the woodsmen. They were close and getting closer. The path was not wide, but it was sufficient for Eliot to fly. The woodsmen were quick, unnaturally so. But he was a lean boy of fifteen years. He ran like a jack rabbit. Lightning struck, negating the thinning daylight. A thunderclap shook the land, then rolled across the sky and down into the ravine. It settled among the river's crests.

Eliot ran. He heard the woodsmen closing in. He felt their cold. Whatever grain of hope he'd had disappeared. He could not outrun them. Ahead, he saw the path open in a clearing. He would face them there. His blade was already in his hand when he left the path and came upon the old woman and her cart.

CHAPTER EIGHTEEN:
THE WOMAN AND HER CART

Just as the first large drops fell from the sky and sighed through the trees, Eliot saw her. He leapt aside to avoid running her over, falling onto the dry sand dimpled by new rain. The woman stood at a crossroads, shrouded with a thick mantle pulled tight about her neck with a cord. In her hand was a tall oaken staff and behind her stood a small hand-drawn cart covered by a stretch of lumpy canvas. She had covered her eyes with a dirty dressing, and her lips were parted to ease her breathing. She looked to be waiting. Her cloak fluttered in the wind, resembling black wings. Perhaps crow.

She took a step toward him, and Eliot smelled lilacs and cinnamon.

"Traveler," she said in a clean, pleasant voice, "you come at last. You are he who seeks the phantom."

Eliot paused. "I . . ." he began. "You should go. Run," he said, but the woodsmen entered the crossroads before he could say more. The woman stood between Eliot and his devils. They would kill her. What should he do? What could he say? He could not protect her against the woodsmen. Could he protect himself?

"Aye," she said, "all things bleed—even ghosts." What did that mean? Eliot wondered. No one moved. The old woman continued, "You seek the phantom." She turned toward the woodsmen. "And you would keep him from it." She sighed. Stalker stepped forward, and she moaned. It was quiet yet furtive. He stopped.

Eliot swayed, his body trembling from exhaustion and adrenaline. "How do yeh know this?" he asked, curious what power this blind woman may wield.

"I hear it in the beating of your heart," she said, turning again to face him. "Smell it there, too." She stepped toward him.

"Who are yeh?" Eliot asked, but not without kindness. *Why tarry?* Eliot asked himself. Because this woman held answers somehow. Keys. The woodsmen were waiting. They seemed loath to cross her. But why?

She was not quick to speak her mind. She pulled at the cord about her neck, loosening the makeshift hood.

"You hinder," the old woman whispered, facing the woodsmen. Turning to Eliot, she said, "Your comrades do not hasten you finding what you seek." As she said this, her cloak fell from her face. She was not old. Her countenance was young, though not attractive. Yet she spoke as though from deep wells of age and experience. "Bad company corrupts good character, know you this, boy?"

Eliot wondered what the woodsmen must think of the woman's words. She must be a seer. That was clear. A soft sliding sound issued from her cart, followed by a dull thud.

Eliot asked, "What do yeh bear in yer cart, lady?"

"I carry both wisdom and folly in my cart. Wisdom and folly. It is what you have that determines which you may receive."

"I carry nothin'." It was true. He'd fled with nothing but the clothes he wore.

"Oh, but you do. Since you were born you've carried it and known it not. But there it be. There it be."

Eliot believed the woman had something he needed. She must. This meeting was not a coincidence. It couldn't be. "Name it, and I will confess."

"It has no name, and I shall not give it one." She smiled and turned her face into the rain. The wind whined in the ravine and for a moment the Traveler's Moon stole a stealthy peek from behind the thinning clouds. "I shall not name it," she said again.

"Then I beg yeh, woman, say yer mind."

"What need you, traveler?"

He did not know how to answer her. He was so very tired, and not just from running. Not just from the woodsmen's magic. He was weary of all of it. He felt it to his bones and back. If she held forth a blade and slit his throat just then, he might consider it kindness.

She reached out, but with a finger, not a blade. Stepping closer, she touched Eliot's bare chest. "Mark me as friend, boy. I mean no harm." Then she turned her head, her movement calculated, to face the woodsmen. "Yet someone's marked you, aye?" Her finger traced the runes on Eliot's skin. Her touch calmed the burning. Still, he could not bear it. He pulled his shirt on. She retrieved her finger and turned again to face him.

"You seek the scarecrow." Her cloak, now more than ever like dark wings, lifted in the gale.

Eliot gasped and his head went funny. But this was not magic, not in his head. He had almost forgotten about the scarecrow. "Have yeh seen him?" he stammered. No, she hadn't seen him. She was blind. "Have yeh heard of him? Do yeh know how to find him?"

The woman with the cart smiled. "No, I have not seen him. But do not worry. I see you well enough. And though I haven't seen your quarry, I have seen how you may find him."

He had been running for his life only moments before. Did the scarecrow still matter? He sighed, an invocation for a good turn. A plea for even a moment's true rest. His desperation had broken through his resolve and seeped out in a viscous flow. The woman opened her hand and placed the flat of her palm against Eliot's chest.

"Strong you are. Mayhap stronger than you think. Certainly stronger than they credited you." She did not turn toward the woodsmen. "I hope you are strong enough. For you must seek the Shining Eye."

Now both her hands were on Eliot's chest, probing him as if to see into his soul with her hands. The woman sniffed, lifting her chin in a slight arc. "Do not think to give up the chase, boy. Do not let these men take that from you, too."

"Why do yeh . . ." he began but stopped. Where her fingers traced, his skin crawled and itched, but the burning subsided.

Eliot removed himself from her reach. He pulled up his shirt to see in the moonlight. The runes were still there, but less angry. Less festered. This woman had called herself a friend, and Eliot was inclined to believe her. Perhaps here was her proof. Could she help him find the scarecrow? Should he even seek it? Did the kohlas still matter? The woodsmen would not let him go. He knew this.

As if to prove this thought, Talker stepped forward. "Lady," he began.

"Silence." Her voice was a razor, slicing off Talker's words. "You will leave this boy be. You will let him finish his errand alone, or you will answer to me." It was implausible to think the woodsmen would fear this little thing, but they did. Eliot saw it in their posture. He saw it in the way they shrunk before her. He'd seen fear in them only once before: for the smoking man.

The lady said to Eliot, "The scarecrow. You must find the scarecrow. You must finish your errand. For your sake, you must."

He felt the abysmal truth in this. He had to finish his kohlas or be beaten by it. Eliot glanced toward the cart as another sound came from it, a wet scrape. Friend she may be, but not one he fully trusted. Shaking his thoughts free, he said, "The scarecrow . . . where do I look for such a thing? What is this Shining Eye? Or who? Am I even close to the end?"

She turned her face toward him, her wrapped eyes somehow seeing him through their bondage, making him feel naked before her. Energy crackled on the air, potent static from the storm. Doubt slithered down Eliot's spine. The woman had a power he could not discern. Friend or fiend, Eliot knew she would take what she wanted if she wanted it bad enough. Her robe billowed, riding a frustrated gust from deep within the ravine. No, Eliot did not trust her.

Then she answered. "Cross here." She pointed across the ravine. A bridge, made of rope, planks, and imagination, stretched over the expanse. "Follow the path, it will not lie. But do not leave it. And do not stop for rest. It would be unwise to linger. Travel through the night. You can make it, I assure you. The path will end at the crack's edge. You will find the way to climb down then. Do so."

"And there I'll find the scarecrow?"

The woman laughed. "No, child. Nothing is so simple as that. You will find a cave at the waterfall's mouth. The Moon Cave. Inside you will find a small boat. Take it. Go into the heart of the mountain, but take no light with you. You will not need it, and it will only lead you astray.

"Look for a man, or something like it. He is dangerous, though you may fail to believe it when first you meet."

"How will I know he is the right man? Will he take me to the scarecrow?"

"He is the only man to fish the Craven's banks."

"Craven?"

"The lake. You will see. Trust is difficult for you after all this time. It always is for the scarecrow hunters." She turned again toward the woodsmen, but neither looked at the woman. She shooed them with her thin hand. For a wonder, they left. Eliot was alone with her.

The wind picked up, pushing against Eliot so he had to lean into it to keep standing. It sent the rain skittering down the neckline of his shirt, cooling the offended flesh.

"He will only give audience to you, not to the fiends who brought you."

"Should I fear them?"

"No. They will trouble you no more. This is my promise."

Eliot held that statement, feeling it for truth. Could she make such a promise? "Who are you?"

"The man will see you alone. It is not his way to entertain the broi-dain. This is not their kohlas." Eliot's mouth dropped.

"How do yeh know of those things? How know yeh of the scarecrow? Lady, who are you?"

The woman pulled her cloak tight against the brute wind and chilling rain, threw her staff in the cart atop her secret wares, and turned to lift its handles. A beam of moonshine peeking through the clouds widened, and Eliot saw her face and thought her beautiful after all. "This is your quest, boy, and he will see you. Aye, he will. Follow the Traveler's Moon, and it shall be."

"Then my thanks I give yeh."

The woman turned to face him again. "Do not hasten to meet the Shining Eye. Hasten only to ready your heart. Something has stolen his teeth, but there are other ways in which he might feed. Care not to spoil your life with haste."

"Stolen teeth? But—"

"The man you seek is a drinker, boy. Long time now has he been weak. He has but lips and tongue, yet his hunger for survival has made him crafty. There are more things to drink than blood."

Eliot felt a shiver along his neck. He understood that now more than ever. "But why is he called the Shining Eye?"

The woman laughed. "Let the drinker tell you his story should he wish to tell it. But be wary, boy. Be wary. Now go." At that she turned into shadow, pulling her cart behind her. Eliot looked for the woodsmen to return, but they did not. The path that brought him here remained dark and empty. The rain was slacking off, the clouds overhead breaking apart.

Eliot looked up into the Traveler's Moon, fat and round, as the clouds ripped before it in bands of gray. Beneath the pale face, the bridge glowed blue in the moonlight, a stark contrast to the darkness below. Should he follow her instructions? Could he? Did he have a choice? He had nowhere else to go. He had no one to go to.

Eliot could just hear the squeak of the woman's cart moving farther in the other direction. He wished she was going his way. Or more for the sweet, heady fragrance of the smoking man's pipe just then. Any possible friend would do. Any at all. But there were none. Perhaps there never had been. He thought again of his mother, and grief scuttled up into his heart. Closing his eyes, he willed her strength to rise within him and be a mantle on his shoulders. *The adeglåst,* he thought. He could have wept, but he didn't. He was late, and the way is the way.

With a glance again at the moon, Eliot steadied himself with a breath and walked into its light.

CHAPTER NINETEEN: MOON CAVE

The Traveler's Moon earned its name. Eliot found the end of the path at the ravine's edge and rough-hewn steps cut from the stone leading down into the darkness. The steps were slick with glistening raindrops, the full moon reformed in each.

"The woman said it right," he muttered. She'd called the gorge the crack. It looked like a crack opening to the center of the world. Though the Traveler's Moon was full and the sky now cloudless, light did not penetrate to the bottom of the gorge, not from the moon's low angle.

Mindful of the slick stones during his descent, Eliot took the path one step at a time. He sought the Moon Cave, whatever that was. And the Craven. And the Shining Eye. And a man with no teeth. What new madness was he descending into?

The climb down was slow but not difficult. Eliot's stomach growled. He was starving. He hadn't eaten in two days. He hadn't slept, even under the woodsmen's magic. He was famished and exhausted. He felt it in his weakness. He saw it in the fuzzy edges of his vision, in how his eyes felt both dry and sticky. His right palm lay against the rough edge of the ravine, steadying himself. The steps were narrow and his balance less than peak. He needed rest, but the woman had warned him against stopping.

Who was she? He wasn't certain he cared, not anymore. He was too tired to think. But it all must end soon. It must. No kohlas lasted forever.

The stone path ended on a wide ledge, a tongue of water pouring over its middle. Heedless of the woman's words, Eliot sat down hard. He was exhausted. His legs burned. Though his chest and stomach felt the best they had in a while, they still itched. He watched the water flow over from a pool just inside the cave opening, shallow and shimmering in the moonlight. The mouth of the cave was jagged angles of rock, save for the topmost part. There, the stone was smooth and carved into a rounded plate with runes chiseled into it. Runes . . . And in the center: a moon track. A lunar helix, with the Dead Moon on the left. The Sleeping Moon, the folken called it. Following this was the Spade Moon, the Traveler's Moon, the Sickle Moon, and again, the Sleeping Moon. The full lunar cycle—new, waxing, full, waning, new—was depicted in runic glyphs. The runes caught the light of the actual moon in its tracing, which brought it to life with azure radiance.

He bolstered himself with a breath and stood. He must be halfway down into the gorge. At this height, he could see more of its bottom. It was still deep enough to keep him clear of the edge. Eliot walked to the cave's mouth and stepped inside. It was darker here, but not full dark. The light of the full moon penetrated inside, a bit at least. He traced the rough stone inside with his fingers. He saw flecks of gold inlaid within deep resonant blue. It was the natural formation of the stone, not a stonemason's craft. That explained the blue in the runes.

Eliot stepped farther in and saw, tied to the narrow ledge with a short threadbare rope, a small boat. In it a single oar. The pool was smaller than he'd anticipated. At the back, he saw where water fell from crevices to fill the pool in two places. Opposite this, closer to the cave mouth, was an opening just big enough for a small boat and a boy almost a man to enter. Through it, the pool became a stream. He heard it chattering against the stone walls of the cave beyond, where all he could see was darkness.

"Bring no light," he said, his voice thick with sarcasm. "As if I have a light to bring . . ." He shook his head and propped his face in his hands. His body was ragged with exhaustion and hunger. He did not want to go on. He wanted to stop. To quit. Perhaps not just for the night. Perhaps for good. But if he did, what would it all be for? Maybe if he only slept a little, he could find his strength. Just till morning. What could it hurt?

He inhaled and held his breath. It stretched his chest. It felt good. After a moment, the air burned in his lungs, and he released it in a heavy sigh. "Get on with it," he said to himself.

Eliot climbed into the boat and untethered it. With the oar, he pushed off from the side and the boat turned, catching in the slight current. Eliot floated out into the middle of the pool, the cave opening lit from behind by moonlight. It looked more than anything like a mouth, hungry with jagged teeth. This was not the first hideous mouth to want to swallow him. *Into its belly,* he thought as he rowed the boat through the small opening in the wall.

Here, the current picked up. Before he knew it, he was speeding along into perfect darkness. A jut of stone caught him on his head, on the knot made by Stalker's sword handle.

"Damn!" Eliot shouted, tears springing into his eyes. His voice called back to him from deeper within the funnel of stone, the word chasing itself out of existence. He lay back in the boat, eager to let the current take him where it would. Perhaps he would sleep. Perhaps he would drift into oblivion.

As it was, his mind played tricks on him. Soon, sparkling jewels lit up the ceiling overhead. They were dazzling. No doubt hallucinations brought on by fatigue, thirst, and hunger. And, if he were honest, at least a touch of madness. He stirred in the boat, righting himself to see better. He was not hallucinating.

Ahead, the throat of the cave and the narrow river flowing through it were lit by a network of glittering lights. He used the oar to steer closer to the wall. Worms. The walls and ceiling were covered with iridescent worms and silky webs, luminescent. They reflected on the rippling surface of the river. Star field above and below him, Eliot felt caught between layers of nightfall. It was hypnotic. Again, he allowed the current to lead the way.

Eliot felt grateful. Such a simple thing as unexpected beauty filled him with hope and gave him faith he could endure. It surprised him to find his face wet with tears, and not tears of sadness. Was this joy? Could he recognize it after so long?

All at once he felt the full burden of his kohlas. More tears spilled down his face, no longer joyful. He let them, surrendering himself. Grief poured from him then, his sobs vaulting against the cave ceiling and echoing through the low chamber. His skiff flowed ahead in a cosmic sea, the river beneath him perpendicular to the one of emotion cascading from his heart. He let it go. He let it free. He gave it full reign.

A mournful wail, billowing the circumference of his grief, burst from his chest, up his throat, and out his mouth. The sound carried the weight of his loss. His betrayal. His confusion. His disappointment. It was a dirge for his childhood. For his mother, his father, himself. His head fell back on his shoulders, and Eliot cried out in his solitude, surrounded by a star field of witnesses who could not betray his melancholy. Then, as quickly as it began, the storm was spent. He breathed deep, his lamentation satisfied.

Eliot wiped his face. He felt better. Lighter, somehow. More centered. Of all the magic he'd experienced, this release had been the surest. His face itched from his tears. He dipped his hands into the water and washed it, feeling even better. His sadness remained, only now it was his rather than the other way round. He was not owned by his emotion. Eliot reclined again in the boat, watching the glittering gems overhead twinkle as they passed.

He must have dozed, the soft lapping of the water a lullaby to one so weary, for he was soon surprised to find himself in a broad lake. The roof of the cave vaulted here, high enough he could not make out the individual glow of the worms or webs, only their sum. The domed vault shimmered with hazy light before him, fading into darkness as it met an underground horizon so far ahead he could not see it. His eyes drifted to the dark waters around him, and he sat up in surprise. Beneath the water's surface he saw shimmering blades darting through the murk. Fish, he realized. Fish so white they appeared translucent, reflecting the glow from the lid of the vault. The sight was beautiful, but still it caused a shudder. He would not dare think what lived deeper in those waters. The woman would not name this lake Craven without reason. For certain, he felt a coward here.

"Ah, hail," called a voice.

Eliot turned toward the sound. It was high, thin, and reedy, and it came from a distance. Over his shoulder, Eliot spied a thin man—old as the stone of the cave, from the look—waving one hand and bearing a torch in the other. He looked small from this distance. This must be the Shining Eye. Eliot looked again at the lid of the enormous cave, at the ambient fish swimming in the abiding night, and rowed his way to the bank.

The man was tall and thin. And so old. The warm firelight from his torch revealed little and seemed offensive in this place. It had too much color. Too much warmth.

"Are you the Shining Eye?" Eliot asked when the boat reached the petrified dock. Broad wood beams fashioned it, likely white oak or hickory. The man reached out and grabbed Eliot's hand, hefting him from the boat to stand beside him on the dock. He was old, but strong.

As Eliot tied off the boat, he noticed a pattern of crystals at the dock's waterline. The pendant of an underground saltwater lake. He turned to face the man. "Are you the Shining Eye?"

"Me?" the man tittered. "No. I'm just me."

"But the woman told me I'd meet a man here; the Shining Eye, she called him. Said he's the only one to fish the Craven. Is this the Craven?"

"Aye, it is. And I'm the only one who fishes here, but I am not the Shining Eye." He looked Eliot up and down, and then again. Eliot's brows lifted.

"Do yeh know the Shining Eye? Can yeh take me to him?"

The man's eyes sparkled with torchlight. "Just come with me, love. I'll take you where you need to go." His voice was brittle, delicate but friendly. The man pulled a cord tied to the dock railing, heaving a heavy cache of silver-white fish from the obsidian water. "Come, supper," he said, a crooked smile on his face.

The thin man turned and started up a steep set of stone steps. Unable to stir himself to follow just yet, Eliot watched him go. His rest in the boat had been welcome, but his calves and thighs burned just thinking about more stairs.

"Come," the man's thin voice called. "I promise you haven't far to go," he tittered. Eliot followed.

It wasn't far. The stairway curved upward, but only a short way, before it emptied on a wide shelf open to the night sky. The moon was still fat, though not still full. Small clouds dotted the sky. Otherwise, it was a blank canvas: the moon too bright for stars. How long had Eliot been in the cave? An entire day? Perhaps he'd slept more than he'd thought.

Eliot did not recognize this place, but he guessed where he was. They were standing on a table wind-carved in the side of a steep cliff. Farther to the east, perhaps the origin of the cliff itself, were toothy mountains. The Western Mountains, Eliot thought. If so, this must be the Crag, a lofty and lifeless cliff face separating Carde from the mysteries beyond: the Lost Lake—saltwater, he recalled—in the land of Goth. The shelf looked over an endless plain, one flat and barren from the look. The end of the great green world. If this cliff was the Crag, that must be the Dead Plain. The plain looked very far away. Eliot turned to see where the cliff ended overhead. As best he could tell, they were situated two thirds of the way up.

Eliot looked to the east. In the distance, he saw the ravine twist out of sight like a snake. But the geography baffled him. How had he climbed down into the ravine only to ride a glittering stream into the Craven, and then climb a short distance to this shelf? It wasn't possible. But it was or else he would be somewhere else. His brain was tired. It was thick and slushy. He had an old man to worry about, not how long he'd slept in the boat.

Eliot took in the scale of things. He felt small here. He could discern no end to the great, stretching world before him. Could he have traveled so far from his father's cottage, to the end of his people's land? Home was so very far away just then.

In back of the table, a square wooden hut stood. *This must be it,* he thought. Would he find the scarecrow inside? The mysterious Shining Eye? Or would he just find more questions? Enchantment skittered along the stone facing of the ledge, the wooden shack, and even on the wind. The place was charmed, that was clear enough.

"This way," the thin man said. Eliot followed.

The power of the place sucked at Eliot's thoughts, a waxy hunger. Relief and fear filled him. Not fear exactly, but it was an awareness that felt so close to fear it might be confused for it. But stronger than this was the gravity pulling him forward. The need to see. To find. To finish. The shack, a wooden structure atop stone supports, was small and stilted, suggesting there may be great water on the rock face at times. There was a rickety porch suspended before it, made accessible from the ground by a rope ladder. Eliot saw a cart path just behind the shack leading away at a slight decline through outcroppings of stone. So there was a road to this forsaken place. He neared the building and saw above the door an image scratched into the wood: an eye.

"I thought yeh said yeh aren't the Shining Eye," Eliot said. The thin man, halfway up the ladder, barked a thinner laugh.

"And I said true."

Eliot shook his head. More riddles. More questions. Surrounding the eye were Lynthian runes. Beside this were arcane words of which Eliot was not familiar. Runes, however, were known to him. He sighed. The floor of the shack was at shoulder height. A crow with a swath of red thread tied around its leg sat atop the shack.

"You look familiar," Eliot muttered.

He was wary of this place. But his thirst for answers far outweighed his trepidation. How much of his kohlas had been a lie? The woman, the crows, and the thin man were all part of a larger enigma. A mystery bigger than his mind could take in just now. He sighed again, shaking his head. He was alone here. Yes, perhaps he had always been alone: the woodsmen had never been his allies. But they had protected him. Whatever they wanted from him, they had not wanted him dead. He was certain he would not have survived the Dark Wood on his own for eight years without the woodsmen. He did not regret the woodsmen's absence, but still: would he survive hand to hand against the scarecrow? He must. Why would a child be sent on an errand he could not survive, much less complete? His father did it before him, and his before him.

"The way is the damn way," Eliot said and spat. He huffed, shaking his head. There was nothing for it.

Eliot climbed the ladder to the porch, reached the door, and pushed it open on silent leather hinges. Inside, a small fire burned low in the hearth. The flames moved in a slow organic dance and the room smelled of cinnamon and burnt hair. Eliot saw no one but felt himself being watched. Where was the thin man? He stepped into the room with caution. The door closed behind him.

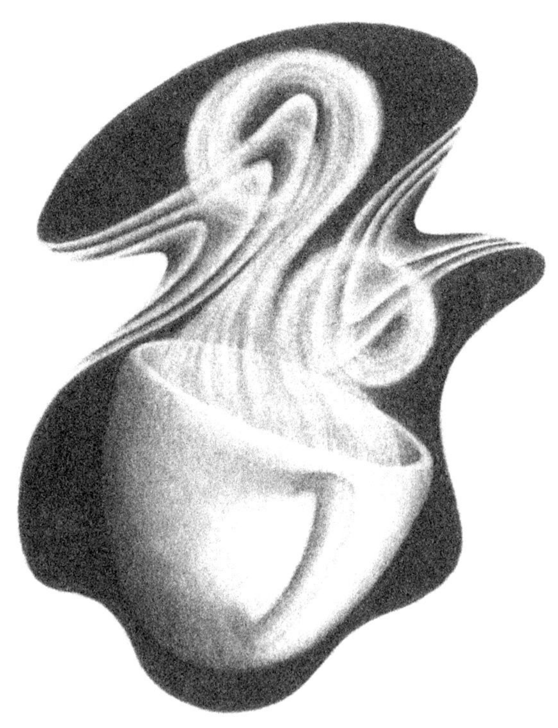

CHAPTER TWENTY:
THE SCARECROW HUNTERS

"Please sit," cooed the thin man's narrow voice. Eliot turned to find him at the door, having just shut it. He motioned toward an uneven wooden chair next to a rickety table. The man moved nearer to the fire.

For the first time, Eliot got a good look at him. He was frail. A torpid man who seemed on the verge of evaporating into the planks beneath his feet. He perched atop a rickety wooden stool and his skin hung loose on his hands and about his neck. His face was jaundiced and sickly. His lips wrinkled into a mirthless pucker: chapped, bulbous, and purple. He had no teeth. His ashen gray hair hung in greasy strands to his shoulders. He turned and looked at Eliot. His eyes were the color of the soot that covered every surface in this hovel.

"Please sit," he repeated, his tone metallic.

"I will," said Eliot as he sat in the small chair, "but know this: I do not fear yeh, though I do reckon yeh someone to be wary of. Do not think to try me."

The thin man laughed. It was the sound of a jagged soul. "Try for what?" His flat eyes bored into Eliot's. "What prize do you think yourself to be, boy?" But he smiled, still friendly. Playful, even. Like a cat with a snake.

Lamenting he had not taken more time before entering, Eliot watched him. So foolish. He wasn't afraid of the man, though he suspected he may be too tired for fear just now. But he was wary, his senses alert. His muscles tight. With deliberation he steadied his breathing, which was coarse and fast. The man seemed to enjoy watching him.

"I always love you dark boys." The man's fondling eyes pushed their way across Eliot's body. Eliot could almost feel their touch, and his skin crawled. The man laughed. "You aren't like those others."

Eliot assumed he meant the woodsmen—the broi-dain, the woman had called them. "No, I am not like those two." Eliot did not want to react to this man's manipulations. *Steady,* he thought. Something occurred to him. "How know yeh of the woodsmen?"

"No, boy. I do not speak of the two who came with you. I speak of the others."

"The other what?"

"Boys, of course. The scarecrow hunters." That phrase—the scarecrow hunters—settled into Eliot like blood soaking fabric. The blind woman had used it, but then it had a different feel. Eliot had wondered how she knew so much about the kohlas, but his curiosity had been overshadowed by the context of their meeting—he had been fleeing the woodsmen for his life. He had been coming to terms with their betrayal. But here, draped in this man's greasy voice, that phrase was heavy with meaning and shimmered with dull clarity. Why did it unsettle Eliot? The thin man smiled, and Eliot's skin creeped all over. He looked Eliot over like a hungry man salivates over a hunk of roasting meat.

"I am tired of riddles," Eliot said and stood. His head was so heavy with exhaustion. His mind was fuzzy. But he would not be manipulated. "Speak plain if yeh wish me to stay."

The man shifted in his chair, and Eliot once again got the feeling he was barely there at all, that he might dissolve into the wood of the shack at any moment. But Eliot could also hear the thin man's bones crack as he twisted. He was substantial enough. If it came to it, Eliot believed he would bleed. All things bleed. The emaciated man waved his thin hands at

Eliot. Sit down, they said. Sit and I will explain. Eliot sat again. The man took up a firebrand and agitated the coals within the fire. Sparks stirred in a magical little dance. He left the poker in the fire and folded his naked hands across his wizened lap.

The thin man turned his head to look at Eliot, the fire reflecting in his black eyes. "Oh, aye," the thin man said. "I bleed, but not as prettily as you."

Eliot's shock drove him from his seat. He stood and faced the man. Before he could do anything further—and he did not know what he intended, but the man had read his mind!—the thin man spoke, waving one wicked hand in supplication.

"Please, please. You are my guest. Do not be offended, not yet." He cleared his throat. It was the sound of breaking glass. Eliot sat. His hackles raised, his wariness was more pronounced. He must guard his thoughts. He pushed against them in his head, pressing them into a back corner . . . But what did Eliot know about mind reading or how to prevent it? The thin man tilted his head, as though studying a particularly curious problem. "You are different somehow from those who came before you."

"Who came before me?" *Focus on his words,* Eliot thought. *On his lies, like as not.* He must do anything but give this man access to his thoughts. Eliot hadn't been the first: he knew there were others who came before him. Countless other scarecrow hunters came before him. Perhaps all had passed through this shack. Eliot wondered, was that the point? To bring them here? If so, the quest had never been a random hunt. And if it was not random, the scarecrow must be part of the pretense. This horrid place had been the goal all along, Eliot reasoned. And he, just like the others, was the prey. The object of the hunt. *Do you still believe you are the hunter . . . .* Eliot shoved those thoughts away and looked down at his arms and legs. Not for the first time, he felt his frail condition. But now he had a horrible realization: he was thin. Thin, like a scarecrow.

"The scarecrow hunters," Eliot whispered. That phrase was haunting. Fear had him now. He had been wary. He had been tired, but he had not been afraid. Until now. He'd walked into a trap. There was no question. He'd been walking into this trap since he was seven years old. But where the final trap-jaws lay hidden here and the mechanism for tripping them, Eliot could not see. The full weight of his loneliness crushed him. He pushed his thoughts into the darker shadows of his mind. Or at least, he tried.

"Now you begin to see," the thin man said.

"Why?" Eliot asked.

"Why is poison, lover. Why is death. Do not ask why. You know why, don't you?"

Eliot shook his head. "No. I don't know why."

The man laughed. "Why? Because it is. It always has been. It always will remain. The way is the way." His mockery stung. The lie grew bigger in Eliot's head. The thin man tapped the wooden stool on which he sat with a grotesque yellowing fingernail. "Come now, boy. You ask why, but you do not understand the question."

"I am tired of riddles," Eliot said, more to himself than the thin man. He tried to stand but couldn't—he felt weariness puddling inside him and weighing him down. Had he believed he might prevail here? *Shh,* he thought. *Don't think.*

"The scarecrow hunters are not so smart, I'm afraid. Blind fools, says I. They are raised to be so by an illogical religion." An oily smirk quilted the thin man's face just then. "Of course, some are smarter than others. Lucky for me. Unlucky for them. The stupid ones, they get to return home. Produce offspring. Send us more delicious morsels." Fear trickled down Eliot's throat as he saw the man's meaning. "Ah, and there it is," the thin man said. "You see at last . . .

"The smart ones are given to me to do with as I please." He giggled. It made Eliot's skin creep into tight knots in his lower back. Ice settled around his ankles. Seeing his fear, the thin man again laughed, rubbing his thin palms together. His delight was rotten. He sucked his lower lip and looked Eliot in the eyes. "I can be creative with the smart ones. And you, my sweet, delicious boy, are a smart one, aye? Mayhap, the smartest yet."

Eliot's stomach turned. Dry heaves shook his body, his empty stomach in spasms. He should go. He should get out of here. But all he could do was thrash and gag. The thin, pale man laughed and licked his chapped lips with a moldy tongue, waiting for Eliot's fit to pass.

"Aye," he said, smacking his lips. "I can make many meals with a boy like you."

Eliot fell out of the chair and stumbled back on his hands, crawling backward toward the door. He had to go. Had to get to the door. Where was the door? There was no door.

"Oh don't worry," the thin man said. "You won't feel most of it. I promise." His sweet, overripe voice dripped with malice. "Or I can make you like it. Would you prefer it that way? Would you prefer I make you enjoy yourself?"

"Yeh can't hurt me," Eliot said, not believing it but hoping his doubt did not show. "The woodsmen will come for me."

The thin man cackled. "The woodsmen," he purred. "The dain are only just smarter than the boys they collect, says I. Oh, they have their uses," he blurted, as if teaching a lesson. "They and the witch serve a larger purpose, and their part, simple as it is, is integral. Though I admit, I'm glad just the two and no more remain."

"Witch?" Eliot's throat was dry. He could not swallow. And his focus was coming unraveled. Was this witch the Shining Eye? If so, who was this deplorable wretch? And where was the damn door?

The thin man looked at Eliot, hunger on his face. Hunger and dreadful pleasure. Again he sucked his lip and giggled. "Oh love, you don't want to know about the witch." His smile slid, his voice lowered. "And don't call me a wretch."

Eliot's breath clamored in his chest, trying to escape. He couldn't swallow. He could hardly breathe. And his thoughts . . . he couldn't keep a single thing in his mind from this fiend. *This filthy, degenerate wretch,* Elliot thought. *This revolting mass of rotting flesh, meat fit for maggots and little else. Deplorable and disgusting,* Eliot thought hard. *You are revolting. Toothless.*

The thin man's eyes narrowed, his purple lips a tight sneer. *He does not like what he sees in my head,* Eliot thought. "You're a fighter. I like that," the man said, his voice melodious. "Makes the meat sweeter . . . inside and out." He smacked his lips again, and his body grew more solid somehow. Eliot felt nausea rip through him and something besides wash over him. Like air on his skin.

The thin man grabbed the poker, using the brand to shift about the burning coals. The flames licked high in the hearth. After a few moments, he spoke again, looking at the flame rather than Eliot.

"The scarecrow hunters come here broken. They come here empty. Husks, really. My work is easy. But you, love . . . though you are breaking, you have yet to come apart. Though you are wasting away, you are not yet empty inside. Not yet wasted enough." Then he laughed. "This pleases me, but also it puzzles me."

"Puzzles yeh?" Eliot was struggling to breathe. Trying to think. Trying not to think.

"Oh, don't be silly, love. Don't you know? Hmm," his voice hummed, "I am puzzled because you are nothing special. You are untouched by faye. Your ehwain tells me you are not born of bardic blood nor taught in khamunic ways. You have no special talent with magic or strength of will, and yet you have withstood the kohlas more than any who've come before you. You've resisted the quest and its glamours. You are frail, but you resist despite that. What glue fastens you, I wonder . . ."

Eliot shook his head. The room grew tighter. The smell of the place was making him sick again. "I resist what?" He had to buy time. He had to think. No, he should not think.

"Your fate." The thin man tossed the brand into the fire again. He huffed like a spoiled child, but Eliot thought this was an act.

"What is the point of all this?" Eliot asked, his voice small and quiet. A sudden anger moved him. "Do not lie. Tell me true: what is the purpose for this hunt?"

"This is your kohlas. This is how all little boys grow to become big strong men."

The mockery in the thin man's voice was clear. It was mockery, and it was a lie. A lie growing too big for the constraints binding it shut. A lie that resonated deep within Eliot. He felt like spoiled meat, spoiled by lies upon lies.

"And the scarecrow?" Eliot looked at the thin man through narrow eyes and willed him to speak the truth. His suspicion regarding the scarecrow was growing more certain: the scarecrow, the broi-dain, the witch, the thin man . . . they were all in league. They must be.

"What scarecrow?" The thin man's question shot through Eliot, a blade of sudden realization. "There is no scarecrow. There never was a scarecrow. Only scarecrow hunters."

The truth, at last. It fell into Eliot with violence. The room spun. Eliot felt unmoored. How deep did this lie go? The lie was not just that the kohlas was unnecessary. That it was meant to ruin men in the valley, not build them. The lie was more sinister: the scarecrow didn't exist. The hunt was a means of seasoning the boys, of preparing them for harvest. But if there was no scarecrow, who had attacked him? Who had Eliot seen at the gorge? Another lie. A cold reality presented itself: he had been bred for failure. This failure. As his father had before him. There would be no escape from a scheme so well executed. One so long honed. But he had to escape. He had to get out of this place . . . .

The blind woman had warned him. She had said something about this man, this creature. His hunger for survival has made him crafty, she had said. There are more things to drink than blood, she had said. Eliot knew he must stay the course. He had to fight the thin man's words, truth or not.

He had to keep the man out of his head. Out of his head? More things to drink than blood . . .

Vertigo flipped Eliot's stomach and for a moment he thought he would heave again, but it passed. He steadied himself. He closed his eyes and took a deep breath before opening them again and looking into the thin man's dead eyes. Mirth filled those eyes. And reprobate pleasure. And insatiable hunger. He was reading Eliot's thoughts even then. He knew what Eliot was thinking, and he reveled in it. Outside the shack, the wind blew hard. On the wind, Eliot heard the crows. *Stay the course,* he reminded himself. *Be smart,* his mother said.

"Are yeh the Shining Eye?" Eliot asked. This did not matter, but the words were all he could find.

"Shining Eye," intoned the thin man. "That name is one I know well, but I am only myself and nothing more."

"I saw yer mark above the door outside. I've seen it before." And perhaps he had, long ago in a forest filled with bones. But he could not say for sure. He had to buy time. He had to be smart. Smarter than the drinker.

"Did you now? You saw my mark?" teased the thin man. "But how do you know it is my mark?" His putrid tongue, yellow and wretched, licked at his broken purple lips, as if it wanted to escape the prison of his vile mouth. As if it wanted to reach the length of the room and taste Eliot's sweat.

"Who stole yer teeth?" asked Eliot. His thoughts were thinning along with his breath. His head swam, the room tilting and spinning.

"Ah," the thin man breathed, his voice dainty and thin. Playful. "That is a story I may tell you at length. But first, won't you have a tea?"

Eliot felt warm steam on his skin and looked to find a cup of hot liquid sitting next to his arm where it rested on the table. The cup had not been there before. His arm had not been on the table. He had not been seated in the chair. But now, all of that was true. "I don't want yer tea," Eliot spat. He tried to stand. Couldn't.

"It is quite safe, I assure you. I would not dare poison you. Not before I've tasted you. Your body, I mean. And anyway, I can not drink from the dead."

"You can't drink at all," said Eliot. "Nor will I drink yer tea." He could smell the liquid in the cup. It was fragrant and pleasing. His mouth watered, his throat spasmed. They wanted the warmth and the moisture. *Don't drink it,* Eliot told himself.

“Don’t fight it,” the thin man countered. “You can drink. I promise it is safe. Oh, and I can drink. I will drink.” The thin man sniggered as though telling a joke, leaning forward. His thin voice fell into deep resonance as he said, “I’m drinking now.”

“Is that what yeh wanted? To lure me here? To kill me?” Eliot asked, his head lolling. He blinked. His eyes were dry and burning. He breathed deep and shook his head.

“Come now. Who spoke of killing?” The thin man’s voice was dainty once again, and he laughed and laughed and laughed.

Eliot’s head was thick with syrup. He could not stand, but he could barely remain seated. *Stay the course. Be smart.* “Yeh’ve had murder in yer eyes since I came through yer door. Yeh cannot kill me. I will not allow it.”

The thin man laughed for ages at this. “Do not mistake hunger for murder. Desire can be a dark magic.” Again, he sucked and smacked his lips.

Then he stood, gathering strength as he did. In that moment, for the first time he seemed wholly there. And savage. He moved toward Eliot so quickly that Eliot had no time to react. He flinched as the thin man crouched before him.

“If killing was my business, boy,” he whispered, “I could have killed you many times by now.” He stooped closer, his tongue reaching for Eliot’s face. His breath was sweet, sour, and pungent. The thin man licked Eliot’s face, leaving a slimy, odorous trail. “So, so sweet,” the thin man laughed.

“If I wanted to kill you, I could have killed you in the Moon Cave, while you slept. While you wept. While you marveled over the fever worms. Or before, when that oaf carved these into your lovely skin.” He found Eliot’s scars beneath his shirt with hungry fingers.

Eliot swooned. The room seemed to bleed out the light, growing dimmer by degrees. The air seemed to absorb into this devil, now close and getting closer. His hands tracing Eliot’s face, his lips. Tracing the runes on his body. The cut. Eliot could not resist. He was so near to Eliot, Eliot felt heat radiating from the thin man. It chilled Eliot’s marrow.

“Or, I could have killed you in the skull woodland when you were full of your fantasy of the smoking man,” the thin man continued. “That is what you call him, aye? I once knew him by a different name. No matter. There I could have ended you. Or better even, when you were first taken to the Place of Skulls, when as just a wee boy of seven you first saw the cyth. And bled on it.

"At any point while you were wandering on your fool's errand. Chasing a fantasy. A scarecrow, ha! I could have killed you countless times." He laughed, high and loud and dainty. "I could have killed you the moment your father passed you over that fence. I could have crushed your neck in my hands." Spittle flew from the thin man's lips, lustful and possessed. The spit landed on Eliot's face, on his lips. On his eyelids. The thin man licked it away.

Eliot felt himself falling, felt himself pulling apart, felt himself wanting to let go. To embrace oblivion. To seek it out. *Stay the course,* he heard himself say. *Be smart. Keep the oath . . .* He hadn't spoken except in his head, but he heard the words. He hadn't just thought them. He'd spoken them aloud, but in his own mind. Frantic, he searched the thin man's face. If this monster had heard those words, he gave no sign. But he must have.

"If killing were my business, sweet, sweet boy, I could have ended you when you were only seed in your pathetic pooey's nibbles. I could have stomped out your light when your mother, that cunt, was given to the Dark Wood."

Shock slapped Eliot hard, a gut punch. His mother . . . *I would kill you for that,* he thought. But he couldn't, could he? He shook his head. He looked at the thin man, face to face . . . Saw the lust and hatred there. Saw his own end. Again, he heard himself inside himself: *Stay the course, be smart, keep the oath, be the oath . . .*

"You would kill me, lover? Oh, I doubt that. I do not mean to kill you," the thin man triumphed, "I mean to play with you. To take my time. And to drink. To savor your taste." Then he pulled back, his vigor spent, and slid back onto his stool by the fire. "Do you know what I mean by play? I have more hunger than just for blood. Just for the life in your body. I want your body, too. And your mind. I will have all of you, every little piece. You know that by now, aye?"

Eliot breathed. He hadn't known he was holding his breath. His head felt huge and heavy, his chest tight and tiny. The thin man laughed. "Drink your tea, boy. It grows cold."

Eliot looked at the teacup, his focus going in and out. It steamed. It smelled delicious. It smelled sweet. It looked warm and soothing. His throat was sore from thirst. It burned from the heat of the room. When had he last drunk? *You can't drink it,* Eliot thought. *You can't.*

"But you can," the thin man cooed. "You should. It will soothe you."

Eliot reached for the cup and pushed the tea away from him for fear of being seduced. It fell to the floor and shattered, the tea sizzling where it spilt onto the plank floor. The sound of water poured onto a hot rock.

“So be it,” stated the thin man, false disappointment in his tone. The room felt tight and stuffy, too warm. Steamy.

“Yer good at . . . shiftin’ . . . attention . . .” Eliot said. Speaking was difficult. “Why don’t yeh . . . answer my question? Who . . . stole yer teeth?” His breathing was labored. *Be the oath, be the oath, be the oath.*

“I do not evade your question,” the thin man replied with reasonable nonchalance, “but I know my teeth are not why you are here. You seek something else. You seek the—”

“I know . . . what I seek,” said Eliot. “But first I would . . . know more of . . . who I’m . . . talkin’ to. Who stole . . . yer teeth?” *Oath, oath, oath.*

The thin man laughed at Eliot, and it was driving Eliot mad.

“That is a tale worth hearing. Still, I am reluctant to tell it.”

“Does the memory trouble yeh so?” Eliot tried to say, but he could not muster the strength. Rather, he gasped.

“Trouble me? The memory does not trouble me, lover,” said the thin man with sincerity. “It is not me for which I am worried. No, it is you, love, for whom I am afraid. I do not know if you can bear the hearing of this particular story.”

Eliot was aware again of the woman’s warning. He remembered her words: There are more things to drink than blood, she had said. He could not quite see the real danger here, but he sensed it was close. The thin man was dangerous, yes, but there was more to it. The thin man was putting on a show, but for what? Why waste this time?

“Closer than you think,” the man giggled. “Coming closer . . . But this is not a waste of time, not for me. I love this.”

Again, Eliot heard the cawing of crows. Many, many crows. There was murder in the air. *Oath. I am the oath, I am the oath, I am the oath. Oath, oath, oath,* he heard himself say. Back in the shadows of his mind.

How could he defend himself against a threat he could not name or see? His head swooned. The room felt hot enough to burn his skin. He felt sick churning his stomach, a noxious belch burned his throat and escaped his lips.

I am the oath.

He must fortify his mind. With what? He tried focusing it into a thin point: on springtime. On life. On his mother’s face.

I am the oath.

He knew the thin man’s abilities must have limits. He must find them. He understood he was being lulled into a stupor. He must resist. He must not give up. He could not.

I am the oath. "Tell me . . . yer story," Eliot said at last.

The thin man stirred before him, shifting to better face him. His posture was prim, his sophistication incongruous with the rest of his decrepit savagery. He studied Eliot. What did he see? Eliot wondered. More important, what didn't he see? The thin man smiled a tight smile, a sinister, degenerate smile. Then he drew a shallow breath and began his tale.

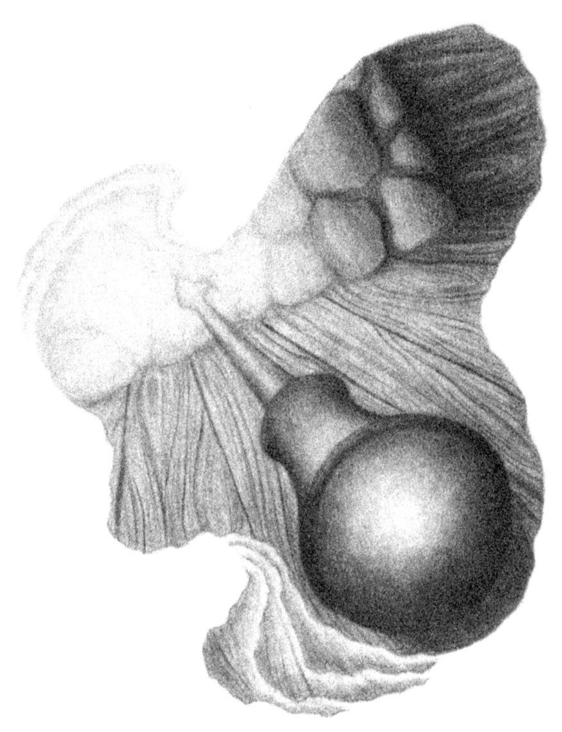

CHAPTER TWENTY-ONE: THE DRINKER'S TALE

"I admit, as tasty and sustaining as your blood might be, it is not what I desire most from you. What I desire most does not require teeth."

Eliot felt himself coming apart. He felt himself being crushed. That he remained seated seemed a miracle. *Be the oath,* he heard himself say deep inside his head. And now it was not one voice, but two. His voice, duplicated. I *should not think,* he thought. *He will hear me,* he thought. *Be the oath,* he said in two voices.

"I hear you, lover. You cannot help but think," the man said. "Though your head is growing more empty. I should hasten telling this story. Otherwise, you'll be unaware of all the fun we're having." Then adopting the tone of a teacher, he explained. "I am rumen. A rumenati. A blood drinker. Yes, under normal circumstances we use our teeth to draw out the blood. But any point will do. A blade. A nail. An existing wound. I am also a caster, but you knew that already. I've heard you wrestling to keep me out of your head. I've cast about in your thoughts, listening as you failed. Watching as you've attempted to sneak away."

Eliot felt pressure near his waist. He felt tugging on his clothing. But there was nothing near him. The rumenati sat opposite him, separated by the width of the tight room.

"And that is peculiar," the thin man said. "That you feel things you cannot see. You are special, lover. I cannot wait for you."

Oath, oath, oath.

The words were tangible as stone in Eliot's mind, but all around them was gauze. Translucent, immaterial. He heard himself speak within his head, a dead echo. One Eliot layered atop another. But outside his head, he felt his body growing heavier. His eyes burning. His chest tightening. He saw the rumenati. He heard him. He felt his hunger.

Beyond that, as though there was another layer of reality, Eliot felt something else. Something moving around him. Something he could not see. Air on his skin. Grime under his arms and between his legs. But more than that. He felt the fabric of his tunic fall away. He felt the waistband of his breeches loosen.

The thin man continued. "Rumen live a long time, much longer than your kind. And I am perhaps older than most of my kind. My teeth were stolen, yes. Come boy, chin up. I prefer when you see me. When you watch me. When I feel your eyes in my own."

Eliot felt exposed. He tried to lift his arms: couldn't. He tried to open his mouth: couldn't. He wanted to jeer at the thin man, to call him ugly names in his head: couldn't. But he could hear his own voice calling to him from a deeper place to be the oath. And he could feel something outside his body move over his skin. He had an awareness of movement in the air. A sensation of nakedness. The rumenati shifted on his stool.

"I had grown weary of tightly packed cities. Of overpopulated villages. Even glutting myself on the blood of others gave me little pleasure. Blood is necessary, but not so much as you might imagine. And I overindulged. I once spent a full year feasting on the sweet blood of children in a secluded mountain orphanage. In another time, I had lain waste to an entire village, drinking it dry one body at a time. Most recently, I had slated my thirst on a harem filled with lovely young things in a regent's court. A remnant of an older age, an age of kings and queens. The harem was filled with boys, girls . . . all tiny things and so sweet."

Eliot saw the thin man's lust curl his lip into a hideous thing. Eliot blinked, but his eyes remained dry. He swallowed, and his throat burned. He gasped, but his chest refused to open. And inside his head, he heard his voices. One sliding away, the other fading out. *Be the oath,* they said. But Eliot could only just keep his eyes open.

Breath. He felt it on his stomach, hot breath. He looked down or tried. His body remained undisturbed in his chair. His filthy tunic bunched around his thin frame, his breeches worn but sound. He saw his hand lying across his lap, dead. He felt his other hand hanging from his side, dead. But he'd felt breath on his stomach. Even now he felt breathing on his skin, moving lower. Between his legs to his inner thigh. To the wound there. Then wetness. A mouth. Lips. A tongue. Hands on his knees, pressing them apart. A mouth sucking at his wound.

"But I confess, love, I need more than blood. I longed for a more intimate setting. For a reprieve from the self-important fools I found among the masses. So I sought simpler folken, and I left the many to seek a few. And we both know Carde is the best land for few. I came to this desolate country because of its thin population. I had not accounted for the stupidity of the folken here, their lack of . . . how do I say this, vitality? Culture? Meridians are so simple, so plain. Near tasteless. A land of traps and millies. But I supposed Carde was perfect for a brief venture. Ah, too bad I never left. I miss extravagance . . ."

Eliot was trapped inside his body. Trapped inside what he could see. And what he saw was an illusion. Behind a thin curtain of glamour, Eliot felt defenseless, claustrophobic. He felt hands on him. Lips on him. Breath moving over him. *Be the oath,* he said, the two voices now one. And the one sliding further away. *Trapped,* he thought. *Trapped inside my body . . .*

"Thirst led me to a small mountain hamlet, just large enough to allow me my drink without arousing suspicion. Yet small enough I could watch with interest every person in the community. I kept my presence a secret. I did not show myself to any living thing, choosing instead to watch from the shadows. Like a cat stalking a bird.

"I became enamored with a young girl there. She was a beautiful creature. Mind you, I had seen beautiful creatures without end, both female and male. But this girl had a quality that set her apart. In total honesty, at first I would not dare drink from her. I would not dare destroy a thing of such perfection. Oh no worries, lover. Calm yourself. You are more perfect than she. See? Yes, I drink from you. Yes, you taste divine. But, shh, we'll get back to that. Don't distract me . . .

"At that time, she was everything. Having become bored, I played with her. I haunted her dreams. I would alight on her bed frame and watch her sleep, slipping my fingers beneath her bed linens. Feeling her soft places. But I did not drink. Not yet. Not even a drop.

"I can feel your soft places, lover. Your rough places. The delicate places in between . . ."

Eliot willed himself to move. His body. His arms. His hand. A finger. Nothing obeyed. His body was dead weight, his mind splintering and falling deeper into nothing. And always, he felt hot wetness sliding over his skin and left to cool. And that breath growing strong, hotter. Amorous and furtive.

Be the oath.

"It isn't the loss of blood that would kill you. No. It would, and that well enough. But there is no need of it. The death happens because of our venom. I should have mentioned that earlier, I suppose. This story is the story of how I lost my teeth, and it comes down to the venom. The toxin is unlike any other poison of which I am aware. And that is why it cost me so much in the end.

"Oh, wait. I almost missed a drop . . . There.

"It is poison, but the venom rarely kills outright. It doesn't act quickly. It is quite slow. If given enough, it renders the victim powerless from the start. Paralyzed. But even a large dose isn't enough to kill you outright. Were I a merciful creature, I could drink a body dry and kill it straight away. But I am not unlike you. No one wishes to drink the few stale drops at the bottom of a water bag. I can tell you, blood drawn from a body is the same. I would not bleed them dry. This would have killed them, indeed. And straightaway. But that would ruin the taste. And I am a bit of a sadist, I confess. But the paralysis, if it lasts long enough, will eventually suffocate the victim. That is rare. I prefer to find more eventful ways for their passing.

"I do get distracted, and I must apologize. You are quite the distraction. But we will need no pretense soon enough. And telling this story takes me back. I admit. I enjoy reminiscing my cruelty almost as much as I enjoy committing it. A good story is a good trophy. I have many trophies. But I need to finish this tale. You and I have business. I can see you are almost ready, love. And I never keep a lover waiting."

Eliot felt his skin prickle with gooseflesh. Felt the need to crawl out of his skin. Out of his body. He pressed with all his might to move himself. Nothing happened. He saw the thin man sitting on the stool, but Eliot felt hands on his stomach. On his chest. Pressure there. Pressure inside his head. Pressure on his crotch. He felt breath close to his heart. He felt a sharp point pierce his skin.

Be the . . .

"During my time in this hamlet, I met a witch. She made her living in a nearby forest and she offered me the power of casting. Mayhap you see the importance of such a thing. I know you are aware of your reality just now, and that fascinates me. You fascinate me, love. Anywhat, in exchange for teaching me this craft, I allowed the witch to collect the venom from my teeth. My body will always make more, so why not? Some of my kind have this ability to cast innately. Sadly, I do not. So I allowed her harvest, and my tutelage had just begun when first I stalked the pretty girl. I honed my skill on the girl. Shame, I never learned her name. Perhaps I should make one up for her. Hmm . . .

"Your chest is hot to touch, and your skin is so clammy, we should get started soon. And you are drooling so. Let me get this . . . My, my, my, Eliot. You are ready, and so delicious."

Be the . . . ? Eliot pushed again and felt his resolve snap. Felt his grip fail. Found the darkness pressing in.

"I would come upon the girl in the forest and stupefy her. I had rarely known the desire that men and women have for each other, but I enjoyed miming the ludicrous act with this girl. I've learned to appreciate a good fuck since then. A useful skill as I imagine you yourself will soon learn. Had I come into this world as a man, I would have been a degenerate of the lowest kind. A reprobate worth celebrating! But I meant no unkindness to the girl. Truly. I loved her, in my way.

"My business with the witch would often leave me with an insatiable hunger. She was the most difficult of taskmasters. But I put this hunger in abeyance, knowing the longer I waited to slate my desire, the more satisfying it would be when fulfilled. Months passed and my thirst bordered on insanity. How sweet then would be the indulgence, aye?"

Eliot felt blackness pressing into his periphery. The sensation on his skin, of being touched and tasted, was dimming. He could not feel the chair beneath him. He could not feel his fingertips. He was losing sensation in his skin. And in his thoughts, his voice was gone. Inky darkness pushed in. But he could hear the thin man. He could see him even as blackness pressed in from the corners of his vision.

"My time with the witch was nearly at an end, or so I thought. I was no longer a novice with casting, and the witch had stored quite a cache of my venom. I decided finally to take the girl and be on my way. To drink her blood into my rumen, the organ we use to store blood we've consumed. To enjoy her blood over the months and years to follow. To watch her die slowly and exquisitely from my poison. Why would I expect anything to stop me? I presumed no one would dare try. We rumen have few natural enemies. Men are sluggish and stupid. There are the Brogden, but we can avoid them. No. I had no reason to believe anyone would thwart my plan.

"I was wrong." The thin man stalled in the telling of his tale. His restlessness lay just underneath his pallid lethargy, but it was there like a bed of snakes beneath a quilt. His voice pealed melodious, like the empty sound of a wind chime or a window harp. Eliot saw all this, but he could not react. His breathing had grown shallow and arhythmic. The double layer of reality, the one with his body naked and exposed, was receding with his sensory perception of it. His mind was emptying. All that remained was this lie. The lie of this, the final step in his kohlas. This glamorous lie of a conversation between two men. The thin man smiled.

"That mistake nearly cost me everything. Indeed, I suppose in many ways it did.

"I was taken unawares. The girl was coming up the small path. I always called her during the night songs, and when the moon was full. I could smell her, though she was still a good distance away. Someone took me from behind with strong hands and threw me to the ground. Before I could turn, they fell on top of me. I was pinned. I'd never known strength like this. I could turn my head but little, yet the light of the moon was bright even in the forest. I made out our shadow on the ground beside me. We could have been fucking if our shadows told true.

"The fiend reached their fingers into my mouth. Ah, the bliss with which I realized I would prevail after all. One scratch from my teeth would paralyze this intruder, for nothing living is immune to it. I would like to tell you my venom protected me, but that would, of course, be a lie. Until those moments, I'd never known how my victims felt. Now I do. And now, I find the life I drink from you even sweeter because I understand your helplessness. And it fills me with desire."

The thin man leaned forward on his stool, inhaling the scent of Eliot's sweat. His blood. His body.

"No, lover. My venom did not prevail against my witch. She had bested me. She had tricked me. She had thrown me to the ground and pinned me there with an unfathomable strength, perhaps part of her magic. It was she who reached bony fingers into my mouth. My venom was gone. She had milked the last from me. I made more, but only later. A searing pain burned my mouth in that moment, and no paralysis came to the bitch. She didn't steal my teeth. She used her magic to burn them out as I screamed.

"Then she left me in a shallow slough of my own fluid and took the girl while I lay paralyzed by my own vulnerability. Unceremoniously, she snapped the lovely young thing's neck and gave the body to her crows. Then she brought me here. It is the witch who has fed me ever since. She it was who introduced me to the succulent boys of Gal-Braith. The scarecrow hunters. And to their chaperones, the broi-dain.

"Forgive one last distraction—I promise, after this, we will begin—but it isn't often I can be so honest with another living thing about my feelings toward my . . . arrangement. It is dreadful having to share you with those dull fiends. The woodsmen have years with you, but I only get moments. I suppose you could mistake us for being similar. We are not, I assure you. The dain are little more than lemmings, following blindly the witch's instruction and their devotion to their Dragon. And they are drinkers, of a sort. But they do not drink blood. Unlike me, they are disinterested in any of the body's fluids. No, they waste the precious delight of your blood for their arcane religion. That, too, is the witch's doing. She is their . . . what? Priestess? They are older than she, and serve an older master. She was created by them, yet she manipulates them. It is too complicated here to explain, and I don't want to put off our engagement any longer. I don't have time to teach you about the Dragon. Perhaps in time I will. We will be together for a long while . . .

"I suppose you've guessed by now my venom has been at work on your skin for some time, long before you came to this shack. I do not know what that oaf puts in his ointment, but it includes some of my own poison. And that Red Death business of the Skree. What else, I can't say. I don't know how you survived it at all. Magic, I suppose.

"No matter. The witch retains most scarecrow hunters for her own uses, sending them back to feed that dreadful forest. All save the smart ones. The ones who think, see, and reason. Who don't fit the pattern. Who could upset the balance. The sweetest ones, Eliot. The ones like you. Not like your father. He was dull as death. You, on the other hand, are succulent. I hold you in my mouth now. I don't want to swallow. I want to taste you forever, but the need to swallow is unbearable. To feel you in me. Your blood is equally delicious. You can tell how much I enjoy you, aye? Oh, if you could see your face just now. Your bruised body . . . It's exquisite.

"Ah, but the witch. I have become her servant. I do her bidding, and she allows me a fair treat." He sighed. "I've lived better, but I could live worse. The scarecrow hunters almost make up for my loss and imprisonment. Mayhap you make up for it all on your own, Eliot. The witch understands this. She is a sly one, that. She is the Shining Eye.

"Come back to me," the thin man said. "Just a bit longer, lover." A gurgling sound, the call of hunger, emitted from his gut. From what he had called his rumen. He wiped his slender fingers over Eliot's eyes, and Eliot's sight clarified. He saw the truth. The chair in which Eliot had been sitting was not there. It never had been. The table was also gone. The small sweltering room of the shack was empty of most furniture. There was the rumen's stool. There was the fire in the hearth, the firebrand. There was the soot. Everywhere the soot. Otherwise there was little save Eliot's naked body on the floor and the thin man crouched above him. Spittle and blood smeared the rumenati's dirty mouth.

Eliot's head . . . it hurt. The heat of the room was excruciating. His chest was compressed. He could not breathe. Hard to see. Hard to think. He felt the thin man's hands. He felt his tongue, and more. But his vision began to fade once again. Like meal sifted through a sieve, it fragmented into dusty darkness. There was so little light, even the fire seemed dimmer. There were faint scrapings, sounds as though filtered through a wall. Something hard beneath. Stone, perhaps. And pain, but not much. Mostly, there was emptiness and dread.

"Your eyes," the thin man said. "Open. See one final thing."

Eliot did, but not by his own power. He hadn't realized his eyes had closed. But in a blinding moment, he saw with perfect clarity: from across the room a door opened, one that Eliot had not seen before. Through it walked a woman with a dark heavy mantle. Her black cloak resembled the dark crows staining the sky beyond the door. She no longer appeared blind. She no longer carried her staff and there was no bandage about her eyes. But this was her, the witch. Not a friend. Not a helper. This was the Shining Eye. And her eyes burned like white flame. She did not move far into the room but nodded to her fool. The rumenati advanced upon Eliot's still body.

"And now, love, you become part of my tale. My beautiful trophy . . ." Eliot saw the thin man coming toward him, toward his face. His fingers scraped the skin of his belly. His breath moved over Eliot's body. "I have one more task for the Eye, one more part you must play, and then you are all for me." His story ended, the thin man's words turned to black, coalescing into a vaporous, lubricious screen through which Eliot slipped. His body went limp as his consciousness separated and fell into nothing. As he fell, Eliot heard the thin man laughing.

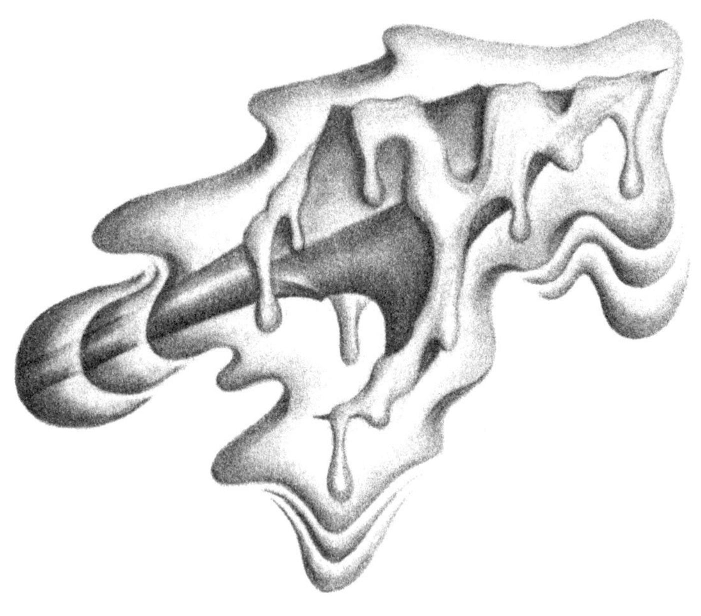

CHAPTER TWENTY-TWO: THE WINDOW THAT WASN'T THERE

Eliot sat up with a gasp, sliced in two. Divided. Madness clouded his thoughts. He felt sick and confused. Disoriented. Where was he? His eyes and mind adjusted to the dark by degrees. How had he come here? He did not know, but he knew it wasn't good. He sat still, but the surrounding space swayed as though agitated. What little light there was came from a window that was not there. It was small and high. He stood and walked to it, peering through. A boy lay on the floor in the other room.

"What am I?" he asked, but that's not what he'd meant to say.

A bullwhip crack brought his attention into focus. He put his hands against the wall, hard as stone, soft as yielding flesh. Slimy with heat. His head burned with pain. He couldn't stand. Had to kneel. Had to push out the pain.

Where was he? Where had he been before? He couldn't remember. He was at the end of something. Whatever it was, it had everything to do with the boy in the other room.

Eliot pulled himself upright again to see through the window. He could just make out the boy sprawled on the dirty floor of the adjacent room. Eliot squeezed his fists and willed himself to stay upright as he watched the boy writhe in agony. He grew nauseous with realization: he recognized himself.

He heard the boy cry out with his own voice. This couldn't be, but it was. *What am I?* he thought again. He was a wasted shell. He was bone thin and shuddering with pain and effort. He knew his vulnerable body. But how was this possible? His mind was here, his body there . . .

Eliot lay on the floor of the shack, unable to move. His mind struggled against madness. It felt like most of his consciousness had been ripped away with violence. In its place was a void.

He could see, but only fuzzy images draped in mist. The thin man laughed and used two spindly fingers to trace the runes on Eliot's chest. He slid his other hand down Eliot's stomach, grazing Eliot's tender skin with his nails. His skin reacted to the clammy touch of the thin man's hand and broke out in a rash of gooseflesh. The rumen licked his putrid lips as he ran his palm up Eliot's stomach and chest until it rested over his beating heart. His other fingers had found Eliot's mouth. They probed his throat. Eliot struggled to fight off the rumenati, but his body could not hear his mind's instruction.

The thin man was crazed with thirst, and for more than blood alone. His giddy laughter proved as much to Eliot. The thin man gibbered spells and tittered. His voice was a violent, desperate wind. Eliot could not resist it. His body buckled under the spell. He felt heat being siphoned out of it, and he realized this—whatever it was in reality—must be the part of him the witch wanted. One final offering from the scarecrow hunter before he became the thin man's toy.

The thin man lapped at Eliot's chest and abdomen, his saliva hot and thick. He gloated, his eyes thirsty as he looked over Eliot's flesh. Eliot could see little, but what he saw did not fill him with confidence. He was thin and starved. His skin was blanched and unhealthy. It stretched over naked bone, patchy with filth. The thin man licked Eliot from naval to nipple, tasting his sickness and frailty. His hand reached between Eliot's legs and squeezed. He threw his head back in ecstasy, savoring the taste of Eliot's sweat. His laugh rang out. *It is my funeral dirge,* Eliot thought. The thin man licked Eliot's body again, but sweat was not what he craved this time. He was mad with bloodlust. Eliot felt his hunger for it. The rumenati bit at Eliot, sucking at his chest with a toothless smack. The frenzy of an addict. Eliot would not last long. If he was to survive, he had to make his body move.

He watched the thin man pull his swollen purple lips and tongue across his skin. He saw and felt the thin man pierce his chest again with a browned fingernail, pulling it in a crescent. Blood welled. Had he the power, Eliot would have puked when the thin man sucked at the wound. But Eliot could only convulse. His body was too heavy to move, too unruly to command. Cumbersome and clumsy. And still he knew some essential part of himself was being drawn out, but his mind was black except what he saw of the thin man's work. But the rumenati's cut evoked a reaction in Eliot's body and mind, pain flaring bright red.

Movement called his attention back to the other room. Then a flash of red. Eliot had felt the tip of a blade slice into his flesh again, just beside his nipple. He had felt wet blood pour from the wound, felt a wet tongue lapping at it. A vacuum opened inside Eliot, only this went against the pull of the darkness surrounding him. It stood in contrast to his body on the floor as he watched through the window. His body writhed as if a snake were coiling up it, but beneath his skin. The sensation was both hot and cold at once. Wherever it touched, it burned. It burned hot. It burned cold. Eliot felt this even separated from his body. And he sensed something else . . . *What am I?*

A scent wafted toward him. From a memory, long ago. In it, he had been a young child. The scent connected to the affectionate, steady voice of his mother. A voice made of love, strength, and fanatical resolve. He knew this smell, though he could not account for its presence in this dank place. It was the scent of his childhood. Juniper blossoms. Rain in springtime. Mud from the creek. Honeysuckle and jasmine. Smoke from the hearth fire. Burning autumn leaves.

Misery tortured his body, and his mind now felt it scratching into view. He saw, for the first time, spindly fingers creeping up his bare legs in the other room. The nails were like blades clawing as they crawled, trailing ghastly arms behind them in the darkness, disembodied and hungry. They were poisonous.

They would rip him apart, and he could only watch. He could not act. *Wait,* Eliot thought. *I must take control. I must be in control.* But any idea of control left him breathless, weak and nauseous. *I must be . . . what? What am I?*

Eliot beat his fists against the window. *I am . . .* He heard laughter, freezing and hateful. Eliot had to act, but how? He could not get to the body. His body! He looked closer. He was bones and flesh, little more. How was he still alive?

I am the . . .

Those hands. He knew those hands, thin and hateful. Thin . . . The thin man. Now he remembered the rumenati. He could hear his cold laughter; he felt it, too. A rabid dog chewing on his bones. A strong wind blew deep inside his mind. Its edge was cold and fierce. This wind was desolation, and it was hungry for him. It was the thin man's hunger for him. Eliot heard the laughter rise again with fury. It was louder. It was closer.

I am the . . . what?

The ragged straps that remained of his sanity flew in tangles, clouding his inner vision. He placed his palms flat against the wall. It breathed, swelling with the inhale. Shuttering with the exhale.

"Think," he said aloud, his voice a wisp. "Think . . ." *I am the . . .*

The darkness surrounding him tilted on its axis, vertigo flushing through him. Something new was here. In Eliot's periphery, warm light blossomed within the chaos. It was light . . . literal light, blinding, brilliant, and yellow. It was growing brighter right before his eyes. Soon Eliot could see nothing but this dazzling light flooding his perception with color. Before, all was grays and blacks. Now it was yellow. The light was internal. It was warm and comforting, though so brilliant it hurt his eyes. He snapped them shut just as his thoughts snapped open.

And with this came another voice that was not his own. It called to him from a place of hope. "I am the adeglåst," it said. "And this is my oath . . ." His mother.

Those words burned with truth. They singed their way through the layers of his paralysis. They cut deeper and bore their way along the outlines of his consciousness, a hot alloy to bind his severed parts.

Then pain seared its way in through the light, bringing Eliot back to the moment. He looked again, saw his body jerk on the floor. He saw his agony. He saw his eyes drawn tight. He saw his thin bloody chest. His heart beating its mad cadence beneath the tight skin. He saw blood welling from his lip. He tasted iron in his mouth. He knew the thin man was in that room, was hovering over him, but all he saw were the rumenati's talons toying with his skin. He'd moved up from his legs now. He was toying with Eliot, his fingers invasive little crabs. Then a fierce gust of evil wind ripped up a linchpin in Eliot's mind. His mother's voice and her words remained inside him, however. Those mysterious words continued their binding work.

He focused on them: adeglåst. Oath. He focused on his mother's voice. He'd forgotten her. He had remembered her. But he could not see where the memory or her words came from. It was there, just beyond a point his mind could reach or make truth of. Still, the memory was true. He felt that.

He watched his body grow still, an empty sleeve again. He saw blood leaking from his body's chest. He watched blood drip from his body's mouth. He could taste it. He heard the cold, dead laughter, coming from somewhere in the shadows of his mind, shrieking in his darkness. The thin man was not yet here, inside Eliot's head. But he was coming. He was beating at the door.

Eliot knelt again. He could not watch. He could not. He peered around at the darkness. He wanted to escape into it. To run away, to be safe. Safe . . . . Again, he heard his mother's voice. "I am the adeglåst," she said. "And this is my oath . . ."

Keep the oath.

Be the oath.

What am I?

I am the oath . . .

"And my oath is unbreakable," his mother said.

All at once, Eliot remembered. He remembered everything. He remembered the woodsmen and their betrayal, the false memories of his mother. His father passing him over the fence. He remembered the smoking man, the woman with her cart . . . the Shining Eye. He remembered the thin man and his glamour. A fury awoke in Eliot, born from new freedom and driven with outrage. It was a fury to match that of a thousand wild devils.

He opened his mouth, sucking in air. As he exhaled, he said, "I am the . . .

. . . Oath."

"Ah," the thin man said, surprised. "You speak. Curious . . . You are a wonder, scarecrow hunter. But no matter. I like it when you interject." He tittered. The thin man moved to Eliot's feet, where his breeches bunched. He sucked Eliot's toes one by one, then scratched his way up Eliot's legs again. His nails clawed at Eliot's skin. His tongue licked. Eliot felt the rumenati's poison working deeper into him. He was aching with awareness of his exposed flesh.

"I am the oath," Eliot said as his limp body seized. Eliot watched it grow rigid, swollen veins appearing like worms under his taut skin. He wrestled with his body's deadness. It twisted but remained insensate. Rebellious. He felt the darkness pulling on it, pushing on it, feeding on it. The thin man's shrill laughter penetrated his head, pulling sharp splinters of pain through his thoughts. Eliot's eyes bulged. His lips drew into thin lines, teeth grinding like millstones beneath. His heart beat so hard he saw it through the skin of his chest. His tightened fists pounded the rickety floor as if beyond his interference.

"No, you aren't like the other scarecrow hunters at all," the thin man said, his voice round with wonder. "You fight. You taste sweeter. More feral . . . and something else. Something alien. You are just a boy, and boys are made for breaking. For sucking. Aye, and fucking. And yet, you continue to fight. For now . . ."

"I am the oath." Eliot heaved, his body jerking with the spasm. He must pull himself back together. His body was tormented on the floor of the shack, and his mind was there but not in control. He had become untethered. He tried to fight off the thin man, but all he could manage was to beat his fists against the floor. To wriggle his body. That was something, at least, but the thin man seemed to enjoy his struggle more.

The thin man laughed. "I will not spoil you completely, love. I will keep you. I must leave enough in your pretty head to tell your feet how to walk and your hands how to work. Under different circumstances, you would go back home and stick your pretty prick inside some pretty girl and make another pretty boy. But Eliot, you are so very different. You were never going back. And I may have toyed with you and discarded you before I tasted you. But now, I will keep you. There will be other boys. There are always others. The valley has not yet failed to give us its boys.

But it has never produced a boy like you. Aye, you could be spoilt, but why spoil you when I can keep you for always?"

Eliot felt the thin man's hands crawling over his body. He spoke taunting words, but Eliot did not fear them. Only his hands, venom dripping from his fingertips. The rumenati was maniacal, and Eliot was little more than a potato sack. *No,* he thought, *I am the oath.* He focused on those words. He beat his fists against the floor. He arched his back. The thin man grew rabid, sucking his chest, nipples, and wound.

"I am the oath!" Eliot shouted, his voice thick and clumsy and not loud despite his effort.

"It's always this way before a feast," the thin man said, breathless. "The anticipation of your blood, big, hot gulps of it, is nearly as good as the taste itself. Nearly. The high certainly precedes it. Even this little lick from your chest is exquisite, painfully so. And it has been a very long time since I drank from a boy of the kohlas. And never from one like you. I must control myself, or I might devour you completely. I wouldn't want that. I must preserve you. I want to savor you for always. Hmm," he purred, "I'm going to enjoy this, scarecrow hunter. I'm going to enjoy you . . ." His mouth found Eliot's body again.

I am the oath, Eliot thought. But the more he struggled to wrest control of his body, the more the thin man grew mad with desire. He bit down on Eliot's thigh. He had no teeth; still, it was repulsive. He dug his nails into Eliot's thin frame. Eliot groaned, the sound little more than a wheeze.

I am the oath, Eliot thought again, *but that isn't enough. I am the . . .*

" . . . oath, and I am unbreakable," Eliot said aloud. The words echoed in the room, silencing the thin man's laughter and bringing the rumenati to look at Eliot, curiosity in his eyes. His mouth and chin were slick from his attentions. With sudden and blistering clarity, Eliot understood, in part at least. His mother had bound her oath within him. It was part of him. He was the oath, and the oath was him. He could not explain this, but the secret was in that warm yellow light. He squeezed his eyes shut. His heart was beating war drums in his chest. Like a rip at the seam of his consciousness, he opened: a bleeding wound. And in that opening, he saw the brilliant yellow light. The vacuum created siphoned the blackness separating him, snapping him back together with a slap. He heard his mother's voice. He felt strength and purpose return to his body. When again he opened his eyes, he saw with blistering clarity. With both his eyes and inner sight. He saw and began to fight.

"I am the oath," he said in a whisper, "and I am unbreakable."

The thin man laughed, leaning forward. But there remained curiosity in his eyes. "What's that? I can't quite understand your gibberish, but please. Keep trying." The thin man's smile was a wicked lesion in his pallid face. "Yes, scarecrow hunter, fight. It makes you taste so much better. Your unwillingness to quit, to give up, makes me love you more. Want you more."

Eliot focused himself into a single thread. A single blade. He sucked air into his lungs and felt them kindle. He narrowed his eyes, boring them into the thin man's. Then he flexed his jaw and spoke louder.

"I am unbreakable."

"You are what?" The thin man recoiled, wonder blotting his face. His smile remained hungry.

Fire filled Eliot's body—a healing, ravenous fire. The strength of his mother and her oath. The strength of the boy of spring. The strength of life and hope. Of birth. Of memory. Of unbending, impenetrable truth. It was fire and light and it filled Eliot's body, and as it did, the witch, still standing by the door but otherwise uninvolved with the thin man's game, withdrew a step, screeching with a savage growl. To her demon, she said, "Kill him, now!"

The thin man could not see what the witch saw. He did not know a beastly force had awakened inside Eliot. He could not see the fire kindled in the boy's eyes. Eliot knew why: the man was blinded by lust.

"Kill?" the thin man whined, turning his gaze to the witch. "But he is mine to do with as I please. You promised . . ." The rumenati saw something in her face, for his countenance changed. He looked again at Eliot, but Eliot was ready for him.

"I am the oath," Eliot said, "and I am unbreakable." He reached with both his hands, his thumbs hardened into spears, and stabbed the thin man's eyes. The rumenati cried out, pounding his arms on Eliot's chest. Eliot kicked with both legs at the thin man's stomach, forcing retched, pink-tinged bile from his mouth. Yanking up his pants, Eliot stood, but the thin man came after him. With strength, the demon threw Eliot into the opposite wall, his body tumbling to the floor and into the fire.

Eliot reeled like a stowaway on a freebooter's ship, rolling out of the flames. His anger pressed itself into strength of will. Perhaps it was that and years of instinct and reflex. Perhaps it was the power of the oath. But Eliot grew steady, feeling his mother's words course through him, calming him. He was finding his strength. And his strength was yellow.

His hands grappled with the wall as he worked to pull himself to standing. He heard the devil's raspy breath behind him, coming closer. In the dim light, Eliot's fingers found a thing most welcome. His fist closed around the firebrand. He turned. The thin man lunged, and Eliot thrust the poker into the demon's gut, piercing its belly. A glut of rancid blood and fluid issued from the wound, and the thin man cried out as his body emptied of its vitality. Eliot pivoted with the stick and rolled the dead thing's body into the hearth. Fire leapt, consuming it.

Then Eliot turned to face the witch.

CHAPTER TWENTY-THREE: THE WITCH

"You are my scarecrow," Eliot said.

The witch did not respond, but her eyes paled. She dismissed his statement with a flourish of her hand. "Eliot," she said, "who are you? Really?"

Her question surprised him. He would not honor it with an answer, even if he had one. He was just a boy from Gal-Braith, like any other boy from the valley who came before him. Yet he wasn't. Apparently, she saw this in him. The thin man, too, had seen something unique in Eliot. Eliot saw nothing special in himself except his mother's oath. When he didn't reply, the witch went on.

"Very well, Eliot. Will you sit?" She motioned to the overturned stool on which the rumenati had sat. In the wake of violence with the thin man, and the violence of his own tortured mind, Eliot felt the sudden calm in the room disconcerting. Threatening. The thin man's lifeless, charred body cracked and popped in the hearth. It smelled like rotten eggs and scorched meat. But other than the burning corpse, Eliot and this woman may have been well met. New friends, perhaps. Eliot inched away from the fire and closer to the door. The witch nodded understanding.

"You will not leave, not without your answers."

"The woodsmen," Eliot said. "They are yours, aye?"

The witch laughed. "No, they are not mine."

"But yeh serve the same master, aye?"

Eliot saw calm in the witch's face, but he sensed something deeper. She was not jeering at him, taunting him with threats, like the thin man had. She reminded Eliot of Talker, with her calm, rational voice. Still, he saw her lip twitch. He saw her breathing was heavy if controlled. She wanted him to believe he did not have to fear her, but what he saw in her was her own fear, well tended. What was she afraid of?

"Who do you think I am?" the witch asked.

"A witch."

"Aye, but what sort of witch?" Her voice was kind.

The question—and her tone—confused Eliot. This had to be her plan. "The bad sort," he said at last. "The sort to feed on witless boys. The sort to allow fiends and," he nodded toward the hearth, "creatures to do the hard work. Aye, while yeh hide in shadow, they prepare the boys for harvest."

The witch laughed. It was altogether different from the thin man's. She seemed amused. Perhaps impressed. "Harvest? You see much, Eliot."

It took effort to appear unmoved by her familiar tone and the use of his name. His body thrummed with nervous energy, springs tightly wound just beneath his skin. She spoke with kindness, his name issuing from her tongue with meaning. Had they met under different circumstances, Eliot might have believed it was genuine affection he heard in her voice. He felt the weight and heft of the firebrand in his hand. It was a minor comfort, but a comfort still. Eliot pressed the witch. "What game are you at? There must be some greater purpose for all this than simple hunger. Yer lust could not justify such ages of toil and deception."

"And why not? If it satisfies our needs for life, what other need be to justify it?"

Eliot knew there was more. "Who is yer master?"

"I am my own master, Eliot."

"That name is not yers to use."

"And will you stop me?" The question was not a threat. She smiled, stepping closer. "No, I think not. I think you do not really wish me to stop using your name, aye? Eliot?"

Eliot shifted the poker to his other hand. He took notice of the sensation of his skin, the current of thought in his head. Did he sense traces of magic there? No. He found the lingering effects of the rumenati's poison—how he'd withstood it, he could not say—but not of his magic. And so far as Eliot could tell, no new magic. The two stood at opposite ends of the small room. He considered bolting for the door, but he knew she would not let him leave. For all he knew, the door was shut fast with sorcery. But it wasn't her sorcery that worried him now. It was her sincerity. Besides, what use would escape be if he was hunted later? He ignored her question.

"Yeh serve yerself, but I think there is more to it. I think yeh have needs more than thirst or survival that drive yeh to this. Aye? Yer fool told me as much."

"Fool . . . you say correctly. Mayhap you've done me a service by ridding me of that decrepit creature." Her head tilted, and she studied Eliot with her dully glowing eyes. It was unnerving. "So be it," she said as if conceding his point. "I am my own master, but not my only master. I serve alongside another. And aye, I know the woodsmen. They do not serve me, nor I them. Rather, we have similar goals. We are . . ." She thought for a moment. "We are symbiont. We share with each other. We depend on each other."

"Share what?"

"That I think you know." The witch kept a friendly air, but her words took on new gravity. At once she was inviting and challenging. "You see much, Eliot. And I see you. We could be symbiont, I think."

The witch's eyes were alight but not bright. He wondered if she dimmed them for his sake, a means to gain his trust, perhaps. If so, it was not working. She was clever, he knew that. He worried that every second spent talking with her brought him closer to becoming ensnared within her trap. He knew she was using magic. She had to be, like the thin man before her. Only her magic was more subtle; he could not detect it. That's what troubled him.

The witch smiled and took a step closer. "You and I have much to share, I think. I am not like the others, Eliot. I did not choose the broi-dain. And I do not think the way they do. I am not limited by their blindness."

Her words had to be a trap. How was she different from the rumenati and the woodsmen? Eliot felt truth in what she said, but even truth can be fashioned into a weapon. She took another step.

Eliot swung wide with the firebrand. It glistened in the firelight with rumen viscera. "All I wish to share is the point of this poker."

The witch smiled as she drew back. "That I see. But what after? Will you return home? Will you scurry back to the valley? Your father is dead," she said, her voice gentle. Sympathetic, even. "You know this, don't you? The fathers always die long before the sons return. That is part of the design. The kohlas feeds us, yes. But the pact requires further sacrifice, beyond what we take."

Emotion pulled the skin tight in his neck. "For what?" Eliot asked.

"The Dark Wood, of course. Low things have an insatiable hunger."

Eliot's eyes burned. His chest heaved. He knew his father was dead, but he hadn't given thought to how he might have died. The witch's words struck him. Eliot shook his head and blinked away tears.

The witch stepped closer, and when she spoke again, her voice was soft. "You and I are alike more than you know, Eliot. I once had a life. It, too, was taken from me. I have . . ." She hesitated, her words thick with emotion. Her eyes had dimmed their radiance, and tears found their way down her elegant face. She looked to the floor and inhaled. When she looked again at Eliot, her tears had stopped. "I have lost much."

He felt her words resonate within him. He felt their pain, and he knew this was no trick.

Everything about her words rang true, but he did not pity her. By now, she'd earned any pain or loss she'd once experienced. She'd stood by, idle and dissociated, while the thin man would have claimed Eliot's body as his own. Would have raped him. No, he did not pity the witch, but he saw her with more clarity. She had what the woodsmen and thin man never had: humanity. She was a villain, he had no doubt. But there was more to her than that simple reduction.

"I can help you," she said. "I can give you a home. A purpose. I can show you love. And . . ." She hesitated, then stepped closer and sighed. "And I believe you can help me. I did not choose to be a part of this, but I would choose you. If you will choose me, too."

What had she endured? How many loves had she known and lost? What force compelled her into service? He wondered all these things. Eliot felt her loneliness. He felt her sincerity. It could be a trap. It could be a wicked spell, but he did not think so. He saw her less and less a witch and more a person. He might feel pity for her, he realized, but he had no pity to spare.

Eliot's heart burned. It was broken, and each piece sizzled with need. With the return of his memories had come the realization of just how empty he had been. The full gravity of all he had lost. He had not just lost his mother. He'd lost the truth of her. He'd lost the father he might have had. He had lived eight years without a kind touch from another person. He hadn't known he needed this before—to be held and wanted—but his bones ached for it. And the thin man had put his filthy, vile hands and mouth on Eliot, a perversion of the touch he needed. The woodsmen, too, had marked him in a way antithesis to love. A spoiling touch. What would he give now for kindness? Tears spilled down Eliot's cheeks.

The witch saw and stepped yet closer. "Will you let me love you?" she asked. "Will you allow me that honor? You are a beautiful and good boy. And strong. I do not know your story, not all of it. But I know this: you deserve love. You have lived too long without it. I, too, have lived long without love. We can love each other, you and me. Do you see this, Eliot? Can you see it?"

Eliot was quiet. He saw it. He saw and loathed the sight in his mind. Even so, he was torn. And tired. So very tired. Did he really want to escape? To run again? After all this, what sort of life could he live?

His tears pulled a sob from his chest. Once begun, it bore forth with feverish life.

"Eliot," the witch said, "you and I are kinsmen. I can love you. I want to love you. And I think you want me to."

She stepped closer until she was just a breath away. Eliot knew she could take advantage of him, but she didn't. Swallowing his emotion, he pulled himself together. He wiped his arm across his wet face and looked down at himself: he was a wreck. His carved skin stretched taut over his bony frame, his chest bleeding from the rumenati's nail. His dark skin bleached of color. His breeches were threadbare, just like his heart. Like his life.

"Tell me, Eliot," the witch said, "can you love me back?" She reached out her hand and placed her palm against Eliot's chest. Eliot recoiled, but she did not flinch away. He remembered her touch at the bridge, how he'd felt healing from it then, and he let her touch him. His flesh reacted with chills. Her touch was sweet and welcome. As healing now as it was before. He felt it sweep through him in a delicate drift. She rested her palm against his bare skin, slimy with sweat and tears.

Her touch did not feel like the thin man's. It did not feel like the woodsmen's. And it did not feel like magic. Maybe she was right. She could love him, and perhaps he wanted her to. Perhaps he needed her to. He knew he should not want this, but he did. He was spoiled. Who else could love him? He wanted to reach out to her, to reciprocate her touch. His fingertips itched for it. He should not want this.

The witch must have felt his uncertainty. She moved her hand and laid it against Eliot's cheek.

"My sweet boy," she said. Her words remained sincere. He looked in her eyes. She meant this kindness. It was truth. "Let me love you. Will you do that? You can become a son to me, and I a mother to you."

The words stung Eliot. "My mother is dead."

"Aye, but I can love you on her behalf. I can step into her place. Is it her strength I see in you? You spoke of oaths. Was it hers which bound you? Preserving you against the broi-dain?" She thought for a moment. "I think so. I would like to have met her, your mother. Will you allow me to take over where she left off?" The witch placed her other hand on Eliot's cheek, cupping his face. Then she leaned in and kissed him on the lips. It was not sensual; rather, it was affectionate.

"You are unbreakable, aren't you?" she said.

No, he wasn't. Not at all. Eliot was broken in a thousand pieces, one for each pale memory he had of his mother. One for every day he'd wandered in the lie of his kohlas. Then again, perhaps this made him unbreakable. Can a shattered thing be damaged further? Can glass ground to sand be broken? His eyes grew hot with tears, but they were tears of anger now. The witch sensed the shift in him. She removed her hands and stepped back.

"I mean no disrespect to your mother. Quite the opposite. I envy her." Her face was still close to Eliot's. He saw compassion there. "Eliot, take your time. You do not have to decide now, but you—"

"Did you know anything of my mother?" Eliot asked. "Before I came into this shack? Do yeh know what happened to her?"

The witch's eyes diverted from Eliot's, but just for a moment. Then they were back and filled with all the kindness and love she'd promised him.

"I am sorry about your mother," she said with conviction. "I know she must have—"

"Answer the question," he said. "Did yeh know of her fate before? Did yeh play a part in it?"

The witch shook her head. "Eliot, the Dark Wood does not answer to me. I cannot command it."

"The Dark Wood," Eliot muttered. "So yeh knew. Aye, yeh knew—"

"Eliot, the only way for us to move past this pain is to trust each other. Can you see that?"

"I am alive today because of my mother. Because she loved me."

The witch smiled. It was sweet. "I know, and I can love you, too," she said. "I can love you better than she did. Do you see this, Eliot?" She reached again to place her palm on his cheek, but her words filled Eliot with fresh fire. He saw his mother's face as she'd turned to him the last time.

"I am the adeglåst," his mother had said. "And my oath is unbreakable."

"No," Eliot said to the witch, his voice low and dark. He stepped out of her reach. "You could not love me better than my mother. I do not know yeh can love me at all apart from yer need to survive me."

"Now you are being silly." Her voice was still kind, but he'd touched a nerve. He sensed it. "This is not about my survival, but yours."

"You would save me then?" Eliot asked, genuine curiosity prompting the question. The witch smiled and nodded. "But I do not need yer savin'," Eliot stated flatly.

The witch's expression changed. It bore her own curiosity now. "Don't you?" she asked. "Eliot, you must see I am offering you something I have offered no boy before you. Otherwise . . ." She stopped herself.

"Otherwise what?" Eliot asked. "Yeh'll kill me?" The witch did not answer. "Yer promise of love is all or nothin', aye? If I choose not to love yeh, I die. Is that it? I've wondered what was motivatin' yeh. I couldn't tell at first, aye. But I see it clear, now."

"Love," the witch said. "Love motivates me, or the hope of it."

"Aye, mayhap you could love me. But yeh'd have to stop fearin' me first."

"Fear?" The witch's tone was tainted with arrogance and surprise. And yes, he thought he detected hurt in her voice. His words wounded her. "I do not fear you, Eliot."

"Don't yeh? Yeh look at me and yeh can't quite understand how I survived yer fool. How I withstood the woodsmen. How I resisted the spell of the kohlas. And I don't rightly know myself, but I did. Yeh see these marks on my body, and yer afraid of what's inside me."

"I am not afraid," she said, growing agitated. Still, affection and sincerity framed her words. "I mean what I say. I believe we can help each other. But I cannot save you unless you—"

"Aye, unless I become another of yer fools. Is that it?" Eliot asked. His grip tightened on the poker, his sweaty hand choking up on the handle. He saw anger rising in the witch's face, her eyes brightening. "Look at me. I'm skin and bones. I haven't eaten in days. I've had no water. No sleep to speak of. Yet I killed that devil. And I resisted his poison." He pointed at the hearth with the firebrand. "I'm so tired I can barely stand. My head hurts. My body aches, and yet yeh fear me. Why?"

"I told you—" she said, her words tight.

"Because of what burns inside me. It's the oath of my mother, the adeglåst." At that word, the witch's expression changed. She recognized it. Understanding settled into her features.

"Your mother did fine work in you, and I wonder over her skill." More to herself, she said, "I wonder how we had not seen this." Then back to Eliot, she said, "But your mother did not survive. Could not. I am not your mother. I will survive, and not only, I can also give you great power and long life. I will not make you my slave, not like the rumenati would have. I do not mean to exploit you. Eliot, you will be my equal. If you trust me, we can be unbreakable."

Again, she reached her hand to touch his chest, but Eliot swung up with the firebrand, a swift arc that only just missed the witch's face, but struck her extended arm. She winced and pulled back.

Again, the witch smiled. This time there was cruelty in it. When again she spoke, it was an incantation.

"Dothra kim doe-rah bee no, rhat! Seigh-doh pley tee rhat!" Her speech made Eliot's head swoon. The fire leapt again in the hearth to gobble at her incantation. The tip of the poker in his hand glowed fresh: red hot. His vision pulsed and his body rocked. He swayed and for a moment feared he would collapse.

She spoke more feverishly, words he didn't understand, her blazing eyes now bright with compressed flame. As she lifted her palms out before her, facing up, the fire sputtered and licked at the wall above the hearth. The plaster rippled, then bubbled. The firelight danced over the contours of her skin, crawling with intention.

"Be quiet!" Eliot cried. "I will kill yeh! I would kill yeh for my father. And for his father. I would kill yeh for myself. For every other scarecrow hunter before me, but I won't. Not for us. Instead, I'll kill yeh for her. For my mother." He swung the firebrand, making another wide arc in the air. Its glowing red tip came within a breath of the witch's nose. She withdrew a step, surprised. Then she laughed.

"Ha!" cried the witch. "Eliot, I could bury you now with a flick. I could drown you in your own piss and shit. Of that I give my unbreakable oath. You know I could, but I want more than your death. I want more for you even if you don't. I am not your scarecrow. The scarecrow is in your mind, Eliot. It is in your heart. The scarecrow is the fear of your people. It is the essence of the failure of your fathers. It is your own failure, and that of your mother. But I can make you more. I will make you more." The witch extended her hands in front of her, her right hand making a circle with the index finger and thumb, the other hand a flat palm facing Eliot. "I want you. I want you to stay with me. I do not lie: I want to love you. Aye, and you will let me. That, I promise."

Unwilling to hear another word, Eliot swung the firebrand. There was a crunch as the bones in the witch's right hand broke. She screeched, and the sound was a chorus of vitriol. Multiple voices cried forth from the witch, and each in its own tongue. Eliot's head flared with pain, but he was again focused.

"Pity your optimism, child. Pity your blind hope. You have no authority. You have no power. And you have no chance against me," the witch hissed. "I will bend you into what I want you to be, and I will show you: you want it, too."

"It is you who have no power. It were broken when my eyes were opened. I do not fear yeh, witch. Even should I die, I win today."

Eliot stood erect, his body rattling with pain and exhaustion. His chest and stomach bare. His breeches soiled and wretched. But for the first time since he was seven, he stood on his own volition. His mind was clear and his alone. His heart was broken, yes. Broken into pieces, but he felt it. For all the good in the world, he felt it. All the shattered splinters, he felt, and the feeling was strength. For once, he was not empty. He was full to bursting.

Eliot continued, "I have lived this lie. And I have lived long enough to call it what it is."

"Do not toy with things you cannot understand, Eliot. Do not stoke a fire that will consume you."

"You are the Shining Eye," he said. "But that is a false name. Your shine is a lie, and I have seen it. And it is not your name that matters now, but my own." He took a step toward her. Incredibly, she stepped back.

"I am Eliot, son of Asha and Laila. I am the adeglåst, and this is my oath. My oath is unbreakable." Eliot felt strength gathering within him. He felt warm yellow light burning behind his eyes, within his chest. And deeper still, white hot light. He went on, the witch shrinking before him.

"I am the adeglåst, and my oath is to breathe. To live, to believe. To see truth. To know love. To resist yer magic. To call it for the lie it is. To bear witness to its death, if only within myself. From this moment on, I play no part in it." Eliot shook his head, fortifying his thoughts. Yellow infused his vision. "My kohlas never were mine. This quest was not my destiny. It is not how I become a man. It is a lie to pillage me, to plunder from my heart the capacity to love, to be loved. And I allow that no more. I deny its poison. I defy it and call myself a free man. Free from its lies. Free from its hate. Even in death, I will be free. Free from you and whatever master you serve.

"And know this: should I survive this day, I will never send a boy to this place. I will never give my son to this damned lie, and that I vow. With my life, I vow it. I am the adeglåst. This is my oath. Try and break it."

The witch gasped and her burning eyes leapt in her skull. A cyclone filled the small shack and shook it. It shuddered on its stone foundation. Outside, the storm of crows swarmed and rocked the shack, a cyclone in their own right. But Eliot continued, tightening his grip on the glowing brand. Shouting above the chaos.

"I do no fear yeh, woman. I do not fear yer dark magic. For I hold the magic of spring in my chest. I hold the magic of faith and love and truth. The magic of life and hope." He did not mean for it, but tears ran down his face. And that yellow light swelled within him. The white light pulsated. He knew his words came from the light. They were not his own, or not just his. "I believe in the power of the sunrise and the pull of the moonbeam. I trust in the cycles of the land and all her children. I trust in the hearts of men and women. In the folken's capacity to love. To overcome. And I believe, once and for all, that I am not the son of this foul quest. I am not the son of Gal-Braith. I am the son of a father who may have loved me well had his soul not been stolen. I am the son of a mother who was strong enough to love me in spite of yeh, to bind herself within me. I am Eliot, son of Asha and Laila. And I am not yers. I do not belong to you or yer dark magic."

The wind in the small room was savage. Eliot had to shout to be heard above its racket. The witch, holding her broken hand to her chest, pointed a warped finger at Eliot. Eyes blazing wildly, she spoke again in that indecipherable tongue, her voice not one, but many. As her words echoed around the cabin, Eliot's guts flipped. He bent with inexplicable pain. His eyes beaded water. His bowels released, filling his breeches with shit. She spoke louder now, almost shouting. Eliot's knees shook. His hands trembled. His bladder released blood and urine. His nose bled and filled his mouth. The witch moved closer, exulting. "Khal-ee-shioh! Quee-ee-shioh! Klaht-ee-shioh! Doohm rhat-ee-shioh!"

The witch grabbed Eliot's neck. Her eyes were a nucleus of fire and hate. Eliot reeled on his heels. His heart raced. His blood pounded. His body shook. But his mind was steady, burning a brilliant yellow flame, and he waited. The witch drew close to his face, the knuckles of her broken hand punching into his chest. They smeared blood from the cut. The crows cawed in the darkness outside. Her chant continued, even louder still. Fuller.

When Eliot thought his body could take no more, she stopped speaking and leaned close, biting Eliot's lower lip until it pulsed with fresh pain and blood. She sucked the blood into her mouth and swallowed it. His vision smeared into a glossy shine. The luster from the witch's eyes burned the skin of his cheeks and forehead. His chest compressed. His throat constricted. He could barely breathe. But in his mind, Eliot saw springtime. He heard summer rain. He tasted juniper-bean pie. He gripped the warm neck of the firebrand. He choked up on the handle, the red-hot tip exposed, his palm smarting from the heat.

The witch licked his bleeding lip, then her own. Her broken hand hovered above Eliot's head in a final, absolute victory. Eliot waited, shutting his eyes tight against the glare of her now blazing face. Behind his lids fire erupted. His stomach clenched. His knees trembled. But in his mind he saw his mother's face, and she was smiling. The witch inhaled. The walls of the wooden hovel bulged inward. The witch exhaled. The Crag seemed to teeter. Her blazing eyes dazzled. She threw back her head and laughed. It was mad and spiraling and chaotic. Then she opened her mouth to speak again her enchantment.

But just as the witch's eyes flashed into an all-consuming brightness, Eliot shoved hard the poker into her neck. They faltered together, two dancers moving in step. Before she could react, he retracted it, and stabbed with the bloody stake, goring out her eyes. Screaming in fury and pain, the witch collapsed to the floor. Her hand lost its grip on Eliot's neck and sliced at his chest and stomach as she fell, large red welts puckering in its wake. Drops of blood seeped from the runes. Gasping for breath but free from her spell, Eliot stood. He lifted the firebrand with both hands and brought it down in a crack on the witch's skull.

The woman whimpered insensate on the ground. Again Eliot lifted the firebrand. He struck her head. Then again. Point down, he drove the stake into her back and through her, into the planks of the floor beneath. The adrenaline that had driven him was spent, his body trembling in its absence. He swayed on jelly legs. The tension from the exchange vibrated through his muscles. His arms and legs twitched with exhaustion.

He went outside the shack. The crows were gone. He expected to find the woodsmen waiting for him, to finish him. But they were not there. Perhaps they lay in wait for him, to ambush and overtake him. If so, so be it. The way is the way.

He found the witch's cart hidden behind the shack. Next to it, a stack of kindling and firewood. A hatchet lay on top. Eliot almost pulled back the tarpaulin covering the cart. He hesitated. He did not want to know what her cart held. Instead, he threw the hatchet on top and dragged the cart up onto the porch, then rolled it inside. With the hatchet, he cut off the witch's head. He removed her tongue. For good measure, he cut off her arms as well.

Covered in the witch's blood, Eliot searched the shack but found no oil. Instead, he stacked kindling and firewood in each corner of the small room, then pulled ratty curtains from two windows—windows he had not seen while under the rumenati's spell—and used them to ignite the piles of wood. Then he used the hatchet to scatter live coals from the hearth across the wood floor. He stood by the door and waited. He had to see the building burn. He had to see the witch's body come alight. Before long, the heat from the fire was too intense, and he went outside.

Folkenlore says if you remove the tongue of a witch and keep it with you always, she will never again have the power to hex you. True or not, Eliot held the witch's tongue in his hand, but he could not keep it. Once the shack had burned to cinders, Eliot threw her tongue and the hatchet over the edge of the Crag.

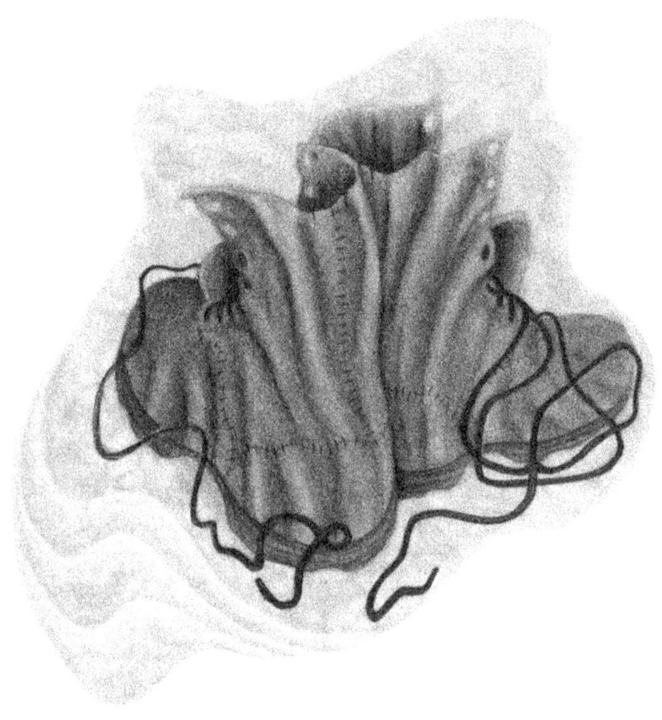

CHAPTER TWENTY-FOUR: BAPTISM

The sky above was blue and bright as Eliot stood on the bank of a pond, its meditative surface virginal and calm. Beneath and around his feet were the strong roots of a large elderoak. The roots created a wall half as tall as a man above the water's edge. Rain, wind, and time had washed the earth away, leaving behind a dais overlooking the pool.

First, he peeled off his threadbare boots, the leather worn through in places. His shirt, sodden with his own filth and that of his quest, dropped to the ground second. His breeches followed, now just rags. He stood naked, his body scorched and bruised, and looked himself over in the serene reflection of the pond's mirrored surface.

He was fifteen years old. The body he saw in the water, however, looked more like that of an old man. His skin was bleached a dirty gray and almost hairless. The tangle of unkempt hair on his head, not often trimmed and only then with a dull blade and duller concern, topped his otherwise axe-handle frame with a mad crown. His eyes were dull spots of light beneath the snag. Sallow skin and layers of filth hid his muscles. He was unmercifully thin.

Truly seeing himself for the first time since childhood, he realized just how close he had been to death. Had there been no other threat, malnourishment would have finished the job well enough, and soon, by the look. He felt it was more than a small miracle he had survived. His belly hollowed as a horrible thought occurred to him: had the woodsmen's magic kept him alive despite his frailty? Did he owe them thanks for his life? He owed them nothing.

Eliot wept. He shed tears for all he had lost, for his stolen childhood, for his father and mother. He cried for other things, things he'd lost but could not know were lost. Forfeit joys he would never have known to mourn. Birthdays he hadn't spent with his parents. Hidain festivals. Winning kisses from girls. Perhaps becoming a big brother. Learning a trade. He mourned what he could never know. Life without shadows and curses. Becoming a father . . . he could never let that happen. He cradled his face in his hands and sobbed. It came out in a flood, all at once. He did not cry a child's cry. It was the deep weeping of a man. It lasted a few minutes only. And just as it came on, it passed out of him. That seemed the way of weeping, he thought. Now he had a life to live, and he had no idea how to live it. Or where to go. Or why. Perhaps he would remain here a while. He dropped his arms to his sides. His naked body pickled with gooseflesh against the breeze.

He had escaped. He had killed the witch and her rumenati. Or at least, he hoped they were dead. He'd watched their bodies burn, but he may never feel confident they were gone for good. He'd considered pursuing the woodsmen but gave up the idea. They would not be so careless as to leave a trail. And if they did, they would leave only the trail they wanted him to find. No. He would not give them another moment of his life. He was finished with them. His kohlas was over. He would disappear, start new. His beginning was now. He may be a fool to leave the woodsmen unattended, but he had lost enough of himself in pursuit of phantoms.

Eliot studied his reflection in the calm water, seeing someone he did not recognize. He was still here. He had survived. He had beat the kohlas. And he was new. "It begins now," he said. He thought about this, then corrected: "I begin now." More tears came, but these were quiet. He took a deep breath and steadied himself, luxuriating in the sensation of being unbound of mind or body. "I begin now," he repeated.

Eliot climbed down to the water and walked into its depths, needing to wash away the years of torment, of living half a life, of walking in a daze. The water was frigid even though the sun was warm. The sun. He had nearly lost the memory of how it felt on his skin. It felt good. Very good. He reached to the bed of the pond, pulling up large handfuls of mud and grass. It was a simple folken remedy, but effective. The pond grass was wasp lettuce, an aquatic leaf used in cooking and medicine. The mud a natural exfoliant. He used these to scrub his body, to cleanse himself of the filth of the kohlas once and for all. The last vestiges of his quest purified. It may be only dirt and blood washed away, but he felt new after. His skin was raw, the scars and cut on his chest sensitive, but even they seemed to breathe at last. The sap from the grass stung, but that was its job. Stinging gave wasp lettuce its name. It would purify his wounds. He would search later for other plants he could apply to his rash, encouraging healing. Crushed daisies or lavender might work. If he was lucky, perhaps he'd find violets. He walked deeper into the pool, surveying the far bank of the pond. Flowering plants may grow near the water in season. As he reached a depth up to his chest, something dawned on him. He looked across the tranquil surface of the pool at the trees budding on the farther edge and the curtains of honeysuckle embroidering them.

He smiled. Spring was a riot.

Eliot traveled south. He'd descended the Crag by the hidden cart path behind the shack. It brought him down to the Dead Plain, but he did not want to tarry among dead things any longer, so he made his way for an elderwood to the southwest. He spent months in the shade beneath the expansive branches. He had fresh water to drink, and fish to eat. And solitude. There was little motivation in him to go further. Where would he go? He'd camped beside the elderoak dais and the pool, loving them for the way they first served him: symbolically washing away his past. Over time his body healed. His mind was another matter. He saw shadows coming after him everywhere he looked. He saw the woodsmen behind every tree. *That nightmare may never heal,* he thought.

Summer rolled across the Dead Plain and warmed the cooler spots in the elderwood, but Eliot did not mind. And when summer spent itself and resolved into autumn, Eliot knew he would not be able to spend the winter here. He would need a coat. New boots, too. Yet he was reluctant to leave. But when the first winter storm blew in with brutal force, it chased Eliot from the elderoak he'd called home for two seasons. He found a homestead, long abandoned by the look. He found a coat and other clothes, too big and only slightly less threadbare than his own. He found no trace of who had lived in the home, but it offered a roof and a hearth, and no one to chase him away. Even before the first hints of spring, a dirty pall that hung over the dead homestead had crept its way deep enough in Eliot's thoughts to make him itch to leave. And he needed better supplies. He would need to find a village.

Throm was a ways place, sitting in the heart of Carde-Meridea and serving as a middle point for travelers. It was easy to find, but it took months to reach. A road that cut through the elderwood took Eliot there. All roads led to Throm in this part of the world. The land rolled with limitless hills so far as he could see. Even from a distance, Eliot could smell the village. Or he thought so, anyway. It was the largest village in Carde after Gal-Galleen. And where Galleen stretched wide in a vast canvas of ports and markets and inns, Throm went up. From this distance, it looked like stacks of two or more villages, one atop the other. A large wall surrounded it. Throm was not so wide as Galleen, but he thought it must be packed tighter with people inside that wall.

Eliot had walked just within sight of Throm but could not bring himself any closer. He could not face that many people just yet. He hadn't been in a village of any size since before his miserable quest began, much less one so impressive. As alone as he'd felt before, he was terrified of meeting normal folken now. What would they think of him? He did not know how to talk to people who weren't witches, evil masters, or their dark henchmen. As much as he longed for kindness and—yes—love, he could not bear the possibility of being met with scorn. Or disgust. Or worse, fear. Eliot was marked by evil. For all he knew, the folken in Throm would smell it on him the second he walked through its gate.

And Eliot didn't sleep well at night. Dark things came in his dreams. He relived his moments in the shack over and over. And other stains from his past: the more hideous moments. It was rare he could sleep more than a couple hours each evening. He knew he must look like a specter. If they couldn't smell the darkness on him in Throm, they would certainly think him diseased. And wasn't he? Sometimes as he woke, he felt a hunger to return to the shack. For what? Nothing remained but ashes. And yet he felt compelled to go there. Worse, sometimes he heard something calling to him. He knew the voice. He remembered the dark mouth, how it opened above him. How it would have eaten him. Nothing in this world could convince him to return to the Dark Wood, and yet part of him longed for it. Part of him felt homesick for the cyth. And a deranged part of him missed the company of his teachers. Eliot was diseased. He could not doubt it.

So Eliot could not force himself to go to Throm, not yet. Not with all the strength remaining to him. Instead, he found the ruins of a small stone chapel on a hill to the north of Throm. The village rose into the sky on a distant hill: a blot against the horizon. He sat, his back against the outside wall of the church. It was a sacred place, or had been once. Perhaps it would bring good magic to wash away the black in him. The day was cool, the sun warm, so he dozed. After a time, he was awakened.

He stood, his body alert. He'd heard something from within the ruins of the sacred place. He listened, leaning his ear close to the stone, warmed from the sunshine. He heard it again. It was an altogether lovely sound, one that arrested his curiosity and begged him to explore it further. A melody that made him itch to find its source. For within the chapel he'd heard a voice, a girl's voice. She was singing.

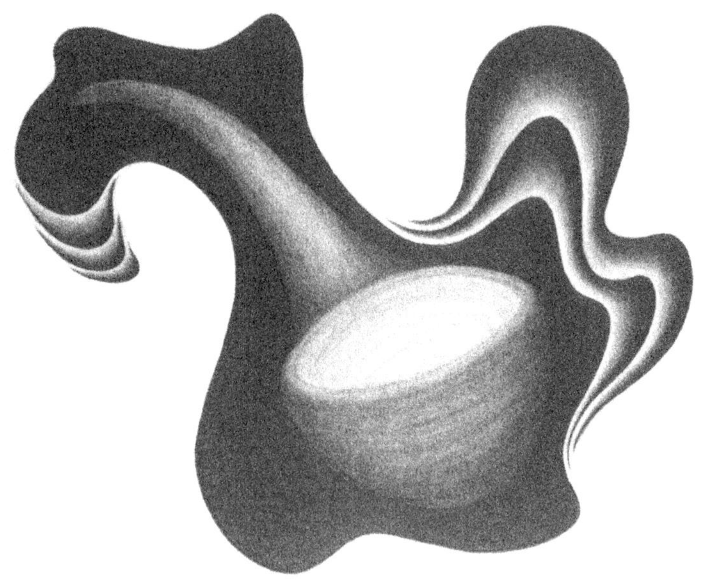

UNBREAKABLE OATH

Her heart was pounding. This was not going how she'd planned.

Asha would be okay. She had to believe Asha would be okay. Her priority was Eliot. The boy was shaking in her arms, their hearts near failing together. She was running. Her thoughts were a jumble of lunatic words, frustrating and conflicting: she just had to run. She had to make a choice . . . and run.

But when she reached the bottom of the hill, she froze. She felt the hair on her neck grow stiff, and her little boy grow tense in her arms. He squeezed her closer. She didn't blame him. She worried she was squeezing him too hard and would break him. But she could not let up. Would not.

The darkness would not take her boy. She would not allow it.

She looked ahead on the trail, past the brook crossing it. A wall of shadow bound the path shut. It was not just darker; the path beyond had disappeared. Worse, she saw the darkness breathing. She turned, looking over her shoulder. The path toward home was gone also.

She couldn't make sense of it at first, the voice that called to her. But she was aware of peril, and the voice had stopped her running. Had likely stopped her from running into the hungry dark. Later, it still made little sense, but at least she better understood. After. After it was too late. But now there was no voice. Perhaps had never been a voice. And she was caught.

To her left, the trees swayed, inspired by the breeze. A welcome sight, but not enough. She could run that way, but she could not see inside the trees. She could not see safety there. The forest to the right of the path was rattling. It was all black and shadow, an ominous, sweltering mass, but it was alive with chaotic noise. It was a wonder her heart kept beating against it. It was loud, so loud. Building and building in a crescendo of agitation. The trees were shaking. Clapping. Beating against themselves in the dark. A noise to raise the dead, or make new dead. And she could not move. Surrounded, madness gripped her. Fear stuck her in place.

She had to move.

Move, dammit, she thought. *Move.* But her feet didn't listen. She squeezed her boy, pressing her face against his sweet head. I *am the adeglåst,* she thought. *This is my oath.* She repeated the chant over and over. End over end in her thoughts. Sealing it. Feeding it. Claiming it. Making it so.

Then the rattling ceased, the forest growing preternaturally still. She gasped. What new devilry was coming? She braced herself against it, whatever it might be, but there was none. Not at first. The voice again called to her, not from within the wood but close.

"Aye?" she said. What nonsense was this? Who was she consorting with? She had to get Eliot to Bickie's. She had to run. Run and save him . . . but she could not move. Palaver was the only recourse. She had no hope it would help.

The voice spoke to her. Told her he was a friend. Laila believed him. That was nonsensical, too. But she did. It was the resonance in her chest that told her the voice spoke truth. The resonance and her oath. They were familiar. She stepped closer. Friend or no, she could not hear.

"Who is it?" she asked. She was aware of Eliot's growing angst in her arms. She must run. She had to. But darkness still walled off the path both ahead and behind. She and her boy were trapped.

No. This would not be how it ended. The dark would not take her boy. It would not. It would . . .

The voice spoke again. This time closer, but not close enough. She leaned toward it, felt Eliot's growing restlessness. His growing agitation and fear. Eliot was safe, the voice was saying. For now, Eliot was safe. The dark would not take him, not tonight, the voice assured her. She put the boy down. This was madness. Utter madness, but what could she do? She could not take him closer to the wood. But she had to step closer. She had to hear better.

"What is it yeh say? Speak plain. I don't understand." Why was this happening? Why had she come to this valley? Of all the places in the world, why had she chosen this one to call home? She looked at her boy and felt grateful she had. Even now, under such circumstances, she was grateful.

The voice was speaking, but against growing conflict: the forest was moving again. A yellow haze bloomed in her periphery. Had it been there all along, ever since she stopped on the trail? Holding her steady? Holding her in place . . . She thought so, only now it grew into her vision. She turned to look at Eliot. He was garlanded by it, a soft golden glow. What was this? It felt like salvation. The voice spoke again, spoke a name. And something besides.

"Who is that?" Laila asked, her voice dripping with frustration. She glanced up and down the trail. The darkness was inhaling, exhaling, and tightening around them. The rattling began again, off in the Dark Wood. Rattling echoes of bones and lost souls. The voice . . . the golden voice with its charms and magic and light. *Focus on the voice.* Eliot, wreathed in golden light, shook in the path, his bare feet littered with dewy grass blades. "I don't know what yeh mean," Laila said. She felt her hope falling away, but she snatched at it. She grabbed it at just the last second and bound it again within her.

Her heart was racing. *Please don't fail me, heart,* she thought. She prayed. She hoped. *I am the adeglåst. This is my oath. My oath is unbreakable,* she thought over and over.

"Say it," the voice said, now clear as a bell chime. And she heard actual bells, faint but there. Faye bells. Zyphlen. "Say it out loud," said the voice. "We haven't much time. I cannot save you both, but I can save Eliot. For now. But you must say it."

Say what? she wondered. "Your oath. Speak it aloud over your boy. Do it now. The slip is slipping."

Laila turned, understanding. Not all magic is evil, after all. Not all magic is dark. She smiled at her beautiful boy—her sweet, beautiful boy of spring.

"I am the adeglåst," she said over him. "And my oath is unbreakable." Fire and ice commingled in her chest, and she felt new magic there. New power. The golden light surrounding her boy of spring sparkled, growing blinding against the dark. She smiled. Tears spilled from her eyes. Her heart flooded with angry, dreadful hope. A hope to eat the darkness.

"I am the adeglåst," she said, stronger this time. "And this is my oath. My oath is unbreakable." But something was wrong. She was suddenly veiled within a golden cocoon of light, but just beyond it was black. Thick inky black. Impenetrable. Eliot was gone. The forest, the brook, the path, they were all gone.

Laila screamed. A sphere eclipsed the light, then rotated. It was a hat. A wide-brimmed hat, and the face beneath was lovely beyond her imagination. The kindest, warmest face she'd seen, a pipe smoldering between his lips. And his eyes were burning yellow fire.

"Laila," the man said. "Your boy is safe, see?" And he lifted his arm. The golden cocoon of light spread, a sleeve reaching out and open. Through it, she saw Eliot running for his life. Up the path toward home. Darkness chased after his ankles, but golden blades of light beat it away. "He will make it. The light will keep him. I am Lightfoot. Do you trust me?"

"Aye," Laila said. "I do. I must."

"Then take my hand. Our time is short. The slip is slipping."

"The what?"

He smiled and shook his head. Unimportant, the gesture said. She took his hand. "But what of Asha? What of the kohlas? Can yeh keep him—"

"Shh, love. There isn't time. Trust . . ." The kindness in his face broke her heart, for she could see his heart was broken, too.

"Aye," she said.

"Speak your oath. Speak all of it," Lightfoot said, and he removed a small glittering blade from an inner pouch of his tunic. He smiled around his pipe, burning hot and fragrant. "This'll hurt, but only just. Aye, even ghosts bleed." He laughed as he opened his palm with the blade, and then Laila's. He put his palm to hers, their blood mingling. "Now, love. Speak it true."

Laila breathed deep, reaching into the farthest, deepest parts of her, to pull out the fullness of her oath. Like pulling water from a deep well. She began:

"I am the adeglåst. And this is my oath. My oath is unbreakable. With my life, I preserve life. With my hope, I birth hope. With my truth, I dispel lies. With my being, I am . . . and I am unbreakable."

Lightfoot joined her, their words a chorus.

"What is bound is bound for life and good. And what is life shall remain. What is good will not be stained. By the adeglåsia, this is my oath. And in hope I call it forth and name it true."

"Now," Lightfoot said, "Name your boy. Say his name. Bind the oath within him." His pipe flared. His eyes sparkled.

"I am the adeglåst," Laila said. "And my oath is unbreakable. Eliot, boy of spring, is my oath. And he is unbreakable. And in him is light and life. Around him is hope and truth. And they are unbreakable."

The blood between their palms moved. It stirred. She felt it, a brazen dance of life between them. Lightfoot smiled, his face radiant with life.

"The slip is failing, and I must leave. I cannot save you," Lightfoot said, "and I cannot save Eliot from what is coming. But you have given him all he needs to save himself. I will do all I can. I will play my part. I give you my word."

Laila smiled. It was sad and honest. "If you help save my boy, yeh've saved me. I say true."

"And it is my great honor, lovely one. But I must ask one thing further of you, love."

"Anythin'," Laila said.

"Say the other name. The one I told you. Bind it by your oath and bind its bearer."

"Why? Who is that?"

"Someone very important. You will love him. Aye, trust me. To say more would break the spell. Just do this for me. For you. For Eliot. And for him . . . "

So she did. She spoke aloud her oath, feeling it take wing. Feeling it grow solid. Twice more, she spoke it aloud. Once again, for her boy. And once for this other, whom she would love. Sadness filled Lightfoot's eyes, but it cast no shadow there. The golden sphere shrunk around them. The blood grew fine and sterling between them. Lightfoot placed a finger against her cheek, and she saw her boy of spring alive and well, a grown man. A husband. A father. And as the darkness swelled in and the light blinked out, Laila died with the image of her boy, happy and safe, in her head. And with the name of someone whom she would love on her lips . . .

Dathan.

From The World of Glint & Shade:

A COLLECTION OF TERMS, LORE, AND GEOGRAPHY

MAP 1

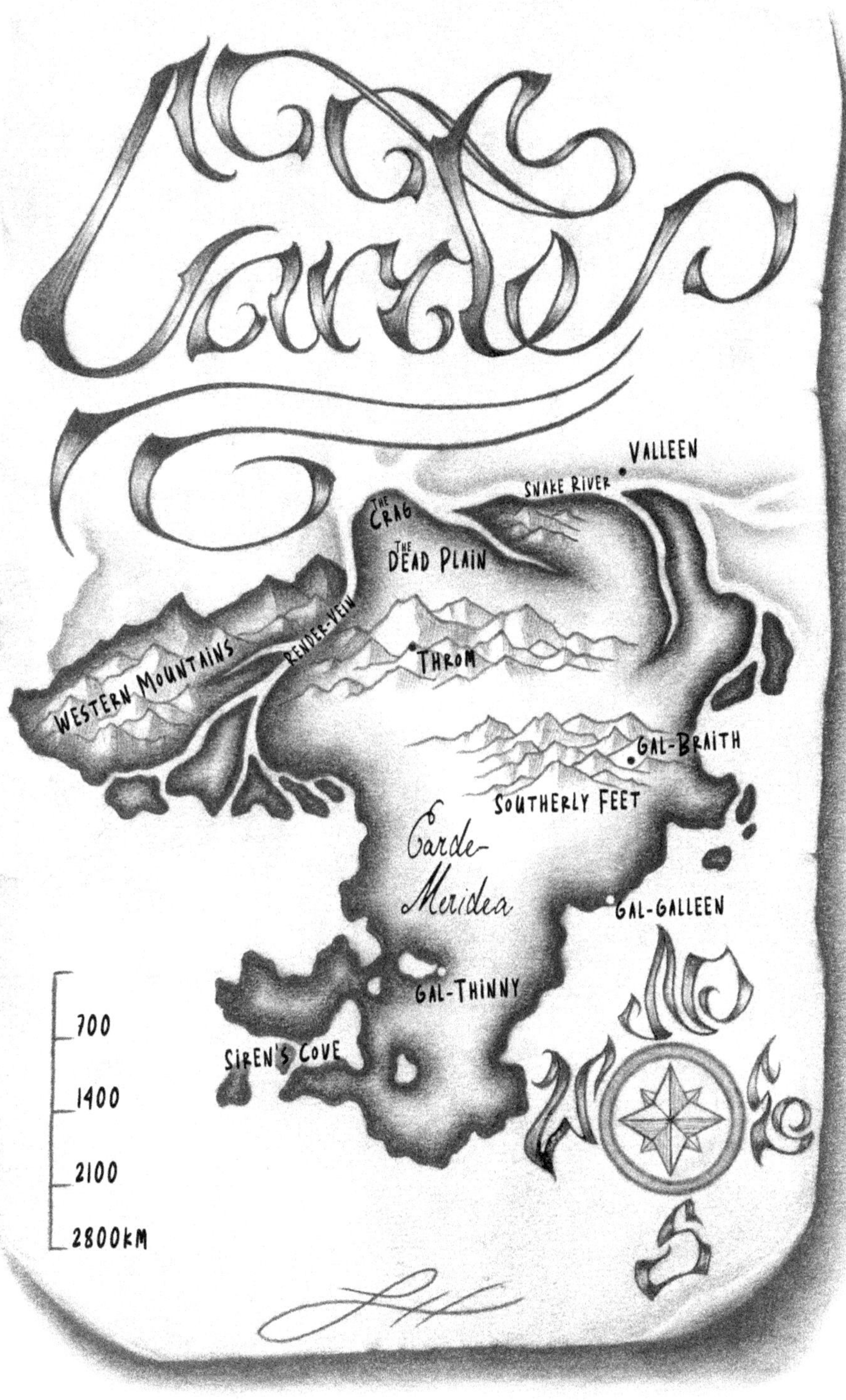
VALLEEN
SNAKE RIVER
THE CRAG
THE DEAD PLAIN
RENDER-VEIN
WESTERN MOUNTAINS
THROM
GAL-BRAITH
SOUTHERLY FEET
Carde-Meridea
GAL-GALLEEN
GAL-THINNY
SIREN'S COVE
700
1400
2100
2800KM

the Forgotten North
the Grea
No
BASTIAN
LE-T
Goth
THE BARREN
MALKET
THE DEAD MAN'S SPINE
THE GRAY LAKE
VALLEEN
THROM
Carde-Meridea
GAL-GALL
N
W
E
S
700
1400
2100
2800KM

MAP 2

GALANTIS
FINGER OF THE QUID
SHOOSHOOS
THE DEAD MAN'S SPINE
THE SEA OF GLASS
THE DIAL
TORBINATH
TRAIGEN
HALENHEAD KEEP
THE GIMMLETT
ALABASTER KAY
Land of Glint & Shade

A COLLECTION OF TERMS

A

adeglåsia RELIGION AND BELIEF — A religious rite. Adeglåsia is the act of pressing an oath or promise into another through the → *ehwain* of each. The word is a → *lynthian* term which can be translated as "oath speak." The practice is found in most religious and spiritual beliefs. The rite is often performed by those sick or dying to pass on a spiritual heritage or mantle to another. It is sometimes employed as a blessing with newborns, though this practice is generally performed only by a → *khamun*. In any event, the speaker (or bearer) of the oath is known as the → *adeglåst,* while the receiver is referred to as the → *adegleen.*

adeglåst RELIGION AND BELIEF — The performer of a religious rite. A → *lynthian* term, an adeglåst is the speaker (or bearer) of an oath during an → *adeglåsian* ritual. The receiver is known as the → *adegleen.*

→ *adeglåsia*

adegleen RELIGION AND BELIEF — The beneficiary of a religious rite. A → *lynthian* term, an adegleen is the receiver of an oath during an → *adeglåsian* ritual. The speaker (or bearer) is known as the → *adeglåst.*

→ *adeglåsia*

Alabaster Kay (also → ***the Kay***) GEOGRAPHY — An island. **Alabaster Kay** is home to the → *Brogden* race and is a large, black-sanded island bordered on the south by the → *Catcher's Sea* and the → *Sea of Glass* to the north. Peculiar in its geography, the Kay has a large river, known as the → *Wodor* (or the → *River Kay*), that encircles a smaller island (approximately half the size of the island proper) where most of the Brogden live. Alabaster Kay is a highly fortified land mass, due in part to its geography.

auroch FAUNA — A species of rare, sentient creatures. **Aurochs** are large, powerful beasts with shaggy pelts and three-pronged hooves. The males have wide, curving horns which can span the height of a man. Aurochs are similar to cattle in appearance (apart from their size, in which case they are up to twice as large as a bull) and in that they are herbivores. However, aurochs are simple yet sentient creatures—though they do not speak in the same way as the → *folken,* they are believed to use a primitive language between themselves (one that cannot be replicated by man). Because aurochs show reason and intelligence, folken can communicate with them through very simple gestures, tone and even some words. In rare cases, some tales suggest certain aurochs have demonstrated a small proficiency in the tongue of men, though such cases are hard to verify. Aurochs keep to themselves and as a result, though they are believed to have a fairly large population in more remote regions of → *Mor-Thandak,* sightings are extremely rare, leading some folken to believe they no longer exist.

Ausrost GEOGRAPHY – A region. The eastern portion of the southern geographical region of → *Mor-Thandak* is known as **Ausrost.** It is surrounded to the east by the → *Sea of Glass,* to the south (along the → *Border Lands*) by the → Catcher's Sea, to the southwest by → Carde (delineated by the → *Snake River*), to the west by the → *Barren,* or the → *Lost Lake,* and to the north the → *Dial,* the great desert.

B

Barren Lake GEOGRAPHY – A lake.

→ *the Barren*

Barren, the GEOGRAPHY – A lake. Also known as → *Barren Lake* or the → *Lost Lake,* **the Barren** is a large, highly brackish lake found in a vast crater, perhaps the result of a volcanic eruption, at the top of the → *Crag* in the → *Western Mountain* range and extending north into → *Goth.* It is actually a series of two lakes and serves to separate → *Ausrost* (in the east) and Goth (in the west). Little life is found in its depths, the full span of which is unknown—some → *folken* suggest it has no bottom. Others believe mysterious creatures known as → *water dragons* live there. An object of dread and superstition, only those without fear or lovers of death venture onto the Barren's waters, one notable group being the → *Skie-Len,* a seafaring band of → *Skree* who consider the Barren a sacred place and believe that dying at its hand is a great honor. During raids, the Skie-Len will shuttle hordes of Skree across the salty waters of the Barren in order to invade the land of Ausrost.

Border Lands GEOGRAPHY – A region. The land dividing → *Carde* (in the south) and → *Ausrost* (in the east) is a dense, grassy desert known as the **Border Lands**. Sparsely populated and considered bewitched by the → *folken* of both regions, it is flat grasslands and is the only way to reach → *Alabaster Kay* by land. It is found at the southern end of the → *Prairie of Gro-Len.*

Brogden ETHNICITY – A tribe of giant-like people. **Brogden** are a race of giant-like people, dark complected, with bright eyes and hair (often gold, also green, blue or purple). Their eyes and hair mirror each other. The hair, always a base shade between blond and brown, has hues throughout that are similar to those of the eyes. This feature is most pronounced with gold eyes. The Brogden are most well-known for three reasons:

(1) Their size. With an average height of 9 feet, Brogden are also very wide.

(2) Their stories. Storytelling is considered their religion, especially telling stories to honor the dead, and is called in their ancestral tongue → *sprechliif.*

(3) Their purpose. Brogden are a race of hunters who track and destroy → *rumenati.*

Brogden hail from the island → *Alabaster Kay* in the → *Catcher's Sea,* a day-long boat ride off the southernmost point (and least populated portion) of → *Ausrost.* Brogden live to be several hundred years old.

broi-dain RELIGION AND BELIEF, MYTHOLOGY — A spiritual order. **Broi-dain** are priests of the → *Dragon*. According to mythology, the broi-dain were an order of priests who served the Dragon of old and helped exile the → *Great Witch*, → *Dal-Reeahs*. As she fell, the witch cursed the broi-dain, and all are said to have perished. Iterations of the tale vary, and specific details change, depending on who is telling. Ancient → *scrips* exist which outline a fuller narrative of the event, though these exist only within secret, spiritual orders.

C

calamity fish FAUNA, in some cultures considered FAYE — A species of fish. **Calamity fish** are small fish with iridescent scales, which are believed in some cultures to hold magical properties. Primarily saltwater fish, though some stories suggest they may also be found in fresh water, calamity fish live in large schools and, when agitated, can be very dangerous. Fishermen seeking to catch calamity fish will often push a large bull or ox into a school of calamity fish. The fish will feed on the animal as it disturbs the school. They eat until they will become so full the fish become as if dead. They float to the surface of the water, where the fishermen scoop them up with nets. They still serve a threat to the fishermen, however. Some choose to kill and scale the fish immediately (since once the fish are dead, their bodies begin absorbing the iridescent properties of the scales and, as an extension, their potency). Scaling calamity fish requires special skills and tools as each scale is razor thin, incredibly tough and quite sharp. The fish are first killed by bludgeoning their head, often by hitting it on the hard wood floor or railing of the ship, and subsequently scaled. However, most cannot scale the fish while at sea. Because of this, and since killing them outright and waiting to scale them would diminish their value significantly, most harvest the fish and collect them in large barrels. After the stupor of their feast has passed, they have been known to come alive and wound or kill mates on the ship. The trade of calamity fish is dangerous and only a handful of fishing vessels who harvest the fish exist.

Carde (also **Carde-Meridea**) Geography — A region. Properly called **Carde-Meridea** (or Carthe-Merithea in the old tongue), **Carde** is the southern portion of → *Mor-Thandak.* Densely populated, it is surrounded to the northeast by → *Ausrost* and to the south by the → *Catcher's Sea,* specifically the → *Gleime'n Coast.* To the west is the → *Gray Lake* and to the northwest the → *Western Mountains,* (in Carde, the Western Mountains are referred to as the → *Northern Mountains* since they lie to the north of portions of the region), and the western tip of the → *Lost Lake,* or the → *Barren.* The largest village in Carde is the sea village of → *Gal-Galleen* on the Gleime'n Coast. Gal-Galleen is a heavily used seaport as it is the only major port in Carde. Generally speaking, Carde is a much poorer region than its neighbor, Ausrost.

cast CULTURE, SOCIOLOGY — A cultural technique.

→ *casting*

caster CULTURE, SOCIOLOGY — One who → *casts.*

→ *casting*

casting CULTURE, SOCIOLOGY — A cultural technique. **Casting** is the act of reading another's mind or of inserting thoughts/ images into another's mind.

Catcher's Sea GEOGRAPHY — A body of water. The **Catcher's Sea** is the southern sea, which borders portions of → *Carde* and → *Ausrost.*

Char-thein RELIGION AND BELIEF, CHRONOLOGY — A sacred day. **Char-thein** is the first day of the week and also the sacred day of the week for the → *Monkshood.*

City Regent (or → ***Regent***) POLITICS — A political office. The **City Regent** is the elected leader of a city or village, most notably in → *Torbinath.*

→ *Regent*

Corkscrew, the ECONOMY — A seaport. Also known as → *the Screw,* **the Corkscrew** is a floating borough which is part of the city proper of → *Torbinath* that features a series of bridges and floating docks to create a large, circuitous spiral where ships, many semi-permanent, dock for trade, thus creating a "corkscrew" effect—bridges of various size and permanence connect the barges and docks while allowing smaller vessels to navigate beneath them. Torbinath is considered the only viable route into the → *Great North* and commerce with the → *Quid** (the only other ways to reach the Great North from the southern regions is via the → *Dial* and the → *Barren*, both of which are considered by most to be too dangerous for crossing). As Torbinath's port, the Screw is the primary outlet for trade and fuels the economy of Torbinath. As the port for one of the wealthiest cities in → *Ausrost,* ships leaving the Screw are highly susceptible to raids by pirates and → *freebooters.*

* Though the Quid are not known for trade, what little trade they do is generally done with sailing vessels in the → *Hundries,* the goods then brought south to the Screw.

Crag, the GEOGRAPHY — A landmark. **The Crag** is a great stone cliff wall facing the → *Dead Plain* in → *Carde* and considered, at best, to be an enchanted place and, at worst, a → *low place.* It is generally avoided by travelers, which is easily done since travel through the Dead Plain (a desert), the only way to reach the Crag, is dangerous. Atop the Crag is a large saltwater lake known as the → *Barren.*

Criers ETHNICITY, CULTURE — A subgroup of the people of the → *Skree*. **Criers** refers to those who create one of two sigils* of the Skree. Criers are members of the Skree chosen at birth who are, during their first year, subjected to mutilations of the larynx. Most of these children die during the initial procedure or shortly after. Since death is practically worshiped among the Skree, this is considered honorable. Those that survive are considered fit for the calling of Crier and chosen by their Dragon God, known simply as the → *Dragon*. A mature Crier has the ability to screech in an inhuman and unnatural way and thus create the second sigil of the Skree, one that is chilling and reminiscent of the cries of a banshee. Indeed, the screeching is believed to call forth the dead or announce the coming of death, since the cries announce the coming of death at the hands of the Skree. However, they seem to have no supernatural ability to call forth the dead in any capacity.

* For the second sigil of the Skree, see the → *Red Death*.

cumatu CULTURE — A rite of passage. A **cumatu** is any rite of passage whereby children symbolically (or practically) pass into adulthood. Cumatu are as varied as there are cultures. Many are associated with religious observances. A cumatu may be a simple ceremony lasting minutes or hours, as in the → *kolinga* in → *Ausrost*, or up to several years, as with the → *kohlas* of → *Carde*.

cyth RELIGION AND BELIEF — A religious object. A **cyth** is a large, flat stone altar, typically surrounded by water, with runes and → *lynthian* carvings covering its surfaces. Often (but not always) found in a → *Place of Skulls* (or a → *Duntwille*), the cyth are used as a platform for sex and sacrificial rituals, especially by the → *dumas*. Their carvings on top were designed to collect the blood and other fluids from the sacrifice and either to direct them to a collection pot or to empty into the surrounding water. The area surrounding a cyth is always a → *low place*.

D

dahnee RELIGION AND BELIEF – A religious order. **Dahnee** are members of an ancient order believed to be one of the earliest religious sects. Dahnee is a → *lynthian* term which means "Coming of the Light" and refers to the belief that the world was once shrouded in a type of darkness wherein the Coming of Light was prophesied and eventually fulfilled. Though not a belief system largely adopted by the → *folken*, there are pockets of the dahnee order which have survived and exist mostly in secret throughout → *Mor-Thandak*. Among the order is believed to exist the most well-preserved → *scrips* from most of the known spiritual tribes.

→ *Order of Light*

dain RELIGION AND BELIEF, MYTHOLOGY – Members of a religious order. Members of the religious order of the → *broi-dain* are known as **dain**.

→ *broi-dain*

Dal-Reeahs MYTHOLOGY, RELIGION AND BELIEF – A mythological figure and religious object of worship. **Dal-Reeahs**, also known as the → *Great Witch* (or → *True Witch*), is a mythological figure of ancient times who was betrayed by many of her own followers, the → *Monkshood*, during her battle with the → *Dragon*. Iterations of the tale vary, and many specific details change depending on countless local beliefs. Ancient → *scrips* do exist which outline a fuller narrative of the event, though these exist only within secret, spiritual orders.

Dark Wood, the GEOGRAPHY – A region. **The Dark Wood** is a large, densely forested region on the northeastern edge of → *Gal-Braith* and is considered a → *low place* by the local

→ *folken*. The Dark Wood is shrouded by superstition and fear and serves as the central hub of the Gal-Braithian tradition of the → *kohlas*.

Darker Half, the METEOROLOGY, CHRONOLOGY – A season of the year. **The Darker Half** is a phrase which refers to winter and finds its origins in the ancient → *lynthian* language used by the → *dumas*.

Dead Man's Spine, the GEOGRAPHY – A landmark. **The Dead Man's Spine** is a geographical strip that cuts across → *Mor-Thandak* northeast from the → *Gray Lake* to → *Galantis*. It is a largely impassible geographical oddity made up of, from west to east, the → *Kathian Mountain* range (home of the → *Skree*), the → *Barren* and the → *Dial*. Effectively, the Dead Man's Spine serves to keep most travelers from conveniently passing between the lands of → *Carde* and → *Ausrost* into the → *Great North* and → *Goth* because of its dangerous (often fatal) conditions.

Dead Plain, the GEOGRAPHY – A landmark. **The Dead Plain** is a vast, desert plain that is considered dangerous and possibly cursed. It stands in the shadow of the → *Crag* in the northern region of → *Carde*. Much of its lifelessness is due to the salty runoff of highly brackish water from the → *Barren*, a large salt lake atop the Crag. It is also noteworthy that the Dead Plain, a wasteland of scrub bush, separates the southern region of Carde from the Barren, the → *Northern Mountains* (known in other regions of → *Mor-Thandak* as the → *Western Mountains*) and → *Ausrost*. It is possible that much of the negative beliefs regarding the Dead Plain is due more to what lies beyond it (the Barren and Northern Mountains, the home of the → *Skree*) than the plain itself.

Dead teeth (or **teeth**) ECONOMY – A currency.

→ *tricks*

Dial, the GEOGRAPHY – A desert. **The Dial** is a large, salt desert that separates the → *Great North* from → *Ausrost,* making up the eastern portion of the → *Dead Man's Spine.* Considered nearly impossible to cross, it serves as a barrier between the two regions and runs from the northeasternmost portion of the → *Barren* to the → *Sea of Glass.* The → *Lady's Smile,* a wide river at the base of the → *Hundroën Mountains,* borders it on the north.

divets NUTRITION – A dish. **Divets** are a rural version of → *doppits.*

Domen-Shoo RELIGION AND BELIEF – A religion. The **Domen-Shoo** are an ancient religion originating in the → *Hundrain Islands,* or the → *ShooShoos,* which separates the → *Sea of Glass* in → *Ausrost* and the → *Galantis* in the → *Great North.* A veiled and secretive religion, it relies heavily on mysticism and rituals. Very little is known about its origins though legend suggests the Priests of Domen-Shoo, who were said to have perpetual flames of → *winter's bane* burning in their temples, were driven mad. Subsequently, they sealed themselves within caves beneath their most sacred shrine on the coast of the northernmost island of the → *Hundrain,* → *Shou-ling.* Winter's bane is still used in the daily rituals of the Domen-Shoo.

doppits NUTRITION – A dish. **Doppits** are fried bread rolls filled with

(1) meats and cheese,

(2) sweet things, like fruit and honey,

(3) savory root vegetables, or

(4) fish and seaweed (in coastal regions).

Doppits are primarily found in larger villages but are also popular is small villages and homesteads to a lesser degree, where they are colloquially called → *divets.*

Dragon, the MYTHOLOGY – A mythological creature. **The Dragon**, known as Gothro, is a mythological creature who was defeated and subsequently exiled by the → *Great Witch,* → *Dal-Reeahs.* Iterations of the tale vary, and specific details change depending on who is telling. Ancient → *scrips* do exist which outline a fuller narrative of the event, though these exist only within secret, spiritual orders. The → *Skree* and → *Quid* are believed to be descendants of the followers who served the Dragon, and the Dragon still plays a large part in the spiritual rites and observances of the Skree.

dragonfern FLORA – A plant. **Dragonfern** is a flowerless plant with leafy fronds that grows year-round in warmer climates. It reproduces using spores (most often red or purple) released from the underside of the fronds. When burned, the dragonfern produces a heady, sweet aroma and is often used in cleansing rituals or on sacred days to purify homes and temples. It is also used in some locations during the → *Hidain* festival of low winter, or → *Feilebroc,* when → *winter's bane* is unavailable in warmer climates.

dumas RELIGION AND BELIEF – Druidic priests. **Dumas** are a type of druidic priest whose task is to perform ritualistic rites and sacrifices, often human. The dumas were found among nearly all the ancient religious sects, so the term refers less to a specific belief system and more to the actual duties specific to their most striking office—sacrifice. Though an archaic term, some lower religious sects still claim some form of dumas, though rarely do these perform human sacrifices.

Dun-twille GEOGRAPHY, RELIGION AND BELIEF – An area of ritualistic magic. **Dun-twille** is the → *lynthian* term for a → *Place of Skulls.*

→ *Place of Skulls*

E

Edön RELIGION AND BELIEF — A spiritual power or a person bearing that power. **Edön** refers to a mantle of power that allows its bearer, mostly women, to use the deep connectivity of all natural things to influence (though not control) the natural world. The term also refers to a person (or group) who bears the power.

→ *Edöné*

Edöné RELIGION AND BELIEF — A religious order. The **Edöné** are a line of people who have a deep and natural bond with the greater connectivity of all things in nature. This bond allows open communication between them and the natural world even to the point of having limited influence over the elements and natural things — i.e. wind, rain, plants, animals, etc. This ability is usually manifested only in females but is passed down from parent to child; male children have shown signs of this ability but usually with less intensity than their female relatives, and generally, though not always, when such a male child, has no living mother or sisters or in cases where the women → *folken* have failed to either bear signs of the → *Edön* or simply resisted its power. The term Edön is often used before a person's name who is believed to be an Edöné, though few people actually know or understand its meaning. The Edöné are largely a private group, are not self seeking, and tend to avoid making themselves known to other folken to avoid attempts on their part to utilize the → *edönic* gifts. They do not collect in like groups but generally live interspersed within larger communities, villages and cities, or occasionally as hermits. However, in times of great need, they have been known to band together for the service of the greater good.

edönic RELIGION AND BELIEF — Referring to a spiritual power. **Edönic** is a term which refers to the mantle of power as it is used by the → *Edöné*.

ehwain RELIGION AND BELIEF — The essence of someone's vitality. A → *folken's* ehwain is the essence of their (or any living creature's) vitality, or their life energy. Believed to be visible to some as color and mist, especially during times of heightened emotion, stress, or vigor, it is most often something felt or sensed rather than seen. When it is seen, it is only by those who are keen on the spiritual elements. Only those with a seeing gift can see it. Regardless of how it is perceived, a person's ehwain can give insight into their intentions, mental state, physical condition and, to a lesser degree, their future. However, the degree to which someone can read and understand another's life energy depends on their innate skill and/or training in the spiritual arts.

ehwain branding (also → ***staining***) RELIGION AND BELIEF — A mark of magic. **Ehwain branding** is when a person's essence has been marked by magic, whether intentional or accidental. This "mark" often makes them susceptible to other forms of magic, particularly those in a similar vein to that which created the stain (dark stains attract dark magic, for example). In addition, it makes some people more sensitive to magic, both in the vein of their staining and magic that is most at odds with their staining, giving them a type of insight into opposing or contrasting forces on the magical spectrum.

→ *ehwain*

elderwood FLORA — A very old forest. An **elderwood** is any very old forest. In general terms, it is usually uninhabited (which explains its virginal state), and the trees have grown large and wild (though the size of the trees varies due to species and geography). Because of the age of such forests, much folkenlore surrounds them. Though not often considered a → *vaultine* proper, elderwoods are believed to possess more magical and medicinal properties in the diversity of the fauna and flora growing within them. This belief stems from the reality that such unmolested forests have been allowed to nourish many natural forces that have been driven out of other locations. Similarly, an elderwood is believed to be a draw for → *faye,* both because of the near vaultine status of the wood and the seclusion. It is common to find witches, → *khamun,* and other seekers (largely hermitic) in the elderwood. Elderwoods are often protected by the → *folken* to preserve good fortune and provide healers with a ready source of vital supplies.

embers pot RELIGION AND BELIEF – A religious object. An **embers pot** is a type of → *Hidain lamp* used during the festival of → *Feilebroc.* Traditionally, it is a clay pot with four squat legs that sits either on the floor or a table and is kept burning for the week(s) leading up to festival day. Often, besides logs or coal, herbs and spices are added for the fragrance and belief that some plants (such as sage, → *winter's bane* or → *dragonfern*) purify the spirit world.

Eri, the (Sisters of) RELIGION AND BELIEF – A religious order. **The Eri** are a sect of seers, all female, who divine using natural herbs and stores. Also known as **the Sisters of Eri**, members of the order use the prefix Eri, from an ancient word meaning awake, before their given name. Generally a peaceful group, though worthy of respect and deference, the Eri are typically visited for medical purposes, endangered pregnancies, unwanted pregnancies, and general hexes to thwart misfortune or spells for luck. Their abilities, culled mostly from the natural things of land and water, are shrouded in secrecy as they do not want attention. However, they do not secret themselves as the → *Edöné* do and rather choose to be an active part of the communities in which they live. Though uncommon, the Eri have a history of being dangerous when cross. The Eri's origins are unknown, but their three Matriarchs are → *Eri-Sofia* (a goddess of intentional love), → *Eri-Timley* (a goddess of wisdom) and → *Eri-Staint* (a goddess of strength). These three Matriarchs are believed to be divinely purposed by the → *Weeping Mother Tree,* the mother of all life and guardian of travelers, both weary and lost. The Weeping Mother Tree, though believed to be the

Creator → *Mother,* is only one of many token spirits the sisters use in their work. Though the Eri do employ incantations and religious rituals in many of their rites, their true power comes from the secret things found in the natural world: many of which have both medicinal value, as in treating ailments and health related issues, and hallucinogen properties, which may induce a trance state.

Eri-Sofia RELIGION AND BELIEF – A religious figure. **Eri-Sofia** is a goddess of intentional love and the first guardian spirit of the → *Eri,* an aspect of the → *Weeping Mother Tree.* Sofia is regarded as the eyes of the Tree, forever watching over those on whom her favor falls.

Eri-Staint RELIGION AND BELIEF – A religious figure. **Eri-Staint** is a goddess of strength and the third guardian spirit of the → *Eri,* an aspect of the → *Weeping Mother Tree.* Staint is regarded as the branches and roots of the Tree, forever protecting those on whom her favor falls.

Eri-Timley RELIGION AND BELIEF – A religious figure. **Eri-Timley** is a goddess of wisdom and the second guardian spirit of the → *Eri,* an aspect of the → *Weeping Mother Tree.* Timley is regarded as the river, or the natural road, of the Tree, forever guiding those on whom her favor falls.

F

faye FAYE – A collective term for magic beings. **Faye** are those creatures who exist as a natural part of the world and do not practice magic so much as be magic. Examples include fairies, sprites and → *listeners.* Other creatures may be considered faye in some cultures while only fauna in others (an example of this is → *calamity fish*). Faye can also refer to geography or flora. Faye do not seek magic or develop magical properties. Rather, magic is a basis of their fundamental makeup. This is the primary way they differ from the → *sōklyn* (seekers of magic) in that faye are born/spawned with magical abilities.

fayelee FAYE – Someone who has faye-like traits. **Fayelee** refers to any natural creature, whether human or animal (and more rarely vegetation) which is imbued with faye-like characteristics, powers, instincts or sight (even the ability to see or be seen by → *faye* creatures) either through mixed blood line, exposure to or training in faye-related magical arts, an → *ehwain branding* (or → *staining*) by a higher magic (whether dark or light), or any other means by which the creature or person is marked as being separate from non-magic → *folken*. A → *sōklyn* (seeker of magic) may be fayelee but seeking magic alone does not make one fayelee.

Feilebroc CULTURE – A festival. **Feilebroc** is one of four → *Hidain* (or Holy Days)—the festival of low winter. It falls on the first day of the second month and marks the coming of spring (is believed to conjure spring in many cultures). Life-size dolls (→ *"goddess dolls"* fashioned to represent the Goddess of Spring, → *Homůnre*) are prepared and decorated with bright colors and → *winter's bane* (when available; in warmer climates, → *dragonferns* are used) and are paraded from house to house until ultimately brought to the center of the village or city and burned. This burning is thought to light the way for the Goddess Homůnre (the incarnation of Spring). Feilebroc is a time of divination that heralds the coming of the end of winter and the beginning of spring. It is a festival of hope since it celebrates the coming of new life (spring) in the dead (or center) of winter. It is also characterized by giving gifts and keeping an → *embers pot* burning. Its twin Hidain is → *Tanneibel*, which is the festival of low summer and marks the beginning of the harvest season (the first day of the eighth month).

Finger of the Quid GEOGRAPHY — A peninsula. The **Finger of the Quid** is a peninsula found in the → *Great North* that reaches into the → *Galantis* and is the most sacred region of the → *Quid.* Its northernmost tip, → *Joolie,* the sacred heart of the Finger, is considered a shrine celebrating the life and power of → *Quiddly-Jool.* The Quid are expected to make a pilgrimage to Joolie at least once during their lifetime.

fire sticks RELIGION AND BELIEF — Religious objects. **Fire sticks** are pots or rods made of clay and paper and filled with volatile materials that spark, sizzle or explode when exposed to fire or pressure. Originating with the Quiddick people, fire sticks are more rare in southern regions because the → *Quid* manufacture them in the northern hemisphere and the Quid, by nature, do not often trade. However, fire sticks are used in southern regions during → *Hidain* festivals. The Quid do not share the composition of the fire sticks as this recipe is fiercely guarded due to

(1) their use in Quiddick religious practices and

(2) the use of fire sticks during warfare, though warring against the Quid is rare as they are largely a peaceful race.

folken SOCIOLOGY – **Folken** refers to all common people.

Forgetful Mountains GEOGRAPHY — A mountain range in → *Mor-Thandak.* The **Forgetful Mountains** is a mountain range that separates the → *Forgotten North* from the → *Great North* and → *Goth.*

Forgotten North, the GEOGRAPHY — A region. **The Forgotten North** is considered the northernmost region of → *Mor-Thandak* (though actually northwest), separated from the other regions by the → *Forgetful Mountains.* Little is known about the Forgotten North or its inhabitants.

freebooters SOCIOLOGY – A people group. **Freebooters** are savage pirates notorious for not only stealing, plundering and burning merchant and private vessels but also leaving no survivors. They are most commonly found in the east in the → *Sea of Glass.*

frick RELIGION AND BELIEF, CULTURE – A religious object. **Fricks** are festival chimes hung during → *Sauingrey* to protect households from the roaming → *faye* or spirits of the dead. Often handmade out of common items, such as metal, pottery or seashells, they are elaborately decorated with paint and trinkets. The sound is believed to ward off mischievous spirits, faye, and dead alike, and is a favorite custom among children. The custom originated as part of several religious practices.

furies MYTHOLOGY – Mythological creatures. The ancient belief was that the natural elements were embodied by sentient creatures who could take the form of colossal beings called the **furies.** Myths surrounding the furies were used to explain many aspects of the land: mountains, rivers and oceans were the result of the titans warring among themselves, for example, while weather often represented their anger toward or pleasure with the → *folken.*

G

Gal LINGUISTICS – Prefix. **Gal** is a prefix used in the names of most villages or cities in the warmer climates of the south (→ *Carde*), especially smaller ones. It literally translates “little” but carries a connotation of respect. In rare cases, it is used before the name of an individual dwelling, but only when the dwelling is large—as with a castle.

Gal-Braith GEOGRAPHY – A region in → *Carde*. **Gal-Braith** is a sparsely populated valley in the → *Southerly Feet Mountains* of eastern Carde. Not a village proper, Gal-Braith is merely a scattering of small farm holdings throughout the valley and is cut off from the rest of the land by the mountains and the → *Dark Wood*. It is home to the region-specific coming-of-age rite known as the → *kohlas*.

Gal-Galleen GEOGRAPHY – A village in → *Carde*. **Gal-Galleen** is a large coastal village in the → *Southerly Feet Mountains* of Carde, and the major seaport of the region. It is primarily visited by travelers traversing the Southerly Feet or the → *Gleime'n Coastline*. Gal-Galleen is a trade hub. It also serves several surrounding rural regions (including the rural valley of → *Gal-Braith*) for trade amongst the farmers. Gal-Galleen is the largest village in Carde and the closest thing the region has to a wealthy city.

Galantis GEOGRAPHY – A body of water. **Galantis** is the northern sea. Little travel takes place in Galantis since it is a foreboding sea with erratic and extreme weather. As a result, very little is known about its northernmost portions.

gilly kisses FLORA – Petals of a plant. When budding, → *gilly weed* produces delicate purple flowers which release their petals. The petals are so fine, they often appear semi-translucent and float in the air. These are called **gilly kisses**. Children often blow the petals free and make wishes as they take flight. They are considered lucky.

gilly weed FLORA, MEDICINE – A plant. A **gilly weed** is a common plant that grows near (and in some cases in) water. It is also found in grasslands during springtime when rain is more plentiful, but the summer sun typically kills them. Gilly weed is often used in tourniquets and as an appliqué after it is crushed and combined with a fastening compound, such as mud or dough, to reduce inflammation and withdraw floral poisons that may have caused skin irritations. When budding, gilly weed produces delicate purple flowers which release their petals. The petals are so fine, they often appear semi-translucent and may float in the air. These are called → *gilly kisses*. Though the petals have no known medicinal value, they are considered lucky.

Gleime'n Coast GEOGRAPHY — A region. The **Gleime'n Coast** is the coastal region in the → *Catcher's Sea* where sits → *Gal-Galleen*, the major seaport of → *Carde*. It is a highly fished coastline with an abundance of seafood.

Glint RELIGION AND BELIEF, MYTHOLOGY — A religious object. The **Glint** is a magical talisman believed to have been created by the → *Great Witch* at the beginning of the current age and is a → *joiner* that allows the wielder to access alternate realities and influence time, though very little is understood about the extent of its power. The mythology surrounding the Glint adopted the specific beliefs of many religious orders through the years and therefore is difficult to define or prove. However, there are a few aspects which seem to remain consistent and are generally observed as being true regardless of regional beliefs:

(1) The Glint is believed to be kept in its place of origin, a → *vaultine* forest.

(2) It is a flat, spherical plate, convex on either side, and is about the width of two adult hands held palm up, side by side.

(3) It is a joiner between realms or worlds.

(4) Its exact location is unknown. Its actual existence is unproven, even though it is considered fundamental to many religious and spiritual systems.

goddess dolls RELIGION AND BELIEF – Religious objects. **Goddess dolls** are dolls made of straw and sticks fashioned to represent the Goddess of Spring, → *Homůnre*, during the → *Hidain* → *Feilebroc* (low winter festival). They are prepared and decorated with bright colors and → *winter's bane* (when available; in warmer climates, → *dragonferns* are used) and are paraded from house to house until they are brought to the center of the village or city and burned. The light of this burning is thought to prepare the way for the Goddess Homůnre (the incarnation of Spring) and mark the coming of spring.

Goth GEOGRAPHY – A region in → *Mor-Thandak*. The western region of Mor-Thandak is known as **Goth**. It is home to the → *Skree* and the → *Kathian Mountains*, separated from the → *Great North* by the → *Nameless Mountains*, and bordered to the west by the → *Gray Lake*, and to the north by the → *Forgetful Mountains*. Goth is a rugged landscape.

Gray Lake, the GEOGRAPHY – A body of water. **The Gray Lake** is the western sea. The Gray is rarely traveled because of the danger of the → *Skree*, who often use it to sail past the → *Kathians* and the → *Western Mountains* to raid → *Carde* in the south.

Great North, the GEOGRAPHY – A region. The northeastern region of → *Mor-Thandak* is called **the Great North**. It is separated from the land of → *Goth* by the → *Nameless Mountains* and from → *Ausrost* to the south by the → *Dial* and the → *Barren*. The Great North is home to the → *Hundroën Mountains* and the → *Finger of the Quid*, both of which play largely into the mythology for which the religious beliefs of the → *Quid* are based. The Great North is home to the Quid.

Great Witch, the MYTHOLOGY, RELIGION AND BELIEF – A mythological figure and religious object of worship.

→ *Dal-Reeahs*

Gro-Len, the Prairie of GEOGRAPHY – A landmark. **Gro-Len** is a large, flat plain in the southern region of → *Ausrost* that divides the land between the mountains of the Lustrè and the wetlands in the north and the coast of the → *Catcher's Sea* in the south. The Prairie of Gro-Len is home to an abundance of grasses and small creatures as well as fresh streams of water, so it is habitable. However, given the size and stretch of it, very few → *folken* call it home, with the only village being the small village of → *Gro-Lenlaight*. Travelers rarely cross the prairie from top to bottom or side to side, so the southernmost portions of Ausrost exist almost as a world unto themselves as a result: the → *Border Lands* between the southern regions of Ausrost and those of → *Carde-Meridea* are virtually unexplored (the superstitions surrounding the Border Lands lend to the sparse inhabitation of the prairie).

Gro-Lenlaight GEOGRAPHY – A village. **Gro-Lenlaight** is a small → *Ausrostian* village in the → *Prairie of Gro-Len* and is, in fact, the only sizable community habitation there.

gu-delak CULTURE – A perceived condition of a twofold world. **Gu-delak** (or the **lak**) is a term used to describe the cultural phenomenon of mirroring between the "upper" and "lower" regions of → *Mor-Thandak*. Specifically, the → *Dead Man's Spine* marks a separation between two halves of the continent, with → *Goth* and the → *Great North* loosely mirroring → *Carde* and → *Ausrost* in terms of culture and observances. The term refers less to a substantial or literal reflection and more to a commonly held concept that upper cultures stand as opposites to those in the eastern and southern regions. However, there are some practical ways the gu-delak plays out, including that of seasons and → *Hidain* observances: seasons, and the festivals linked to them, are mirrored between the two halves. The singular religious and/or spiritual similarity between the halves is lunar observances, though interpretations may vary drastically since reading the moon is often linked to seasonal or festival timing.

H, (I)

Heigh, kin LINGUISTICS, SOCIOLOGY – A greeting expression. "**Heigh, kin**" is an expression used to greet welcome friends and families on special days such as → *Hidain,* weddings and funerals. It roughly translates to "Welcome, good and kind friend." It is typically answered by repeating the phrase, or with an added note of good will, such as, "...and may your days be gentle," or "...may your hearts be light (or sunny)." It varies from region to region and based on the current day of celebration or mourning.

Hidain CULTURE – Festival days. **Hidain** are High Holy Days. There are four: → *Sauingrey,* → *Feilebroc,* → *Lunauinbroc,* and → *Tanneibel.*

Hidain lamp CULTURE – A religious object. **Hidain lamps,** also called → *tween lights,* are set during high festivals and serve a variety of purposes. Tween lights come in many different forms, but the most prevalent are any bucket or container that can be filled with burning candles, tallow or twigs. Common examples include hollowed-out gourds, clay pots, holes dug into the earth (generally surrounding a home or sacred place) and typically filled with burning logs, skulls (though these are reserved for the darker arts and are most often used during → *Sauingrey*).

high place FAYE, GEOGRAPHY — A place characterized by → *faye* magic.

→ *vaultine*

hommie LINGUISTICS, SOCIOLOGY — A way of addressing or referring to a person. **Hommie** is a respectful term of endearment, formal in nature, used by children when referring to adults, especially close relatives.

Homůnre, Goddess RELIGION AND BELIEF — A religious figure. **Homůnre** is said to be the incarnation of spring and often the object of celebration during → *Feilebroc*, the → *Hidain* festival of low winter.

Hundrain Islands GEOGRAPHY — An island group. The → *Hundroën Mountains* in the → *Great North* extend into the → *Sea of Glass* (separating it from → *Galantis*), creating a series of sharp islands known as the **Hundrain (Islands)**. Often shrouded in fog and known for sinking ships, these islands, known as the → *ShooShoos* among sailors and the Hundrain to land dwellers, are believed to be cursed like the mountain range from which they rise.

Hundroën Mountains GEOGRAPHY — A mountain range. The **Hundroën Mountains** are a mountain range in the → *Great North* that separates the → *Galantis* in the north and the → *Sea of Glass* in the south. Considered to be nearly impossible to cross, the mountains are considered cursed, personified as being malicious and full of trickery and treachery. The most notable lore concerning this phenomenon regards a party of fifty travelers who set out to cross the Hundroën, also known as the Hundries, in order to seek a fresh water supply. The party returned seventeen days after setting out with a madness that led them to not only slaughter everyone from their home village but eventually themselves as well. The event is known as the Hundries Massacre. The Hundroën Mountains extend into the sea, creating a series of sharp islands, often shrouded in fog, known for sinking ships. The → *Hundrain Islands,* known as the → *ShooShoos* among sailors and the Hundrain to land dwellers, are believed to be cursed like the mountain range from which they rise.

husking CULTURE – A festival tradition. **Husking** is part of the celebration of the new year, a practice among agrarian cultures where → *juniper-beans* are dyed with colored oils and pigments and collected into large barrels filled with water. The barrels are placed most often in the village center where, over the course of festival, there are scheduled feasts and dances where the villagers will celebrate together. Throughout festival, each time someone passes the barrels, they knock against them with either fist, boot, or stick—there are dances designed to celebrate this practice. This knocking—or husking—is not simply an act of celebration: it softens the tough juniper-bean husks. It is also believed to bring good fortune in the upcoming new year, so the more one knocks, the more good fortune they are likely to have in the coming year. Festival culminates with the barrels being turned over. The beans have now separated from the husks and are collected: some are ground into butters, some are baked into pies, some are roasted, some are jarred for storage, and many are eaten raw. The husks (or hulls), now multicolored and shiny from the husking process and oils used for dyeing, will be left on the ground to be dried by the sun—a symbol of throwing off the old self for the sake of health and good fortune. This is also the location where the new year will be celebrated. Dancing on the hulls creates a colorful dust that covers the revelers feet and legs and is also considered good luck. The festival is primarily celebrated in southern cultures (→ *Carde*) though there are variations of it in northern cultures as well.

Husking Festival CULTURE – A festival. The **Husking Festival** is a celebration of the new year held (mostly) in the south (→ *Carde*).

→ *husking*

J

joiner RELIGION AND BELIEF, MYTHOLOGY — A spiritual object. A **joiner** is anything that is used as an "adhesive" during spiritual transactions. Blood may be used as a joiner, as well as any other "payment" or connective object or sacrifice. A joiner may also be a conduit through which magic passes from one person, place, or thing into another. Perhaps the most famous joiner is the → *Glint.*

Joolie RELIGION AND BELIEF — A religious site. **Joolie** is the Quiddick (→ *Quid*) shrine to → *Quiddly-Jool,* found in the northernmost tip of the → *Finger of the Quid.* It is also the northernmost part of → *Mor-Thandak.*

juniper-beans FLORA — A legume. The fruit of a hardy vine, **juniper-beans** are purple seeds relatively the size of a peach pit and vaguely shaped like a bean. Their outer shell is a tough, leathery substance that must be soaked in water in order to be removed. Once the shell is removed, juniper-beans can be cooked, roasted, or eaten raw. Their flavor is slightly sweet, comparable to sweet potatoes. Common lore among the → *folken* is that juniper-beans are good luck and promote prosperity and fertility. Juniper-beans are the object of the new year festival tradition of → *husking.*

→ *Husking Festival,* → *husking*

K

Kathian Mountains, the GEOGRAPHY — A mountain range. **The Kathian Mountains** are the mountain range that separates → *Carde* and → *Goth* and include the → *Western*

Mountain range (or the → *Northern Mountains,* a term used by → *Meridians,* for the southernmost peaks of the range), the → *Dragon's Belly* and the → *Mountain of the Dragon.* The Mountain of the Dragon is the home of the → *Skree.* By extension, the Kathians are often equated with the exiled, fallen body of the → *Dragon* Gothro, with the Dragon's Belly, a wide valley splitting the range in half from the → *Barren* to the → *Gray Lake,* and the Mountain of the Dragon serving as its "head". The Kathians are often referred to as the wilderness of the high county.

Kay, the GEOGRAPHY — (1) An island. (2) A river. As an island, **the Kay** is another name for → *Alabaster Kay.* It is also one name of the large river that divides Alabaster Kay into two land masses, an island within an island (→ *Wodor*).

khamun RELIGION AND BELIEF — Religious figures. **Khamun** are any holy → *folken,* mostly ascetic in nature (renouncing material comforts and leading a life of stern self-discipline out of religious devotion). Khamun may be men or women and the term is not specific to any one belief system, though it suggests believers who strive to be at one with nature (the → *Mother*), such as the → *Eri* or the → *Edöne.* Through the years, most belief systems have adopted the term.

khan RELIGION AND BELIEF — A religious figure. **Khan** is a term specific to → *Lustrain* and the surrounding mountain region in → *Ausrost* to refer to any → *khamun.*

kohlas CULTURE – A rite of passage. **Kohlas** is a → *cumatu,* or rite of passage, for boys of age seven that is peculiar to the rural regions of the → *Southerly Feet Mountains* in the land of → *Carde,* specifically the valley of → *Gal-Braith.* A boy begins his kohlas on the morning of his seventh birthday. It is an adventure he must complete on his own without the aid of his father, mother, or any other adult or peer. It is believed to be the proper way a boy grows to become a man. In most regions, children take on adult responsibilities as early as age seven—a transition age viewed as the "sprout" of adulthood, but this rite is peculiar to the rural southwest. The boys of the kohlas are expected to leave home on a mysterious journey and remain gone for several years, returning only after they have reached full physical maturity. Wards who do not interfere with the boy's challenges accompany them on their quest. The kohlas is never spoken of openly as it is considered too sacred to do so. The kohlas is intrinsically tied to the valley's religion. Because of this, the kohlas is both revered and feared.

kolinga CULTURE — A rite of passage. **Kolinga** is a → *cumatu,* or rite of passage, for girls age thirteen that is peculiar to → *Lustrain* and the surrounding mountains in → *Ausrost.* The kolinga is a ceremony that marks a young woman's passage into adulthood. Origins of the rite are unknown, but historical records show the ceremony was once supervised by a particular sect of → *dumas* known as the → *Monkshood.* However, over time the Monkshood died out, and local → *khan* took over the duties. In older times, the girls would be given a sleeping tonic upon entering the ceremony and would often not wake for days after. The exact details of what transpired during the ceremony were never revealed beyond the dumas, and the girls themselves could offer no practical insight into the rite.

L

listeners FAYE — A kind of spirit. **Listeners** are invisible spirits believed to hear the hidden secrets of those on whom they spy, to what end no one can say. The listeners may be found anywhere but are more likely to settle in magical places, sacred places, or even → *low places,* and are associated with a mythological place called the → *Weeping Forest.*

Lost Lake GEOGRAPHY — An intracontinental lake in → *Mor-Thandak.*

→ *the Barren*

low place FAYE, GEOGRAPHY — A place characterized by dark magic. **Low places** are locations believed by → *folken* to hold concentrations of evil or dark spirits. They can be created in many ways, but the three primary ways are

(1) a long-standing tradition of performing dark rites or ritualistic sacrifices to dark deities or spirits,

(2) the haunting of a shade who in life had held great power as a witch, warlock, or other magical being, or

(3) the mass extinction of a group of people through great tragedy or evil, including murder.

It is common for the origins of a low place to be unknown or mysterious, particularly if the cause happened before recorded history. Technically, a low place is a form of → *vaultine,* albeit one that is created (whether intentionally or unintentionally) and one known for dark magic and negative energy.

Lunauinbroc CULTURE — A festival. One of four → *Hidain* (or Holy Days), **Lunauinbroc** is the last day of the fourth month of the year (or the eve of → *Summer Han*) and marks the beginning of summer. Special bonfires are kindled—flames, smoke and ashes are believed to have protective or destructive powers. In some regions, people leap over or pass between flames to signify prowess, strength or bravery, and this act is also considered lucky. The dew that falls on the morning following Lunauinbroc is believed to hold magical properties. Lunauinbroc also refers to midsummer festivals. It is a time of divination. In the northern hemisphere, it is celebrated at the other end of the year: the last day of the eleventh month. Its Hidain twin is → *Sauingrey* (celebrated on the eve of → *Winter Hu*); both are celebrated on the last day of the month preceding the seasonal turn.

Lustrain GEOGRAPHY – A city. **Lustrain** (pronounced "loostrain" with a slight trill on the r) is a city known for and named after its mining and distribution of the primary source of currency in → *Ausrost* (→ *tricks*). It is a wealthy city nestled within the mountains of the → *Ti-Fleek Lustrė* (eastern range) and is mostly cut off from the rest of Ausrost by the mountains and the → *Barren* (to the north). It is a highly fortified and distrustful city given its vast amount of wealth because of its control of the currency supply throughout Ausrost and, to some degree, all of → *Mor-Thandak*. Lustrain is home to a large population of poor → *folken*, the vast majority of which work as indentured servants in the Ti-Fleek Lustrė mines.

lusts ECONOMY – A currency. Pronunciation: "loosts".

→ *tricks*

Lynth LINGUISTICS, RELIGION AND BELIEF – A language. **Lynth** is an ancient language spoken mostly by → *dumas*, → *khamun*, and other devout religious and spiritual followers. Mostly arcane, it was never widely spoken by the → *folken* but was reserved for religious rites and → *scrips* and is now nearly extinct. However, many lynthian terms (or variations of them) remain in the vernacular of the folken, particularly in religious terminology.

M

Meridea, the GEOGRAPHY – A region.

→ *Carde*

Meridian(s) SOCIOLOGY — A people group. **Meridian** refers to people from → *Carde-Meridea.*

milly LINGUISTICS, SOCIOLOGY — A derogatory term. **Milly** is a derogatory term used to suggest someone is immature or otherwise inexperienced. It is often used by adults when speaking to youths, but it is particularly offensive when used to describe someone who considers themselves a peer or equal.

Monkshood RELIGION AND BELIEF — A religious group. The **Monkshood** are an ancient priesthood who myth suggests were originally followers of the witch → *Dal-Reeahs,* but they turned on her, leading to her exile. Legend also purports that some of the Monkshood who remained faithful to the witch were bound by her magic and turned to a human-animal hybrid called the → *wolfenkind,* though only the most superstitious → *folken* believe this to be true. Though their origins and purposes are widely debated, the Monkshood did indeed exist and may yet have followers.

Moon, Dead ASTRONOMY — A phase in the lunar cycle.

→ *Sleeping Moon*

Moon, Drodein ASTRONOMY, CULTURE — High moon. A **Drodein Moon** is when the → *Traveler's Moon* "crests" on both → *Sauingrey* and → *Char-thein* (the first day of the week, and also the sacred day of the week for the → *Monkshood*). It is considered the most powerful day of the Monkshood faith. Drodein is a → *lynthian* word that means both "death" and "resurrection," depending on where you place the stress. When the stress falls on dro- the word means "death," subsequently with the stress on -dein, it means "resurrection." A Drodein Moon is a very rare occurrence. The rituals that accompany it reflect its rarity, and thus, its vitality.

Moon, Farmer's ASTRONOMY – A phase in the lunar cycle.

→ *Spade Moon*

Moon, Harvest METEOROLOGY, ASTRONOMICAL CHRONOLOGY – A signum of the seasonal cycle. The **Harvest Moon** refers to the moon during autumn.

Moon, Lover's ASTRONOMY, CULTURE – High moon. The **Lover's Moon** is when the → *Pregnant Moon* "breaks" on → *Lunauinbroc*. It lasts for three days and is considered fortunate.

Moon, Malkein ASTRONOMY, CULTURE – High moon. Malkein is an ancient → *lynthian* word meaning "magic." **Malkein Moon** refers to a period where the → *Sleeping Moon* (or → *Dead Moon*) "crests" on any of the four → *Hidain* (High Holy Days). It is believed to thin further the veil between realms, heightening the magical properties of the time. The exact meaning of a Malkein Moon is determined by which Hidain it falls upon: a Malkein Moon during → *Tanneibel* is a good omen, one during → *Feilebroc* is a bad omen, one falling on either → *Sauingrey* or → *Lunauinbroc* must be interpreted congruent to other factors. The "reading" of even the simplest Malkein Moon is complicated, as influential factors vary. Weather patterns, religious beliefs and regional superstitions play a role in the interpretation.

Moon, Poison ASTRONOMY, CULTURE – High moon. When the → *Traveler's Moon* (a.k.a. → *Pregnant Moon*) "breaks" on → *Sauingrey*, it is known as a **Poison Moon**. A Poison Moon is considered a special moon when magic, especially dark, is more potent.

Moon, Pregnant ASTRONOMY – A phase in the lunar cycle.

→ *Traveler's Moon*

Moon, Quiet METEOROLOGY, ASTRONOMICAL CHRONOLOGY – A signum of the seasonal cycle. The **Quiet Moon** is the moon during winter.

Moon, Reaper's ASTRONOMY – A phase in the lunar cycle.

→ *Sickle Moon*

Moon, Sickle ASTRONOMY – A phase in the lunar cycle. The **Sickle Moon** is the waning, last quarter moon and is also known as → *Reaper's Moon.*

Moon, Sleeping ASTRONOMY – A phase in the lunar cycle. A new moon, also called a → *Dead Moon* (also, in some regions, Slumbering Moon), is called the **Sleeping Moon**.

Moon, Spade ASTRONOMY – A phase in the lunar cycle. **Spade Moon** refers to the waxing, first quarter moon and is also known as → *Farmer's Moon,* or simply **the Spade**.

Moon, Thunder METEOROLOGY, ASTRONOMICAL CHRONOLOGY – A signum of the seasonal cycle. **Thunder Moon** is the moon during summer.

Moon, Traveler's ASTRONOMY – A phase in the lunar cycle. A full moon, also referred to as the → *Pregnant Moon,* is called the **Traveler's Moon**. It is considered to have magical properties.

Moon, Waking METEOROLOGY, ASTRONOMICAL CHRONOLOGY – A signum of the seasonal cycle. The moon during spring is called the **Waking Moon**.

Mor-Thandak GEOGRAPHY – A continent. **Mor-Thandak** is a large land mass surrounded by ocean on each side: the → *Gray Lake* to the west, → *Galantis* to the north, the → *Sea of Glass* to the east, and the → *Catcher's Sea* to the south. Mor-Thandak is divided politically into five regions: → *Carde-Meridea,* → *Ausrost,* → *Goth,* → *Great North,* and the → *Forgotten North.* The most northern region is the Forgotten North. It is removed from the southern regions by the → *Forgetful Mountain* range. Very little is known about the Forgotten North. Carde-Meridea (or → *Carde*) is the southernmost portion of Mor-Thandak along the western coastline. Ausrost, in the southeast, is the most densely populated region and contains the wealthiest cities and villages. Goth (making up the majority of the west) is situated above Carde and is home to the → *Skree.* The Great North lays above Ausrost. The name "Great North" is a misnomer since the Forgotten North is farther north and west of the Great North, though the most northern part of Mor-Thandak is → *Joolie,* the uppermost tip of the → *Finger of the Quid* in the Great North, a peninsula in Galantis. Most people of Mor-Thandak live in the southern two regions of Carde and Ausrost, and most travel takes place within and between these two regions.

The land of Mor-Thandak is divided into three geographical areas: the Forgotten North, separated from the southern areas by the Forgetful Mountains, makes up the first and least-known area. Goth and the Great North make up the second: these regions are sparsely populated due to the barbaric nature of the Skree, and to a lesser extent the → *Quid,* and the harsh conditions of the land. Goth and the Great North are separated from the southern regions by what is known as the → *Dead Man's Spine:* from west to east, the → *Kathian Mountains,* the → *Barren* (or → *Lost Lake*), and the → *Dial.*

Mother, the RELIGION AND BELIEF, MYTHOLOGY – A religious figure. Perhaps the oldest of all known belief systems, **the Mother** is thought to be exactly as she sounds: the mother of all life. Essentially, she is the world itself and all natural (including magical) things that are part of it. She is sometimes referred to as Mother Sky or Mother Tree (or variations of either, such as → *Weeping Mother Tree*), but she is also referred to simply as the Mother. Though her religion was a thing unto itself, many other belief systems have adopted the Mother as part of their own beliefs.

Mountain of the Dragon, the GEOGRAPHY – A mountain. Found in the → *Kathian Mountains,* **the Mountain of the Dragon** is an actual mountain which is the home of the → *Skree* and the fabled place of the exile of the great → *Dragon,* Gothro.

N

Nameless Mountains, the GEOGRAPHY – A range of mountains. **The Nameless Mountain** range is a series of mountains that create a border between the regions of → *Goth* and the → *Great North.*

Northern Mountains, the GEOGRAPHY – A range of mountains. **The Northern Mountains** are what → *Meridians* (→ *folken* of → *Carde*) call the → *Western Mountains,* as they lie to the north of their homeland.

O

Order of Light (Order) RELIGION AND BELIEF – A religious order. Most commonly referred to as just the Order, **the Order of Light** is one of the oldest known religious sects. Members of this ancient order are called → *dahnee,* a → *lynthian* term which means "Coming of the Light" and refers to the belief that the world was once shrouded in a type of darkness wherein the Coming of Light was prophesied and eventually fulfilled. Though not a belief system largely held by the → *folken,* there are pockets of the dahnee Order which have survived and exist mostly in secret throughout → *Mor-Thandak.* They are believed to own the largest and most well-preserved collection of → *scrips* of all known spiritual tribes. Their traditions are passed down secretly among those chosen to be part of their ranks. A person can choose to become part of the Order, but a rigorous series of tests (which require years) are necessary, and most do not pass these and are eventually expelled. If chosen for the Order, a person is chosen shortly after birth. The parents are given the choice of whether they will allow their child to become part of the Order (since once a child joins the Order's ranks, they never leave it). The basis for choosing members of the Order is known only to its members, though most who are chosen now are chosen from among villages and/or family groups who believe being chosen is a great honor. Members of the Order are considered wise and merciful and are occasionally sought to help resolve issues between warring peoples' groups. Their monastic communes are mostly hidden from the outside world and are protected by ancient magic.

outlander ECONOMY – A profession (infml). **Outlander** is a term used to describe career sailors.

P

pasture next, the CULTURE, LINGUISTICS – The afterlife. **"The pasture next"** is a colloquial phrase used to describe the afterlife. Origins of the phrase are debatable. However, it seems to derive from a common trope among most → *folken* religions that the afterlife will reflect the quality of the life lived and the character of the man or woman who lived it. Such beliefs often use symbolism of a pasture to represent "what comes after," whether good or bad. It is unclear if the phrase originated from the collective metaphor of a pasture afterlife or if it led to such imagery.

Place of Skulls GEOGRAPHY, RELIGION AND BELIEF – An area of ritualistic magic. An area of ritualistic magic, often involving bleeding, sacrifice or sex acts, a **Place of Skulls** is found in the heart of a → *low place* and features a great amount of skulls, both animal and human, as well as other bones. A stream or other source of natural water often penetrates its center. If no such water source exists, a cistern or other reservoir, whether natural or artificial, will be close at hand. A Place of Skulls will also include a large, flat stone altar, known as a → *cyth* and typically surrounded by water, with runes and → *lynthian* carvings covering its surfaces. Most such places have been abandoned and reclaimed by the land and any low forces that still exist there, since the Places of Skulls were largely used among the → *dumas* only. The cyth were used as a platform for sexual and sacrificial rituals, their carvings on top designed to collect the blood and fluids of the sacrifice. In the lynthian tongue, the Place of Skulls is called → *Dun-twille*.

poke POLITICS – Hired fighters. **Pokes** are fighting men employed by → *Regents* or other local officials and/or civic leaders to help govern. Because there is no standardized system of government, the role of pokes varies from village to village. Generally, they work to enforce local laws, may be hired out as fighting men or bounty hunters, and are either paid wages, given room and board in exchange for their work, or a combination of both. Pokes often have unsavory reputations, as there is a stigma associated with them of taking bribes. Those men most often attracted to the position often cannot find gainful employment through other means because of a history of violence or, ironically, breaking the law.

pooey LINGUISTICS, SOCIOLOGY — A form of address. **Pooey** is a vernacular term meaning father (or, by extension, grandfather).

pug rabbit FAUNA — An animal species. **Pug rabbits** are large carnivorous rabbits (typically the size of a medium to large dog) that live in warrens, are nocturnal and hunt in packs. They generally populate the grasslands of moderate climates.

Q

Quid ETHNICITY — A people group. The **Quid** are a race of people who live in the northern hemisphere, beyond the → *Hundroën Mountains.* A decidedly stern race, the Quid are believed to be distantly related to the → *Skree* because they share similar physiognomical attributes as well as similar religious beliefs which are shrouded with secrecy to those outside the Quid (though the deities worshipped by the two groups do differ in name and certain aspects). The Quid are typically an albino people, though hair and eye color vary. The most striking difference between the Quid and all peoples of the southern hemisphere is the mirror of the seasons: winter in the north is summer in the south and vice versa, and their → *Hidain* reflect this. Another peculiarity to the Quid is their ability to build explosive clay pots filled with volatile substances that spark, sizzle or explode when exposed to fire or pressure—these are known as → *fire sticks.* The Quid are the only known race of people who do not fear the Skree but are not their allies.

Quiddly-Jool RELIGION AND BELIEF — A religious figure. The preeminent object of worship of the religion of the → *Quid,* **Quiddly-Jool** was an ancient witch priestess who was believed to have vanquished an evil dark lord in the guise of a great serpent (or lizard in some versions).

R

razor-bone FAUNA – A fish species. **Razor-bone** refers to a type of fish that has a fin that is a very strong and sharp extension of its spine. Due to this peculiarity, razor-bone fish are often captured for the sake of harvesting the blades of its dorsal and caudal fins for use as tools or weapons. A school of razor-bone can be deadly, though the fish themselves are not aggressive.

Red Death, the CULTURE – A powder used for burning, or the smoke of it. The term **Red Death** refers to one of two sigils* of the → *Skree.* The Red Death refers to the burning of a fine powder specific to the → *Kathian Mountains* that releases billows of thick, red smoke into the sky, and is also the name of the powder itself. The powder is volatile and corrosive and is considered among the Skree to be the "breath" of the → *Dragon,* or the fossilized saliva of the Dragon. Some believe the powder holds magical properties. It is highly sought by apothecaries and sorcerers throughout → *Mor-Thandak,* since it is very difficult to obtain outside the Kathians. It can be found among roving bands of Skree, though getting it this way is most often considered far too dangerous, or through the primary way it is acquired: when it is left behind as a light residue once a village or city has been eradicated by the Skree. This latter practice is the typical way it is collected, though Skree raids are far more rare than in past ages.

* For the second sigil of the Skree, see → *Criers.*

Regent POLITICS – A political office. **Regent** (or the regentry) refers to any leadership or governing power in a village, region or city. Because governance varies throughout → *Mor-Thandak,* there is no prescribed manner by which the regentry may govern. Equally, there is no standard for enforcing the regents' rule, but often fighting men, or → *pokes,* serve in the capacity of law enforcement. Regent (or the regentry) may also refer to any leadership or governing power.

→ *City Regent*

rip FAYE — A space portal. **Rips** are portals through which people may pass, allowing them to skip to another point in space. These rips are largely anchored; meaning, two rips always connect to each other in the same space of geography. Rips are believed to be caused by a thinning of the veil in a particular location which allows the link to a similar spot in another location to occur. The cause for such thinning varies. As a result, rips can be very dangerous if the thinning was caused by low and malicious means or by a temporary phenomenon. The rip itself is not a threat (unless it is volatile and "blinks" out suddenly), but the energy inhabiting the area may be. Rips should not be confused with → *slips,* a different type of portal suggested to offer a similar movement not only between points in space but also time.

River Kay GEOGRAPHY — A river. The River Kay is a large river on → Alabaster Kay that divides the island into two land masses, an island within island. It is also known as → Wodor.

rumen FAYE* — (1) A creature, or (2) a similarly named organ of that creature. **Rumen** is

(1) an alternate term for → *rumenati* and

(2) an organ specific to rumenati that collects the blood consumed by rumenati. It holds the blood until it is needed for nourishment, at which point it is regurgitated into the mouth and swallowed into the stomach proper. Blood can be stored in the rumen for an indefinite amount of time.

* Rumenati origins are unclear, though their physiology appears to be biological rather than magical. However, given their uncanny

"powers," they are loosely considered → *faye.* This is only marginally true, since faye tend to be of a more natural order.

rumenati (alternate: → ***rumen (1)***) FAYE* — A creature. The **rumenati** are a race of semi-immortal blood drinkers who live on the consumption of blood, primarily human. There are many myths surrounding the rumen, though little has actually been proven regarding their origins. They take great pleasure in causing pain in others. They are more powerful at night, though they can move about in the day. Their teeth and nails contain a poison much like spider venom, incapacitating their prey so the rumenati can eat at their leisure. They do not swallow the blood straight away but collect it in an organ specific to the rumenati—this organ is thus called a → *rumen (2)*—where it is held until needed, at which point it is regurgitated and swallowed. The rumen have some power of persuasion and other magical or supernatural abilities. One is born a rumen—humans cannot be turned into rumenati.

* Rumenati origins are unclear, though their physiology appears to be biological rather than magical. However, given their uncanny "powers," they are loosely considered → *faye.* This is only marginally true, since faye tend to be of a more natural order.

S

Sauingrey CULTURE — A festival. **Sauingrey** is one of the four → *Hidain* (Holy Days) and occurs on the last day of the 11th month of the year (or the eve of → *Winter Hu*). It signifies the end of harvest and the beginning of winter, or → *"the darker half."* During Sauingrey, special bonfires are lit. It is a liminal time when spirits and fairies are believed to move more easily in the world. Souls of the dead revisit homes. Divination rituals are common, often involving nuts and apples. In the northern hemisphere, Sauingrey is celebrated at the other end of the year: on the last day of the fourth month (→ *gu-delak*). Its Hidain twin is → *Lunauinbroc* (celebrated on the eve of → *Summer Han*); both are celebrated on the last day of the month preceding the seasonal turn.

Screw, the ECONOMY – A port.

→ *the Corkscrew*

scrip RELIGION AND BELIEF – A spiritual text. **Scrip** refers to any spiritual text but is most commonly associated with ancient writings of any sect.

Sea of Glass GEOGRAPHY – A body of water. The eastern sea is known as the **Sea of Glass**. It is a large sea that spans the eastern shore of → *Ausrost*, from the → *Galantis* in the northern hemisphere to the → *Catcher's Sea* in the south. The Glass is an ocean stretching from the southern tip of the → *Border Lands* at → *Alabaster Kay* in the southern hemisphere to the → *Hundroën Mountain* range in the north. Though most portions of the Sea of Glass are safe enough to travel, the farther north you go the more dangerous the voyage becomes: weather is erratic, hidden land masses contain indigenous people and animals that can be very dangerous, and the sea itself is often filled with → *freebooters* (pirates who steal and generally leave no survivors).

shade FAYE – A → *faye* phenomenon. A **shade** is any spiritual being that once inhabited (or can inhabit) a physical body. Examples include ghosts, spirits and demons.

ShooShoos GEOGRAPHY – A group of islands.

→ *Hundrain Islands*

Shou-ling RELIGION AND BELIEF, GEOGRAPHY — A religious site. **Shou-ling** is the most sacred shrine of the Priests of → *Domen-Shoo* in the → *ShooShoo* islands. It is located on the northernmost coast of the northernmost island.

Skie-Len ETHNICITY, CULTURE — A people group. **Skie-Len** are a seafaring band of the → *Skree* who considers the → *Barren* a sacred place and believe that dying at its hand is a great honor. The worst kind of → *freebooters,* the Skie-Len may also travel through the other seas surrounding → *Mor-Thandak.*

Skree, the ETHNICITY — A violent people group. **The Skree** come from the → *Kathian Mountains,* sometimes referred to as the wilderness of the high county. They are a violent group of people who at various times send campaigns out for the sake of harvesting slaves from the eastern and southern regions of → *Ausrost* and → *Carde.* The Skree are cannibals, and a portion of their slaves are used for food (much like cattle with other people groups) while others are sold. The Skree's harvest season, a period of eight weeks believed to fall on the weeks leading up to → *Sauingrey* (the Skree's most sacred day of the year), involves the sacrificial offering of one Skree warrior (male or female) per day. Considered a high honor to be chosen for the offering, the chosen Skree's body is eaten by their kinsmen. The Skree's home base and temple are in the heart of the → *Mountain of the Dragon,* found in the uppermost range of the Kathian Mountains. Because their homeland is almost unreachable by the → *folken* of the southern lands, due primarily to the treacherous northern mountains, the → *Barren,* or → *Lost Lake,* and the ferocity of the Skree themselves, not much is known about daily Skree life in the Kathians other than their reputation for being merciless murderers and slave traders. However, the Skree are believed to descend from the followers of the → *Dragon* Gothro (a mythological deity figure believing to have come to this world following the witch → *Dal-Reeahs*) and are believed to continue serving him still. The Skree's two sigils include the burning of a fine powder specific to the Kathian Mountains that release billows of thick, red smoke into the sky, known as the → *Red Death,* and the wailing of the → *Criers,* Skree chosen at birth and subjected to a series of mutilations to the larynx to give them the ability to screech in an inhuman and unnatural way. By these means, and through the small amount of information known about the Skree and the legends surrounding them, the Skree instill fear in others. The Skree are albino and shave most of their hair, which is so light blond it appears white. The men often wear long, pointed beards or goatees, the women (who fight alongside the men) often have a single braid growing from the base of their skull. During campaigns they smear intricate patterns on their bodies with the Red Death powder, their skin layered with heavy scars due to the burning nature of the caustic powder, and use slivers of bone to pierce themselves on their ears, face, chest and torso, leaving only their arms and legs unadorned. They fight naked to the waist, even in winter and even the women. Many sharpen some or all of their teeth into points. The desired effect is for the very sight of them to instill poignant fear in their beholders even as their sigils and reputation have much the same effect. The Skrees' weapons usually consist of broad knives, for close fighting, and spears, about four feet, with a sharp blade fixed to one end and a hook on the other.

slip MYTHOLOGY – A cosmic appearance. A **slip** is an opening in the fabric of time which is believed to allow people to travel forward and backward in time, or across space. The rules regarding slips make them appear unlikely to manage and highly dangerous. Largely, slips are believed to be nothing more than mythology. They should not be confused with → *rips,* actual portals allowing movement through a thinning veil across space.

Snake's Tongue, the GEOGRAPHY – A landmark. **The Snake's Tongue** is the largest fork in the → *Snake River,* which delineates the beginning of the → *Border Lands.*

Snake River GEOGRAPHY — A river in → *Mor-Thandak*. The **Snake River** divides → *Carde* and → *Ausrost*. It originates at the → *Crag* on the southern tip of the → *Barren* and is subsequently brackish for a good ways south. As it flows south, it is fed by freshwater streams until it is mostly freshwater before emptying into the → *Catcher's Sea*. It also serves to delineate the beginning of the → *Border Lands* at its greatest fork (known as the → *Snake's Tongue*).

söklyn CULTURE — A seeker of magic. **Söklyn** is a term which refers to any person who seeks magical abilities or power, whether through the discipline of a specific religious or cultural order or simply as a means to an end. The term is broadly used.

Southerly Feet Mountains, the GEOGRAPHY — A mountain range. **The Southerly Feet Mountains** is a range of small, rounded foothill mountains in the eastern region of → *Carde*. It is home to → *Gal-Braith*.

sprechliif CULTURE, LINGUISTICS — An oral tradition. The ancestral → *Brogden* term for telling stories, particularly to honor the dead, is **sprechliif**. Telling stories is considered the religion of the Brogden people.

staining RELIGION AND BELIEF — A mark of magic.

→ *ehwain branding*

Summer Han METEOROLOGY, CHRONOLOGY — A part of the seasonal cycle. **Summer Han** refers to the six months of every year considered to be summer months. The eve of Summer Han is celebrated as the → *Hidain* festival of → *Lunauinbroc*. (Compare → *Winter Hu*.)

T, (U)

Tanneibel CULTURE – A festival. **Tanneibel** is the festival of low summer and one of four → *Hidain* (or High Holy Days). Tanneibel takes place on the first of the eighth month of the year and marks the beginning of the harvest season. Traditionally, Tanneibel was celebrated with ritualistic athletic competitions (often to the death), feasting, matchmaking and trade. Tanneibel still offers athletic competitions, but in a lighthearted, festive way. Feasting, matchmaking and trade continue to be part of the festivities. An offering (or sacrifice) of the first fruits of the field is often made, though to which deity(s) depends on the region. Much of the festival, especially the rituals and offerings, takes place on the top of hills or mountains. Tanneibel, like its Hidain twin, → *Feilebroc* (low winter, celebrated on the first day of the second month), is a time of divination.

Throm GEOGRAPHY – A village in → *Carde*. A large village in the heartland of Carde, **Throm** is one of the primary villages in the south, second only to → *Gal-Galleen*. It is unique because it is the last village proper heading northwest toward the → *Western Mountains* as superstition and fear of the → *Skree* prevent major settlements farther north or west in Carde (there are a handful of smaller settlements, but these are generally little more than outposts).

Ti-Fleek Lustrẻ, the GEOGRAPHY – A mountain range. **Ti-Fleek Lustrẻ**, an ancient phrase meaning "Teeth of the Lost," is the name of a mountain range nestled within the cavity of the → *Barren*, also known as → *Lost Lake*. The range gets its name from the considerable impression it makes from the north: reflecting on the surface of the dead water, Ti-Fleek Lustrẻ creates a pair of jagged "teeth." Rather than opening on the lake itself, they appear to be poised to open on the world beyond, adding to the mystique of the Barren. Ti-Fleek Lustrẻ is actually part of the → *Western Mountain* range but is separated by the southernmost expanse of the Barren.

Torbinath GEOGRAPHY – A city. **Torbinath** is a coastal city on the northeasternmost corner of → *Ausrost.* It is on the → *Sea of Glass* and offers the largest entry port into the southern regions from the → *Great North.* Its most well-known feature is the → *Corkscrew,* a floating city as part of the city proper that features a series of bridges and floating docks that create a large, circuitous spiral where ships, many semi-permanent, dock for trade, thus creating a "corkscrew" effect—bridges of various size and permanence connect the barges and docks while allowing smaller vessels to navigate beneath them. Governed by an elected official known as the → *City Regent,* Torbinath boasts one of the few large cities in Ausrost that has one central governing figure who is, in broad terms, elected by the people. Torbinath is considered the only viable route into the Great North and commerce with the → *Quid* as the only other way to reach the Great North from the southern regions is via the → *Dial* (a desert that is believed to be uncrossable, though there are documented cases of individuals successfully making the crossing, though rarely with health and sanity intact), and the → *Barrens* (a series of two large, salt water lakes that are considered "barren" of life sustaining food and too near the → *Skree* homeland to be considered safe).

tricks ECONOMY – A currency. **Tricks** are a coin-based currency found in → *Ausrost* but also widely used in → *Carde* (as they have no monetary system of their own). The value of tricks is based on the weight of the individual coins (which come in a variety of sizes and shapes as there is no uniform way of creating the coins), making the exchange of coin for goods and services a tricky (hence the name) scale-based process. Tricks are made of chunks of metal called lustrẻ which are mined primarily in the eastern portions of the → *Ti-Fleek Lustrẻ* mountain range surrounding the city of → *Lustrain.* Tricks are also referred to as dead teeth (or teeth) or → *lusts* (pronounced "loosts").

True Witch, the MYTHOLOGY, RELIGION AND BELIEF – A mythological figure and religious object of worship.

→ *Dal-Reeahs*

tween light RELIGION AND BELIEF, CULTURE — A religious rite.

→ *Hidain lamp,* → *tweeny*

tweeny RELIGION AND BELIEF, CULTURE — Referring to transitional times. **Tweeny** is a → *lynthian* term which refers to the "time between times" that is believed to hold magical properties. Daily examples are sunrise, sunset, and the time between wakefulness and sleep. In a broader sense, a tweeny time is any time of transition: between seasons, at the beginning or ending of a storm, puberty, life to death, etc. Though the concept's origins are lynthian, it is widely adopted throughout most regions and religious systems.

V

vaga SOCIOLOGY — A group of people. **Vaga** refers to a seafaring group of nomads. Though their origins are unknown, it is believed they inherited their dark olive complexion from a tribe of → *outlanders* who came to the mainland from an unnamed island in the → *Catcher's Sea* far south of → *Carde.*

vault FAYE, GEOGRAPHY — A place with magical properties.

→ *vaultine*

vaultine FAYE, GEOGRAPHY — A place with magical properties. **Vaultine** refers to a geographical area where magical properties have pooled to create a potent region where ethereal sensibilities are heightened and the separation between spiritual and physical plains is lessened. A → *low place* would technically be considered a vaultine; however, the two are often considered opposites. Vaultines are often associated with positive energy or good magic, but they are yet wild and magical in inception and nature and must be treated with utmost respect and care. Vaultines are also referred to as → *vaults* and, occasionally, → *high places.*

W, (X, Y)

wasp lettuce FLORA – An aquatic plant. **Wasp lettuce** is an aquatic leafy grass used medicinally. Its fronds are rough and can be used to exfoliate the skin. The sap creates a stinging sensation due to its antiseptic qualities. Wasp lettuce can also be eaten. It is typically boiled or stir-fried in animal fat. The leaves can also be used as wraps for → *doppits.* Wasp lettuce leaves, when eaten, are said to aid in digestion and for soothing mild stomach irritations.

water dragons FAUNA – Aquatic creatures. **Water dragons** are large, saltwater serpentine creatures who are believed to exist in the depths of the → *Barren* (and according to some beliefs in the unknown seas above the → *Forgotten North*). Little is known of water dragons, including whether they exist or not. Legends surrounding water dragons were passed down orally through most known people groups, thus suggesting they did exist at one time. Considering how little travel takes place on the Barren, outside that of the → *Skie-Len,* it is conceivable that a leviathan type creature inhabits its waters.

ways place GEOGRAPHY, ECONOMY – A settlement where multiple roads meet. A **ways place** is any place where multiple roads, particularly through roads, meet. It is called a ways place because it is easy to choose any through road in order to reach a specific destination. Such hubs often grow into villages or cities known for trade and news. In more rural areas, ways places will often have little more than directional signs or even a supply cache where travelers are expected to take and leave supplies as needed. To a lesser degree, a ways place may also include a shrine or other hallowed space for local deities or religious factions.

Weeping Forest, the FAYE, GEOGRAPHY – A forest characterized by magic. **The Weeping Forest** is a → *vaultine,* mythological forest so named for the sound its limbs make when stirred by the wind: a song of weeping. Believed to live wherever it chooses, independent and sentient, the Weeping Forest is said to have no permanent location. The limbs of its trees are said to collect the secrets of those visiting the forest and sing them aloud to share them with the invisible → *listeners* seated among the lofty branches. Neither a good place nor an evil place, the Weeping Forest is wild and magical in inception and nature and is a pooling of magical forces that creates the power of the place. Travelers cannot find it but must be drawn into it by the Forest itself. Some believe the origins of the Weeping Forest are linked to the → *Weeping Mother Tree,* though it is largely accepted that the two are now distinct entities.

Weeping Mother Tree FAYE – A religious figure. **The Weeping Mother Tree** is a kindly spirit believed by the *Sisters of* → *Eri* to protect travelers, the weary and the lost and to give some the ability to see into the fabric making up all things and/or into other realms. The origins of the myth of the Weeping Mother Tree, considered by the Eri to be the Creator → *Mother,* are not well known; however, the essence of the tale is that a tree, the mother of all life, once wept a river for those lost and weary, for those who could not find their way. The river symbolizes hope and deliverance derived from the Weeping Mother Tree's tears. It is also believed by some the Weeping Mother Tree forged the → *Weeping Forest.* The Creator Mother is a token spirit of the Sisters of Eri (one of many).

→ *the Mother*

Western Mountains, the GEOGRAPHY – A mountain region in → *Mor-Thandak*. **The Western Mountain** range separates the southern region of → *Carde* from the northwestern region of → *Goth*. The farther north one travels through the range, the more impassable the mountains become. Though the Western Mountains only refer to the southernmost series of mountains in the range (above that are the → *Kathians*), it is part of a vast range of mountains culminating in Goth with its highest peak: the → *Mountain of the Dragon* (birthplace and home of the → *Skree* people). For many southern → *folken,* often superstitious, the range is considered the far north with nothing beyond it but myth and danger. Thusly, it is referred to as the → *Northern Mountains.* The full mountain range is known properly as the Kathian Range.

Winter Hu METEOROLOGY, CHRONOLOGY – A part of the seasonal cycle. **Winter Hu** refers to the six months of every year considered to be winter months. The eve of Winter Hu is celebrated as the → *Hidain* festival of → *Sauingrey*. Winter is also called the → *Darker Half*. (Compare → *Summer Han*.)

winter's bane FLORA – A grassy plant. **Winter's bane** is a heavy grass that grows in areas of wetter climates. Though it may be found year-round, during winter it produces tiny white florets that release light seeds on the wind, creating a flurry similar to that of snow. The stalks and leaves of winter's bane, which grows in large tufts especially near open water, are used during the festival of → *Feilebroc* because they self-pollinate during the winter months and foreshadow the coming of spring. Winter's bane, in all its parts, is deadly if eaten; however, when burned or smoked, it has some medicinal value as well as hallucinogenic properties. Even when burned or smoked, it must be consumed in small doses, or it may cause severe health problems and even death. Winter's bane has a distinct and pungent odor, even more so when it is burned. The plant figures prominently into the mythology regarding the Priests of → *Domen-Shoo*, who were said to have perpetual flames of winter's bane burning in their temples. It is also widely believed that the Priests of Domen-Shoo were driven mad and ultimately sealed themselves in caves beneath their most sacred shrine on the coast of the northernmost island of the → *Hundrain* in large part due to their ingestion of the plant. In most contemporary uses, burning winters bane is considered cleansing.

witch's tongue CULTURE, RELIGION AND BELIEF, LINGUISTICS — A saying based on folkenlore belief. **"Witch's tongue"** is a common phrase, particularly in rural regions, which refers to the folkenlore belief that if one removes a witch's tongue and keeps it, the witch will no longer be able to curse or otherwise trouble them. Though it is rooted in superstition, the most common uses of the phrase now are primarily metaphoric. For example, if someone owes a fellow a large sum of money which he cannot pay, a friend may say, "Well yeh may as well take the witch's tongue of it," (or the witch's portion, in some regions) a phrase which implies an undesirable course of action may be necessary to pay off the debt (i.e. servitude). The general idea here is that a tough thing cannot be concluded until after it is started. Another use of the phrase is simply stating "he has the witch's tongue," or more simply, "he'll have the tongue" (or similar variations). The suggestion here is that some difficult and perhaps dangerous task must be done, but the end of it will "pay off" (or justify the discomfort). Metaphorical uses aside, the belief that a witch's tongue prevents a witch from hexing the holder of the tongue is common among the → *folken.*

witchlight FAYE — A magical appearance. **Witchlight** is a magical aura that is thought to be a portent of coming evil or death, a residue of the stain of evil or death on a place or person, or a warning of the possibility of evil or death. Though there is no hard and fast description of the appearance of witchlight, it is believed to take many forms and is characterized only by an unnatural light in an otherwise normal setting: a glowing fog or water, beams of light with no source, glowing skin or eyes of the dead or bones, a hovering shimmer, etc. Though witchlight is most often associated with negative tidings, there are those who suggest that it may also bear good news, offer direction to lost travelers, or bring comfort for the bereaving.

Wodor, the GEOGRAPHY – A river. **The Wodor** is a river on the island of → *Alabaster Kay*. It divides the primary island from a smaller island within its interior. Sometimes known as the → *River Kay*, Wodor is one of several natural barriers the → *Brogden*, the sole inhabitants of Alabaster Kay, use to fortify their homeland.

wolfenkind MYTHOLOGY – Form-shifting, mythical creatures. Mythical human-animal hybrids, part human, part wolf, who are decedents of the faithful followers of the witch → *Dal-Reeahs*, the wolfenkind can change between the two forms at will and religiously follow the lunar schedule. → *Sauingrey* is their holy day. Even though the wolfenkind are not believed to exist, their myth is one of many reasons Sauingrey is considered the darkest of the four → *Hidain*. In some regions, there are those who worship the myth of the wolfenkind and act as though they were part wolf: hunting in packs and eating their prey, usually animals, raw.

Z

zyphlen FAYE – A → *faye* phenomenon. **Zyphlen** are fairy bells, referring to a sound which accompanies the magical workings of the faye or any of a plethora of magical natural creatures (i.e., those that are a natural part of the world and do not practice magic so much as be magic). Largely only held as a superstitious belief, the concept of zyphlen finds its origins in nearly all the ancient dumaen (of the → *dumas*) → *scrips* of the → *Eri*, → *Edöne*, → *dahnee*, → *Quid*, → *dain*, and → *Monkshood*. In this regard, the overwhelming presence of zyphlen throughout the many ancient and sacred texts suggests the reality of the phenomenon, at least in the past.

AFTERWORD AND ACKNOWLEDGEMENTS

This story began as a dream. A literal dream. That was in the summer of 2001. I was in a tweeny time . . . in between careers and staring down the long empty barrel of my future. I felt disembodied and had no idea what I wanted to do with myself. I was directing a summer camp for underprivileged children in North Carolina and planning to return home to Georgia at the end of the summer and substitute teach while getting my teaching certification, but those plans failed. Even if they hadn't, the plans felt like a stab in the dark. A best guess at what I should do next. Then I had the dream that inspired this novel. In the dream, I was a little boy. My father brought me to an old wooden fence on the edge of his farm and handed me over to the creepiest two men I'd ever seen. I was supposed to help them hunt down a scarecrow. I'd already seen this happen to my father in the dream. His father had brought him to the fence when he was a boy. Later, after my quest was over, I brought my own son to the fence. Only I couldn't let him go with the hunters.

I woke up from the dream while fighting to rescue my boy from the clutches of who would become known to me later as the woodsmen. I woke up not knowing if I'd saved my son.

The dream helped shape me. It changed the way I saw myself and my future. I decided to take a different path after that. I came back to Georgia and began working at a youth home for teenage boys who would otherwise be incarcerated. I'd work there full time for the next fourteen years. The dream was a big part of my reason for seeking out that job.

I first wrote The Scarecrow Hunters in my journal. This was simply an act of recording the dream. Later, I wrote it into a short story. Then I deleted that and wrote it again, still as a short story. Then a novella I meant to include in a series of three or four novellas set in the same world, but featuring different characters. The second novella in that series would feature a girl I'd learn later was named Grey. It wasn't long before I realized these weren't separate stories, but part of the same story. My Scarecrow novella became a novel, and later, that novel became two novels: The Scarecrow Hunters and A Greedy Shadow. Eliot has been with me since 2001. The novel has been evolving on the page for at least a decade. Today, sharing Eliot and his story with anyone who cares to read it feels like the culmination of a twenty-year journey, because it is.

Thank you for joining us. Eliot and I hope to see you again soon.

—Eric Shane Love—

October 3, 2021

Though it is impossible for me to list all those friends and enemies who helped me get this story out, I do want to acknowledge those who perhaps served as anchor points for me along the way. Here they are in chronological order:

DAD — For showing me what a father should look like.

NATHANIEL — For giving Eliot his name.

BRIAN — For being the only person in the middle of things who took the time to illustrate Eliot's story. He gave me the crow that lives on the back cover. Brian is also a damn fine older brother.

LOGAN — For finding Eliot's soul and showing us what it looks like.

ANJA — For being the first person to be honest with me about the words I'd written, and for loving Eliot as much as I do. And also for being a super-duper beta reader who loves to point out when my stories are too Disney.

PARISA — For shining a light in my and Eliot's Dark Wood and helping me find Eliot's way. A good editor is nothing short of good magic.

ABOUT THE AUTHOR

Since January 2016, I've been a freelance videographer, photographer and social media content creator. I live in a rural Georgia town about an hour and a half inland from Savannah. Before 2016, I worked nearly fifteen years at a small, non-profit youth home for troubled teenage boys. I was a mentor, educator and the creative director during that time. I've always had a love of writing. As early as sixth grade, I wrote stories about my classmates, passing them around the room to get feedback.

A few random, interesting and trivial things to know about me: I'm in a band with my brother, Brian: Tiger Creek. I sing and play keys. I am a classically trained vocalist, though that has almost no bearing on the classic and 80s rock, and, less fortunately, the spattering of country songs we perform in the band. Halloween is my favorite holiday. Christmas is a close second. I have three dogs and a cat: Maddie, a 150-year-old basset hound, Bella, a mutt who gives me the best cuddles, and

Hot Breath Eugene, an enormous pit bull/mastiff mix whose head looks like a basketball with eyes. Maddie is the Queen, Bella is the Princess, and Eugene alternates between being the Court Jester and the Village Idiot. The cat's name is Chuck, and he is irreparably deranged. That's why we love each other. He's the Crazy Witch who lives in the forest outside the city walls, so to speak. All my pets are rescues. I also have about fifty plants in my house. I have a tendency to take much longer to tell a story than is necessarily required, and sometimes those stories don't have endings. I get that from Debbie, my mom. Also, I hate technology.

Sign up for my newsletter and have access to a behind-the-scenes look at my writing process, read exclusive content, and learn about the lore and geography of Eliot's world at my website: ericshanelove.com.

www.ingramcontent.com/pod-product-compliance
Lightning Source LLC
LaVergne TN
LVHW020538100826
845148LV00010B/1513

* 9 7 9 8 9 8 5 3 1 7 3 0 5 *